WHISKEY TANGO FOXTROT

WHISKEY TANGO FOXTROT

DAVID SHAFER

MULHOLLAND BOOKS

Little, Brown and Company

New York Boston London

Copyright © 2014 by David Shafer

Mulholland Books/Little, Brown and Company
Hachette Book Group
237 Park Avenue, New York, NY 10017
mulhollandbooks.com

First Edition: August 2014

Mulholland Books is an imprint of Little, Brown and Company, a division of Hachette Book Group, Inc. The Mulholland Books name and logo are trademarks of Hachette Book Group, Inc.

The publisher is not responsible for websites (or their content) that are not owned by the publisher.

The Hachette Speakers Bureau provides a wide range of authors for speaking events. To find out more, go to hachettespeakersbureau.com or call (866) 376-6591.

ISBN 978-0-316-25263-8
LCCN 2014937564

10 9 8 7 6 5 4 3 2 1

RRD-C

Printed in the United States of America

To Fiona
Without whom zip

WHISKEY TANGO FOXTROT

MANDALAY, MYANMAR

The little room was so hot that Leila tried not to move inside her clothing. She'd chosen the plain tan shirt with the piping on the pocket because bureaucrats are swayed by even the smallest impression of martial authority. Ditto the shiny black shoes. But the lady who took in Leila's laundry had really gone to town on the shirt, and the result was like a suit of armor made from paper bags. Leila could feel a line of sweat trickle south down her back. A large beetle somehow injured buzzed and rattled in a corner of the stifling room.

It had been nearly two hours since one of Colonel Zeya's underlings had instructed her to *Wait here, someone will come for you! You please must not leave this room!*

Fine, she'd thought then. Leila Majnoun could wait. She wasn't going to fall for that make-the-Westerner-sit-until-she-is-undone-by-her-own-impatience trick. She pulled out her notebook. She favored Gregg-ruled steno pads; went through them at a rapid clip. She wrote in a swift and flattened cursive that was nearly illegible to anyone but herself and maybe her big sister, Roxana. She wrote mostly in English, but she also used Pashto, and some stenoglyphs that she'd invented along the way.

3

Leila was no Luddite, but she trusted her paper notebook over any of her electronics. They usually let you keep a notebook even when they took your passport and pocket computer. Though in a secure airport interview room once, they'd taken Leila's notebook from her hands. That's as dicey as it had ever gotten for her. Soon after that, she'd done a job that put her in proximity to commando-type soldiers, and one of those guys had his instructions in a sort of sheet protector Velcroed to his inner wrist. The commando wrist slate—that's the kind of personal organizer she could use.

Leila let the tedium flow around her like lava while she filled her pad with notes that would help her get through the next week of this frustrating job. Her title was director, in-country, Myanmar/Burma. But back in New York there was a country director, Myanmar/Burma. The silliness of the titles should have been her first clue that Helping Hand was a bush-league NGO. Though deep-pocketed, apparently—HQ was two floors of a skyscraper in midtown Manhattan. They'd hired her to do the advance work on what they said would be a twenty-year commitment to public health in northern Burma. She was supposed to be *establishing a country program!*—and her New York bosses said it like that, like she was a general in a tent or something, when what they really meant was rent an office, buy some desk chairs, and find out who else was working there and what wasn't getting done. But beyond that, her two or maybe three New York bosses couldn't even agree on what the Burma mission was. One of them thought Helping Hand should be identifying strong female candidates for full-ride scholarships to the school of nursing at Boston College. Another one thought the organization should be setting up village-based primary-care health clinics. Mainly her bosses sent her conflicting e-mails and sabotaged one another's goals.

And in truth, Leila had herself underestimated the difficulty of achieving anything in a place like Myanmar. She had done war-torn, she had done devastated, but this living-under-tyranny thing was a superbummer. The Myanmarese (Myanmartians, she called them in her head; the stenoglyph was an *M* with an ovoid helmet and antennae) spent all their energy protecting what little they had or avoiding persecution; there was nothing left over for hope. And no one on the outside cared that much, or was even sure of its name. Was it called Burma, which had something to do with Orwell? Or Myanmar, which sounded like a name cats would give their country? The rest of the world just avoided this place, as on the street you'd avoid a stinking, pantsless drunk—because where would you even begin?

And where was that stupid little colonel? Leila was running low on anti-impatience techniques. The room seemed to have been designed to distill boredom and discomfort and focus it on the occupant. It was like being under some sort of time-stretching ray. There was the stippled layer of dust on everything; there was nothing to read but the No Smoking sign; there was one plastic fan in the corner, its electrical cord shorn off as if with a serrated knife. Smells seeped from the wooden benches and plastic blinds—cigarette smoke and greasy food and the vapors emitted by anxious humans.

Once she had done all she could reasonably do on the work flowchart, Leila just sat and thought about her family. A low-level concern for them had been rising in her lately. Roxana had written that their kid brother Dylan's new GF was a battle-ax. Dylan hadn't mentioned a girl to Leila. Also according to Roxana, their mother had had two suspicious falls in the last nine months, the second one resulting in a broken wrist. Leila couldn't tell by e-mail how exactly Roxana had meant *suspicious*. Like, neurologically? Or alcoholically? She noted again that no one ever informed on Roxana like this. Birth order did seem to trump the other personality predictors, Leila thought. Would that be forever? What about after their parents died? How far away was that? None of the Majnoun children had spawned yet. Was that breaking their parents' hearts? Her mom's, yes, probably. But her dad was a beloved middle-school principal in Tarzana, California. Maybe that job satisfied some of his grandpaternal needs?

Leila decided she would wait ten more minutes and then go in search of someone, maybe Colonel Zeya himself. Though good luck finding that guy. He must have an office in every dingy little government building in Mandalay, and a henchman to keep people out of each one. This was the third time that Leila had been promised her shipment, a shipment that represented six months of work on her part. But this was the first time she had actually been brought to the airport. On the previous occasions, she had been summoned to the terrestrial passage entry station behind the clamorous bus depot, and those had turned out to be shakedowns—demands for the payment of newly discovered taxes and import duties. Most NGOs allowed for a certain amount of this. But Helping Hand was not playing along. New York said that to do so would "abet endemic corruption"—or perhaps this was just Boss 1 screwing with Boss 2—and at first refused to release the funds that might win Leila her shipment. Only by haranguing Boss 3 was Leila able to convince HQ that the extra money was in this case a cost of doing business.

Still; still. Leila had moved similar shipments hundreds of times. This was a container of palletized medical equipment—fourteen short tons—that she'd coaxed without incident from Miami to Doha to Yangon and then to Naypyidaw, the bizarre new capital that the generals had erected suddenly in the middle of the country. But then her shipment had been waylaid and effectively ransomed by an invisible mafia of Myanmarese customs officers who could be reached only by phone, and even then only via their underlings' phones. Once Leila figured out which government building contained the Department of Leila Antagonism, she and her driver, Aung-Hla, took the half-day trip to Naypyidaw and attempted a frontal assault. But the stupidly hatted officials she located—though shocked that she'd found them—only asked her to return with obscurer forms and more exact change.

She worried that her shipment was getting picked through and pilfered from. It was high-end stuff. If the bozos at HQ had their way, the crates would probably be stamped EXPENSIVE and ALREADY LOST and SORRY ABOUT COLONIALISM. Worrying about it kept her up at night.

Though there were other things that kept her up at night also. The subtropical heat, the mouse-size cockroaches, the regretful thoughts about Rich. And how much regret are you allowed when you're the one who did the dumping? And the loneliness. Sometimes—often—her day was a screen, a phone, a couple of merchants, and three meals by herself. That wore thin.

A man was coming toward her. One of Zeya's underlings, but not the one who had deposited her in the infernal waiting room. She recognized this guy from an earlier fruitless wait; he'd brought her a Coke once. She did not stand up but tried to look unbothered as he approached.

"Follow me, please," he said. It was five degrees cooler outside the little room, and that relief slipped down her collar and into the humid biome beneath her shirt. Leila could hardly wait. By the end of the day, she would have the crates de-palletized, inventoried, and stacked in the storeroom she'd rented beneath her office. She was having an effect; she was causing things to happen. Huzzah!

She tried to tamp down her excitement. *Not until you see it. Not until you touch it.* And was there something troubling in the way this lackey was walking through the little corridors of the big building? Some slump in his shoulders?

Shit. He didn't want to get where they were going. He was actually slowing down.

And then her worry bloomed into certainty. Somehow she knew. That huzzah had been premature. *Of course* the colonel had screwed her again; *of course* her shipment had not arrived or would not be released. The hot wait was just a two-hour insult, and she was an idiot for sitting through it. What the fuck? She was trying to help this place, and she had a way to be of help.

They entered a room and passed a klatch of officers taking tea at a plastic table, and Leila could feel their eyes on her. At every door, there was a boy with a rifle, sweating under a helmet. The menace was present in everything here; it was like walking by a man holding a stick, the man silent, the stick raised above his head.

They arrived at the underling's desk, and he indicated a chair where

Leila should sit. She didn't sit. "My boxes aren't here, are they?" she asked the lackey in Burmese. She didn't know the word for "shipment."

He turned around, shook his head minutely, failed to meet her clamped gaze. Yeah, he hated this. "You will sign?" he said in English, pushing toward Leila a sheaf of papers. She'd seen those before. She'd signed them already.

She picked up the papers on the desk. Oh, fuck it. If they weren't going to release her shipment this time, she was going to make trouble.

Leila leaned in to the man's desk. She was too small to loom over anything, but she could lean in. In English, and too loudly, and in her best imitation of importance, she said, "I am an officer of an agency recognized by the UN"—a meaningless statement, but it had *officer* and *agency* and *UN* in it. "You cannot prevent me from taking custody of my shipment." She actually stamped her foot.

The underling blanched and receded. At the far end of the room, the klatch quit stirring its tea.

Then Leila said very quietly, in Burmese, "I know this is not your fault. I will leave you. But tell me where Zeya is now. He is the one I need to speak to."

Leila worked alone; she had to be both good cop and bad cop.

The man squinted at her. She often got that squint when she used Burmese; her accent was probably pretty bad. But then his eyes widened and softened, and she thought that he was going to take this deal.

In a quick and quiet utterance, in a mix of two languages, he said to Leila, "It is day three. He is with the bird people on day three."

The Burmese numbered their days of the week. He meant Tuesday. But what the fuck were bird people?

Sticking to Burmese, Leila said, "How do I get my boxes? Why does Zeya make it so hard for me?"

And the underling, in English, and looking sorry to report it, said, "Lady, they do not want you here. Maybe, if you pay the taxes, and you do not bring in too much, you will get your boxes. But I think they do not want you here no way."

*　　*　　*

Leila refused to return to the city with the Ministry Department driver who had brought her to the airport. She thought if she could make her way to the passenger terminal, she could find a taxi. That terminal was half a mile away; she'd noted the distance when they drove in. So she stomped out of the hangar and walked back the way she'd been driven. It was not a road for walkers; it was a dusty hummock with ditches on both sides, the ditches trickling with sewage and trash. Her shoes were all wrong now; they made her gait scuffly and her progress dusty. Still, she was free of all those clownish apparatchiks.

Well, not free, exactly; a teenage soldier in baggy pants and an M1 rifle followed fifty paces behind her. But sulkily; more kid brother than armed goon.

The paper-bag-armor blouse was brutal. She thought of unbuttoning, but then reconsidered. She was alone except for the boy soldier at her back. She'd gone this long without getting raped, and it was her daily, specific intention to keep it that way.

She looked back to check on the boy soldier, and her eye caught something behind him: a small plane was landing. But it was a snazzy white jet, Leila noticed, not a Burmese military aircraft or one of Air Mandalay's goofy French turboprops. The jet came to rest in the middle of the tarmac. Then three big SUVs emerged from the hangar in which Leila had just wasted two hours; they zipped toward the jet in tight formation, like cockroaches racing across a kitchen floor. Two men— soldiers—got out of each vehicle, and each pair received a metal crate that was lowered by winch from the rear door of the jet. The crates went into the SUVs, two men lifting each crate. A set of stairs sprouted from the front of the aircraft, and three passengers—male, was about all Leila could determine—briskly descended and got in the back of the lead SUV. Then all the vehicles sped off, and before they'd even disappeared around the corner of a distant building, the little jet had turned its nose and was taxiing to a takeoff. The whole operation took less than three minutes—the most efficient maneuver Leila had ever seen in this country. Those crates were probably full of Johnnie Walker and porn on VHS, headed to a general top-heavy with medals. Meanwhile, her medical supplies were rotting in lockup. Leila was pierced by that mix of anger and sorrow that can make a person give up on a thing. What outright bullshit, she thought.

At the passenger terminal, Leila made directly for the taxi queue. But coming from the wrong direction, she snuck up on the taximen, who were lounging in the shade of the tall, mimosa-looking trees; they roused themselves to semi-alertness for her. How did they keep their shirts so white? she wondered. The men here wore brilliant shirts and long, faded sarongs—lungis, they were called in Burma, big-knotted in the front so that each man seemed to be wearing a sort of codpiece. She briefly hoped that Aung-Hla would be waiting with the other airport men. But, no, Leila didn't know any of these guys.

It was from a similar shade-lounging posse that Leila had chosen Aung-Hla, months ago, when she'd started traveling out of Mandalay on Helping Hand business. For the first of their many trips together, he had kept some distance from her. He answered her questions briefly and mostly declined when she asked would he like a Coke or a sandwich when they stopped for food, preferring to spend his time checking the fluids under the hood of his white Toyota. Or he would wipe down the worn-soft vinyl upholstery and whisk-broom the carpets. She had never ridden in a car so well cared for. Aung-Hla's car was similar to the one that Leila's mom and dad had driven when she was a girl. But theirs had been beige and ragged and sticky with melted things. Was it a Tercel? In the back of Aung-Hla's taxi, she was put in mind of her girlhood ride, the slope of the shoulders of the bucket seats ahead of her, the nearness of the central hump, the frequency of the vinyl piping, and that smell of—what? Tracked-in sand? Low-voltage electrical current? Thin carpet on hot metal?

After they'd taken about ten trips together, Aung-Hla opened up a bit. Nothing much, but he laughed at a joke she tried to make; he introduced her to another taximan he stopped to talk to; he pulled off the road to show her a magnificent view. Then Leila snapped a good photo of his taxi, shot in that three-quarter-angle way she knew was flattering to vehicles; she showed Aung-Hla the photo on her laptop screen, and he just about keeled over. He had no e-mail address to mail the photo to, so Leila printed him a copy from the color printer behind the desk at a hotel in Yangon. He rubber-banded the photo to the visor of the car that was its subject. Soon he was telling her names of things—of trees; of his three daughters, photos of whom were also rubber-banded to the visor; of the characters in the Theravada scenes painted thickly on the plaster facades of dinky roadside shrines.

Then he must have seen her face fall when, breaking a long drive to the northern city of Tamu in the kind of petrol-station-cum-lean-to café that art directors are always mocking up for jeans ads, Leila had once again tried to order the delicious chicken-broth-and-rice-starch-cube soup she could find easily in Mandalay and had once again received what appeared to be the culinary result of someone taking a phone book to a plucked chicken. She was so hungry that day that tears sprang to her eyes when a plastic bowl of oily chicken slurry was put before her. After that, Aung-Hla ordered for her, and he watched as the cook prepared her food. She could see him reject the contents of certain plastic vats and approve the use of others. It embarrassed her that she had caved on this. She knew that she should order her own food and place her own phone calls and generally navigate strange places without giving the men around her the satisfaction of seeing a woman ask for help. But Leila could also recognize when the solution to a problem required more skills or resources than she had. Like the chicken situation, for instance.

Soon, Aung-Hla was sitting with her at the same table beneath the thatch-and-canvas shade beside the sun-blanched road. She taught him a card game. He told her about Uposatha, a sort of Sabbath in Theravada Buddhism. He also turned out to have more English than he had let on: very spotty or halting grammar but a fair range of nouns. In fact, Aung-Hla was a quick study, like Leila, and she taught him how to form the future tense for the verb *to go*. He had several perfectly practiced idioms that he deployed slightly incongruously or that he overused. He said, "Hold, please," and "Ready, set, go," and "I won't allow it."

But Aung-Hla was not at the taxi queue, and Leila rode back to Mandalay with a driver she did not know, in silence. An accident on the so-called highway from the airport clogged what little traffic there was, and Leila averted her eyes when they finally passed the wailing and mangled mopedist whose day and probably whole life was going a lot worse than hers.

She tried to will herself into a better attitude. This was a setback, no more. She'd overcome worse. Part of her wanted to be all *You have no idea who you're fucking with*. But she couldn't summon enough of that moxie; they apparently knew exactly with whom they were fucking: a lone white girl whose organization lacked the pull, the will, or the cash to get fourteen short tons of medical equipment out of lockup. In fact, it was *Leila* who didn't know who was fucking with *her*.

I think they do not want you here no way. The guy had looked scared when he'd said it. A pronoun without a referent. Always troubling. And if bird people were involved, things were way more complicated than she had figured. What could the man have meant?

She went back to her office—two rooms above a grocery store beside an important traffic circle on a wide, dirty avenue downtown. She changed out of her stupid shirt and shoes. She made motions at her desk like she was doing work. But it was an act, and soon she remembered that she was without an audience. So she left her office with her laptop in a plastic shopping bag and started walking toward her favorite tea shop. She would order mint tea and those digestive biscuits they had there called Number Nines. She liked the bustle of the street. If she was moving quickly, not speaking, and wearing something reasonable, Leila could blend in here. She could blend in in lots of places; one advantage to being Persian.

But blending in was a kind of hiding, right? She was too alone here, she thought. The aloneness had been the point when she accepted the job. A year in the hot far-away. After the Rich breakup, she wanted out of New York; she wanted to go back in the field. Leila had no social deficits; she existed in the happy and crowded range of the spectrum. The rules did not escape her, nor did ways to bend them. But she thought that maybe she didn't like all that many people. *How many people are you supposed to like?* she wondered. *Below what number are you attachment-disordered?* She liked colleagues in a drinks-after-work kind of way. But in general, they were net-unhelpful during the workday, and often annoying, with their egg salad sandwiches and their bike helmets perched on their monitors.

But in this situation, Leila could have used some help. Besides Aung-Hla, her only friend here was Dah Alice, a precise-English-speaking, crane-like woman, the director of a local orphanage and charity. Dah Alice had been kind to Leila since her arrival and had seriously helped Leila with the find-nursing-students part of her assignment, by introducing her to faculty at the nursing school. But Leila was reluctant to admit to the older woman how much trouble she was having in her work; she didn't want to be the clueless complainer.

Especially since Leila had discovered this about Dah Alice: Though the orphanage was her main thing, her charity had a wider social-services role—some public-health outreach, some adult-literacy programs. The more capable and effective she was, the more threatening the generals found her, so they kept their shifty eyes on her; she had to do her work *and* keep her head down. Asking Dah Alice for help with the denied shipment—that would be a bridge too far; it would put her on the spot. People living under tyranny ask fewer favors of one another.

Leila's favorite tea shop was down a street that had no outlet and no Anglicization of its name on the metal enamel street sign affixed to the pocked pink two-story building on the corner. The Burmese script looked to Leila like a loopy cuneiform or like the schoolgirl doodles that once crowded the margins of her notebooks: it was a series of horseshoes and bubbly *Es* that apparently contained, for the twenty million readers of the language, useful information. If Leila couldn't decipher a particular written Burmese word, she tried to notice and remember what the symbols looked like to her. A moon over three tennis balls, smiley face, backward *E,* fucked-up @ sign: that was the name of the street of her tea shop.

Even ten yards down this narrow street, the heat was cut by shade and leavened with streams of cooler air that trickled from low doorways. People wandered in and out of the buildings down the length of the street. A nonsense-named dead-end street in a second city in a klepto-cratic East Asian punch line, thought Leila. But it's busy!

A man in shades and a crisp white shirt had followed Leila a few steps down the street from the avenue—a too-eager money changer hoping she'd been inviting his trade, she thought. He saw that she was intent on something else, so he stopped at a T-shirt-and-teapot stall and heartily greeted the vendor.

Leaning on the wall or squatting on the sidewalk, men sold soap and batteries and barrettes that were spread on rugs more valuable than any of those things. An old woman folded lace on a stoop. An older woman was making and selling whisk brooms. A decidedly antique little man was polishing shoes, his hands black and nimble. Two monks mumbled at each other. Leila remembered not to smile too keenly, to just keep her face open and make soft eye contact with anyone who wished to do the same. A few did. She had been coming down this street twice a day for a couple of months now. The lace-folding lady gave her a little chin-raise, and a child in a Hard Rock Cafe T-shirt beamed and waved.

In the tea shop, Leila sat with her back to the wall. It annoyed her when aid workers acted like Army Rangers, but one eight-month stint in Afghanistan had drilled a few cautious habits into her. The waiter, who may have had a little crush on Leila, raced over to take her order, though by now he probably could have guessed: mint tea and a plate of Number Nines.

What was that smell? Was it cumin? Burlap? Chinese dish soap? Whatever, it was delicious, and it soothed her. That's what she'd miss when she left this place: the smells. Leila smelled whatever came near her; not just food, but book pages and faces and phones. Her sniffing technique was discreet but effective. Certainly she never had to pass anything under her nose, sommelier-like, as her little brother, Dylan, had to do to match her skills. That's what the Majnoun kids did on slow Saturdays back in the day: they played smelling games. Roxana might hide a Starburst candy behind her toes and wave her foot in the air in front of her siblings, who then had to guess the flavor. Leila could tell you who had been sitting in the red corduroy chair an hour ago. Dylan did not dare steal Leila's stuff because once she had claimed she could smell his hands on her library books. Bluffing or no, she'd been right.

Leila's particular sensitivities seemed to cycle between the wafty, closer smells — mainly food and human — that draped over a moment, and the dusty, distant smells that could be carried by coat sleeve or breeze. In the former category was the knapsack that still smelled of curry, the hairbrush left too near the stove, and the human hangover behind the counter at Kinko's. In the latter category was the subway-tunnel vent mixed with newspaper that had snaked around her corner in Bushwick, and the tang of handrails, and the seep of wet gravel, but it also included the thinner smells that came from paper and paint and industrially produced hard surfaces. This cycling was in some way related to her mood. Only very rarely did her nose prove too powerful. She was usually able to shut it down or tune out the worst, as when a pair of dirty underpants sat down next to her on a bus. So it annoyed her when pregnant women went on and on about their powers of smell, about how they just had to leave the room because someone was eating a banana or whatever.

Her tea arrived, the little cup and pot and plate of biscuits arranged just so on the dinged aluminum tray. Her waiter practically bowed as he retreated.

No, she couldn't ask Dah Alice for help. And she doubted Aung-Hla could help in this situation. He knew how to bribe traffic cops but this was probably out of his league. Though maybe he would know what bird people were. Then there was one American in Mandalay she'd spoken with a few times. Fred. Was it Fred? He was some sort of visiting fellow at the university, fluent in Burmese and Kachin and Shan. Maybe he knew something about how to get around crooked customs officials; he said he'd been in Mandalay for a few years. But despite his exotic multilingualism, he didn't strike Leila as all that bright. Besides, she thought with a cringe, when they last spoke, she may have been a little snooty to him. He had asked would she like a tour of Mandalay Palace. But she'd just arrived and thought she had a lot to do, and she'd seen about a thousand palaces anyway and Fred didn't look like someone she wanted to hear talk about fenestration or crenellation or whatever.

Leila stayed in that tea shop until three in the afternoon—more or less the end of the Burmese workday. For most of that time, she drafted an e-mail to Dylan. He had a correspondence-return rate of about one in three, but you really have to stay on kid brothers and she wanted to know about this girlfriend and was Mom drinking too much and who was Roxana's fancy new employer.

Then she called Aung-Hla on her disposable Burmese phone. Comms were kind of a hot mess on this job. Though in fairness, that wasn't due to Helping Hand; that was more due to working in a failed socialist-military autarky. Leila had a smartphone that could receive some but not all calls from abroad, plus the office landline she was legally required to keep, plus the satellite phone that Helping Hand was very proud of, plus her local cell. Foreigners were't allowed to sign contracts, though, even for a cell phone, so Leila's local cell was always a prepaid burner bought on the street. Eighty minutes for ten bucks. But she got a different number each time she bought a new phone. (Which was actually a *used* phone. Take that, first-world recyclers!) The constantly changing number meant that it was pretty much just an outgoing-calls device, as though she were carrying a little phone booth with her at all times.

She needed to reconfirm tomorrow's trip with Aung-Hla. When she'd told him the destination—a town in Kachin State called Myo Thit, five hundred kilometers north—he had looked apprehensive. Leila knew that things got a bit extra-repressive up there, because of the separatists, but Myo Thit wasn't the deep north, she thought, and it was right on the main highway. If they started early and turned around quick, maybe they could do it in one day.

When she got Aung-Hla on his phone—he shared it with another taximan—he said yes, he would meet her in the morning, but he said no way they could make it there and back in one day. He actually said, "No way this can be done."

"We will find a hotel, then," said Leila, "a place to stay in Myo Thit." She could hear his hesitation over the line. Was he embarrassed? Should she not have said *we*? Or was it a question of his time, his fee? "I will pay you more. Double the usual rate." She immediately regretted that. It probably seemed to Aung-Hla that money was a lever she could pull whenever she wanted to. She would like to explain to him about her student loans.

"The same rate," he said, and she winced. "But the hotel. I think it will not be salubrious."

She and Aung-Hla would find somewhere to stay, she told herself later that night. It was an important trip. There was a woman in Myo Thit she needed to meet.

The nursing students that Leila had so far identified as strong scholarship candidates were all from relatively prosperous Burmese households. These were women able to put themselves forward, and they were fine applicants. But Leila also wanted to find the women who usually missed these opportunities. Probably because of her sister, Roxana, because there had been someone who'd intervened in Roxana's case when she was young, someone who had said to the Majnouns, Your daughter is disabled, but she is also a genius.

The woman in Myo Thit was called Ma Thiri. She was a twenty-eight-year-old nurse with a below-the-knee prosthetic who had single-handedly opened a medical clinic in a small village in a poor and dangerous region in a destitute and benighted country. The prenatal care that the clinic provided had demonstrably reduced infant mortality in the population. To Leila, this sounded like a woman who might seriously benefit from three years at an American nursing school.

Jeez, it was hot. Implausibly hot for midnight, Leila thought. Her upper arms stuck sweatily to the skin of her rib cage, except where her T-shirt blotted their meeting. There was a ceiling fan in her two-room flat; it was on now. But it whorled and kerchonked around at such an unstable and idiotic rate that what it gave in breeze it took back in worry. When she'd first arrived, the bed had been centered beneath the fan, but she couldn't sleep a single night with that seizing squid above her, so she'd moved the bed, a steel beast, to the window, ten feet away. Even so, Leila found the clatter of the fan anathema to sleep, so she had developed a bedtime routine that involved shutting off all the lights, taking a cold, drippy shower, and then, last, killing the fan.

The water from the plastic showerhead spit and dribbled, pooled in Leila's clavicles, then ran down between her breasts, sluicing before it the film of sweat and yellow dust that coated her daily. For a moment, in the dark shower, she was a completely solved problem, happy as a beetle on a leaf. She thought of California, her motherland, or mother-in-law-land, really. She was on a Huffy bike, pedaling hard, her little brother standing tall on the pegs of her back axle. She was walking the Redondo Beach boardwalk in a beloved yellow windbreaker, her whittled big sister roller-skating beside her.

Then, leaving the shower and ghosting naked across the dark room, Leila killed the fan and sparrowed into her sagging netted bed. The sheet reached her ribs and lay on her like moonlight. Worries began to circle her. But she listened to the breath that she borrowed from the air and she lay still. She let the worries circle. You can't move a muscle if you're trying to fall asleep in Mandalay in April.

Aung-Hla was outside her place at six in the morning, and they made good time until they came to a lineup of cars waiting at an unexplained roadblock. There was no traffic coming the other way. Leila watched Aung-Hla. Was he concerned? No. So she tried to sit patiently. After half an hour, two big SUVs came roaring down from the other direction, and when the SUVs had passed, the checkpointists reopened the road. Leila and Aung-Hla didn't make Myo Thit until one o'clock, and, from the moment of their arrival, the town struck Leila as a menacing place. The dogs flinched at unthrown rocks. Doors shut ahead of her as she walked down the street. The man who sold her a Coke wouldn't meet her eyes. And at the teahouse in the dismal main square, she saw Aung-Hla being given grief, presumably for driving a foreign girl.

When Leila found the small clinic, she had to wait an hour before Ma Thiri had time to sit down with her. This annoyed her, but she tried to get over it; the woman was clearly busy with patients. Surely, that was more important than talking to some rich foreign girl who would be gone tomorrow. Isn't that how Leila would have seen it if they'd swapped places? Because Leila knew well that that's what she was here, that was how she *presented:* as rich. This question, in all its forms, vexed and pestered her: How much did money matter? Clearly, a lot. Being so poor hurt. This clinic was pretty dirty. Obligingly, a patchy cat skittered through the little waiting room. Yeah, rich/poor still meant everything. Did that make her a Marxist?

But then sometimes Leila saw that there was *something* about living closer to the ground and nearer to need, something that bestowed grace on a soul. Or was she just romanticizing poverty? That was super-annoying, when people did that. This ineffable thing she was admiring in the downtrodden Burmese—she didn't want it enough to give away any of what she had.

They spoke in Ma Thiri's small examination room. The walls were covered with exhortations to wash your hands and some junta-required agitprop about working together to overcome adversity and negative elements. But also some medical-anatomical and pictographic self-diagnostic posters that would probably get a school nurse in Kansas run out of town.

Leila's Burmese was about as good as Ma Thiri's English, so when they spoke, that rare thing happened: they shared languages; they shared all that work and risk. In all her previous interviews, Leila had found it difficult to avoid the women's desperation, the plain truth that they would do anything to get what she was dangling before them. So it took her ten minutes to even understand that maybe Ma Thiri didn't want her scholarship. Once Leila understood that ambivalence, she heard herself become incredulous.

"Why not seize this?" she asked. "You can return here with more knowledge and more skills."

"But and what because if I do not return here?"

It was a jumble of words, but there was Ma Thiri's sad smile at the end of it, and its meaning was clear to Leila. Just as Leila had been doing moments before, Ma Thiri was wondering at the puzzle of rich and poor, and she was saying that she was afraid that the West would ruin her for the tougher life that was hers to live.

"You must resolve to return, then" was what Leila said to her (or, actually, *You must extra-decide to return, then,* as she didn't know the Burmese for *resolve*).

But there was this amazing thing that Ma Thiri had already accomplished—the clinic—and that was mostly what they talked about. She said she'd done it for her mother, who had died from—a word that Leila didn't understand but didn't want to ask her to repeat because she got the important part: that it was preventable, and that Ma Thiri was still mad about that.

There was some money from a Christian charity, and perhaps more coming; there was another nurse who might begin work soon. Ma Thiri sighed. Then she smiled. "You will give me a man, also, at this hospital school?" She mentioned the dreamy doctor from a years-old TV show, and Leila laughed.

No. There were too many who needed her here, Ma Thiri decided, right there in front of Leila. And because Ma Thiri was speaking in this stripped-down way, she did not disguise the brag inside her reasoning.

"I am too important here," she said. "No one else can do this." And it turned out that there was a sister and brother to think about as well, and an ailing father.

"Yeah, I have those too," said Leila. But it wasn't like Dylan or Roxana had ever kept her anyplace, or held her back; it wasn't like her dad was sick.

By the time they were done, Leila had gotten Ma Thiri to say she would give the idea more thought. But Leila knew that this woman's mind was made up and that this concession was a politeness. Leaving the clinic, she felt like a confused Ed McMahon walking back to the van with his enormous cardboard check.

That night in Myo Thit, Leila was the only one in her hotel. Not just the only guest—the only human soul. The man she'd assumed was the proprietor left the building, and the lady who had been washing sheets on the roof left the building. Leila lay beneath a mosquito net on a dank foam mattress in a giant room with five other beds, each one shrouded in netting so that it was extra-easy to imagine behind their scrims ghosts or rapists or murderers with machetes or ghost rapist-murderers with machetes. From the bathroom came the blink and buzz of a fluorescent tube and the plang of a dripping valve. A wet brown moth probed her net's perimeter. Every hour a generator chugged flatulently outside. She wished she had objected more fiercely when Aung-Hla insisted on staying in some taximan dormitory down the street. How much cheaper could that place be than this one?

In the eventual morning, Aung-Hla came to collect her. She told him about spending the night with no one in the building, which she shouldn't have, because it made him ashamed for having left her there. He yelled at the proprietor, using a kind of Burmese Leila couldn't even catch scraps of.

"Let's blow this Popsicle stand, Aung-Hla," Leila said to her driver in English when they pulled away. He laughed, probably figuring that she had just said something clever.

But at a checkpoint ten kilometers outside of town, two young soldiers decided to scrutinize Leila's foreign-visitor terrestrial-passage permission form. They made her sit in a white plastic lawn chair in their stifling wooden shack beside their bent, barber-pole-striped, concrete-counterweighted road barrier while they wrote down every number she had on paper that she could attach to herself, including the digits from an expired membership card to the YMCA pool in Oakland, California. They made Aung-Hla sit in his taxi.

After half an hour, Leila saw that Aung-Hla was standing just outside the door to the shack. He motioned to her—silently, pantomimically—that they should go. She stood up. He came in and started speaking to the young soldiers quickly and with force, cutting them off when they tried to answer back, the way you need to speak if you have any hope of bluffing armed teenagers. He gathered up the contents of Leila's travel wallet from the soldiers' laminate desk and sort of reverse-shepherded her out of there, then retreated with Leila to the taxi outside, the soldiers close behind. He saw Leila into the backseat, and, still talking sternly to the soldiers, Aung-Hla himself lifted the barrier across the road. This was too much for one of the soldiers; he unholstered his dull brown pistol and started yelling. Aung-Hla pointed directly down the road and said something ferocious-sounding to the gun-holding boy soldier. It must have been ferocious, because it quieted him, and Aung-Hla took a moment before he turned his key and pulled away from the checkpoint at a dignified speed. Leila fought the urge to sink low in her seat as she had seen people on TV do to duck bullets.

Once he had them out of range, Aung-Hla drove at an increasingly less dignified speed. Leila could see the fear in the back of his neck as they rounded the rutted roads. Those soldiers were drunk, or maybe high, Leila came to understand via Aung-Hla's explanatory charades from the front seat. He made the drink-from-an-upturned-bottle-the-neck-of-which-is-your-thumb gesture. He made the drawing-on-a-joint-pinched-between-thumb-and-index-finger gesture. Then he raised an index finger before him and ticktocked it back and forth, like a metronome on ninety beats per minute, to indicate *no, negative, not to be done, nope, don't, dangerous.* He did it well, this manual negation, keeping his hand still beneath his tocking finger, keeping eye contact with Leila in the rearview.

Aung-Hla left the main road and turned up a wide gravel one that ribboned up a clear-cut hillside into the forest. Leila noted that she was now trusting her driver way past the point of soup. Aung-Hla was trying to explain to her where they were going. Here is what she got: "The drunk soldiers' bosses work up here. If I complain about the drunk soldiers before they report a gate-jumping taximan carrying a white girl, we will be fine. No trouble."

Maybe Aung-Hla knew someone up here. His brother-in-law. Or nephew. Or great-grandfather. Kinship words in Burmese were a bitch.

When another checkpoint hove into sight, Aung-Hla tossed into the backseat a sort of cotton sarong and told Leila to cover up. She wrapped the sheetish thing around herself and cowled the top part into a hood. Aung-Hla pulled to the side of the road in front of the checkpoint, cut the engine, and told her to stay in the car. In perfect English: "Stay in the car," he said. He left the taxi and strode up to the checkpoint house, which was a more impressive affair than the last: it was made from a modified shipping container and raised off the ground; a sweaty air conditioner was bolted to its back, and a telescoping mast lifted a mean-looking and satellite-laden antenna twenty feet into the air. The antivehicle device was not a crappy lift gate but a metal deck with those retractable one-way teeth that you just knew would rip the shit out of your tires. Leila saw Aung-Hla greet one of the checkpoint men with body language that was hearty but submissive. He was led inside the container office by the man he greeted, but he managed to give Leila a no-look thumbs-up sign just before the door closed behind him.

Leila sat in the car. It was only ten in the morning, but after a few minutes, the car was so hot she felt like a Pop-Tart. She looked hungrily at the shade beneath a nearby tree. But Aung-Hla had told her to stay put, and she intended to stay put. She drooped the cowl of her sheetish thing over her brow, tried to keep exquisitely still. Heat this hot was conducive to Buddhism, she realized; it encouraged stillness. Her exhalations stirred the cloth near her chin. Her eye found the photo of Aung-Hla's daughters rubber-banded to the visor. They were seated triangularly against a fake alpine backdrop. They were, at time of snap, what—six, eight, and ten? Then she saw the already-fading printout of the digital photo she'd taken of the car she was sitting in. (In the picture, there was a weeping green tree behind the car, and clean black tarmac beneath its wheels. She had done a good job with the composition.) There was an analog clock Velcroed to the dashboard. The vinyl warmed; the car ticked hotter.

A big Mitsubishi pulled up to the checkpoint. The tire-hungry teeth of the drive-over plate were retracted posthaste, and the Mitsubishi clanked across. Two men debouched from the rear of the car. Leila thought they were a strange pair: one looked Burmese and about fifty; the other looked like a hipster in a Starbucks—T-shirt, square glasses, big headphones, a laptop satchel. They both walked quickly into the container-fort-office thing, the older man holding the door for the younger. Leila was roused from her mild meditation by the event. Then two more white dudes got out of the front of the Mitsubishi and each man started—digging something from his teeth? No, they were both installing plugs of chewing tobacco in their lips. Leila had tried that once; puked. The men were fifty feet away. They were talking, but she couldn't hear what they said. Leila tried to lull herself back into the fugue. She was getting better at recognizing situations over which she had no control.

The two men were leaving their vehicle and walking nearer to hers. They made it to the shade tree she had been coveting. Once they reached it, they didn't so much stand under it as lurk beneath it. They had the hunch of security men but wore no insignia or uniform. They were fifteen feet beyond her open window. They both wore black, wraparound glasses, from behind which, she was sure, they were scanning the perimeter. One, the younger man, clocked her, and then Two, but they both seemed to look right past her. Through the sheer fabric of her wrap she could see them plainly, but they were talking as if they were alone. They spoke English in American accents.

". . . little prick thinks we're butlers?" said One. He spit a brown splat on the dirt at his feet.

"Doesn't matter what he thinks we are," said Two.

"I mean, he's fucking tech support. He's here to install software. You know that?"

Two snapped: "No, I do not know that. You don't either. You know he's the package. You get him in, you get him out. That is all you know."

"I know that little shit sent me back for his suitcase, for face cream or whatever. I know that," said One. "This whole shit is bullshit, is all I'm saying."

Two said nothing to this last critique. But he spit, better than One had, a glob missiled at the ground. A tiny shake of his head told Leila he was rolling his eyes behind the viperous shades.

One hadn't finished. "We're not allowed to carry. That's bullshit. These eight-week rotations are bullshit. And the food is definitely bull-shit. If that was chicken, I'm Pat Sajak."

"You getting paid?" Two asked One. Veins stood out on his arms, his neck.

One was indeed getting paid, apparently, for the line quieted him. But he was still mad, Leila could tell, watching from behind her veil. He was standing in a tough-guy pose, and when he spit, he squinted like he was pissed at the tobacco. "That job with the Pakis—now, *that* was a job."

"Boy," said Two—they both looked like hammers, but Two was older—"if you just want to be muscle, you got about five years left in this business."

"Nothing wrong with being muscle." One sounded hurt. "Better than being a fucking taxi driver."

At that, Two shot a quick glance at Leila. He was appraising her. Had she looked listen-y? She needed to appear oblivious. From her fancy knapsack, which was out of the men's sight, she took the sunflower seeds that she'd brought from Mandalay. Noisily, she rustled them out of the newspaper envelope they were wrapped in, but she brought them to her mouth delicately, one by one, in the slightly feral way she had seen women eat seeds here. It seemed to work — Two quit looking at her and plucked flecks of tobacco from his lip. Leila dialed her ears up to ten.

"I'm just sayin'," said One, sulkily. "I didn't sign on to be a bellhop in Burma."

"We're in China," said Two.

"Yeah, right. China," said One.

Aung-Hla came out of the office, down the metal steps. He was effusively thanking the man in the office. The security men tracked him to the car. *Don't speak English to me,* Leila was thinking hard at Aung-Hla as he opened his door.

"We are hunky-dory," he said to her loudly, smiling because he had just accomplished something rather complicated. The security men stiffened at the English. Two looked at Leila again, harder now.

"No more English, Aung-Hla," she snapped at her driver, in Burmese. She pitched her voice high and nasal, in a way she hoped sounded convincing. Burmese was a tonal language, but Leila, like most Indo-European speakers, was reluctant to attempt the tonal part, because she thought it made her sound like an aggrieved crow. "Those men no good," she cawed quickly at Aung-Hla. "Talk Burmese to me. Now." And he did. He understood her meaning and spoke a rapid Burmese paragraph, which she did not understand.

"Leave now. Us both," she said. And they did; Aung-Hla executed a quick three-point turn and they headed back down the road they'd come up. Leila found her fancy running watch in her knapsack and pressed the MARK POINT button.

She tried to explain to Aung-Hla what had happened. It was difficult. She didn't know how to say *contractors* in Burmese, or *mercenaries.* She managed *soldiers who don't work for the government.* And when she told Aung-Hla that Americans were not allowed to work in Myanmar, he said, "But you work here."

That night, after they got back to Mandalay and Aung-Hla had dropped Leila off, she filled out the Helping Hand paperwork that would allow her to pay Aung-Hla as not just a taximan but a "required national." She put the equivalent of three hundred dollars in an envelope, managed to copy Aung-Hla's name in Burmese script on the front of it, and put the envelope in her knapsack. She looked forward to giving him the money and tried to think only of the benefit it would bring him, not of the stark difference in power between them that it would make plain.

PORTLAND, OREGON

Turning his head to look at the Fremont Bridge sparkling in the sharp light of the November morning, Leo felt his chin rasp across the collars of his two woolen shirts and his canvas work coat. The outfit thickened the upper half of his tall thin frame, which even at rest had a teetering quality. Hunched into the wind, proud over the handlebars of his bicycle, he looked like a heavy kettle on a high shelf, and most in his path gave him wide berth. But it was early yet, just light and still cold; there weren't many in his path.

As he did most every day now, Leo wished that he were biking over the Fremont Bridge instead of the bridge he *was* biking over, the Broadway Bridge, which was a more workmanlike affair, maroon and million-riveted; a bascule bridge with chunky block piers like galoshes. The Fremont Bridge was so beautiful, massive and graceful at once, a marvel of engineering. A brisk wind in the seagullosphere snapped the flags at the apex of its arc. The river below was a deep, churning green.

One morning six months back, Leo had found his car skewed and curb-jumped before his house. *So it was no dream,* he'd thought, filled with shame and dread and panic. It was easier to quit driving than drinking, so Leo had transformed himself into a committed cyclist. But now, the fact that there was no pedestrian or bike path on the Fremont Bridge was an affront to him. Leo knew well that driving over the top deck of that bridge, especially at speed, was a real zooter. A state-subsidized roller coaster for the auto-addicted, he thought to himself as he looked at the Fremont's graceful trajectory, which lay along a much shorter path between his home and workplace—another affront, to be denied not only the most glamorous but also the most direct route to his destination. Why should so much of the might of the state go to flinging out these ribbons of concrete so that citizens can zoom around in their private metal zoom-arounders?

He was getting indignant. Leo was good at indignant. Also burdened; he could do a good burdened. But indignant was one of the few aggressive postures he could strike convincingly—something having to do with the mix of blue-blood Yankee yeoman farmer and *Mayflower* screwball and tough prairie Protestant in his pedigree. A crackpot uncle of his, in Maine, had twice handcuffed himself to heavy equipment to obstruct the construction of cell phone towers. There was a gene Leo wouldn't mind expressing.

Yes, he thought as he passed too close to a shuffle-jogging man upholstered in a damp terry tracksuit, *pedaling over the Fremont Bridge in the morning would be an excellent start to the day*. Maybe he should lead a political campaign to get a pedestrian and bicycle right-of-way added to the bridge. Maybe by his efforts the bridge would become a century-defining nonmotorized boulevard and, upon his death, from kiteboarding or something, would be named after him. A man who looked like a teddy bear was cursing at him. Why?

Now a gust came up off the water and flung the tassel-terminated strings of his woolen hat behind his head. He biked faster. The gust brought him news—yeast and pine gum and benzene and bleach and fir and mud and pulp and slurry. Atop the Fremont Bridge, you could probably smell for miles, thought Leo as he coasted across the humbler bridge, filling his lungs with air and his eyes with light.

Then a cloud scudded before the sun and the bridge quit humming beneath him and the wind ceased to carry meaning and in countless other ways the grandeur fled, like shining back into shook foil. The strange brew of neurotransmitters that had encouraged the bike-activist fantasy sloshed up against some limiting mechanism and began to recede; the recipe was tweaked, and chemicals brushed past one another, exchanging glances, methyl groups. Leo started the process, which would increase in period and intensity throughout the day, of telling himself that he was a loser and a failure.

Where to begin? People who get bike lanes added to bridges are committed people, five-year-plan people. Tireless campaigners who probably cared more about ideas than they did about themselves. How do you care about something more than yourself? Leo wondered. Daydreaming about bridges bearing his name? Please. He hadn't voted in years, he wasn't wearing a helmet, he had only one brake, he was late for work, and he worked at a preschool.

"Fuck. I hate myself," he whispered, spit drying on his chin.

Leo waited at the traffic light at the end of the bridge. He marveled at the vast post office—was that Soviet architecture? Brutalist? The place seemed big enough to hide a mining operation. The light turned green and he went right, dropping down into a neighborhood sprung full from a salesman's case. A dry-cleaner, a dog boutique, a sandwich shop, and an optician were the only businesses along one block. In front of the dog boutique, a FedEx truck chugged at idle, its hazard lights bleating carmine auras into the morning mist. He ghosted over silky new pavement through an empty public square that featured a sunken, dry fountain and pebbly planters full of exotic grasses and reeds. On four sides rose new apartment buildings, the kind with exposed structural elements and balconies at dramatic angles and valuable parking and panoptical security systems. These were condominiums for the creative class, or for any taxpaying and easily policed types of citizens: potentate drifters, wealthy retirees, and leisure merchants. But the whole thing was about a minute old, and only a few souls had moved in.

Leo's preschool, Brand-New Day, was on the far side of all of this new development, but he had never tried to bike through it. The way around wasn't much longer, it had a wide bike lane, and it took him past a favorite coffee shop.

But a late arrival to work today would put him in even hotter water than he was in already with his fake-smiling supervisor, Sharon. Just yesterday, she had tried to impress upon him that it would be a Brand-New Day for him employment-wise if he didn't start attending to the areas that she had earlier mentioned were areas he might want to look into improving around.

"I think that, instead of lateness, you could be aiming for on-time-ness" was one of her points.

And Leo, who more and more these days was overcoming his natural restraint, had said, "Or punctuality. I could aim for that instead of on-time-ness."

A route through the pretend neighborhood could save him the five minutes he needed. The danger was dead-ending against a freeway sound wall and having to circle back. He briefly considered the stakes, then cycled deeper down the quiet streets of terra condominia.

Yeah. Too quiet, thought Leo. In a year or two, the facades of these buildings would no longer enjoy that blush of blank beauty. Soon each window would instead emit its own signal—here, probably the flaccid ficus trees and stereos of the urban professional, exercise machines and transfixed house cats—semaphoring to passersby some information about the lives stacked up behind the glass. But maybe one day, thought Leo, these buildings would be re-tasked—laundry might be hanging from those balconies, Caracas-style, or more buildings could be warrened atop these, like in Hong Kong. For that matter, the sunken civic Zen patch back there could become a Byzantine souk, tent-poled haphazardly and covered in rugs looted from the surrounding design stores. Maybe we'll all be living a lot closer together in the future, in a sort of pleasant, Burning Man–ish kind of way, Leo thought. Or maybe in a totally *un*pleasant, refugee-camp sort of way, with viruses we haven't seen the speck of yet, viruses that make your face fall straight off, and our drinking water brought in by tanker trucks. If it were like tha—

There was no one even near Leo when he flew from his bike. His mind cast about for a culprit, for someone to blame other than himself. The bike just ceased its forward motion and he did not. How surprising, how nifty physics was. And as he trebucheted toward a four-inch curb, aware at once that his meeting with it would be physically calamitous, he remembered that he was wearing no helmet, and his surprise turned to fear. A month ago, at a party to which his friend Louis had brought him, Leo had heard (well, overheard) the host claiming that he wasn't afraid of death. That particular claim seemed to Leo to be demonstrably false. So, costumed as Jesus (for this was a Halloween party), Leo had decided to explore the man's reasoning. *Not afraid of death, huh? My, that must make you a real psychopath.* But he had seen almost immediately that he should not have told the man that he was like a Holocaust denier. "I said *like* a Holocaust denier. *Like,*" he protested lamely when Louis escorted him out of the party and told him to enjoy the bracing walk home, dressed as Jesus.

No, thought Leo, as he landed his right hand, fingertips first, on the cold nubbly of the curb, *I am definitely more than a body, but I believe I am less than a soul.*

Then, with a fluid agility that hadn't been his in years, Leo tucked his head and vertical body behind the leading edge of his rounded arm. Some latent muscle memory from five months of jujitsu at the McBurney YMCA on West Sixty-Third Street when he was ten? Leo seemed to recall that this YMCA had in fact served the adventurous class of men described in the song. Now, he felt a point beneath his stomach become the axis of his spinning mass, and he knew to use that dragony breath to take the hit when, after about 120 degrees, his trunk met the sidewalk, hard. Next was his hip and ass, which rolled over not just the concrete but also a busted padlock on the scene by chance. Then came his knees and feet, with a thwack. That was followed by his trailing left arm, which lay down gently, and his gloved palm, which landed and sprang back, the way a *conguero* lands a hand on the taut hide of his drum.

Leo stood up. He was fine. Just fine. Right as rain.

Leo stood up again, this time more carefully. Okay, maybe *fine* was an overstatement. But ambulatory and intact. A bit exhilarated, actually.

His bike lay twisted in the street behind him, its front tire still clamped in the groove of the new light-rail system tracks they were laying all over town. Only now did he notice the yellow-and-black warning signs that would have made him aware of the hazard his bike had to cross. The graphics depicted pretty much what had just happened: a bicycle with its front wheel caught in the maw of the track, the blockish pictogram rider hurtling over the handlebars. An honest piece of graphic art; a tiny, two-line picture poem, thought Leo, and he started to upbraid himself for his carelessness and lack of attention.

But wait. On one corner—the direction from which he'd come— the warning sign was there, but it was swathed in black plastic, taped up tight.

The thought came like a revelation: *This was no accident. They obscured that sign because they want me eliminated.*

Some part of him said, *No, don't be ridiculous.* But then why was only one sign shrouded?

The dips and swoops, the rapid-cyclings, had been with him for a while now, but these revelatory thoughts were new. They arrived at the peaks of the swoops. That's when things really started ringing, when it seemed that he was at the center of things, that the very planet was pulsing with connectivity, and he was one of Tesla's bulbs.

Was it really so far-fetched? That there would be some agency tasked with keeping tabs on wayward members of the intellectual elite? No, it was actually quite reasonable, Leo thought. Big Data and all. So, yes, it was possible that he was being singled out, being watched, being followed. It was probably connected to his blog, on which he'd lately been considering what exactly a shadow government would look like, how it might work. Maybe he'd been getting too close.

On the dips, he saw that such notions were perhaps paranoid delusions and that he might need psychiatric help. But he was unwilling to submit his mental processes to the purported care of professionals who might have all sorts of limitations and biases and, yes, agendas. And the swoops outnumbered the dips, so why complain? Shimmering on the bright edge of every day was the possibility that he was going to discover a grand unifying theory. That was not a condition to be treated; that was something to hold on to.

He started again toward work, wheeling his injured bicycle beside him. There was no way he could avoid being late. But he hardly cared now. He had been granted grace and had avoided death. Life was not a dense thicket of pain and scrabbling; it was a wild and godly fable in which he figured prominently. This news spread through his body like a flush. He was reconnected with the great river of life that flowed all around us all the time. The sky domed huge and gray-blue, and the trees, shaken by a gust, rattled a tattoo to him.

Brand-New Day was in a building that had once been a genuine warehouse. You could still make out SCHMIDT'S SPOOL AND SPINDLE in huge, ghosty letters across its facade. Five years ago the warehouse had been converted into the offices of a briefly white-hot Internet business that turned out to be a bellwether of the dot-com bust. Brand-New Day had inherited the late-bubble furnishings and appointments of the previous tenants, and so it resembled a start-up run by toddlers. Chop the legs off a couple of poured-concrete conference tables and you get some deluxe arts-and-crafts zones for little Mirós. Why not give every child a cubicle instead of a cubby? (Because children crapped in their cubicles was why not, it turned out.) The skateboard ramp in the foyer was filled with sofa cushions and called the romper zone. Employees sailed across the polished concrete floors on Aeron chairs while their charges crawled over and drooled on and beat with sticks black-leather benches and cubes and sectionals.

The Aeron chairs were nice. Leo was the author of a game called Rolling Death, staged in the outdoor play zone, in which a staffer, "restrained" in an Aeron chair by the kids, would zoom maniacally around the OPZ yelling, ideally, "I am Death. I touch you, you die," while the kids screeched and careened, addled with joy and running with snot, and dodged the caroming desk chair. Leo wasn't the only one who played it now either. Another staffer named Lisa did a great Rolling Death, as did a tiny Dominican lady named Cecilie, who laughed more wildly than the children as she zoomed—they raced from her as if from a plague. The game was a desperate favorite of just about all the children at Brand-New Day, though when he played with the twos-and-threes, Leo zoomed more slowly. Just the whisper of maybe playing it could get fourteen five-year-olds to collect from the floor a morning's worth of paper scraps and gluey cotton balls.

The management was in a bind re Leo and his methods. He was sometimes a liability, especially when prospective parents were touring the facility. Why were the threes-and-fours listening to the Clash? Why were the fours-and-fives engaged in what appeared to be a mock trial of a stuffed gorilla on a Big Wheel? Sharon claimed to have no problem with Rolling Death per se (she was quite fond of *per se;* also *at this point in time*), but she wanted the name changed.

"How about Huggy Monster?" she suggested to Leo once at the seven-thirty goals meeting.

"Not as much at stake in that case, I think," he said.

The truth was that the outdoor play zone was actually a covered parking lot that backed up to an enormous freeway pier and was surrounded by chain-link and surfaced in orange matting. A few play structures couldn't dent its overall vibe of incarceration. When only the twos-and-threes milled outside in heavy diapers, or when a sparse crew of toddlers fought for possession of two blanched pedal cars, the outdoor play zone was truly grim and resembled a transfer point for tiny high-value detainees. Only a game that got the kids whooping, like Rolling Death, could transform the OPZ into the squealing theater that made parents certain they had done right to choose Brand-New Day, despite its cost, which was more than pretty much all of them had ever thought they would spend on child care.

And the parents, once they had interacted with Leo a few times, liked and trusted him. The mothers especially. They saw that their Lukes and Lolas ran to him first thing every morning. They watched him sit in tiny chairs and murmur to children who were protesting their parents' departure. None of this wide-eyed condescension; no *Is that your bear?* shit. Rather, an intense and sincere interest. He rinsed their soiled clothes and hung them to dry over the sink; he slipped their best artwork into manila envelopes so that it would not get crumpled. And the parents liked the way he filled out the daily journal sheets that went into each child's mailbox at the end of the day.

TODAY WE PLAYED WITH _____. *Blocks. Who woulda thunk?* Leo might write. Or, for TODAY WE ATE _____, he'd riff on the day's offerings. Sometimes he'd produce a critique: *Fish sticks flaccid, but juice boxes especially cold.* Sometimes he'd mash up imaginary combinations, aiming for gross, as a child would. *Orange Roughy and Band-Aids. Mousse de Purell. Baby Carrots in Rubber Cement.* Or he'd pair a wine with the meal: *Riz Brun. Petits Pois. Château Latour 1959.*

But then, beneath those idiotic prompts, in the lower half of the page, he'd add a few sentences about the weather or a reference to current events, something to peg that piece of paper to the adult world. Or maybe something about the mood in the room that day. *Carla's vomiting in the sink transfixed the fours-and-fives and put them off snack.* Or, *The squall that came at midday soothed everyone here. Rain on windows trumps contested sock monkey.*

Then he'd copy that master thirty times, standing over the copier as proud and eager as Hearst before his presses. Afterward, he'd add child-specific notes to a few of the editions, and then he'd distribute them among the mailboxes at the front. He liked to see the mothers and fathers jam these pieces of paper in their pockets and bags. He hoped that their lives would be improved some small amount by his words, by what they read about their children, for whom they toiled. Often he saw these notes crumpled and thrown away unread; there was a recycling bin next to the front door. Some parents had probably never once read a daily journal sheet.

That was okay. Leo was aware that taking pride in such a thing was ridiculous—that to do so exposed him to ridicule. But since everyone pretended to believe that you should take pride in whatever you do, most people were caught by something in Leo.

That happy fool at day care is referring to Afghanistan today, a man might say to his wife from the kitchen. And she to him, sweeping Cheerios from the sofa: *It's* preschool, *you idiot. What'd he say?*

When coworkers chided Leo about his devotion to the daily journal sheets, he tried to take it in stride. But really. Why did grown-ups find it necessary to tease fellow citizens who actually gave a shit?

"Enter the aphorist," Eric would say whenever Leo came into the break room. Eric was the only other penis-laden BND employee and he seemed to not quite understand what an aphorist was, or maybe he hadn't actually read the daily journal sheets, because Leo's reportage was anything but aphoristic. Whenever he was reminded that it was largely fools and galoots who ran the world, Leo resorted to subvocal mantric recitations of the true-yet-banal moral directives that he had picked up from the few AA meetings he had ducked his head into after the blacked-out drive home: Reserve Judgment. My Side of the Street. Principles Before Personalities.

But why did it not occur to any of his colleagues that not enough was being written about these kids? That children—even these economic-pinnacle children—were cashless and unlettered, after all, and if some decent record was to be kept of their day, someone would have to do it for them? Leo didn't consider his account even adequate, really. So much was going on around him that escaped his notice. They were a flock he watched over; corralled, actually. He was a subcontracted shepherd, and his authority over them came from his greater strength, from the fact that he could quickly extract and, if need be, carry and, if need still be, restrain a child swinging a Wheat Thin like a shiv. The kids were hardly ever offered a choice—a real one, anyway—and Leo pretty much had to leave them alone to see them express preferences and drives. In these moments, or when he knelt among them silently observing a quarrel or a peacemaking gesture, he was aware of their society. But mostly, he was as clueless as a towheaded television reporter in Tahrir Square, and he did not hold himself up as a toddler sage or anything.

Leo made certain not to slack off in the other areas of the job. His coworkers could count on him to do his fair share or more of the daily labor required to run the floor at BND. The job consisted largely of light to medium housework and physical interventions in minor civil disputes. Leo was good at it, and he was well liked by pretty much everyone at BND.

Until Sharon came around. She started in on him at once about the lateness. *Can't you see that no one else around here cares?* he wanted to say to her. *I'm fifteen minutes late and you're thirty pounds overweight. Can't we just call it even?* He did not say this. He loved his job and feared that Sharon was looking for cause to fire him. But really: No one else cared that he was late. Leo was almost always the last to leave. And there were about nine doors to check and lock and three notebooks to sign out of before the last to leave *could* leave. Once a week it was Leo who would stay late to receive the cleaners, a spectral team of Tyvek-suited Mexicans. A day-care facility was light duty for these guys, probably. Leo imagined that they usually cleaned up after suicides and fires.

Two or three times a month, Leo could count on staying late with a hyperactive boy named Malcolm whose mother would tear up at half past seven in a heaving BMW, desperate with apology and excuse. Such a parent was, per BND policy and contract, supposed to be charged a dollar per minute for any child care provided after 6:00 p.m. That was just stupid and punitive, though, so Leo would back-time Malcolm's mom's arrival to, say, 6:15. The last time that she had been late, she put cash in Leo's hand under a dark and soggy sky outside. He'd accepted it accidentally, because she'd slipped it to him so discreetly, as if he were a maître d'. There followed an awkward operation in which Leo tried to give the money back, and he'd succeeded only when he'd finally pressed it against her. Which in turn complicated things, because there was a little spark, and they were both suddenly and briefly aware of the fun they could have fucking.

There was definitely something off about his equilibrium, Leo thought as he wheeled his lame bicycle up to the door of Brand-New Day. The right side of his body was beginning to feel like meat wrapped too tight in cellophane, and his hands were clumsy working the key of his bicycle lock, as if he had two fingers instead of five.

That fall really gave me paws, he thought to himself, and he chuckled, which hurt his ribs.

He gave up on the lock, thumbed a code into the keypad around the side of the building, and rolled his bike into the play area. Employee bicycles were not supposed to be stored in the play area, another Sharon-promulgated rule.

Louise, a self-assured five-year-old on a Razor scooter, was the first to see him. "What's wrong with you?" she asked.

"I fell off my bike, Louise," he said.

"Did you have a helmet on your head?"

"No. I forgot it," Leo said.

"You shouldn't forget it, Leo," said Louise sternly, and she Razored off.

Then Bennett and Milo, inseparable four-year-olds, stamped up to Leo, huffing, in spotless Nikes.

"What's wrong with you?" asked Bennett.

"Nothing, Bennett," Leo said. "How are you doing today?"

"Okay," said Milo. "You fell off your bike?"

These kids were rhizomic, thought Leo. "Yeah, but I'm okay."

"Can we play Rolling Death?" asked Bennett.

"Maybe in a little while," said Leo.

"When?" asked Milo.

"Gimme a minute, guys," said Leo as he slid down a wall to sit on the ground. His neck felt like a stem. He tried to keep his head between his shoulders and directly above his body. He was weirdly aware of his skin as the sack holding his person. It was *un*pleasant.

Alka approached him. She was a little Indian girl, all eyelashes and shoelaces. "Are you okay, Leo?" she asked.

"Yeah, I'm okay, Alka," he said. Then, because she was a child and would not call him crazy for saying it, he added, "But I think that they just tried to kill me."

"You should be careful," said Alka.

"Mos' def, Alka. We should all be careful."

It was probably due to his disembodied—or, rather, too keenly embodied—state that Leo was unaware of Sharon, who had come up behind him.

"Can I speak to you inside, Leo," said Sharon.

"They tried to kill Leo," said Alka.

"No, that was just a joke, Alka," said Sharon. "Leo was joking. Why don't you go and play with Cecilie." Sharon was in a purple pantsuit. Alka, all of five, heard the edge in Sharon's voice and shoved off. "Leo. Inside. Right now," said Sharon.

Every successful person knows that he's supposed to have a story about having been fired. But if one is telling such a story, it is presumed that the teller has overcome the embarrassment of the event and is telling it beneath the smiling light of a vindicating future. However, Leo had been fired from, or failed at, a few jobs now, so the walk from the outdoor play zone to Sharon's front office was a long one indeed, especially because his feet seemed to lag in their response to his brain's commands, which meant that he was staggering.

The other play facilitators weren't looking at him. Or maybe they were just engaged with those children who stayed in a mild post-traumatic state for twenty minutes after drop-off, the ones you really had to look after. Samuel was not one of those children. Samuel, a stoic riddle of a child who happily did blockwork while classmates shrieked murderously beside him and who would probably soon receive a distinguishing diagnosis, had dropped his gluestick and was beelining toward Leo.

"Hold on there, Samuel," said Leo to the boy as he approached. But

Samuel ignored him and flung himself at Leo, open-armed. Leo picked him up and held him strongly, though in doing so, he noticed, painfully, his torqued spine. So, gently, he put Samuel down. Sharon was standing at the open door to her office. Leo trudged in.

Sharon's office was full of beanbag frogs; she thought frogs were winning and childlike. She gestured for Leo to sit, and then she sat too, among her frogs, and put her arms on her desk.

"Leo, I think we both know why you're here," she said.

Yeah, but he wasn't going to help her do this. "Promotion?" he said.

Her fingers were laced pudgily on her huge desk-blotter calendar. "You've gotten stranger and stranger these past few months, Leo. I'm afraid I just can't have you responsible for these children. I am going to have to ask you to leave."

"Ask me? Really?"

"No. Tell you. Okay? I'm telling you to leave. Let's not make this unpleasant, Leo. Brand-New Day has no further need of your services."

His face went hot and the small room got smaller, like someone had twisted the zoom lens on his vision. He felt like a child. Tears—oh hell, not *tears*—came to his eyes. He was going to lose something dear to him. The mayhem of cleaning up after crafts, the riot of Rolling Death, the quiet of nap. The children. They didn't care what a hash he'd made of the past ten years. They were joy uncorrupted, bad liars, openhearted. They were his fan base, his gorgeous, dirty rabble. They loved him.

"But who will write the daily journal sheets?" he tried to say but squeaked instead, the words rushing, high-pitched, to beat out the sob rising behind them.

"I want you to leave the building when you leave this room, Leo. Do you understand?" she said.

Leo tried to collect himself. He paid close attention to his breath. He set his mouth, looked at his hands. Then something strange happened: anger began to eclipse the pain and confusion.

"You'll have to pay me to leave, right? You can't just fire me like this?"

"I think if you look at your contract, you'll find that we owe you two weeks' pay."

His contract? He had forgotten he had one of these. "Okay. I'll take that now."

Sharon looked at him as blankly as one of her frogs.

"I mean *right* now. You got nine hundred and sixty bucks in that desk?"

"Of course not. I'll have Linda send you a check."

I'll have Linda send you a check. And just like that, Brand-New Day would be done with him. Oh, it made his blood boil; it made him light-headed. So few people could give these children the kind of care he'd been giving them. He was sure of that. Never lying to them; engaging them with all he had. *I'll have Linda send you a check.* He wanted to rifle through Sharon's desk drawers, her purse. He wanted to take whatever money she had, kick her in the pantsuit. He wanted to break her stupid fat fingers, scatter her zillion folders, command the fours-and-fives to set on her like jackals. Uh-oh. He had mumbled some of that aloud.

Behind the rage was another feeling: a keen pleasure at feeling en-raged. He tried to hold on to the rage and the pleasure at the rage, because beyond these was a deep lake of sadness at the fact that he had just lost a job he loved, that he would not see these children again, that tomorrow the hours would yawn in front of him. Others would go to work and he'd have to pick his way across the moody rubble of the day. Plus, he didn't have any breathing room in his budget. He spent every cent that came his way. And the last time his sisters had given him money, they'd made it pretty clear that they were tired of bailing him out.

He stood up too quickly, and the chair he had been sitting in tipped back and fell over. Sharon jumped in her seat. Leo enjoyed her discom-fort. Was she actually afraid of him? Good. Let her be. Puffed with anger and gutted with grief, he opened Sharon's office door to leave.

"I don't want you upsetting the children, Leo," Sharon said to his back. "You understand? I just want you to leave now. Don't worry about the take-home notes. I can write those."

Sharon would write the daily journal sheets? She'd fuck up a shopping list. His hand found a beanbag frog. He turned and hucked it at her. The frog whizzed through the close air of the office. It thunked squarely into Sharon's eye and landed flat on her desk.

They were both shocked. Only the thrown frog was unfazed. It was still smiling the way frogs certainly do not smile. Then that moment broke, and Leo, proud of the first violent act of his adult life, skedaddled.

"That's assault! You assaulted me, you little prick," Sharon yelled after him. She was picking up her phone.

But he was moving now. Toward the exit. He stopped to face the big room once. The grown-ups were brittle, the children oblivious. He raised a clenched fist high. "Give 'em hell," he shouted.

At the far end of the room, Samuel raised his small fist in return.

NEW YORK CITY

Right this way, Mr. Deveraux."

The assistant led Mark down low-ceilinged corridors to a greenroom and held the door open without entering himself. Mark peered in. Leather couches; an expansive array of granola bars and iced bottles of juice and water and bagels and tea bags in foil envelopes; *Margo!* magazines on a hyperabundance of end tables; an attractive man stirring coffee daintily and looking engrossed in the sheaf of papers before him. Mark didn't enter the room either.

"Yeah, listen," he said to the PA, "I believe that my representative told the person that she liaised with here that I would be needing a private room to prepare? With a window? For meditational purposes? Do you think you could see about that?"

The PA nodded slowly and blinked twice. He looked at his clipboard. "Ah, sure." He exhaled. The microphone part of the headset he wore looked like a big fat fly hovering before his mouth. "Would you like to wait in there and I'll see about that?"

"That's okay. I'll wait right here." Mark watched the PA retreat and he considered the possibility that he would have to go on TV in his current too-sober state. Other than this potential crimp, though, everything was pretty much as he had hoped it would be: the black car sent for him; the attractive assistant who sat primly in the backseat with him (she wore a gray skirt and a pristine mountaineering parka that kept Mark from scoping her northern hemisphere, and she worked the thumb wheel on her BlackBerry as though it were a rosary); the way that, once he got to the studio, there was a sort of event horizon that preceded him by fifty yards within which everyone appeared to be aware of him and of who he was.

He realized that he recognized the good-looking man in the green-room—a celebrity chef who claimed his name was Nicholas Rugby. Mark had received a copy of his book from three different people last Christmas. It was called *Eat for the Real You* and featured shallow-depth-of-field photography of noodles, and breezy instructions rich in kinetic verbs. He could go in there now and introduce himself and they'd probably both pretend to respect each other's work and maybe become celebrity friends and Mark could have Nicholas to dinner and Nicholas could make his famous noodles, famously, in the open-plan kitchen Mark was going to install in the apartment he'd just bought in Brooklyn. But no—Mark was getting more nervous by the moment. Maybe after the taping there'd be time for that. He would wait in the hallway now, wait to be shown the private room that these days was his due.

In the year or so since he had begun his steep ascent through the strata of this particular type of fame, Mark had found that those charged with his comfort actually liked him to express specific wishes. A seat number less than ten and on the right side of the airplane. A lectern no taller than forty inches. Idiosyncrasies were also appreciated. He kept about ten pens on his person and had notepads jammed into every pocket. The jamming-in part was important. Mark pre-rumpled the notepads—bent the cardboard backing and curled the pages—so that when he pulled out a pad, it looked positively fizzling with ideas. Marjorie Blinc, his cunning consigliera, encouraged the behavior, especially the pre-appearance requests. "Don't be a jerk about it, but be firm," she said. "Let me be a jerk about it." There were a few stipulations she had written into his standard

contract that Mark had balked at: lemon rounds, not wedges; hypoaller-
genic makeup; fair-trade green tea. These, she explained, were gives—
items that he was *not* to insist upon, which lack of insistence would make
him seem like a much more reasonable person than his contract made
him out to be.

"If it comes up, go ahead and say you had no idea that the agency
wrote lemon rounds into your contract," she told him, "and that you find
such a requirement ridiculous." At first, these machinations had embarrassed him. Then he saw how well they worked. And soon he ceased to
think of them as machinations. The fact that he accepted, graciously, either a lemon wedge or a lemon round in his sparkling water he took as
evidence of his own lack of attachment. He knew that there were people
who actually did care about such things; he was not one of them.

But this need to be alone in a room with a window was not a give. In
a few minutes he would be talking to ten million people. Come off well
here, and his name and work would bloom like ink in water. There were
people waiting around to see if the success of his book was repeatable, if
his philosophy was scalable. Blinc's agency had already gotten him more
money than his mother had spent on his upbringing. But Mark was no
fool. Someone else would come along with something new and knock
the charm right off him. Before the magazine-reading classes tired of
him, he needed to leverage his fluke fame into something more bankable.
He needed to pluck from this tempest the idea he still believed in and
carry it to safety. Do that, and he wouldn't need Marjorie Blinc or her
squads of editors and forecasters. He wouldn't need the craven SineCo
squillionaire James Straw, whose early devotion to Mark's book—he'd
decreed that it should serve as management doctrine for his tech empire
and bought a copy for every one of his employees—was the reason that
Mark now had an agent and publicists and an accountant and (ever since
he'd begun to receive scrawl-penned letters from one particularly enthu-
siastic and unhinged fan) a security consultant.

Gray Skirt was coming toward him now at a brisk clip. Her boots
made a *tack-tack* sound that preceded her.

"Is there a problem with the greenroom?" she asked, appearing to care.

"Oh, no. No problem. It's just that I'll need a few minutes of solitude before I go on. To meditate. To get centered. A room with a window, if at all possible."

"I think we can accommodate you," said Gray Skirt, smiling in a tight-lipped way.

Yes, I think you can too, thought Mark, giddy with the sense, as he was so often these days, that the world would and could accommodate him. Was it zero-sum? A pretty girl was going to lead him to a private room in a TV studio; did that mean that someone else, somewhere else, was *not* receiving such treatment? He thought not. Although there were probably not enough private jets for everyone. Mark had now spent tens of hours aloft in a few of these—he had *slept on a couch* in a tube going five hundred miles an hour high above the blue earth. But for that matter, even being able to fly coach represents an unearned economic advantage, doesn't it? Or, hell, just driving a car. Who among us deserves all he has? Mark recognized that there was hypocrisy at the center of his current life ("A young wise man without pretensions," *Time* magazine had called him, although last week, he had been hunting wild boar, drunk, on Straw's Carmel ranch), but he was doing nothing more than asking for the things he wanted. Which was what his book, *Bringing the Inside Out,* had turned out to be about. Still, when he remarked to Gray Skirt that the studio was a bit nippy, he did this by way of flirtation, not in anticipation of being handed a cashmere sweater from a closet stocked with them.

"Here, take a *Margo!* sweater, courtesy of Margo," said Gray Skirt. "Margo keeps the studio at this temperature to boost alertness. It was one of many changes she made around here after she read your book."

Was she fucking with him? Mark wondered. If not, then he was dealing with a real fawn, which was exciting. He scanned her again for any obvious defects that might have escaped his initial survey. Somewhere between black car and chill studio, she had swapped her extreme parka for a sort of power shawl, which was somewhat more revealing. She had pretty, coltish shoulders and thick black hair. But still. She might very well be fucking with him. There was a lack of feeling in the way she deferred to him, although that could have been due to the fact that she was Margo's third—or maybe even second—lieutenant, and therefore more powerful and important than he was. If she was only chafing at the task assigned to her, that would be fine. He could probably win her over by acting as if he didn't care that she outranked him. But he wished to eliminate the possibility that she was one of the—it must be many—people who believed that his book was totally fatuous. Did she know that he could not now recall how he had arrived at any of his so-called conscious-clusions; had no idea, really, what the word was meant to mean? Ditto *flowtachment.* Did she know that, after he and his eight agency-supplied editors had been over the copy hundreds of times in the four weeks it took to produce the manuscript, Mark could not see in the book's anodyne, aphoristic nonsense any of the ideas that had made "Motivation in an Unjust World" a good essay?

"Motivation in an Unjust World" was the essay Mark had written two years ago. The gist of it had been wrung from him in a single night, at his kitchen table, on an IBM Selectric, which hummed like a generator on a ship. Bombed on OxyContin and Pouilly-Fuissé chardonnay (and Riesling, when the chardonnay had gone), he had written ten pages without getting up. They were confused and chaotic, but there was a bright strand of logic running between the paragraphs, which drew a reader through the whole thing.

Or would, Mark felt sure the next morning, if he could just flatten out a few of the steeper arcs between ideas and find a way to avoid sounding so strident there at the end; in fact, do away with any whiff of strident and replace it with the detached tone he had somehow managed in the first third.

He set about the rewrite that day, after a cigarette and a walk around the block, and at the same kitchen table, stinging coffee and buttered toast in the a.m., slick Guinness and buttered toast in the p.m. By the next day he had ten thousand words on how a person—no, how Mark, how *he himself* should arrive at right decisions. Kant was in there. Elie Wiesel was in there, and Hannah Arendt and John Rawls. James Baldwin and Walker Percy were in there too. The trick was to stay hammered enough to write courageously but sober enough to see the screen and avoid porn. The trick was to write for an audience of one. *I will not be rewarded for acting honorably,* he stressed in the essay. *Rewards come from without, and what is given to me is never really mine. Even my breath is borrowed.*

The points he made were like lily pads on the surface of a lake—the monstrous lily pads he had seen once in a Florida swamp. You wouldn't want to get too comfortable on those, but you could maybe alight on one briefly and move on to the next.

It was pretty basic stuff about how you're never going to be certain, and there are too many variables to control for, and that probably the work of life is all about balancing, which is a task that never really gets any easier, so the most you can ever hope to do is be kind and be careful, and trying to be those things actually, literally, turns out to *be* its own reward. But he managed to hit just the right notes. Nothing had ever come to him like this before. Writing it, he felt the weight of self lessen and saw the gates of truth swing open. Even the scrape of the chair legs across the vinyl floor told him to keep writing.

Or was that the crushed-up Ritalin? The slush of ethyl alcohol in the alleys and boulevards of his brain? His roommate had left for the summer; his girlfriend had left him two months ago. The people he knew were getting married, getting better jobs, getting out of the kind of housing you find by pulling tabs off signs in laundromats. He had few friends at work, because work was a biotech company for which he wrote press releases and annual-report copy, and it was made up mainly of hyperintelligent Indians and hypergreedy non-Indians, very few of whom wanted to start drinking directly after work in the Plough and Stars as Mark wanted to do, desperately and daily. So he was alone in those days and had no one to check his slide into the fog and no one, as it happened, to read what he wrote. When he pulled up at the

close of a particularly breathless paragraph (... *because there* are *judges.*
Somewhere. In your particular heavens, in your beating heart. In the knife
you drag across the toast, in the hands you lay on others. Judging and being
judged at once, we cancel ourselves out, as in sleep, and in that hush is our
salvation. At our best, we solve for x, and x = 0), it occurred to him that
he might be writing nonsense. So he took a walk around the jagged
June of Somerville, past the Virgin Marys in their half-buried-upright-
bathtub shrines, past the old Portuguese ladies who, scarved and scowl-
ing, pushed squeaky carts around the neighborhood. Another cigarette
and then a cup of coffee squirted from the machine in the Kwik-Mart
on the corner. And, for later, a couple of Budweiser tall boys and an ice
cream bar from the cases beside the coffee-squirting machine, and then
he waited at the counter behind the old man who fat-fingered quarters
from his swollen palm for two scratch tickets and a pack of Old Golds.
And then he went home, climbed the two flights of sagging wooden
stairs, and played a CD too loud for two p.m. as he lay on his sprung
couch, in and out of a reverie.

No. It was real. *This is real,* he thought. At least as real as the deft illusions his loser magician father had taught him before fucking off, when
Mark was twelve, to drink himself into a soggy death in Berlin. Real
like those illusions in that the effect was real, so who cared about the
method?

But Mark plagiarized at school, lied to girlfriends, dodged his
mother's phone calls, pretended to knowledge he didn't have, kept for
himself a BlackBerry he found in the break room at work, cheated deftly
at cards, put recycling in the trash, didn't really care about Africa or
children, forgot birthdays, and stepped over the indigent in the street.
He was vain and bigoted and selfish and put the maintenance of his drug
habits before his personal relationships. So how could he have gotten
his hands on a complete moral code? The habits and attitudes that he
had somehow managed to pin in paragraphs like iridescent flies on black
foam board—they were thin on the ground in his own life.

Maybe he was turning over a new leaf. Maybe the power to change was being delivered to him, or he was finding it in himself. So he pounded a Budweiser and devoured the ice cream bar and went at it again.

The problem, he was now certain, was that everyone—no, *most* people; no, he, *Mark,* was operating under the mistaken belief that there was an autonomous self sitting in a little driver's seat behind his eyes. And that everyone was—no, he was, *Mark* was, forever overestimating his own importance, his own agency, his own centrality. *Until I can live in the knowledge that the Self is more or less a happy accident, I will never be free.* Let the reader decide if that was the problem in his or her own case. Speak only for yourself. But also: *I am you and you are me. If you would prefer not to be me, tough. Those people who roll their suitcases faster or slower than you in airport concourses? They are not just extras; they are the thrilling protagonists of their own stories. Those dullards in NFL-branded jackets who jaw loudly into their idiot phones on the T? They are you. They who jabber about their dead kin on CNN? They are you too. U2 is you too*...no, ex that out. Come back to earth. What was it he was trying to say? Was there any more alcohol around here?

"Will this do?" asked Gray Skirt.

There was that tone again. Was it mocking? He just couldn't tell. She was standing at the open door of a small room, gesturing withinward. There was something curlicued about the flourish of her gesture, which finished palm up and elbow sharp, as if she were serving from an invisible tray. He realized she hadn't squarely met his eye all morning. Mark quickly scanned the room. White file boxes were stacked tight as Legos against one wall. Four vacuum cleaners leaned like sentinels against another. Watercooler jugs lined a third. But there, on the fourth wall, was a window. High up, but a window, and he could tell that it would open.

"Yes, thank you very much. This should do just fine," said Mark. "The natural light helps to clear my mind."

"Of course."

"Would you see that I'm left alone for, oh, ten minutes?"

Gray Skirt checked her BlackBerry. "You can have eight, I'm afraid. You're needed in Makeup."

"Right." He was pretty sure by now that she was unimpressed by him. But that whole issue had receded in importance. What he needed to do now was smoke this joint in his pocket out that window there.

The door clicked behind Gray Skirt, and Mark assessed the window. Shit. It was, like, six feet up. Holding a water jug by its fat neck, he rolled it across the floor until it sat beneath the window. Balancing one-footed on the jug, he looked like a high-school trophy, though holding a joint instead of a volleyball. The window was an in-swing affair, and opening it with too much force, he lost his balance, fell backward, and landed hard on his wrist and ass.

Eyes on the prize, though. The joint was still in his hands. He righted his water jug and rolled a second one beside it, then stood on the two of them like a rodeo act on two horses' backs. This was more like it. He thumbed his lighter, and the joint crackled in tiny fire. He craned his face out the window and smoked with intent. Inside of a minute, he felt the drug come on, covering his worries and drowning his doubt, just as the tide comes in to cover the jagged sticks and stones of the lapped shore. The bleat and rumble of midtown came up to him on a warm breeze. An air conditioner somewhere near ticked and whirred. He looked at people making money on telephones behind glass across the avenue. One man did jumping jacks before a huge TV. He saw a pigeon whorl and flap and hide its gray self against the grit of a roof.

But then flapping up beside the pigeon came the worry that maybe he was unprepared for this *Margo!* thing. He'd done a few TV spots already, but they were brief appearances, medium-market morning shows, for which he had to fill only a few minutes, the beaming hosts thick and flat with praise for Mark's work. For the corporate retreats and seminars he led, he needed only platitudes. Substance is fine, but it's presentation that hooks an audience, eye contact and lots of hands, a talent he'd inherited from his father.

Below him, a cop car was bellowing and whooping at the truck blocking it from the avenue; the truck crept into the stream, against the light, and the cop car sharked around, went hurtling uptown. Above, a jet escaping LaGuardia left a rumble in its dust—a tube of people, remember, being missiled around the globe. What fun, what a world. No, he wasn't going to blow it. People hawked crappier stuff than his all the time. And he was no fraud, just a little tired of his own shtick. Wasn't that evidence of his integrity? Here was his chance to step it up. His mother would be watching—she'd have the whole tire store watching, probably. She loved Margo. When he told her that he was going to be on the show, she'd actually dropped the phone—he'd heard the phone bounce on the floor and then heard the cat food scatter across the kitchen linoleum.

"You have something to say," he said aloud to himself, standing on his pedestal jugs. "You have something to offer." And he turned his shut lids to the distant sun and let its rays soak his sight; sparkly amoebas swam in a pink sea. He took ten deep breaths.

Then his phone rang, and he startled, nearly fell from his jugs. He looked at the call to reject it. But the name displayed—though it caused him to wince on the inside—was the one name he could not reject. He stubbed his joint into the corner of the window frame and flicked it toughly into empty space. He pressed ACCEPT.

"Hello?"

"Mark. James Straw here."

"Mr. Straw!" Mark exulted. He started loading his mouth with the little dissolving mint strips he used after smoking.

"Marjorie Blinc tells me you're going on that woman's show today."

"Yes, sir. Margo. Backstage now, actually."

"I told you, Mark. Don't call me sir. I feel that we've become much closer than that." Straw had said this a couple of times, but he had not yet said what form-of-address level they had reached.

"Indeed we have . . . Mr. Straw. Indeed we have."

The dead air that followed was weird. Straw usually let you know quickly what it was he wanted. After a moment, Mark had to prompt him. "What did you want to speak about, Mr. Straw?"

"Calm down, boy," said Straw cheerily. "I'm calling you to wish you good luck. Big day for you, I know. I want to help you get that laserlike clarity that you've given me so many times. Even I get some nerves before a board meeting, or with that nasty business with Congress last year. *You* taught me a way through all that.

"Now, I've heard that this Margo lady can be tough. One minute she's saying, *That's so sad, that's so interesting,* and then, *wham,* she's caught you in some lie." Mark hadn't even been considering that. "Well, I want you to know that I *know* you can shine on her show. And just to be safe, I've made it very clear to Margo's organization that everyone at SineCo— and I, personally—have every faith in you and your work."

"Well, thank you, Mr. Straw. That, um, that means a lot to me."

Someone knocked at the door. "Mr. Deveraux. Two minutes."

"They're calling me now. I should go."

"Of course. Of course. Listen, Mark?"

"Yes?"

"I probably don't have to point out that today would be an excellent opportunity to engage in some of the cross-integration that we spoke of. That you agreed to."

It was a moment before Mark understood. "Yes, of course. I'm excited about that part." Shit. What exactly had he agreed to?

"Excellent. Excellent. Well. Look it in the eye, Mark. Look it in the eye!" This was one of the maxims in Mark's philosophy: Whatever you want, you should *look it in the eye.*

There were clipboards and headphones all around him as Mark was shepherded from Makeup to the little on-deck circle backstage. He heard Margo say his name and imagined his mother's thrill and pride at hearing it also. The chief clipboard told him to go, and he went. Into the spotless pretend living room of the stage; into the one-way gaze of ten million people.

He gave Margo's hand a squeeze, did the wave-into-the-lights thing, seated himself in the guest chair with slightly exaggerated settling-himself motions, and—this was the easy part—nodded bashful confirmation while Margo told the story of the sudden, stunning success of his book.

The way Margo made it sound, Mark might have found the cure to a terrible disease or brought clean water to Africa. She said he had changed millions of lives. Then she mentioned, as if it had just occurred to her, that she was an early promoter of *Bringing the Inside Out*.

"I'm not sure that had anything to do with its success," Mark said, interrupting her, and he smiled, mid-sip, over the rim of the mug of fair-trade green tea that had been awaiting him on the little celebrity side table. Margo seemed caught short. Was he really saying this? Who would think it wise to cross her?

Then he winked at her. Mark had an excellent wink. There should be no cranial scrunch in a wink, no lip work. Too slow, and it's silly; too fast, and it's a tic. (Mark also had a great whistle; it could summon taxis from across the avenue.) Camera two caught Mark's wink perfectly, and camera one recorded something like a blush rise on Margo's face.

"Okay, you're joking, I guess," she said.

"Yes, Margo, I'm joking. You pretty much made me."

"Oh, I think your work made you, Mark. Wouldn't you say so?"

"I have and do and will. But who would believe us if we pretended that I've earned all this?" He put down his tea and made a gentle gesture at the lights and cameras.

"Well, as you say in your book, you *futurized, committed, and strove*." She paused, looked at Mark. He lifted his hands a little bit, turned his palms up and his gaze down, and raised his eyebrows: the picture of a man sincerely doubting what he has just heard. Margo took up his slim book with both hands. "You did those things"—here she read from the flyleaf—"and what you wanted flowed to you 'like water down a mountain, like information out of a search engine.' I think that many, many people have found those words inspiring. Don't you?"

"Apparently, yes." Mark leaned forward, put his elbows on his knees, and templed his long fingers. He drew in breath to speak, but then held it, creating the kind of pause that, on television, feels like weeks. "And

I thank those people just for listening to me. It is such an honor to be listened to. You know that, Margo." Another pause, and something like a tiny wince on his face. "But I need to come out right now and say that my success, the success of this book, is hard for me to credit. I am all the time full of doubt, and I'm uncomfortable being described as the man with the answers."

"Mark Deveraux is all the time full of doubt?"

"Oh, absolutely," said Mark, perking up.

"Doubt about what?"

"Doubt as to, you know, the general shape of the curve, the fairness of the judges, the notion that we can make ourselves better."

"But you made yourself better. You say so in your book. You write that you were a, what, a..." And Margo started to flip through the pages.

"A 'whining, blaming, suffering zero,'" Mark supplied.

"Yeah, that. It's so cutting. And then you discovered consciousclusions," she prompted. "You made yourself better."

"Well, I *got* better. Did *I* do that? Who can say? And did I discover anything? Certainly, I gave voice to something. And it's resonated. And, again, Margo, I'm so grateful to each and every person who read or listened to a single word of mine...It's just that I need to be clear..."

"It sounds like you're backing down from what you said in your book, that the power to change ourselves is in all of us." Margo straightened her back and raised her chin.

Mark took in another one of those breaths. He leaned close to Margo so that his butt lifted off the cushion, his right hand sharp-angled to the little table between them. And then he tapped the table, hard, with an index finger. Four times: *tap-tap-tap-tap.*

"I'm. Not. Backing. Down," he said, one word for every tap. It was the strangest gesture that anyone had seen on the *Margo!* show since a chef had lit his sleeve on fire and then swatted it out with a duck breast. Mark's arm retreated; his body settled back in the chair. "Look, Margo. We're changing all the time. There is no stasis. But that's incredibly good news. It means that we can always become better."

"More successful."

"Ahhhm, yes. More successful." Mark had gotten a little lost. But now he saw a thread. "When I wrote what I wrote, I did so as a different person. I did it by faith. Do you remember, Margo, when you woke every day wondering whether you were on the right path?"

Margo actually nodded, involuntarily.

"Now I have this affirmation all around me," Mark continued. "You know: the money, the people asking me what I think, what I want. And now I see that it was living in the doubt that gave my thoughts strength. It was having to place that bet on every day."

"You know what, Mark?" said Margo. "I do remember those days. I once had to sell my piano to make a month's rent."

"Your piano? Oh, what a shame. Tell me about that piano."

"It was a no-name upright that had spent forty years in a church basement. It had these beautiful flowers carved into the front of it and a sounding board that was too warped to stay in tune. But I loved it." She smiled broadly, and was beautiful.

"I've read that you have twelve pianos now. Is that true?"

"Oh, Mark, I love music."

"But what wouldn't you give to have that first piano back, right? Well, get this: It's not coming back. We're all looking for our madeleine."

"Yes. We're all looking for someone, aren't we," agreed Margo.

"Of course we are. We are borne back ceaselessly."

"That's beautiful."

"Thank you," said Mark, graciously. "Yes, we are borne back ceaselessly. I suppose that's how it will always be. My method for personal success requires that we futurize ourselves; that we see ourselves in the future being as we wish to be. But we can't shut the door on our past. We have to be whole people.

"You see, Margo, I've been confused recently. Just now, before coming on with you, I was meditating, trying to futurize. But I've been thinking of my father lately. It was on this day, ten years ago, that he died."

"I'm so sorry," said Margo.

Mark did not know the date of his father's death, but it seemed to him perfectly plausible just then that it *was* the anniversary of his father's death. And, though he hadn't consciously thought of his father in weeks, when Mark heard Margo say the word *sorry,* he knew she was for real, and he felt a stone of grief rise in his throat. "So I guess that's what I've been going through. And it's been making my practice more difficult. The very practice that I'm trying to teach to others... now I find that I don't always have access to it." The stone in his throat was melting away. But Margo was hanging on his words now. He could feel it: ten million people wanted him to cry.

So he thought of his little dog, from long ago. An off-brand terrier named Monopoly who used to poke through the tall grass and broken bottles with Mark endlessly in the long lot that gave way to scrubby pine woods behind the Gasso station. One night Monopoly puked grass and chicken bones on Mark's new Star Wars bedspread; Mark was livid, chased the dog outside, roughly, and went to sleep without her. Two raccoons, hopped up on garbage, opened her up during the night, ripped apart her soft, low-slung belly with stinking teeth and sickle claws. Mark may have heard the attack, Monopoly's yelps colored his dream and woke him briefly. But he didn't go to his dog because he was a little boy and afraid of the night outside: the sodium lights and bashed trash dumpsters with drooling stains; the chill, wet ground and the warm tar streets. Maybe he made up the part about hearing Monopoly's murder; he would never be sure. Nor would he ever tell any of this to anyone. And he never forgave the Star Wars tchotchke mill, or Luke Skywalker, the soiling of whose prissy image had caused him to betray his dearest friend.

Mark closed his eyes and shook his head slightly. "I must now seem an odd sort to be talking about how to achieve success and serenity, Margo." He bit his lower lip with whitened teeth, Clintonishly. He remembered how Monopoly sat still beside him while he built elaborate marble slides around the kitchen with lengths of pine siding he found beneath the house. How, when she woke beside him in the morning and stretched, she seemed to rub her eyes with the backs of her sandy paws. A wave of pure grief climbed through his chest and throat and settled in his jaw, where the camera caught it quivering. Tears came to his eyes, and when he spoke next, his voice was thickened by the humidity in his head. "I'm sorry. I suppose I should have prepared better." Margo's studio audience was rapt, enraptured. Across America, women saw a strong man crying about something abstract.

"No, please, Mark. You're doing us an honor," said Margo. "This is part of the Thorough Honesty that you yourself say we need if we're to reach our own consciousclusions."

"Yes, I suppose so," he said. "And you know, Margo, I just have to . . . no, *we* just have to . . . add this knowledge to our work together. This . . . this doubt, this fear, this insecurity—this is a consciousclusion also. We fold this in, and our Knowledge Blanket just becomes that much stronger."

"Oh, the Knowledge Blanket! I love that concept, Mark. I pull mine out all the time."

"As often as you can, Margo. As often as you can."

"So what will you do with it?"

"With what?" Mark sniffled.

"With that consciousclusion? That we are brought back ceaselessly? That even you can be muddled by your dead father, by a man who—I hope you don't mind me mentioning—left you and your mother when you were young."

"Oh gosh, no, I don't mind. Mention away," said Mark, who had puffed and massaged his middle-class upbringing at the insistence of his editors. He'd punched up the red dustiness of his southern Louisiana birthplace; he'd menialized his mother's jobs, exaggerated the number of times they'd moved, called financial aid a scholarship. He left out the two weeks every year that he and his mother took driving vacations, she with a checklist of cultural and natural attractions she thought her son should see. He left out the tennis camp and the orthodontia.

"I suppose I'll need to learn how to honor the part of me that is still a sufferer and, yes, a blamer. I have to listen to that part. To say: *I believe you, sufferer, I hear you. But you can no longer hold me back.*" Mark seemed to brighten at the thought. "Because we all have our things, you know? And if you're going to bring the inside out, you need to bring it all out; you need all the information. Once you're free of secrets, you can be free of shame and certain that what you have is yours, that it's not going to be taken away; certain that you deserve the success that lies within you, within all of us."

"But how are we supposed to do that?" asked Margo, now leaning in to him. "I wake and I read the paper and I feel overwhelmed. The environment. Global warming. Poverty." Everyone listening to Margo remembered to be overwhelmed by these things also. "Think of the hard-working mother or father or struggling artist who wants to be a help and be a more actualized, more present person. What is he or she supposed to do? You're someone who went from poverty to Harvard, and then from being a—what? You wrote test questions for a living, you worked demolition jobs, you used marijuana?"

"I did all those things."

"Well, now you're in demand wherever you go. To motivate people. To make companies and families and individuals work better. I hear that you're life-coaching some very important Hollywood stars. And, I mean, you look great...doesn't he, people?" Margo looked out at her audience. They whooped and hollered, because Mark did look great. "And I understand—and I want everyone to hear this, I want *you* to hear this, Mark, since you brought up the subject of money—that you've put most of the profits from the sale of your book into a foundation, the Bringing the Inside Out Foundation. Isn't that right?"

Ah, yes. The Bringing the Inside Out Foundation. *Most* of his profits? Well, it was a complex arrangement. The accounting people had explained this to him. Like a big sheltering stand of trees to keep the leaching wind of taxation away from the little berm of his money. "Well, yes, Margo, of course. I mean, I really am trying to teach something here. Though clearly"——he wiped the mist from the corners of his eyes one-handed, thumb and forefinger pinching the bridge of his nose——"I have a lot to learn myself.

"Yes," Mark continued, "the Bringing the Inside Out Foundation is dedicated to helping young people become informed digital citizens. There's so much opportunity out there that they should know about, so many chances to connect. So we provide these kids with all the tools they need. Including these new devices from SineCo. Actually"——he held up the spire of his index finger——"I have one here." Mark dug through the pockets of his bespoke corduroy jacket, elaborately. "It's more than a phone, certainly, and, well, it seems to me that it's more than a computer even. Jeez, where is it?" He pulled out his keys and plopped them on the table like any working stiff would. Then a Velcro wallet, which he stared at as if he'd never seen it before. He gave Margo a look like *Can you believe all this stuff that ends up in my pockets?* He pulled out two crumpled pads ("Two pads. Always got 'em. Could be brilliant stuff, you never know"); pens ("Pens. Too many is never enough. Why is that?"); a napkin ("Napkin. Maybe I got lucky." Margo swayed back, laughing at the very idea); a breadstick ("Oh, look, a breadstick"); and, shit, his tiny stone pipe. ("Lucky stone.") He switch-palmed the pipe to his left hand and quickly dropped it into the Slydini pocket he had had sewn into the lining of his jacket. Making a big production with his right hand, he dug in his inside breast pocket.

"Ah. Here it is." He drew out the Node, SineCo's newest gizmobauble, the perfect size, the perfect weight. No seam or tiny screws, no back to pop off, entirely sealed in the factory. Battery life of seventy-two hours. "Thing's amazing. Cheap too. I mean, low-cost. I mean, relatively. So easy to use. Maybe I'll ditch these notepads soon. And the kids, Margo. They can just run circles around me. They have rich online lives, interconnecting with each other and other kids all over the world. And making music and poetry. It's just amazing."

There was the cross-integration. He had rendered unto Straw what was Straw's, and Straw would be pleased.

"That does sound amazing. Doesn't that sound amazing, people?" she asked the audience.

The audience whooped and cheered, because it did sound amazing.

"Okay, so you do all this great work, is the point," said Margo. "But how? Tell me, tell us, one thing that we can all do to become more goal-attaining, more solution-centered."

"One thing?"

"One thing."

He felt warm all over, disembodied, at home before these cameras. One thing? Before he said it, he knew it would be the title of his next book, a book that would take him beyond talk shows. He returned his gaze to Margo and seemed about to speak. But then he paused again. Gray Skirt, beside one of the camera operators, maybe rolled her eyes.

"Try again tomorrow," Mark said.

QUIVERING PINES

Leo Crane."

The doctor spoke the name written inside the wings of a beige folder, open like a menu in his hands; he said the name like it was just words, which Leo supposed it was. The office was small. Leo was sitting on another piece of disempowering institutional furniture, a too-low, too-high-sided, tautly upholstered chair that encouraged surrender.

"So. How're you doing?" said the doctor, looking at him now.

How'm I doing? thought Leo, sarcastic within his still-aching head. Wasn't that a dumb question? Isn't it safe to say that a person being intake-interviewed at rehab would be mortified, crestfallen, and anxious? That's how *he* was doing, anyway. He raised his arms a little and swiveled his gaze to take in the office: the large window, through which he could see the green swale of grounds outside; the doctor's hulking computer monitor; a desk phone festooned with Post-it notes; a pen cup that said *Pens*. And was that a Viagra-branded tissue-box cover on the table in the corner? Holy shit, it *was* a Viagra-branded tissue-box cover. All this meant to Leo that he had lost. He had been fighting, and he had lost. Here he was, on the sidelines, a loser man-child in a cubular chair.

"Keith said you were reluctant to participate in Group today," prompted the doctor. "Why is that, do you think?"

The doctor-type people here were always employing that fake-wonder-y voice. It was true that Leo had been as silent as a panther since his arrival, barely twenty-four hours ago. He just shrugged at the doctor's question. How far back would he have to start? He was sober for the first time in weeks, but what had replaced the dark sloshing was a profound confusion about whom and what to trust. Best to keep his mouth shut. He found most questions unanswerable, or answerable in too many ways.

And something in the shell of his mind was saying, *Just because you've made a hash of your own life doesn't mean someone else's ideas are any better.* Especially not those of a man with a pen cup marked *Pens*. Was this guy even a doctor? Leo looked around the little office for a diploma.

Hmm. Clinical psychologist. From an institution Leo had never heard of. Oh, and insult to injury: *Bringing the Inside Out* was prominently displayed on the doctor's laminate bookshelf. Proof pretty much positive that this doctor was ill-equipped to dispense advice on any of the important questions.

Long ago, back in college and for some years thereafter, Leo had been best friends with the author of that fatuous work. But once Mark flukishly became famous, he dropped Leo, had some sort of *assistant* return Leo's calls. The wild success of *Bringing the Inside Out* had bothered Leo deeply. Was that all you had to do to make it in this world? Sling shit while smiling? It was strange too; the Mark that Leo remembered would have eviscerated a book like that. Booklet, really. It was about one hundred pages, with wide margins. Presumably, he'd made a fortune from it, which was also deeply annoying.

Leo found his voice. "You a fan of Deveraux?" he asked the doctor. He raised his chin toward the bookshelf.

"I think there's a lot in that little book, yes. Are you familiar with his work?"

"Very," said Leo, the sixth word he'd spoken since his arrival.

He watched the doctor try to leverage this opening, his index finger running through the pages inside the folder again. Leo could guess what was in there—a grim précis of his last few months as reported by his sisters and whoever else had done advance work for the intervention.

Yesterday, when he'd answered the door and found his three sisters standing on his front porch, Leo had known straightaway. None of them lived in the state. And though the days of the week had lately come to mean little to him (just as seeing the clock-based time was inevitably a surprise), Leo did know that each of his sisters had a real job. Ten a.m. on a Thursday was not a drop-in hour, even in Portland.

Two of the sisters were busy tending to a family fortune built by their grandfather, the board-games magnate Lionel Crane. The company had been known as Crane and Herron until Lionel Crane and Nat Herron had come to a bitter falling-out, in 1975, over a golf score. Neither man had any idea what an apology was, so a disagreement (about whether a deep tractor wheel furrow on the twelfth hole of the Millbrook Golf Club constituted "ground under repair") had bloomed and grown septic until the two men were unable to talk to each other in anything but Attorney. That had been a one-day news story in its time—the expensive sawing in twain of the company that made the classic game Board Room (in which players forged allegiances with one another to force others out). The two men fought especially over the rights to the company logo—a crane and a heron intimately entwined on a light blue field—and ended up having to sever the two birds, graphically. The resultant CraneCo (now signified by a winking crane in a top hat, a less compelling logo) went public ten years later and had grown steadily as a youth and family brand.

Rosemary, the eldest of the Crane children, was the chairman of the board. She had never had any problems in the success department. And to Leo, she sometimes seemed more like a forbidding aunt than a big sister.

Heather, the youngest Crane daughter, had started at the company right out of college. It was she who had negotiated the purchase of a small computer-games company that brought onto the CraneCo platform surprise hits like Wackadoodle! and Catch the Bunny. People in the industry apparently thought she was some sort of games savant, like she could look at any collection of random objects and design a game around them. This was funny because Heather was crap at games and puzzles and the abstract figuring they required, always had been. When they all played games as children, Heather's older sisters generally stomped her. She might sometimes win a game of Mastermind or Battleship—she was good at plodding through possibilities. And she could hold her own when it came to the character-based games like Masterpiece or Clue or, one of the siblings' own, Rescue the Baby, which involved putting infant Leo in his crumby baby seat in some sort of perilous position (often it was quite perilous—on top of the fridge, or alone in the dumbwaiter) and then devising elaborate ways of saving him.

Daisy, the middle sister, was Leo's favorite. As a child, she was earnest but had a very low tolerance for bullshit, and she'd always had a mouth on her. Once, she either ruined or saved a wedding documentary by looking right into the camcorder's lens and, when prompted by the off-screen uncle videographer—*What do you think about this great wedding, Daze?*—saying, *I think this cake sucks. And that old preacher guy talked for like a fucking hour. That lady Uncle Farouk married is mean.* She could also lie, brazenly, and was always proposing theoretical scenarios of death, like, "But Daddy, what if you fell off the skimboard and hit your head but then you drowned but then the fish ate you but before you were all the way dead?"

In her way and in her twenties, Daisy had exhibited some of the same problems that Leo had grappled with, though she had gotten off the ride well before the point at which Leo now found himself, or she had devised better coping strategies, because she was a physician's assistant and the mother of two; she lived in Austin, and generally seemed to have figured out how you become a levelheaded citizen and a reliable person. But she had always been the sister willing to cut Leo the most slack.

So she was the only one he made eye contact with when he saw them there, a sedge of Cranes on his porch. Presumably, shifts had been covered and child care arranged and plane tickets bought and cars rented. *Uh-oh,* he thought. *They must mean business.*

Of course it had come to this. In the months leading up to their appearance, he had already fielded quite a few calls from them, calls in which he'd had to deflect their love and concern, minimize the increasing oddness of his blog posts, and promise to show up for the appointments they'd made for him with various doctors and therapists. But he'd missed all those appointments and quit taking his sisters' calls around the time that the mania had crested and the other thing had started to bite. Still, he had enough wit shreds about him that morning to at least try to mount a defense, or another deflection.

"Surprise party?" he'd asked them at the door, and he gave his mug a little shake, which he shouldn't have done, because the ice cubes therein announced themselves with a cold rattle, and it was Daisy, closest to him, who bent over his mug, took a quick whiff.

"Is that gin?" she asked. "Gross, Leo."

"Has this sort of thing happened to you before?" asked the doctor. "Have you ever gone up and down like this?"

"I've been up and down a few times," he finally offered. He had, over and over. But never like this.

"You seem to have a hard time holding on to a job."

"But I get by."

"You mean you're wealthy?"

"I mean I have a supplemental income."

The doctor perused a page. "Your family makes toys?"

The CraneCo thing caused some to think that Leo had grown up like the kid on *Silver Spoons,* riding a little train through a mansion. In fact, all it meant was that he had about eighteen hundred a month, unearned. Plus what he got from the deeper-pocketed sisters, who loved him. The doctor couldn't hide a tiny, smug smile—people always like to see a rich kid brought low.

"Games. Not toys. It's a public company," Leo said.

"So you don't need to work."

Leo gripped the armrests of the stupid chair. "You're right. I'm lazy and spoiled."

"That's not what I was saying," countered the doctor. "But, I suppose, if you heard me saying that, it's something we should talk about."

"No need."

"Do *you* think your life is easy? Do *you* think you're lazy?" pressed the doctor.

Well, obviously, yes, my life is easy, Leo thought. But only on one level. But that is probably the level at which ease has the most meaning, the most purchase. But lazy? No, probably not lazy. Lazy people, Leo figured, would presumably derive some benefit of leisure from their lack of industry. And since leisure was not a feeling he had ever really even approached—hounded as he was from crack of morning to lip of sleep by a pack of worries and their contingent sub- and meta-worries— Leo reasoned that he could not fairly be called lazy. His problem came from being unable to trace a straight line from present state to future goal.

For Leo, the single salient observable fact about the future was that it never turned out to be what you thought it would be. So different were the expected and actual futures that he found it hard to credit the idea that the Leo of two or five or nine years ago was even the same person as the Leo of today. Sadly, this meant that most information needed to be learned over and over again, that the same experiments needed to be run again and again, with different variables controlled for.

He had been unable, as yet, to put this highly nuanced information to any professional or artistic use. And for the past fifteen years, his life had consisted mainly of holding on while he rode the sine wave in his brain. But from a young age, he had received the impression that this moodiness was a womanly trait, and if a man admitted to it, he should do so only in a paragraph about how he had overcome it, or how he intended to overcome it.

There were hard-to-credit upward swoops in his outlook, brought on by love, wind, proteins, neuro-slurry, patented pharmaceuticals, the pH of the tap water, the buzz of sodium streetlights, or some deeper current. At these times he took risks and adopted a sort of shine and swagger.

The worst was that bookstore he bought. He was twenty-six, and he'd emptied his trust fund like a kid shaking a ceramic piggy bank (plus took on as much debt as the bank would let him). What a shitshow that turned out to be. He thought the bookstore would lead to a journal edited by himself. Writers would clamor to submit. He would know everybody. He moved into a room above the store and stayed one long cold winter, his room heated only by a leaky woodstove, his store patronized by kind locals who had loved the former owner's freakish breadth of knowledge; weekend celebrities in thousand-dollar jeans; drowsy students looking for a two-dollar *Siddhartha;* morose and august humanists from the college.

But not enough of any of these.

After nine months, having grossed $6,700 in his career as a bookstore proprietor, the bloom way off the rose, Leo sold his entire stock to a dealer from Florida, who arrived in a Range Rover and paid by check. Rosemary bought the building from Leo and sold it quickly, at a loss.

After the bookstore flop, he'd worked at CraneCo, briefly. But the company couldn't really find a place for him, and he was embarrassed every moment of every day. So, though it was his birthplace and motherland, his Fern Hill, and though the cool dank zephyr that preceded a subway's arrival from the mouth of its tunnel comforted him, he fled Manhattan and moved to Portland. A place that was kinder to people like him.

He drove a wine-delivery truck, he drove a taxi; he was a mediocre waiter, a drunken barback. The periods of hope and courage came less frequently. And as his twenties became his thirties, the landscape came to feature swamps of gloom dotted with marshy hummocks of anxiety. He worked on getting better. He tried jogging; he limited his drinking; he sprinkled seeds into his yogurt. A girlfriend got him into yoga. He practiced having a good attitude. But it was trench warfare. He lost his yoga mat and had to buy another one. Then he lost that one and couldn't see buying a third. He watched other people claim to enjoy drinking; they baffled him. The same people spoke of hangovers almost fondly, as evidence of their propensity to dissipation. His own hangovers were whole days mined with grim, churning thoughts. He saw therapists and psychiatrists; he tried Wellbutrin, Klonopin, Effexor, Celexa, Paxil, Xanax, Zoloft, and Lexapro. Also meditation, core work, and juice fasts. He cut out meat. Kept a garden. Clawed through months of clean living, then fell back into blurred days like an acrobat into a net.

"Tell me about the people who you say were watching you," said the doctor.

Oh, that. "You mean the paranoia, right?"

"If I call it paranoia, you will think I don't believe you."

"You don't."

"You haven't given me anything to believe or not believe."

Fair enough. But Leo did not know whether the constellations of meaning he had picked out were to be believed, exactly. Now, remembering some of his theories, he could see that they were incredible. But this was neither here nor there—the beautiful and true is often incredible. What he felt most keenly was the sadness at the fact that he was no longer certain. He had no wish to convince anyone else—certainly not this doctor—that, for instance, his ex-girlfriend's ex-husband worked for whatever part of the government was tasked with compiling dossiers on wayward members of the intellectual elite.

"You told your friends that you were being followed. Why did you say that?"

"Well. For a while there, I was being followed."

A riffle of annoyance appeared on the doctor's face. The doctor's face. The face of the doctor. A face is just a skin mask with two black holes for seeing and a wet cave for eating and speaking. Leo looked away, not out of disgust, but because he was suddenly aware that this might not be a doctor after all.

Actually, Leo *had* been followed. He knew this in a way that he did not know other things—he did not *know,* for instance, whether his ex-girlfriend's ex-husband worked for the government. He could see now that the man was perhaps your more garden-variety jealous dick. She wasn't even his girlfriend, really. She was Marilyn, the hot mom from Brand-New Day. They had tried a thing for a few weeks. It was mostly sex in the late afternoon and expensive dinners out, sometimes followed by drunken arguments on sidewalks or in her vast, sisal-carpeted apartment, usually about the morality of her profession—advertising—which Leo felt compelled to point out was a form of intellectual prostitution, but once about her very recently ex–husband. She claimed she didn't really know what he did for a living.

"I don't know. Consulting. He consults about stuff," she had yelled at Leo as she stood naked in front of her refrigerator, digging in the back for more wine.

Now the doctor went deeper into his file. "And what about these?"

Oh crap, thought Leo. Doc had printouts of his blog. How was that possible? He had erased all that. Leo wasn't exactly tech-savvy (he mourned the passing of MacWrite), but he knew what a Delete All Files button was meant to do. Without leaning forward, he tried to look harder at the papers the doctor was fingering. They looked like screen-grabs, not downloads. Who could have given him those? Heather? One of Rosemary's assistants? That was a bit much, didn't they think? If they wanted to throw the blog in his face, they should have done it when they were in front of him.

The blog was even more embarrassing than the bookstore, though less financially ruinous.

After being fired from Brand-New Day, it was the children that he missed most. The not having anywhere to be at 7:45 a.m. was okay, actually. But the not seeing what Viola or Gus had chosen to wear that day (a tattered Disney dress; an adult swim cap and a Mylar cape); the not being someone whom tiny people trusted — that really sucked. The thing he missed second most, however, was being the publisher, editor, and staff of the daily journal sheets. So it wasn't even a week after the dismissal that he started a blog, republishing the paper under its new banner, *I Have Shared a Document with You.*

He considered going down to Brand-New Day so that he could keep reporting on the children's lives. He reasoned that as long as he stayed out of the building and the outdoor play zone, Sharon couldn't stop him. There was the First Amendment, after all. But when he ran this legal theory by his friend Louis, whose wife was a public defender, Louis said, "You go down there and lurk behind chain-link to report on children, Leo, and you will be screwed beyond what you really understand."

And that sunk in, for some reason.

So what had been a take-home one-pager from a preschool was transformed into an online account constantly updated by its unemployed and oversynapsed and self-intrigued author. He was on the swoop of swoops, all the world's connections laid plain before him. He wrote daily and linked to hundreds of articles, on solar panels and hydroponics and hieroglyphics.

But then the sad curve of his decline began to be plainly evident in that blog. When his creative imaginings started to turn paranoid and bossy and solipsistic, his friends grew concerned. Katharine, the public defender, tried to intervene.

"Some of it's pretty good," said Katharine. "But a lot of it is . . . well, it's unpolished, and some of it's just too weird." They were standing on Leo's sagging front porch. It was early morning. "It's okay to have these patches, Leo. It's common enough. You'll get through it. But there's no reason to put it all in hard copy, to make everyone watch."

"Transparency is a virtue, Katharine," said Leo, who had mostly heard the *common* part.

"Yeah, *ish,*" said Katharine. "One day you might feel differently about some of the stuff you're putting out. Actually, you almost certainly will."

Leo considered this. Maybe she had a point. But if embarrassment was due him later, it was due him later. *This here now is for this here now*. It is so easy to walk through the world when you ignore embarrassment and look people straight in the eye. Looking people straight in the eye also rattles them a bit.

"Well, aren't you afraid of the secret world government that you say keeps track of everything we do online?" tried Katharine.

"I take precautions," said Leo mysteriously.

"*You* take precautions?" said Katharine. "I downloaded Skype for you. You wrap your computer in tinfoil or something?"

Leo scanned the area. "My real name appears nowhere on the blog," he said. It was true; Leo always signed his posts with made-up names.

Then Leo's friends started making unannounced visits on flimsy pretexts. Then his pot dealer *cut him off*. Out of concern! Like pot dealers are bound by the Hippocratic oath. Probably it was one of those friends who'd called his sisters. People really *were* watching; even paranoids have enemies.

Katharine's sarcastic crack about did he wrap his computer in tinfoil made Leo realize: the noms de blog were not cloak enough. The Internet was probably controlled by the other side—of course it was!—and they would shut him down, remove him from the equation somehow. *I Have Shared a Document with You* had to come offline; it could not be broadcast. It would have to be a *hand-cast;* paper hard copy, a true dissident organ.

Around there, the pivot point came. A sudden change in lighting, perspective, tempo; a moment in time. He was in his attic reading his broadside, the first (and only) paper edition of *I Have Shared a Document with You*. He had fifty copies, printed on an artist friend's ancient letterpress machine.

But then he glanced out the window and the sky looked bad, like menacing bad; a moving front, gray and striated, coming in hard over the West Hills. A darkness grew in Leo's chest; a voice—the only floridly psychotic thing that had ever happened to Leo—said, *That's right. Kill yourself. Before you lose the nerve.*

It made sense, was the strange part. Leo could handle being a depressive. Possibly he had chosen it, in one way or another. And he would find a way to handle it for the rest of his life. But if he was a real nutter, he should find a way to kill himself; that was the deal he'd made with himself.

He climbed out onto his roof, a steeply pitched and many-angled place, and gorilla-walked to its apex, then stood tall like a weather vane. Yeah, that weather system was aimed at him. It was roiling and zombific and loaded with tons of very bad news about his future. He swayed forward a bit, imagined the tumble and empty air.

No, not enough empty air. He'd come out alive, with tib-fib fractures and a head injury; he'd be forever the unsuccessful suicide, the chickened-out.

So he scuttled back into his attic and lay on the floor. He *was* chicken; he didn't want to die.

That's the good news, he told himself. And he remembered his mother telling him that he was not excused from the table. (He was a terrible eater.) Now he heard her voice. Not in the psychotic way, but in the keen-recall way, from heaven or space or the compost or whatever. *You are not excused,* she said. She was tough; she had probably faced those flames bravely when they had come for her.

But if he was to live, how was he going to live with *this?*

He saw that the dissident broadsheet and the blog and all the stupid little fascinations were distractions; they were deeply beside the point. In back of all the wild imaginings, he had been taking shallow breaths and keeping one eye on the door.

In the newspaper—the real one—Leo read about outbound Africans who hid in the wheel wells of jumbo jets. He read about the ones who fell frozen onto Queens, their bid for freedom having far overshot the mark. But maybe some made it through; maybe they bounced off the awning of a Dunkin' Donuts and found new lives as plasterers or lawn-mower men or newsagents, scarfed and hatted and peering at you from behind racks of gum. Panting and wading and grasping, the driven of the earth move across it in unflagging defense of their right to keep living. So what of people like Leo, adrift on privilege and spangled with choice, who let life's flame gutter on its wick?

In the weeks that followed, his thoughts became as dark and jangled as wire hangers at the back of the closet. Oh, how the monsters had come in to stomp around his head. The morning was bearable, the afternoon insufferable, and the evening a damp relief.

He bought his pot from a sketchy character who made you come to him. To his house over by the freeway, its windows blacked out, the fish tanks unclean.

Leo nailed a sheet over his front window. He stopped answering the phone and then the door. The world outside was full of antagonists. He stayed tethered to his bong.

The sisters had timed the intervention well. A week earlier, he might have stood his ground. In the event, he did try. He tried It's None of Your Business, which they rejected out of hand. He tried I Might Still Be Able to See Myself Out of This, which did not convince them. It was clear that they weren't going to leave until he agreed to something in-patient. Rosemary mentioned some very illustrious places back east. He actually thought about it.

But he didn't want doctors poking around in his dome. He'd probably end up with electrodes on his forehead and no memory of the past few months, months that, though they had been a dense thicket and maybe full of figments, he didn't want taken away. There was possibly some information there; maybe some of it wasn't total nonsense. Besides, without that, all he had was this, which was shit.

So, in what had seemed at the time like a brilliant idea, Leo decided that he'd avoid the nuthouse by agreeing to rehab. The gin in the coffee mug was his opening. And in truth, he was sounding less crazy and more drunk than he had a few months ago. When Heather said, "What about all that stuff you wrote on your blog? About the shadow government, the plan to sneak tyranny into our lives through convenience, the massive plot to control all the information in the world?" Leo tried to make it sound like he had written all that *in the voice* of someone who thought like that. He said he was doing this because he was planning on writing a novel about that kind of thing. It even seemed to him like that was something he could have been doing.

It wasn't too hard to get Rosemary and Heather behind the idea of a rehab instead of an asylum. Daisy sensed another deflection.

"You're a bad drunk, brother," she said, "but there's something else going on here."

Luckily, the recycling bins on Leo's back porch spilled with empties that were incriminating in their type and number: jug-size cheapos of gin and rum, a platoon of dead soldiers, sake bottles and sherry bottles and peach brandy bottles.

That was enough for Daisy. "You the only one living in this sorority?" she asked him.

It was only when he was slipping up the pretty driveway in the white minivan that Leo started to have misgivings about his plan. There might be a slight frying pan / fire problem, he realized. Who knew what kind of recovery they dished out here?

"See, Leo," said Heather from the front of the van, "it's not a locked facility."

This had been one of his conditions. And it was true that Quivering Pines appeared to be an expensive and orthodox, gender-segregated Twelve Step drug and alcohol rehab in a strip-mall hamlet a half hour south of the city. It looked like a community college with really good landscaping—there were cacti in large planter pots beside the driveway. Perhaps that was meant to give the facility a desert resonance; the desert was supposed to be so conducive to recovery and transformation.

The first night he was put in a sort of observation bed. A man who looked like an onion searched Leo's bag for contraband, then gave him a Big Book, a slimmer volume on Twelve-Stepping in general, and a notebook, the kind without perforations, so that a torn-out sheet has raggedy edges.

The doctor was reading aloud from Leo's blog now. Specifically, from "Another Unjust Dismissal," Leo's account of being fired from his friend Gabriel's construction crew. Gabriel had hired Leo a few weeks after the Brand-New Day firing, a few days after Marilyn told him she never wanted to see him again. It wasn't total charity—Leo knew his way around Skilsaws and speed squares. But the doctor had secondary sources. He picked a page from the folder and read its excerpts. Was that Gabriel's account? Daisy's account of Gabriel's account?

"It seems that Gabriel had every reason to let you go," said the doctor.

It was true. He'd been drunk. On a roof. With a nail gun. He would have fired himself.

Their time up, the doctor said they would meet again on Monday. "I hope you'll use the weekend to come to terms with your circumstances. I think you'll find that you're really quite lucky you got here."

Lucky? Leo left the little office in a haze of despair. Those blog posts read back to him—he really had been orbiting Planet Crane for a while there. That guy, with his pen cup marked *Pens,* probably was a doctor.

He crossed the quiet quad; barely noticed the beautiful day around him. He thought with relief that at least you couldn't screen-grab something that was never on a screen, so the doc hadn't seen that one issue of *I Have Shared a Document with You.*

If the doc got his hands on that, it'd be electrodes for sure, in Leo's near future.

MANDALAY, MYANMAR

Leila looked behind her and saw the little white Datsun again, her two Burmese minders in the front seats. Heckle and Jeckle, she called them. They'd shown up a couple of days ago, the day after she returned from Myo Thit. It had occurred to her that she might just sneak up to their vehicle, rap on the window, and say, *Maybe you guys should address the open-sewer issue and high infant-mortality rates before you spend any more money on the network-of-spies-and-stooges thing.* But her Burmese wasn't up to it, and these guys were hard to sneak up on. They were always right behind her, and sometimes they were there first.

Okay, boys, she thought, lacing up her sneakers on the steps outside her apartment, *you feeling up to a 10 K?*

Leila ran every day, first thing in the morning. Running was the only way she could make her body and mind operate at the same speed, which turned out to be the only time she could ever truly relax. And the thinking she did while running seemed to be more effective thinking; it was more likely to lead to decisions instead of just to more thinking. In Mandalay, running was also a good way to separate herself from the Lonely

Planeteers, who would go down any rutted track if they were promised a shrine or a ruin and none if they were not.

Leila could not ignore her surveillance detail. The two men were always thirty yards behind her or in the far corner of her tea shop. And at first she was truly spooked. But they followed her in such a strange and polite way. They were not so much covert as discreet; there was no menace in their hovering.

Still, they were a pain in the ass, because everyone around her knew they were there too. Leila's trying-to-blend-in days were over. Who wants to chat with the American girl being trailed by the secret police? Even her man at the tea shop treated her more cautiously. He still brought her Number Nines, but without his usual flourish.

She knew she had to stay away from Aung-Hla until she could sort this out. If he got pulled into it, it would be her fault, and the three hundred bucks that she hadn't managed to get to him yet—that wouldn't cover it. She had seen him a couple of times over the past week, but they only waved at each other across the dusty street and she thought maybe in his wave he was saying, *Yeah, you might as well keep your distance.* Dah Alice was off-limits also, which was seriously inconvenient. Leila could really have used her counsel now.

The problem was that Leila couldn't figure out what she had seen in the forest, what those men had been talking about, or where they were headed. The other problem was that she didn't even know whether she should try to figure it out. It wasn't like she needed more work on her plate.

Besides, Leila had crossed paths with mercenaries a couple of times before, in Africa and Afghanistan. And her politics allowed for nuance; a security contractor *could* be fulfilling a legitimate, non-nefarious role. (In fact, she maybe owed a serious debt to a handsome Englishman in his sixties, a G4S "consultant" on her Sierra Leone job who'd sat up front with the driver; he had once talked the Suburban and all its occupants through an armed gang at a badly misjudged checkpoint. He had used his wits alone to do it, but Leila remembered his jaw muscles and the calm threat in his eyes that told the men outside the vehicle, *You do this, I have a hundred colleagues who will be here in an hour.*)

And yet her scavenging mind returned to the men lurking under that shade tree by the second checkpoint, to their wraparound sunglasses, to the air of menace they gave off. If it had been those two following her instead of Heckle and Jeckle, she would be truly freaked.

When she tried to plot the location of the forest checkpoint on a map, she couldn't find the road that Aung-Hla had taken to get off the highway and up into the forest. It wasn't on maps. And it wasn't just her shitty tourist maps it wasn't on; it also wasn't on Sine maps or on any of the other mapping sites. It couldn't be found using the expensive, proprietary satellite-mapping service she had access to through Helping Hand. She had even visited the dismal library at the university to look through their big atlases. There was just no road in a place where she could pretty much swear there had been a road. And yet she'd marked the GPS point on her running watch. What do you do when the Internet calls you a liar?

Gotta know when you're just busting your knuckles, Leila's father used to say. He affected chestnutty speech like that when they were all new in America and his English was poor. Leila and her brother and sister would bring slang home to him, some of which he deployed, to his children's great delight. They taught him to use *fill your pants* when he meant "be scared," and he missed the joke, had thought it had something to do with running away. He used the expression for months. Once he realized his mistake, he was more careful and would have his children's submissions vetted by an adult American English speaker.

Leila was busting her knuckles here, surely. The heat had definitely been turned up on her lately, and she suspected that it had to do with what she'd seen in the forest. But if there was something criminal going on up near Myo Thit, it would take more than a Sine search to get to the bottom of it—some information just doesn't leave the safe or the briefcase or whatever. She almost wished there were a way to let them know—whoever *they* were—that she didn't understand what she had seen and would leave it alone if they'd leave her alone. That might be a bit like volunteering your lunch money to a bully, but she had a job to do here: getting her medical supplies out of hock and finding scholarship candidates, neither of which was easily accomplished with Heckle and Jeckle dogging her every step.

What was up that road that deserved a visit from that entourage? Gems? Teak? That was one way that generals were screwing this place and enriching themselves—by selling all that to outside interests. But the generals were in bed with the Chinese and the Russians on that; it seemed unlikely that American mercenaries would be guarding any of those schemes. And what was up with that snazzy little guard post? Its retractable antenna and tire munchers? And that strange thing the angry one had said, about the hipster in the headphones: *He's fucking tech support. He's here to install software.* What the fuck?

Maybe ten kilometers, at a good pace, would jog something loose. Plus, it was amusing to see her minders keep up with her. In town, they were pretty slick. If she tried to shake them or make them work hard, they always found a way to handle it. They'd huff over footpaths and duck into doorways and reverse down chicken-clogged streets. She made them peruse souvenirs while she did the same. This seemed to amuse the souvenir vendors, in on a joke they would never have been allowed to make.

But during her morning runs in the shaggy, scraggy riverside parks on the west side of the city, there wasn't much to hide behind. One of the men would stay in the white car and on the nearest-to-her road that was Datsunable while the other ran behind her. It was ridiculous. It looked like there were two recreational runners in Mandalay, but one wore tan slacks and ran thirty yards behind the other.

This morning she really pushed herself. Jeckle kept the pace just fine. She stopped once to stretch, when a sudden stitch chomped at her abdomen. She made her short self tall, and then bent in half. The river before her was flat and gray. A mild pong came off its dirty banks. Jeckle had to stop also; he pretended great interest in a fence post. Leila could see Heckle in the little Datsun, a quarter mile away.

What the hell—she waved at Jeckle.

That surprised him, and she thought she could see the bind he was in; all the binds he was in, a guy like that. *Take that, stooge,* she thought.

But then he waved back.

There was plenty she *didn't* know about her situation right now. But that these guys wouldn't wave back—that was something she had been certain of. Jeckle had waved like he was a *friend.*

She turned and started back. Jeckle ceased to be intrigued by the fence post. And on the way home, Leila did run very fast, and she did indeed jog something loose. It wasn't some genius discovery. It was just a step back, a different vantage point. All those little homilies about how you had to think new thoughts in order to solve problems—they were true. It's just that the homilies seldom told you *how* to do that.

She knew some people who might know how to look into something like this, people who might even *want* to look into it.

She knew a reporter at the *Los Angeles Times,* and there was a boy with whom she had been briefly, fiercely, in love who was now important at the BBC. One summer, eons ago, she ate a lot of mushrooms with a girl who now ran the news desk for a big NPR affiliate. Another time, she had answered a medical distress call from a Reuters photographer in an African capital. (After a fish soup that he'd known from sip one he should not finish but had anyway, this man staggered back to his hotel room and clung to the towel rack as his insides cascaded out of him. He would have died there in that bathroom, from swift and acute dehydration, had he not called Leila. She came like a shot, commandeered a hotel car, and sang a Leonard Cohen song to him as they sped together through the blue night to the hospital.) Her little brother's best friend, who as an eleven-year-old had been besotted with Leila, now did forensic corporate accountancy at some very high level for big-ticket clients. She knew someone at the *New York Times,* an investigator at the UNHCR, and a CIA librarian. She knew a beat cop in Queens, a CDC virologist, and a speechwriter for a congressman.

So that afternoon, all of those people received this e-mail:

Hoping that one or some among you might help me figure out whether there's anything fishy going on near this site that I kind of stumbled upon. That's not really even a cliché—I pretty much did stumble upon it. I think one of the big security companies (could be Exigent or Spire or Bluebird?) is protecting something in the middle of the forest, where there aren't even supposed to be any roads. The place is in northeastern Myanmar, on the Chinese border. It's hard to say who or what you'd be looking for. Maybe any new or high-value facility or activity within about ten kilometers of a Burmese town called Ashang. Or possibly near a Chinese town called Baguanzai. A GPS point you could start with is 24°22'40" North, 97°32'39" East. Whoever is doing work up there, I think they're flying in tech-support guys with bodyguards. I know, right? I said it was fishy.

As ever, if you want a vacation in a despotic backwater, I remain your willing hostess,

Leila

PS: Despotic or not, Mandalay is quite beautiful; the offer is real. LM

Ned Swain was almost two weeks into the battle of not smoking cigarettes. It was not going well. He tried controlled breathing; he tried to smoke the craving, not the cigarette; he tried to act like someone who did not want a cigarette. How do such people act? Probably, such people did not have bosses like the odious Nigel. Nigel was twenty years older than Ned, smoked Lucky Strikes, and looked wretched up close. When Ned really wanted a cigarette and really wanted not to want a cigarette, he looked at Nigel.

Usually, Ned would not have been in Nigel's daily company. But Nigel had lately been ordering Ned to report to the chilly, windowless office in the hotel that provided the station's cover. He said he wanted Ned to compile new region notes. This was like being told to clean the VCR heads or copyedit some never-read HR boilerplate. The truth was that Nigel was clearly baffled by the new platform software and wanted Ned to bump all the systems back to the previous upgrade. But Nigel couldn't just ask Ned to do that—to do so would acknowledge his own technological deficits and violate about ten security protocols—so he had

Ned show him over and over again how to do the new key-chaining and biometrics. Ned made sure to always appear willing. It's handy to know your boss's passwords.

But these days Ned was hyperaware of every cigarette around him. Did he hate them or love them? Where does love become need become hate-because-needed? When Nigel hunched over Ned's desk to issue his pointless instructions, Ned definitely hated cigarettes. The stench was keen; it rolled off the older man like a viscous sludge.

"You'll want to see if the Cambodians will confirm this," Nigel said one morning from close behind Ned's desk, rattling a recent edition of *New Light of Myanmar*.

This was like saying *You'll want to wipe your ass after you shit.* Nigel was constantly giving Ned instructions on the most easily intuited parts of his job. Ned dug his fingernails into his palms and thus succeeded in not pointing out that every single bit of reportage gracing the pages of the junta's absurd and idiomatic daily English-language organ was subject to confirmation.

When Ned was himself a cigarette smoker, this close-quartered micromanagement had been a minor point in the long list of grievances he had against Nigel. But as Ned approached week two without Camel one, he was finding it harder to mask his distaste for the man.

Where to begin? Ned should have been in the meat of his career, but instead he was boxed in by a sociopath, made to do busywork in an obscure corner of the Service. Nigel didn't want anything of any use getting out of Mandalay station without his being able to take credit for it, so he sabotaged the work of every analyst they sent him. Being posted to Nigel's region was like being moved to a broom closet, but a broom closet where they could keep an eye on you.

Ned was a grade 4 field analyst for a clandestine U.S. military outfit called the Central Security Service. Though the name made them sound like mall cops, the CSS in fact outranked every other intelligence service and agency save one (that one was possibly mythical; it was said to have no name or emblem). But if Ned had to finish out his career working under people like Nigel, he'd rather just quit the Service. Did they let washed-up spies become schoolteachers?

There was no way to take Nigel head-on. You did not go straight at a grade 5. You went straight at a grade 5, he got on a secure phone and dinged your rating twenty points and you were now qualified to hold how many posts in the CSS? Oh, none.

So Ned did what people in stressed marriages and small offices have been doing since forever—he discreetly nudged at the edge of certain situations in order to elicit from his antagonist a rash move or utterance. He waited for his openings. He'd been doing this for a couple of years now.

So when he saw the flick-burst transmission about the possible OpSec breach at the gatehouse near the border, Ned saw an opportunity. It came in on Nigel's computer station after Nigel had left the office. Nigel ended most workdays around three in the afternoon, but he always left his station open, because he couldn't be bothered with all the key-chaining required to open and close it. So Ned saw the flick-burst before Nigel. He could have dismissed it, but instead, he made sure that Nigel saw it.

Ned thought that if Nigel was rattled, he might get sloppy and over-share about the Bluebird site. That's just the kind of thing that Nigel would do. He was evil, but he was lazy too. He had already let Ned know that it was Bluebird securing *something* in the forest at the border; Ned wasn't even supposed to know that. Whatever Bluebird was doing up there, it was grade 5 to Ned's grade 4.

Ned didn't consider that he might be putting the Majnoun girl in danger. It didn't seem like much of an OpSec breach anyway. So the girl saw a couple of Bluebirds escorting a client to this big secret site? She was there by accident and she hadn't gotten near the site itself.

But the news rattled Nigel more than Ned had meant or expected it to. Whatever the Bluebird client was doing up there, Nigel clearly felt that the Service was required to provide something more than the standard DADI protocol (deflect attention, discourage inquiry). He bumped the girl's electronic surveillance to 6, which was pretty expensive in bandwidth alone. He ordered terra-surveillance from the locals and demanded that Ned update him daily on her movements and comms.

"Sir? If I may?" said Ned, in the voice and affect he used with Nigel. "I don't think we need to worry about her. She has no idea what she saw, and she's not going to do any serious snooping around. She's having enough trouble here already. Zeya is seeing to that."

"Have Zeya increase pressure on her. We need to mitigate risk to the zero point," Nigel sputtered back, his small hands shaking. "You understand me, Swain?"

As he had risen through the ranks of the CSS, Ned had gradually come to know the score. Being a truly clandestine agency (the unpublished and unpublishable shield used by the CSS was a falconer's glove below a falcon holding a telephone receiver), the Service had to work within unique budgetary constraints. Still, it also had to fulfill its mission, which, after 9/11, had been rewritten: *To build and maintain the world's supreme electronic intelligence-gathering apparatus and cyberdefense infrastructure.* Ned could rattle it off; every analyst could. So the Service made common cause with a few private-sector endeavors—mainly tech and pharmaceutical, but patriots all. These were the partners. The partners provided the Service with intellectual capital and leading-edge technology. And the service that the Service provided to the partners? A little cover for the advanced research and complex commerce that, in order to be valuable and effective, must take place in zones unattached to a particular jurisdiction.

"We just throw a little shade on things when it's in our interest, or when it can be said to be in our interest," one of Ned's supervisors told him once when he was having a hard time appreciating that particular shade of gray.

It was said that Nigel had been an excellent spy once; his speedy rise through the darker channels of espionage was the stuff of legend. In appearance he was nondescript, in manner receding. He could become a fucking coat tree or melt into a marble column. Then—*bam*—he was right there, telling you just exactly how you screwed up.

But that was all years ago. Nigel was well past his expiration date. No one in the Service wanted to risk the capital that would be required to oust him. So he could pretty much do what he wanted until some major part of him broke. And what he wanted to do was drink in the hotel bar. To Ned, it seemed he hadn't ever given a shit about anything that happened in Myanmar.

So why had he roused himself for this Bluebird thing? It looked like Nigel *worked for* the Bluebird client; it looked like the power was going the wrong way. Because Majnoun should not really be the Service's problem. If some nosy civilian girl could derail your thing, you need to address the thing, not the nosy civilian girl. That was the deal, Ned thought.

Ned's plan was working, somewhat. The rattled, worried Nigel was indeed more indiscreet about grade 5 matters than the bored, drunk Nigel had been. There definitely was something happening in the forest. Maybe a SAG (subsidiary agency of government, or "shadow-ass government," as the joke went) was building an offline server, and Bluebird was protecting it during construction? But why would any U.S. agency—even some creepy unnamed SAG—see fit to build such a facility on the Chinese border?

Then Ned opened his workstation one morning and saw Majnoun's e-mail, and his heart sank. He had seriously failed to anticipate that she would crowd-source a request for further investigation of the forest site. People generally quit after a few fruitless Sine searches. Not this girl. And what a list of names in the *To:* field. Those were some *inconvenient* recipients.

Because her e-mail had mentioned Bluebird specifically, there was no way Ned could keep it off Nigel's computer. He just had to wait until Nigel opened his station that morning and saw it for himself.

"Christ. That little slit has gone and done it," barked Nigel at

10:27 a.m. Some scalding Nescafé splashed out of his mug and into his lap; he leaped up and cursed secondarily. Ned could see him blame that on Majnoun as well.

"What's up, boss?" Ned asked. In speech and manner, Ned never betrayed even a trace of his antagonism toward Nigel. He was always cheery and dim and acquiescent. *You have to be the easiest one in the room,* one of Ned's mentors had taught him. *You have to be like a cornflake in milk.*

"She fucking e-mailed the coordinates of the new . . . of that secure site. How the fuck did she come up with coordinates? Didn't the locals dud her devices before they let her go north?"

They had, but they had apparently forgotten about her fancy little running watch. Ned had noticed the oversight a few days after her return.

After another minute of cursing others and dabbing at his stained crotch, Nigel shut himself in the microSCIF — the phone-booth-size sensitive compartmented information facility that every covert station had been issued last year. Actually, it looked just like a phone booth, though the phone on its wall had a screen as well as a handset. Ned had caught only glimpses of the inside. It was for grade 5 use only, and there was no way around the biometrics (short of actually gouging Nigel's eyes out of their sockets and chopping his hands off, a fantasy Ned sometimes indulged).

Nigel was in there for twenty minutes, and when he came out he looked even grayer than usual. He smoked one cigarette and then another; Ned could see gross little wheels turning in his head.

"Listen, Swain. I need you to go down to the Internet place on Eighteenth Street. You're going to meet a guy there."

"Who's the guy?"

"He's SAG. Don't worry about that. Remember you said the NGO girl went north with that driver of hers?"

Ned nodded.

"You can pick him out? The driver?"

Ned nodded.

"I need you to meet the guy and show him which one is the driver."

"Uh. Okay," said Ned. He was stalling, though. Even a cornflake in milk would balk at some instructions. There are only a few reasons you identify a foreign national for a SAG asset, and none of them are happy ones. Nigel would know that Ned would know this by now.

"He's a terrorist, Swain. He chose the wrong side."

And what Ned saw in Nigel's eyes just then—the hardening, the heartlessness, the sharp point of paranoia—it gave him a fright like he hadn't known since he was a boy. Neither one of them thought the taxi driver was a terrorist. The words were just a conjurer's spell, a Patriot Act *sim sala bim*. And the part about choosing sides? That was meant for Ned, and it was delicately laced with a predator's menace.

The guy at the Internet place on Eighteenth Street did not look like a SAG asset. Generally, SAG assets looked like they were just dying to beat the shit out of someone. It would be very hard to pick one out at a hockey game, for example. But this guy was wispy and almost pretty, though once he was sitting in Ned's car, Ned saw that he had the BMI of a shotgun shell and that his every movement came out of nowhere; he even opened the glove box in a deft and deadly way.

The asset was in the passenger seat, Ned driving. When the asset looked right, Ned stole a glance and saw that the guy had a picture of the taxi driver strapped to his forearm, under the long sleeve of his pirate-type shirt.

"Picture's crap. That's why you're here," said the asset without looking at Ned.

Ned drove slowly. He needed to think. You never knew when these things were going to come up. Knowing what you *should* do was seldom of any use. Saying to the man "I'm sorry, sir, but I joined the Service to keep my country safe, not to chauffeur assassins. Please exit the vehicle" wasn't an option; Ned had blown past that point a while back. They passed the faded movie house, the flower market, the rubble-strewn park with the diesel-powered merry-go-round.

He thought of Leila. He'd been listening to her all week, though he'd made contact with her only twice, months ago. Once when she first arrived, and then once when he'd found her in the university cafeteria and talked to her about aspirated consonants. While it was part of his job to bore people into never suspecting him of anything, he couldn't help being a bit hurt that he had been so successful in her case. She was very pretty: compact and Persian and poised. It would have been nice to get a nod from her. He thought of one of these guys prowling around Leila.

"If he's working today, he should be up here," said Ned. They were coming up on the pagoda beside which some of the taximen queued. But the traffic had grown thick around one of the circles. *Back home, on traffic reports, this is called stop-and-go traffic,* thought Ned. The asset wasn't saying anything, just mowing down locals from behind his cheap-looking shades.

"What about Majnoun?" asked Ned in the manner he used when he wanted to sound capable of violence. He imagined that there was something really gross in his mouth; the effect was to make his voice flat and his eyes dull.

The asset looked at Ned; sized him up. Then he just shrugged.

"There's the driver, I think," said Ned, still with the imaginary gross thing in his mouth, and he indicated a knot of men beneath a weeping tree. The SAG asset lasered his gaze through the windshield. The traffic moved again and they were able to approach the target, at which point both Ned and the asset could see it wasn't Majnoun's taximan. The asset relaxed, if that was the word. Ned started taking them on a loop around.

After half a block, he tried again. "Probably can't take Majnoun now, right? I mean, the day after she sends that shit out?"

This time the guy liked it: the lack of subject, the deference, the lame use of *shit*.

"Yeah, that's what they're saying. She just raced right to the top of their pile, though," he said. "Anyway, the girl's got protection right now. Two dudes from that Gettwin Nikaya monastery on her all the time."

It took Ned a minute to understand, because the asset had mangled the Burmese.

When he got it, all he did was raise one eyebrow. He wanted to appear to be thinking, *What, and you're afraid of a couple of monks?*, when he was in fact thinking, *Monks from the Cathubhummika Mahasatipatthana Hnegttwin are protecting Leila? What the fuck?* Ned had thought those two minders were Zeya's men. The Hnegttwin were pretty hard-line theologically — they worshipped the spirit, not the image, of Buddha — but they were no Shaolin Avengers.

"No one's scared of a couple of monks," said the asset, on cue. "But, you know, with these type of people, the monks are very important. They have a lot of power."

Ned sat up for this lesson in the South Asian psyche.

"Like in Afghanistan. With their warlords and shit," said the asset. "You might have a guy totally in your sights and then it turns out he's Abdul Whatever's lieutenant's fuck boy. So you can't go near him."

They were parked now, with the taxi rank fifty yards off Ned's right flank. The asset crooked his forearm in his open window, a pen in his grasp pointed toward the rank. One by one, he pointed the pen at the drivers, twisting the tip of the pen delicately, as if waiting for the last word of a stanza to come to him. Ned could see now that the asset was examining each man's image as it resolved on the screen inside his not-at-all-cheap glasses.

"We shouldn't let her go," said Ned, bringing it back to Leila, though the asset seemed to have finished with her. "The girl's a bad combination. Clueless and connected, you know?" He had to be very careful here not to out-Herod Herod; the asset must know he was a grade 4. But Whatever was going to happen to Leila, Ned wanted to be in on it.

The asset stiffened. "I got him," he said, twisting his pen tip and squinting at his tiny screen. Then in one of his too-swift motions he had his shades off and was handing them to Ned. "Confirm," he said.

The asset had frozen the image on the screen. Ned squinched his mouth up, like he couldn't be sure. "Here, lemme have the lens."

Ned saw the tang of resistance, and then its evaporation. The asset gave him the pen. *You don't have to fight them,* his mentor had taught. *With some men, you can establish dominance by making them give up a small, closely held thing.*

Ned refreshed the screen; aimed and zoomed the pen.

Yeah. Shit. That was Aung-Hla. Thirty-nine, father of three, kept his Tercel sparkling.

"You're really gonna let her walk?" Ned asked, aiming the pen at each of the other men in turn.

"Don't worry about it, bro. Your boss is in on it. Dude can cook up some nasty shit. He's using that new outfit, you know? The Ruiners?"

He'd heard about them. But Ned thought the Ruiners sounded too bad to be true: a cadre of grade 5s sitting in Aeron chairs on the thirteenth floor of a twelve-story building in northern Virginia. It was said they had full access, through every lens, tap, screen, or pipe. It was said they could reach into your life as a child reaches into the world of her toys. Not just pull, but push. They could rewrite your life; play with you, punish you, or crumple you like paper.

"It's not him. It's not the driver," said Ned.

"You sure?" said the asset. Like: *You're really gonna take a stand here?*

"Yeah. It's not him," said Ned, and shrugged. There was a sort of aikido in the effective use of condescension. It was a question of careful dosing, and placement. "I see why you thought so, though. All those guys look alike."

Leila hated the Monday-morning conference call. The New Yorkers as usual forgot that for most people on the call, Monday morning had come and gone. In Mandalay, it was 9:30 p.m. and Leila was wondering whether she would eat chicken soup at the blue place or noodles with green shoots at the place with the tattered awning. And whether either would still be open when this call ended. The New Yorkers were all take-charge and macchiatoed and *Great to have you with us, Pat*.

When Leila dialed in, her connection was terrible, whirs and clicks. She cut the line and dialed in again. The same whirs and clicks. Though maybe not as loud this time, and easier to listen to than fifteen coworkers jostling for position. So she didn't cut the line again. She pressed SPEAK-ERPHONE, returned the handset to its base, and listened absently to all the good intentions and machinations as she wrote in her notebook about who else she might send that e-mail to, whether the Zeya henchman who'd mentioned the bird people could have meant Bluebird, and what she was going to get her dad for his birthday, which was in a month. When it was her turn to report, she kept it to a minimum.

Leila had already decided that this call was not the venue to bring up the freeze-out she was taking from the Burmese. It had gotten worse just in the past few days. Professional relationships that she had spent months cultivating were snapping shut one by one. Heckle and Jeckle were still there—she caught glimpses of them—but they'd receded and been augmented by a rotating cast of plainclothes men who stood on the corner outside her office smoking cigarettes and speaking nonfurtively into walkie-talkies the size of cowboy boots. These guys did *not* wave back. She hadn't seen Aung-Hla in days, and when she asked the other taximen about him, they shrugged dumbly. The only one who would speak straight with her said, *You don't need to know everything.*

And then this morning a young man from the Ministry of Immigration had arrived by moped and served her with notice that in a week her visa would be rescinded and her presence in the country would become illegal. So she would need to loop New York in soon. But she had never figured out whom to trust in Helping Hand and she suspected that the organization would dump her and her projects just as soon as it learned she was politically toxic. Leila needed a few more days to work out an exit strategy. She was trying to find a way that she could get Dah Alice to take over the Helping Hand projects. She didn't know whether she could pull that off or whether it would even be a net gain for Dah Alice's organization. But there was money waiting for those nursing students; there was the ransomed medical shipment; there was the small, well-outfitted office. Maybe that should be Leila's model for global improvement— collect privilege and office supplies from the first world and then cast them off in the third.

"Leila, can we expect to see the paperwork on those scholarship candidates soon?" asked a guy called Tim or Tom Timmiken over the bad line.

What up with that guy? From what she understood of the Helping Hand chain of command, he had no business sticking his nose in this. The problem appeared to be that back in New York, during her three-day Goal Definement and Orientation training, he had hit on her, poorly. She had clearly signaled zero interest. But he kept flinging doors practically off their hinges to open them for her. She saw him check the jut of his jaw in nearby mirrors. She'd read from a binder during the taxi ride they shared while he'd displayed to her both his forearms and his world-informedness by leaning forward and talking geopolitics with the Pakistani driver, who clearly couldn't give a shit.

"Yeah, I'll send that through just as soon as I can, Tahhhm." She tried to elide *Tim* and *Tom*. Hopefully, a *whir* or *click* obscured her obscuring.

She was thinking maybe she could find her dad a complete encyclopedia, like a *Britannica* eleventh edition, or maybe a vintage *Hoyle's Rules of Games* or the kind of *OED* that comes with a magnifying glass when she realized the others had signed off the call and that she was the only one left on the line. Broadcast by the speakerphone and without any competing sound, the whirs and clicks were very loud.

An hour later, she was in the lobby of the Excellents Hotel calling her brother, Dylan, on an avocado-colored phone that sat on a doily at one end of the bar, its handset as heavy as a hammer. The Excellents had been Leila's home for a few weeks when she first arrived in Mandalay. The staff there knew her and appeared to like her; when she came in and nodded at the phone, the desk man nodded back with a smile.

The Excellents was a colonial building, crumbling in a heartbreaking sort of way. Like a wouldn't-make-it-ten-more-years kind of way. The stairways sagged like swag; the doorways skewed parallelogramatically. Wherever a foot had scuffed, a million feet had scuffed before, so there were wear patterns in the wooden thresholds and even in the stone stairs. She climbed onto a stool and dialed her brother, using a phone card she'd bought in the street. The barman brought her a glass of terrible white wine.

Dylan wasn't sure the whirs and clicks meant anything. That's probably why she'd called him—he was skeptical and slow to worry and hard to impress.

"Can't they just kick you out?" Dylan asked her. "Why would they bug your phone? It's not like you have any nonprofit trade secrets."

"They did."

"They did what?"

"Kick me out."

"Hold up," said Dylan. "They kicked you out?"

"Well, I mean, I got a letter today saying they're going to. In seven days my visa gets yanked."

"Plus those guys following you." He seemed to reconsider the whirs and clicks. "Leila, whom did you piss off?"

She liked her brother's care with grammar. Six years younger than Leila, he was the only Majnoun kid born in the United States, the only one who had absorbed no Farsi. As a boy, he'd played the sheriff, the space sheriff, and the policeman; he whipped out his bus pass as if it were a badge. He'd once applied to the FBI, but at an early interview he had miscalculated the candor required and overshared about his collegiate use of psychotropics.

"I don't know," said Leila. "This prick of a general, certainly. But maybe other people too. Did you read that e-mail I sent you?"

"When?"

"Like an hour ago."

"No, I'm at the store. I'm on break." Dylan had washed out of law school and then slipped into something pretty bleak. There was a brief hospital stay, and then a long year and some heavy meds while living in his old room at home. These days, he seemed mostly back together, but he was on a much gentler career trajectory than the one he'd abandoned; he worked at Whole Foods, in produce.

Cyrus and Mariam Majnoun had been hit hard by their son's slide off the striving-immigrant-professional-vindication track, and Leila thought that their undisguised disappointment in him had probably prolonged and intensified Dylan's episode. Plus, it was annoying, because they had two totally successful daughters, women who would have been happy to take some of the burden of achieving off their brother. But it was a son thing, apparently.

"Read the e-mail I sent you," she said. "Can you talk this time tomorrow?"

"Yeah, sure. But sis?"

"Yeah?"

"Why not just come home? I mean, if they're going to kick you out anyway."

"Well. I guess I will come home. I mean soon."

"But how about just come home tomorrow? It sounds like they got you pretty much boxed in. Anyways, I really miss you. And Mom's driving me bonkers. She's always calling me a fruit vendor."

It helps so much to know that you are missed, thought Leila. What keeps the truly alone even attached to the earth? "Call her a housewife," she said. Leila knew all the reasons that Dylan could never do that, but she thought he'd find the idea funny.

"Yeah," he said. He hadn't found it funny. "Lately, she's not really doing that part."

Leila wanted to ask what he meant, but she could hear the forced exhale that meant his cigarette was finished; his break was over. Where do you smoke at a Whole Foods? she wondered. Inside a dumpster?

And when she'd gotten off the phone she'd thought about Dylan's question: Why not just go home tomorrow? Or as soon as she could, anyway? She hadn't really considered that. It just seemed to her that if they were pushing you, you should push back. You should not stand in front of a gun, obviously, but neither should you let a threat alone compel you to move. And if they really wanted to kick her out, she thought she should make them go through with it. At least that way, she'd get a ride to the airport.

But maybe that's not how life works at all. Maybe you're not supposed to put up so much resistance. Maybe a lot of that is pride and ego and pointless in the end. In which case she'd been misled by all that required reading and by the Die Hard movies.

Ned was sitting in a cracked plastic chair on his minuscule balcony drinking a whiskey and smoking a cigarette, his first in two weeks. The evening's haze smeared the city before him, and a rich umber sunset flamed the river beyond. The sensual reward of the cigarette mixed with the moral defeat of the cigarette. His head swam.

Ned actually came from a distinguished line of U.S. intelligence operatives. A distant but direct ancestor had spied for George Washington in New York City during the Revolutionary War, and Ned's grandfather was an OSS legend who'd once had a fistfight with a member of the Central Politburo. If they were looking down now... Well, Ned tipped a little *splish* of whiskey from his glass to the cement at his feet—an offering, an apology. Because his forebears would deffo not approve of what the CSS, in the form of grade 5 Nigel Smith, was doing to Leila Majnoun.

Ned had done a couple of hard-core things in the field, but only against truly bad characters, men who posed a threat. And in both cases, the action he'd taken had been swift. Whereas what Nigel arranged for the Majnoun girl was an escalating series of logistical punishments, like a premoral boy funneling ants into solvent. It was almost like he wanted Leila to not just shut down but feel the edge of what he could do; he wanted her to suspect but be unable to confirm a link between her having asked questions about the forest site and all the shit that was now raining down on her, on her family. If you inject that kind of confusion and doubt to a person's life, you can really derail it.

Ned had risen quickly in the clubby little world of espionage. He was smarter than most of the other guys, a lot of whom were alcoholics in regimental ties. After two years of training, he had begun his career in China region. There was still real spy stuff happening there: boxy cars following other boxy cars along deserted roads, agents meeting people in washrooms, that sort of thing. In China, Ned was called Chuck, a contracting officer for apparel-manufacturing concerns. People just said the craziest shit to Chuck. Ned wrote it all up; his reports were vivid and tight, his insights keen, his observations actionable. Bethesda noticed.

But then it seemed like maybe it would be twenty years before he'd be allowed to advance a grade in China region, so Ned concentrated on his languages and his open-source analysis skills. When he was passed over for three consecutive cycles, he decided to leave field analysis and return to analysis.

Back in Bethesda, his pay slip said he was a statistician for the Congressional Budget Office (he even had some of that work on his desk, a tradition among CSS analysts). He drove an old Saab. He read and read and read. It was like being a professor but with no students, which he understood from professor acquaintances was pretty much the way you wanted it. He had a wicker lampshade over his kitchen table; stalagmites of magazines and journals grew in his living room. He lived across the street from a doggy day-care place, and sometimes when he left his driveway in the morning, a beagle would be keening. He tried Internet dating. He worked on collation and discrete DiP software for Open Source, on the fourth floor. His parents sent him pears on his birthday.

If he hadn't made such a scene about Dear Diary, he'd probably still be there; he'd probably be a grade 5 by now, and maybe he'd be able to effectively oppose people like Nigel and whoever else was putting the Service in the service of a growing web of ambiguously allied clients. These thoughts, and the whiskey, stirred the silt of Ned's regrets and resentments.

The Dear Diary episode had nearly cost him his career. He'd gone out on a limb, and the limb had snapped off beneath him, and he'd been left looking like a neophyte who'd wasted the skills and assets of the Service by chasing a phantom menace. The Myanmar posting was punishment for all that. They'd done more than boot him from Open Source; they'd sent him into Nigel's toxic little corner of the field.

"I believe outcome is being achieved, sir," Ned had told Nigel that morning at the daily report he was now required to present on Leila Majnoun. "She has accepted the fact that she's leaving. She's received no useful response from the original recipients."

"That's because I'm making sure she doesn't," Nigel said huffily, puffily.

Ned nodded—*rightyouaresir*—and continued, "And she sent that e-mail to only one other person."

"Who?"

"Her brother." To underscore that the brother was unconnected, Ned added, "He works at Whole Foods."

"I know where he works," Nigel snapped.

Another little nod from Ned. "Anyway, I don't think she'll contest the deportation."

"I don't think she'll *contest* it either," said Nigel, mocking Ned's word choice. "I think that that nosy cunt will begin her self-deportation in about"—he grandly looked at his heavy Rolex—"five hours."

Ned put on his blankest face, but Nigel did not elaborate, and Ned did not inquire. Part of this game was letting Nigel enjoy the belief that he was as unreadable as the Sphinx when all Ned had to do, really, was wait him out. All morning, the man could barely contain his glee. Midday, he took a call in the microSCIF, and when he came out he was humming.

Then, a few hours later, another SCIF call, and when he came out he attempted to turn on the office TV but got confused by the remotes.

"Swain, did you alter the settings on this thing?" he barked. "The channel won't change."

"Let me see if I can figure it out," said Ned, accepting the remote like it was a partial differential equation. He made an *aha* face and switched the function selector from TV to CABLE. "I think that's it," he said.

Ned snatched back the remote and thumbed his way up to CNN. There was an ad playing—*If you've experienced these symptoms, talk to your doctor about Synapsiquell*—but Nigel waited so eagerly that Ned stayed right beside him. Then there was another ad for a wealth-management company—a fit and shrewd-looking older man walked along a private beach with either his adult daughter or his very young wife. Whichever it was, he was proud. Offscreen, a distinguished-elder-black-man voice stressed the importance of *protecting the legacy you've built*.

Then the show returned, and the camera swoosh-tracked to the anchor desk in that urgent way, and the handsome anchor was squaring the corners of the papers before him. He appeared to be especially troubled by the upcoming story.

"We're starting to get some more details on this very troubling story out of Tarzana, California," said the anchor—TARZANA was highlighted on the map of LA County that appeared beside the anchor's head—"where authorities early this morning removed computers and other electronic equipment from a middle-school principal's office." A wide shot of a parking lot, then a zoom in on three or four men in blue windbreakers carrying boxes to the trunks of white Fords. "This after a police tactical unit arrested a man today in a predawn raid in a neighborhood near the school. While authorities have not yet confirmed any connection between the two events, neighbors told a reporter that the man arrested was Tarzana middle-school principal Cyrus Majnoun"—the anchor paused minutely at the foreignish name.

Cut to a man in a bathrobe outside his house, speaking to camera: "It was nuts. It was guys in body armor. They knocked the door down.

I even thought, you know, *You got the wrong house. That's the principal's house.* But then they came out of there with *Madge-noon.* I never saw anything like it before. It was nuts."

Then back to the anchor. "Authorities aren't commenting on the arrest or the seizures at this time. But viewers may recall that a school district in nearby Orange County was rocked last year by a scandal involving a high-school principal and Internet child pornography. We'll bring you more on this story as it develops."

Nigel clicked off the set, looking like he'd just taken a pie out of the oven. "Ha!" he crowed. "See, Swain? That's how you put a stop to all this Nancy Drew bullshit. Let's see how curious she is now."

And for a split second, Ned may have let the mask slip, because Nigel felt the need to say: "You should be proud of the work we did here, Swain." He put no extra emphasis on the *we.* He didn't need to. Was there any doubt that if something like this collapsed, it would collapse not just on Nigel but on everyone around him?

Thus the cigarettes, which Ned bought on the way home. And then the pre-dinner turn to whiskey. How had it come to this? thought Ned, and he meant all of it: the avoidance drinking, the loneliness, the being stuck under the thumb of a man he despised and implicated in an immoral conspiracy almost certainly unrelated to national security. Ned knew all about the greater good, and something about Patriot Act back channels, and he was annoyed by liberals who walked around all un-blown-up claiming that they liked their civil liberties more than their security. But he'd thought there were some controls in place, that there was still a grown-up in the room.

Ned was smoking as if to make up for two weeks of not smoking. What was the recipe for Camels? They were fucking delicious. What was this "Turkish and American blend"? It was chemicals sprayed out of nozzles, wasn't it?

Leave aside for a moment the morality of what Nigel was doing to Leila, Ned thought. Leave that aside and it was still very wrong just in terms of resource allocation, wasn't it? Unless Leila Majnoun was a future Hitler come back in a time machine, Ned couldn't really see how such a vicious and elaborate operation could be justified. Nigel's interest in her was unprofessionally vengeful. And what he was doing was probably illegal. The word still meant something, or was supposed to, anyway. Extralegal was fine; illegal was not. Plus, it was just terrible espionage—there must be a huge number of people involved in something like what he had just witnessed. Oh yeah—he was one of them.

And that's when Ned had a thought that was one of those across-the-line thoughts. What if *he* told Majnoun what had been done to her? What would she do with the information?

The line crossed was treason, actually. Because there was no ombudsman at the CSS; there was no mediator who was going to take his complaint up the chain of command. The papers he'd signed at his commission to the Service made it very clear: If he did what he had just considered doing, he was on the outside; if he was on the outside, he was a risk; if he was a risk, he was a threat; if he was a threat, he was a target.

He couldn't just tell her straight out. If he told her that 85 percent of electronic correspondence (worldwide) and 100 percent of electronic correspondence (English-language) was run through a threat-sieve network commissioned by the U.S. government but increasingly outsourced to a consortium of private companies, she would not believe him. But if he gave her just enough so that she could go looking for the rest? She was smart, and apparently determined. Give her something to run with—one of the Dear Diary portals he'd identified but had never been allowed into—and she'd probably chase it down. And with her Farsi and Burmese, her monk minders and her Rolodex, she was just the kind of asset that Dear Diary might hook and land.

And if Dear Diary did open a door for Leila, Ned could follow her in. After the e-mail, Nigel had bumped her to level-8 surveillance. At that level she could have a low-altitude UAV snooping her every step; her financials would be flagged; her scent would be waved before the computers. If it came to it, she could be extraordinarily renditioned from, like, a women's toilet. So keeping an eye on her should be cinchy. But he'd have to get clear of Nigel for a few weeks. Taking time off work when you work for the world's most elite clandestine agency is *not* a cinch. You can't just cash in sick days and forward your voice mail. If you say it's a vacation, there'd better be sand in your shoes when you come back, and if you say it's a family illness, they'll be wanting to see those biopsy reports.

He'd find a way. Maybe he could work from Sydney station. The more he thought about it, and the more he drank, the more likely it seemed to him that Leila Majnoun was his ticket into Dear Diary. The obsession had nearly derailed him, and he was still looking for a way back to it.

Okay, so he had an ulterior motive. But his anterior motive — to see that she had at least the chance to fight back against Nigel's plan — that was sincere.

He marveled again at her choice of phone. Ned had ghosted every single one of her devices, and he had real-time access to 80 percent of the phone lines in Myanmar. If she'd been on any one of those, he could have been listening to her now. But the phones at the Excellents were trunked from one of the last predigital exchanges in the city; they used twenty-pulse-per-second crossbar switches and crossbar tandems. Of course, he could get the feed from the other direction, but to do that he would need to involve Bethesda, and the feed would be copied to Nigel's station per protocol. Ned didn't want to risk giving Nigel anything else on Leila or drawing any more heat on her than she was already taking, so he had to settle for recording and subsequent collection. The device he had installed in the handset of the Excellents' lobby phone was the size of a grain of basmati rice. It was unpowered and nontransmitting. He would collect it in the morning.

But he was worried about the morning, worried that by the time it came, he would have lost heart or come to his senses. He needed to do something tonight; he needed to commit.

* * *

Ned bicycled swiftly through the hot dark streets to Leila's little apartment above the tailor shop. He passed by twice, looking for her plainclothes detail and/or minder monks, but he saw no surveillance. What tails she had would be outside the Excellents right now, where she was. He stashed his bike and slipped up to her building along its darkest flank. His heart was beating as it hadn't in twenty years of espionage. His heart was beating as it hadn't since he and a girl from a million years ago used to climb over eight feet of chain-link on a Saturday night to sneak into the marina and onto her parents' cabin cruiser.

He reached her front door and slipped the note beneath it.

I think your father was framed, it said. *Meet me at the Excellents tomorrow. 8p.*

The next day, Ned stayed away from the office. The hangover was not terrible and not unwelcome — it kept reminding him of what he'd done last night. He didn't regret it exactly, but in the cold light of day, his plan looked rickety and tenuous. He would never have pulled the trigger if he had waited until morning.

First thing, he collected the device from the phone at the Excellents, replaced it with another. Then he brought it home and listened to it while he drank coffee and ate cheese.

It was worse than he thought. The dad's arrest sounded brutal. The SWAT team had scared the shit out of the mother; the brother had been injured during the arrest, presumably trying to defend his father from what must surely have seemed to him a nightmare. Cyrus Majnoun was charged with the possession and distribution of child pornography, aggravated by his being a school principal. After hours of interrogation, he'd suffered a mild heart attack. He was hospitalized and stable now.

Leila was definitely angrier than she was hurt or scared. Her voice seethed out of Ned's laptop. She had really burned up that Excellents' phone last night. She'd spoken to her brother and her sister and then an attorney in California and then three more attorneys in New York, and then with her brother and sister again on two extensions of her parents' home phone. Ned could hear the glasses rattle in the Majnoun kitchen when the little brother closed the fridge door.

If any of the Majnoun children doubted their father's innocence, not one betrayed a hint of it. Leila was the most galvanized. At one point, Dylan referred to "clearing" their dad's name, and Leila responded, "Clear him, D? We're going to see him reinstated, apologized to, and recompensed. Like, recompensed in a way that will make the FBI wish they'd never heard the name Majnoun."

Roxana said she had begun to organize parents and faculty at the middle school.

"Will they support him?" Leila asked her sister.

"Hard to say right now," she answered. "I think most of them know it must be a setup or a mistake. But we need to figure out why he was set up, and by whom. There are a few people saying terrible things already, and those voices will only get stronger. We need something to say back to them, some alternative theory. It helps that there are no victims. If he were a predator pornographer principal, he would have hurt a child by now; some victim would have come forward."

Ned was impressed by her detachment, her analysis. This was the eldest child, the armless genius.

Dylan was to going to assist the attorney and start pushing back against the FBI and the prosecutor. "That lawyer you found, Leila, he says we need to get our hands on the seized computers as soon as we can. It looks like their entire case is digital. But the guys we're going to need, the forensics guys, they're very expensive. Like four-fifty-an-hour expensive."

Leila had told them she'd be home in three days. To Ned that meant that his only chance to talk to her would be tonight—if she even showed up.

Roxana quit the line before Dylan, and Ned heard Dylan ask Leila, "Sis, there's no way, you think, any of this could have anything to do with, you know, the trouble you've been having in Burma? Or that e-mail you sent me?"

Ned leaned in to his laptop.

"No. No. The Burmese already kicked me out. And whatever I saw in the forest—and even if it *was* something that I wasn't supposed to see—I wasn't able to do anything with it."

But she had considered it. She had paused between the two *nos*. And that was *before* she had received his note.

Ned decided he would treat the meeting as a potential romantic opening, because that's what his Burma-region persona would do — Ned the tone-deaf postdoc interested in diglossia and the ninth-century pagan empire of the Irrawaddy River Valley. Leila would be wondering why he was trying to help her, and a crush was the most plausible motivation. A girl like Leila would have run into that plenty. So he spent an hour primping for their date. He held various shirts against himself in front of a mirror. That made him worry again that he would never be called handsome because he had a slightly too-large head, and that this was what had kept him from any great love in his adulthood. He splashed on cologne.

He was at the bar of the Excellents Hotel an hour early, ordered a drink, and sipped it slowly. He wondered if she'd show up and what he would do if she didn't. The bar was really just a corner of the lobby with a driftwood sign whereon *Bar* was written in cursive, with rope. There was a nautical theme to the hotel that presumably had once been more thoroughly carried out but now was limited to a few things like the ropy signage and a clutch of naval-battle prints curling in their frames. Maybe some dusty rear admiral, ex of the East India Company, had built the place to make it more likely that steamer-trunked friends would visit him in this too-hot outpost of the Empire.

At 8:05, Leila walked in. She looked around as if scanning for a trap. She saw him. He waved.

She approached and recognized him. "You're Fred. From the university."

"Ned."

"Did you write this?" She held up his note. She didn't sit.

"I did," he said. "You want a drink?"

She ignored that. But she sat down. "Tell me what you meant by it."

She looked rough, like she hadn't slept. "Okay. You know how you were writing to people about the security contractors in the forest?"

"Do *I* know that? How do *you* know that?"

It all hinged on this. "I do some work for a guy who I think is, like, a spy. Like, a CIA guy or something."

"You're a spy?" said Leila.

Ned laughed. "No, I'm a linguist. But I do some translation work for this guy. And he has crappy security on his computer. And I snuck a look. You saw something you weren't supposed to see. They want you gone." One truth and several lies.

"What did I see? What are the contractors doing up there?"

"I don't know." Sadly, this was also true. But it didn't matter for his purposes here. He gave her a mashed-up version of a possible explanation. "It's some huge corporation. I think it's like a Chinese company that wants to test some totally gnarly genetic pesticides on live forests. They want to do stuff you can't do even in China. So they're doing it here and pretending it's China. Is your dad okay?"

"What's the company called?"

"New Solutions?" He said it with a rising terminal intonation. "I Sined it. I think it's just a name. Like, it's owned by something bigger."

He needed Leila to think he was less intelligent than he was. It was the most basic requirement of field analysis, but it was actually quite rare:

the ability and willingness to appear dumber than you were. That's why he'd started out in field analysis: the acting part came naturally to him. He could slacken his mouth a little bit when necessary. He could even deaden his eyes.

Yeah, look at my slightly too-large head, he used to think. *Pay no attention to what I'm doing.*

"So who's your spy friend?" asked Leila.

"He's not my friend," said Ned. "You know that skinny old dude who runs the Paradise Hotel?" More intentionally dull speech. Ned could have offered much more artful descriptives for Nigel: Decrepit. Glossy. Ghoulish.

"The Canadian?"

"Is he Canadian? I didn't know that."

"He sounds Canadian. You say he's a spy?"

"Yeah. I do translating for him, for the hotel. I think he works for the CIA or something."

Leila looked blankly at Ned. "So, what, you rifled through his desk on my behalf?"

"No. No. He had me fixing his computer. He's useless. He couldn't open his e-mail. But he left me alone in his office, and . . . well, I saw the name of the outfit you work for, and I thought, *Why would he care about that?* And then, behind a really dinky firewall, I saw those e-mails you wrote, about the site in the forest." Ned leaned forward. "Dude can read your e-mails." He sounded incredulous at the idea. "And I saw that he had written to someone and said that you would be removed from the equation. That's what he wrote, *removed from the equation.* And there was some stuff about the project you saw, but I couldn't really understand it, other than what I've already told you. I only had about an hour."

She seemed interested. Very suspicious, but interested. "So how do you know my dad was framed?"

"Well. I guess I don't. Know that, I mean. But here's a situation where someone who works either for the CIA or for, like, a bad corporation, someone who can read your e-mail, that person wants you to leave Burma. I saw the news about your dad . . ."

"How did you know he's my father?"

"Majnoun. I'd never heard the name before. And I saw a picture of your brother. You two look alike. Anyway, if they can read your e-mail, I doubt they'd have any trouble putting porn on someone's computer."

She was evaluating. Her brain practically whirred.

"You want that drink?" he asked.

She shook her head no.

"Are you going home?" he asked.

"Yeah." It was the first time that her voice had softened with him. "My dad had a heart attack. He's in the hospital."

"Shit. I'm sorry. Listen, I may be able to help you."

"Really?" She arched an eyebrow. "How?"

"I think I know about some people who are good at getting to the bottom of things like this."

"You mean like the police?"

"No, not at all like the police. It's a sort of a network for, like, people who think corporations are bad and do bad stuff."

"Are you part of this network?"

"No."

"So how do you know about it?"

"They helped out a friend of mine once," he lied.

"And how will they help me?" asked Leila.

"I don't know exactly. But if you get screwed by a government or, like, a corporation, they help you get back at those people."

"That's it? That's all you got for me?"

Ned looked hurt. "Yeah. I guess so. But it's something."

With a nod, she allowed that it might be. "Okay. How do I get in touch with this network?"

Ned wrote the address of a website on a piece of paper and pushed it across the table to her. "It's a house-swapping site. But ignore that. Just write, like, a paragraph in one of the windows about what happened to you. Then they're supposed to get in touch with you."

"But if the CIA can read my e-mail, they're going to know I'm doing this, right? I mean, what you're saying is very, very weird. You must know that."

"I know that. Look, I may be totally wrong about this. But I've just heard that these people can help. I mean, when you're in a jam."

"Like the A-Team."

"Pardon?"

"Forget it."

Leila picked up the scrap with the website address. She stood up. "Okay. Well, thanks," she said, giving little. Then she sandaled out of there, briskly, into the hot night.

Leila left the Excellents and headed back to her office. Sixteen hours until she had to leave the country. She had a lot of work to do before then.

That Ned guy didn't seem like the sharpest tool in the shed, actually. Maybe sort of spectrum-y. And the waves of cologne off him had been overpowering. Was that Drakkar Noir? What he'd told her was almost certainly nonsense. For one thing, why would a CIA agent have some dude fix his computer?

He seemed well intentioned, though. He had said *sorry* about Leila's dad. Hearing the word, she had almost cracked and started crying.

Dylan had asked her last night did she think their dad's arrest could have anything to do with her e-mail. She reviewed again the reasons she'd told him no. Yeah, they were valid. Back in her office, she tossed into the trash the piece of paper with the website address Ned had given her.

She began to pack up the office. She didn't know what kind of a packing job was required. The office was rented for a year, and Helping Hand had paid up-front. It seemed unlikely that she'd be returning, but someone might. New York was being squirrely about whether they would even want her back. During an hours-long call earlier that day, the region director kept referring to the Mandalay office as a "partner program," which was troubling. It seemed like maybe they would dump the whole thing. Leila thought of all the young women whom she had encouraged to dream of a first-world medical education; she thought of their hopes withering like, well, like raisins in the sun.

You should always look behind yourself to see if you have accidentally hurt someone. Her father had said that to her once. He did not say you had to fix everything you screw up; he did not say you must never hurt anyone. None of those unfollowable directions. Just that: *You should always look behind yourself.* She was old enough now to read the secret meaning embedded in all real advice: that the giver has fallen short of it himself, and that falling-short still rings in him and shapes his soul. When had her father not looked behind himself? It must have been when they left Iran.

She packed like a dervish. Pens and cords and cables went into ziplock bags. Reports and binders were puzzled and staggered to fit in boxes. Maps rolled into cardboard tubes. What about the office computer? She transferred all the program files from the desktop to her laptop and trashed everything on the desktop. That didn't seem like enough, considering the weird shit that was going down. What if they were getting rid of her just so they could punish the women she'd interviewed? So she did her best to scrub the hard drive. How do you do that? She found a menu item called Overwrite Deleted Files, and the computer did its spinny pizza thing for a few minutes. Was that enough? She considered taking a brick to the tower, or tearing out its innards. But she didn't know which was the hard drive and which the logic board or whatever. Besides, that would make her look guilty or afraid of something, whereas what she wanted to do was stare down her antagonists, be they Burmese corruptocrats or—as that guy Ned would have her believe—the CIA.

Why didn't she know more about computers? That knowledge suddenly seemed more important than feminist theory or eighties' song lyrics, both of which she was well acquainted with. Computers had risen around her all her life, like a lake sneakily subsuming more and more arable land, but she'd never learned to write code or poke behind the icons or anything like that. She was like a medieval peasant confounded by books and easily impressed by stained glass.

She took Ned's piece of paper out of the wastebasket, uncrumpled it: Ding-Dong.com.

Really?

On her laptop, on the floor of her empty office, leaning against a wall of stacked boxes and sitting beneath the breeze of a plastic fan, Leila sent her browser to Ding-Dong.com. It was indeed a house-swapping site, or appeared to be, anyway. A rather high-pressure vibe on the front page, actually: *The #1 site! Destination: Change;* click-on-able testimonials beneath pictures of happy people enjoying the decisions they'd made. In the first fill-in-able text box she came to, she wrote her e-mail address and then this:

> Weird guy in bar told me to try your site. My name is you don't need to know my name. I may have some information about a major US company doing contract security in Burma, which is violation of US law, FYI. Also maybe they know I know and have screwed with me because of my knowing. Screwed me immigration-wise and maybe more, which would seem to indicate criminal government collusion. If you can help, get in touch with me. If this makes no sense, please ignore it. If this is a joke or a trap, fuck you, you should be ashamed of yourselves.

She double-locked the office, went home, and packed up her little apartment. Her things fit in four large suitcases and a big duffel. There was more to do, but it had to be done in the morning. She lay down and caught a few hours' sleep.

She woke to her alarm. While the kettle boiled, she checked her sites and her e-mail. No response from the house-swapping people. She was disappointed but also somehow relieved. She ate an orange and drank some tea. She stuck a thumb drive in her laptop and copied onto it all of her nursing-scholarship-related files. She tried to check in to her Mandalay–Yangon flight, but she couldn't. She checked in to her Yangon–Doha and Doha–London flights. She got into her running clothes and tucked the thumb drive in the tiny net pocket in her shorts.

She started off at a reasonable pace along one of her usual routes. Two fat policemen in a car trailed her by half a block. No Heckle and Jeckle these guys; they lurked and lurched in plain view but were too lazy to ever debouch. She was about to take advantage of that.

She suddenly ducked left, then sprinted down an alley that led to a small dirty park that at certain times of the day harbored clutches of public alcoholics. She calmed her heart and breath to listen. In the early-morning stillness, she heard only birds. Would it be that easy?

No. She heard the policemen's car *knocket*ing over the bad street above her. They'd guessed at her outlet. She turned and whipped away, ran across the park and up a flight of stairs that led to a semicovered, court-yarded one-block-square market; a bazaar, but a less exotic place than the word evoked. She bought her burner phones in this market; she knew its multiple exits. There were hundreds of tiny stalls arranged into categorical districts: Battery Allée, Hosiery Town, Simcardville. But at this hour, all the stalls were shuttered, plywood faces to narrow aisles. Leila knew, though, that many stall keepers slept with their wares, so she did not feel alone. She ran quietly through the empty aisles, locating the policemen's car as it prowled around the perimeter of the market. When they turned one corner, she went out the other way, and quickly ran down a long set of cracked steps. After four minutes at pace, when she figured she had half a mile between her and them, she slowed.

And she was about to congratulate herself on a job well done when she spotted Heckle *ahead* of her.

Leila didn't break stride. Heckle held back and then dropped in behind her, as if he'd never left. Maybe he never had. She was coming up to Dah Alice's little compound—a plaster wall around a concrete house and ratty carport and shade tree and dappled patio. She had to make a decision quickly. She removed the thumb drive from her jogging pocket. Was there any way to pass this thumb drive to Dah Alice or her house without being observed doing so? Still running, she saw that the patio door was open; a person inside. Dah Alice, probably, making mohinga for breakfast. The compound had a wooden gate at the street. Pretend to stretch against the gate and slip drive in mailbox? No mailbox. Slip drive onto gatepost? Shit. Passing compound. Turn around, pretend to cough, hurl drive toward patio door? A Hail Mary?

Fuckshitfuck. Now well past house, thumb drive still in sweaty fist, Heckle still on her like the clap.

Leila was fifty yards down the dusty road when she heard her name called. She turned and there was Dah Alice leaning on her gate like an Okie. Dah Alice waved, scooping the air with her tawny hand as if to paddle Leila back to her.

Leila turned and jogged to Dah Alice. She passed Heckle. It was as close as she'd ever been to him. He had a handsome, planar face but rough skin; he smiled at her and kept on running.

The two women spoke across Dah Alice's gate.

"Alice"—Leila dropped the honorific, trying to convey the urgency—"I came to see you, but I did not stop because I thought those men seeing us together would cause you trouble." She waved up the road to indicate Heckle and then vaguely offstage to mean Jeckle, wherever he was.

"Those men are friends, Leila," said Dah Alice. "I asked them to watch you. There are others watching you who are not good."

"I don't know what is happening," said Leila.

"So often it is like that," said Dah Alice.

"Not like this. This is different."

"This is how we live, Leila."

Leila didn't know if they were talking about the same thing. But there was no time. The policemen would still be looking for her, the ones who were not good. "I'm leaving today," she said. "I don't know when I will come back."

"Are you going back to Hollywood?" asked Dah Alice. Leila had never managed to clarify for Dah Alice the difference between LA County and Hollywood.

"Yes, I am. My dad is sick now. His heart. And I've become a liability here anyway."

"I do not know what a lie-a-bility is, but maybe that's just what you are supposed to be," said Dah Alice.

"No. It means I'm not helping. I'll come back, though. When I can."

"Oh, Leila, do not say this," said Dah Alice. "But you keep learning your Burmese, yes? Maybe one day you can show me Hollywood?"

"I would love to, Alice. One day, yes." She put the thumb drive into Alice's papery hand. "Here is all the information I have on those women for the scholarships. I erased it everywhere else, I think. Can you keep it safe? Maybe tell the women that I will try to see that this still happens?"

When Leila got back, the two fat policemen were parked outside her apartment. She thought about giving them a little rub-it-in wave, but then thought better of it; she still had a few hours in the country. Just as well. Inside her apartment, a cigarette lay smoking in a tea saucer on the kitchen table. Creepsville.

She washed quickly and finished packing. Then she checked her e-mail again. Hello: mail from Ding-Dong.com. She opened it. Something strange happened: her laptop screen blinked blank for a second, then came back on, as if from a mini-reboot or a petit mal seizure. When it returned, the Ding-Dong e-mail was open.

Got your message. Can you meet us in Heathrow tomorrow morning.

Leila was going to be in Heathrow tomorrow morning. She had a seven-hour layover. She closed the e-mail without responding. But it didn't close back down into her e-mail program. It shut itself into a little owl icon that appeared on her desktop.

LONDON

Mark woke from the clammy reaches of his skull into the gloom of the flat. He stirred the duvet around his legs, cast the lumpy feelers of his parched mind across the pillow and into this new day. The first task was to locate himself. Lately, determining where he was when he woke was a process. Blearily, he took in the room. Outside the window, a bit of leaking cast-iron gutter rat-a-tat-tatted drips onto the brick sill. Ah yes: the SineCo flat in East London, his current home base.

He had been writing last night. He remembered having strong feelings about something. He spidered half his body out of the bed and collected a legal pad from the floor. He rubbed his eyes with the heels of his hands and read what he'd written.

You have to try every day. Life is ten trillion decisions. Wouldn't you like to notice that you're making them?

And:

The loss you feel over and over again is the same (but from the other side).

There was also some stuff about how this, what we're living, is just Middle Life, between Pre-Life and Afterlife. Plus some doodles that any teenager would call substandard, mainly heavily drawn arrows meant to stand in for logical leaps too beautiful and complex for words.

Fuck. It was all shit, all of it. And there wasn't even enough of it. The trap he'd laid for himself with all of his dishonest behavior and vanity was going to spring on him.

Uh-oh. A morning like a cliff edge. Must endeavor not to think until poisonous slurry has finished slopping about my brain. Just make some coffee. Tomato juice in a cardboard box in the fridge. A worthy sort of muesli in the cupboard. You have to move forward, like a shark, even if you are a self-hating shark with a wicked hangover.

He tossed the legal pad aside, flung off the duvet, and tacked toward the bathroom.

On the toilet, he cast his mind into last night's turbid little sea. He had dined with his agent, Marjorie Blinc, at an unmarked restaurant. After two tumblers of bourbon, he'd ordered what turned out to be Chicken Architecture—a torqued tower of stacked planes: chicken, skewed ellipses of latticed potato, chicken, red cabbage, chicken. It was a dumb thing to order when you were having what turned out to be a business dinner. His meal kept toppling beneath his knife, and he would end up with a shard of potato lattice stuck out of the corner of his chewing mouth, like a cow. Blinc ordered seared tuna that looked like five pretty matchboxes on a wide white plate.

He'd been nervous going into the dinner—that's why he'd opened with the circus whiskies. In six weeks, he was supposed to deliver to Blinc his second book. Sadly, it was to be called *Keep Your Promises, Not Your Secrets: Ten Steps to Committed Living*. At dinner, he had tried to tell her that he might need a bit more time with it, and that maybe it would have to be a different kind of book than a straight-up, ten-step self-help book, and that he would like to revisit the issue of the title. At that, Blinc put down her last half matchbox of tuna and said, *Oh, this is all in the contract.*

That fucking contract. He couldn't comprehend it; it was all *in consideration whereof*s and *for a period not to exceed*s. When he had shown the document to an attorney friend of a friend, the man had looked at him askance and said, "I don't understand. You didn't sign this, did you?"

Mark had laughed and said no, but his stomach had lurched straight down.

Mark was basically a sharp and levelheaded person. He didn't come from money; he came from a scrabbling, single-parent home and his mom had taught him frugality, so he usually managed not to get screwed by the cable or the insurance company. He sometimes even remembered to redeem the mail-in rebate coupons that came with his juicer or his German dishwasher. But then he'd gone and signed a fat contract without really reading it. He hadn't even correctly understood Blinc's role. He had thought she was his agent. Her company was called Conch Shell Communications. But he had lately come to understand that she was his employer. Apparently, Blinc *had been* his agent, at first. And she had gotten him a big advance for the first book, and an even bigger one for the second. So big, in fact, that he had neglected to clarify some basic issues. Like: Blinc had sold the second book to Conch Shell Media. But Conch Shell Media was the publishing arm of Conch Shell Communications; Blinc was the CEO of both companies. What the fuck?

Blinc was, it had to be said, quite a conjurer. She was the one who'd shazammed his little essay into a book that had brought him fame and wealth. But the steep angle of his ascent turned out to be mirrored by a descent of similar slope. In the year since his appearance on *Margo!* (which he now recognized as the apex of the ride), Mark had watched, distraught and powerless, as his star faded swiftly. Blinc herself, who a year ago, Mark could have sworn, had looked at him with respect and desire in her eyes was now bored and possibly peeved with him.

He'd spent most of his Conch money already on his loft in Brooklyn and its unnecessary renovation, which had careened quickly over budget. Now he needed money in a way that he had never needed it before. Along with the loft renovation, there was his restaurant habit, his girlish love of a good shopping spree, his mom's mortgage, her car, and her medical. Also the tax hit that he had had no idea that high earners took.

Thank the Lord, then, for James Straw and the money that the man shed like rain off a roof. How strange and wonderful it must be to possess that kind of wealth, thought Mark, emptying a hot thin broth of himself into the toilet. Straw's wealth was the kind that grows like mold by the strange biosis of finance capitalism. The London flat belonged to Straw or to one of his companies or corporations, but the man probably didn't know where it was. He'd lent it to Mark as casually as someone might lend a neighbor a flashlight from a kitchen drawer; Straw had poked a bony finger at his intercom and hollered at it: "Have Nils arrange for Mark to take one of the London flats."

This whole beautiful mess, actually, was because of Straw.

"Motivation in an Unjust World" was published on Mark's friend's blog, way back when that sort of thing was avant-garde. The essay spread swiftly; its dissemination was now cited as an early example of viralism. Some wag called him the American Camus, because "Motivation" was high-minded yet populist; abstract but instructive. Another said he was the first public intellectual sprung from the Internet. The mainstream outlets, not wishing to be left behind by the blog thing, said he was the voice of Generation X at a time when that generation was putting aside its childish things.

Mark enjoyed it immensely. He gave interviews; was referenced by Letterman; addressed a graduating class. His employer, discovering that one of the in-house writers had become an Internet sensation, gave him a fat raise. But Mark knew that the attention would pass; he hoped only that he could write something that good again.

Then one morning his phone rang and a female voice said, "Please hold for Mr. Straw." Straw came on and invited Mark to *drop by*, and within an hour, a black car was at his door, and he was whooshed to an unmarked part of Logan Airport, and then he was aloft, ensconced in leather and walnut. Two pilots and a cabin attendant and however much jet fuel it takes to cross the country so that he, Mark Deveraux, could be same-day-delivered to James Straw, founder of SineCo, the digital-search-and-storage conglomerate.

Then Mark was driven to a downtown arena, and led up through endless corridors and into Straw's owner's box. Straw thanked Mark for *coming by,* as if the Gulfstream V were a crosstown bus. Silent attendants delivered crab, cognac, profiteroles, cigars. Straw's basketball team, the Seattle Search, was soundly beaten that night by the visiting Oakland Tribe; fans began leaking out of the stadium in the middle of the fourth quarter, their big foam cursor-shaped fingers pointed sadly at the floor. Only after the game did Straw come to the point of his summons. He wanted Mark to adapt "Motivation in an Unjust World" into management philosophy; he wanted Mark's ideas to guide his company. He outlined his vision for SineCo as a company with ten times its current clout and his plan for a global, integrated information-and-services-delivering platform that would replace the Internet and personal computers.

"What is the Internet, anyway?" Straw posed the question to himself. "It's a TV and a telephone, is all it is, really." He made a little *meh* gesture to indicate how underwhelmed he was by the Internet. "I could build something that would *in fact* change the world."

Mark could not immediately see any connection between his essay and Straw's business plan. The cigar was making him wobbly. But it was true that "Motivation" contained the idea that you had to start from scratch. And after a couple of hours and some very old scotch, Mark saw that maybe it wouldn't be that hard to reshape his essay into something less abstract, something that could help people get results in their work lives, their personal lives, whatever. Straw had definitely found useful advice in there, and he was a potentate executive world-bender.

"Just think about it," said Straw as the two of them left the arena via its carpeted concrete arteries. Then there was the car-jet-car trip home, and when Mark got out of the black car in front of his dumpy apartment in Somerville, he could have told you something was afoot, that some ray of reward had finally found him.

Indeed, it was only three days later Straw called again. "There's someone I want you to meet!" he bellowed down the blower.

Mark met Marjorie Blinc in a deep-cushioned booth of a hotel restaurant. She was hot, forty-four-year-old hot, and was flanked by a pretty young assistant. Her pitch was succinct: Right now he was valuable, she said. It was still within his power to leverage this essay of his into something more.

Mark was flattered, but he was no idiot. "You mean within *your* power, right?" he said. Then he told her that what was good about the essay was that it was finished. "I said what I wanted to say. I don't have anything else to say about that right now."

At that, she seemed ready to get up and leave. She leaned back and appraised him. "I may have been wrong about you. From 'Motivation' and from what James said, I figured you for ambitious."

Mark understood only now, a couple of years later, that he had been too easily handled in that plush booth; all it took was an eighty-dollar bottle and a woman saying, *Come on, or are you chicken?*

"Oh, I'm ambitious," he'd said to Blinc then, and that was the pivot. Right there.

"So why would you pass up this chance to make an impact on the world?"

Within a week he had signed her dense contract. Blinc cut him a check large enough to make the years of working at jobs beneath him seem like *Karate Kid* training, training he hadn't seen the point of but which was suddenly paying off. He imagined now would come the part where his powerful agent would phone him daily and ask did he have a new draft.

But that's not what happened at all. Instead, a team of Conch editors took his work away from him and "shaped" it. They didn't even require much input from him.

When Mark received his pages to proof, he saw that they had made it into the same stuff that had been offered by self-helpers since forever. The book said that if you wanted to change yourself, all you really needed to do was shout orders loudly down your brain stem. There was the ridiculous concept of consciousclusions, and there was something called "synaptic toning," which appeared to be, more or less, self-administered cognitive-behavioral therapy. There were some allegedly never-before-revealed tricks for accessing your vast, untapped stores of time, will, and attention. You could find hidden hours in every day; hidden seconds in every minute.

Soon enough, he realized that "Motivation in an Unjust World" was not going to survive intact its conversion from essay to mass-market paperback, that its form would have to change from question to answer, because people don't pay money for questions. He figured that this was between him and his sense of artistic integrity. And artistic integrity is a fine thing, but so is financial security. And so is a twenty-three-hundred-square-foot loft on Water Street.

He did object when he heard that they intended to give his book the inane title *Bringing the Inside Out,* but on that point also he was ignored into submission. It was only when he learned that the book would have a subtitle "suggested" by James Straw—now it was to be called *Bringing the Inside Out: Toward a New Operating System*—that Mark discovered SineCo owned something called the Conch Group.

But Blinc wasn't kidding around; when the book came out, it was everywhere. She had first-rate news outlets running copy about Mark that *she* had written. She got him in *Seventeen* and *Esquire* and the *Observer* in one week, so that even if you had no intention of ever buying or reading his book, you probably knew who he was. And then Blinc leveraged that name recognition into more exposure, and on it went, for about six months, until it didn't anymore, until he could see his little blip leaving the screen.

This second book could be Mark's second chance. Or his third, or his ninth, or his millionth—what man could say how many he'd been given? But the dense, drunken drivel he'd found on the pad this morning—that wasn't going to do it.

Mark felt a little less wretched when he finished in the bathroom. He showered and shaved. He did his sit-ups and push-ups—half the usual, because he thought he might puke.

He had to get a grip on this hangover before it chewed up his whole day. *Do what's right—right in front of you.* That was one of the lines he used at the executive-optimization workshops he led.

Mark was one of Conch Shell Media's featured speakers. The fame that his book had brought him left a sort of residue that made him valuable in that line of work. And he was good at it. He had the gift. Maybe something from his father, who at birthday parties had been known to hold a den or patio in thrall, the children *and* the adults rapt, with his charm and tricks and eyebrows. Blinc had given Mark a message shaper and a room coach and voice teacher. He took all they had to give in a few days. He was no retired software CEO trying to make extra money amusing Republicans over rubber chicken; he was Mark Deveraux, and he liked being in front of a room.

But his star seemed to be fading in this arena as well. Blinc still booked him, but he was definitely getting down-venued. A year ago, it was Abu Dhabi and Basel; now it was Cleveland and Leeds. Once, he had been paid thirty-five thousand dollars for an hour-long talk. Now it was five grand, sometimes ten. And it wasn't just talking; he had to lead workshops or be on panels.

Mark drank his scalding coffee like he was slapping himself across the face; he coaxed down some of the worthy muesli. He was due at Straw's office at four. He had the rest of the day to write. *You could do this blindfolded,* he told himself. *You just need to crank out some really good stuff about Increasing Agency through Self-Investigation; about the Excellent Self that lives within all of us; the steely hero of our souls, etc.*

He sat down. He opened his computer.

Okay. Ten Steps to Committed Living. Let's see.

One: Quit Being Such a Scattered, Drunk Loser.

No. That was putting rather too fine a point on it.

The cursor blinked at him like a satellite.

Oh, he was longing again for *Try Again Tomorrow,* the book he *wanted* to write, the one he had *meant* to write. That book would be himself laid bare. But not the vain, lonely, hollow, fraud version of himself he had somehow ended up selling. The himself laid bare in *Try Again Tomorrow* would be the brave, witty, wise Mark, the one who had always been able to see the truth and describe it more cleverly than others; the one who had stepped up when his dad split and had always helped his mom around the house and who had seen her one really bad boyfriend for the nasty snake that he was and run him off, at some physical risk to himself.

But that wasn't the kind of book he was contractually obligated to deliver inside of six weeks. *Try Again Tomorrow* would spill out at all its edges, ragged and bloody and loud. *Ten Steps to Committed Living* was a book that would need to *pretend* to be about taking risks and failing better and all that but would in fact have every edge sewn up tight and every doubt banished before the start.

Step One, he made himself type, **Take Risks and Do Not Be Afraid of Failure**. But then he didn't know what to type next, because most of the risks he'd taken had led to dead ends, and he was terribly, viscerally afraid of the failure that loomed before him now.

Could he write them both? This *Ten Steps* shit and *Try Again Tomorrow*? The latter for later publication, as a non-bullshit companion work, a shadow volume, an apostasy? With it, he would rescue his reputation, reclaim the place that "Motivation in an Unjust World" had briefly let him hold. He would tell the truth about life: that you have to *stop* thinking that you're the able captain of a ship called *You,* with a wheel, or a rudder, or a tiller, or whatever. You have to realize that you are instead a leaf in a stream. And he would tell the truth about himself: that he was a vain, depressive, selfish drug addict who had become, by accident, a briefly, wildly successful self-help author. That alone was interesting. He just had to be honest about it.

But *how* honest was always the question, wasn't it? No one likes an oversharer. And such a book would most likely be contrary to Blinc's plan. Blinc was not someone you wanted to piss off unless you were very sure of your position. If he got Straw really on his side, though, he could probably risk crossing Blinc.

Oh Christ—there is no way a man can write when he is this wound up. Mark stood and did a quick, nervous circuit of the fancy flat, as if the walk would do him any good. SineCo used this flat for short-term executive tenancy. It was furnished in sterile posh. The books on the shelves were set dressing; the food in the kitchen was delivered once a week. What was Mark's he'd brought in two duffels. So it was an addict's conceit to pretend he didn't know what he was looking for.

Mark would have preferred pot to hash. But he didn't know anyone in London and had to score his drugs by seedier means than he was accustomed to, and from a more limited menu. On the black granite countertops of the kitchen, he went through the tedious process of rolling a few hash-laced cigarettes. It was ten o'clock in the morning.

The situation was definitely worrying. It wasn't just the Blinc problem. If it were just that, he could at least imagine some post-Blinc situation. But was he even a writer at all? Not long ago, he had been so sure of it.

He certainly *felt* like a writer. He dressed and comported himself in a way that he thought writerly. And in his own swirling dome, he could still do a good job of putting abstract ideas into words. And he was willing to say what others thought it was risky or impolite to say. So, no, his wasn't an idle, druggie sort of drug use. It was a means to a desperately needed end.

The problem was, though, that these days, when he felt he needed to write, when he felt like he was getting a handle on an idea, it turned out he just wanted to drink or smoke or get fucked up, alone. The pen would lie limp in his hand, the typewriter would hum patiently, the cursor would blip accusingly, and he'd set upon the alcohol in the minibar or the pantry or he'd find a dark bar on a bright street.

And something was changing in his drinking. The lucid, potentially productive patch was shrinking to minutes, and the descent into the slur and fug of drunk was becoming steeper. A month ago, he'd made a few phone calls he could not remember making. That was—for forty-eight hours—a sobering experience. Since that night, he had had to put in place certain rules limiting interaction with nonstrangers after six p.m.

Because by that time he was almost certainly stoned and drunk and casting off to drift alone in a sea of memories and impressions, hoping to return to shore with something useful. But lately what he found flopping at the bottom of the dinghy in the morning was too small to keep.

Mark didn't mind being the kind of alcoholic with a lot on his mind, the kind who maybe fumbles with his keys. But that self-abduction shit—where you take leave of yourself, and a ghoul takes over instead, and the night comes back at you the next day, memories like shredded documents; the gut wrench of wanting to know exactly what you did and not wanting to know at all—that *was* the kind of alcoholic he minded being. And once he'd become a recognizable low-order celebrity, the damage that an unsecret blackout drunk might do to his career...the thought made him sweat.

So he forced that kind of behavior into submission by hating himself incandescently for days after those drunks transpired. And it worked. He had not self-abducted for a while now. If he felt it coming on, he taped a sheet of paper to the inside of his door with a command in Sharpie: *Don't*. So he had been able to forget about his ghoul, to think of him as a tormentor from an earlier time, like a bully from the eighth grade. When a zillionaire actor was caught on cameraphone drooling racial slurs, Mark joined in tsking and glee, though in his secret heart, he felt for the poor bastard.

The thing was, there *was* some overlap in the behavior patterns of the productive artist and the self-aware addict. That was problematic. Or anyway, it contributed to Mark's confusion: Was he a serious writer or a freakishly lucky drunk pillhead? There was a lot riding on the answer.

He left the flat to smoke, bringing his laptop with him. This was a good idea. Who could work in that strange, silent apartment? It was a beautiful day outside, people charging all around.

The spliff did indeed get things going again. Though there was a syrupy quality to the hash high that he didn't like, a gumming-up, like ten thoughts were happily walking along but then suddenly had to squeeze through a narrow gate. He was almost run down by one of those black cabs, coming as they do like Valkyries, and from the wrong direction. That got his heart pumping.

Mark loved London. In the two months he'd been here—trying to write, not writing, drinking alone, and attending almost daily to the needs and ego of his patron Straw—Mark had crisscrossed the place heavily. He liked to go on long, ale-smeared journeys across its broad gut, as unbusy as an indigent. Today, though, he was going to stay on task: find another coffee, maybe a muffin, and then a quiet place to write.

He was outside some sort of toy museum near Bethnal Green. Intriguing. It wasn't really quiet, but there was a café.

He started treating his hangover with careful, holistic self-retoxifying—drinking a string of bitter coffees and ducking out for cigarettes and then another spliff. After a while, he felt okay enough for a chicken salad sandwich and a couple of minibottles of white wine. And he was writing. As his mood improved, he thought he might see a way to write the book Blinc wanted. There were rules to life, certainly. Or probably. And there was nothing wrong with trying to divine them.

After every five hundred words he'd take a wander, past a taxonomy of wooden yo-yos and cases displaying examples of something called toy theater, which was apparently big in the nineteenth century. Then he'd write another five hundred words and then return to an artifact that had caught his eye, like the Victorian board game for children called Virtue Rewarded and Vice Punished.

Remember what it was like when you were a child was his starting point, and pretty soon he'd cranked out a thousand words. It's not that children were innocent, obviously (he had just seen one boy in the café find the tipping point of his little sister's stroller), but they poked at life scientifically. They analyzed data and drew conclusions; they started from scratch. *After some point early in our lives, we forget to do that,* thought Mark. So in a certain way, growing up was the *opposite* of the loss of innocence.

He thought of the possessions he'd loved when he was little. There was a toy called Stretch Armstrong, a rubberized, Speedoed wrestler doll; you could stretch him to great lengths and he would reshape himself. But you could not stretch him as far as Mark had tried to stretch him once, with the aid of some clothesline and two cinder blocks. What a disappointment that was. Stretch turned out to be filled with some sort of lab-accident green goo.

What else had he loved? His dog, his mom, and a doll named Sasha. Mark had loved Sasha in the way that little boys were not supposed to love dolls. Maybe it had something to do with the little sister who had been stillborn a few months before his father left. When people asked him if he was an only child, he said yes but he sometimes thought no.

He had certainly become something of an only adult, though. What had happened to his friends? He had had friends. Back in college and for a few years after that—people who would have come over in the middle of the night; people to whom he would have gone in the middle of the night, and did. But in the museum, sitting there with a clutch of cool postcards from the gift shop, he realized that he had more postcards than friends to send them to. He could not now see where he had gone wrong. True, he'd tossed away a few girlfriends, each one at somewhere near the point when you have to step up or get gone. But that was, finally, out of consideration for them.

"You don't think you're better off *alone*, do you?" his Lost Girlfriend had asked him once. He'd taken too long to answer that, and he'd seen her go cold.

But aren't you supposed to learn to take care of yourself? Isn't that what his mother had showed him?

And Leo Crane. What had happened there?

They'd met in Harvard Yard, on a sharp autumn day at the end of the last millennium; their friendship grew quickly and easily. Mark loved Harvard, but he hadn't really liked being waist-deep in rich kids, all the prep-school princes who'd taken taxis to their orthodontists or who thought they were Keith Richards because a doorman could get them coke. Leo could have been like that but wasn't. They tumbled through college together—careless, confused, and intent. Leo needed someone who could talk fast and wouldn't back down; Mark needed a bit of restraint.

Leo, whose family was full of love and money but was also full of expectation, was jealous of Mark's scrappier growing-up. Mark loved the Cranes for their erudition and for the array of guest rooms on offer in their gloomy Beaux Arts mansion on Riverside Drive. The Cranes probably hoped that some of Mark's sharp charms would rub off on Leo, who had a habit of hanging back.

Had he ever taken advantage of Leo? Mark thought not. He borrowed money a few times, but he'd paid back almost all of it. And anyway, anyone who knew the two of them in those years could have told you that Mark did more emotional heavy lifting for Leo than straight guys usually do for each other. Like when Leo's mom and dad and the greyhounds perished in the fire. Or when it became apparent that Leo's bookstore was doomed, and Leo's sisters called Mark and asked him to go up to Rhinebeck to talk him down and out of it.

But Mark and Leo had drifted apart in their thirties. This was more Mark's doing than Leo's—he'd just quit trying, let entropy and avoidance do their thing. He felt a bit shitty about that. But the same mental issues that had made Leo a cool, brooding undergraduate and an edgy twenty-five-year-old made him an annoying thirty-six-year-old was how it seemed to Mark. It was fine and valid to be a manic-depressive, but if you were also independently wealthy, that should be seen as a sort of karmic compensation; after a while, you shouldn't really complain out loud.

Plus there was the Leo-like character who had ended up in *Bringing the Inside Out,* which had probably given offense, of course. Mark hadn't meant to leave him in there, but Blinc's editors loved that chapter, and in the end Mark had brought that character forward. So he'd had to drop Leo once the book blew up. He actually dodged his calls, left e-mails from him unopened.

Though, in a sense, he'd found Leo again.

At a creative executive conference in Phoenix six months ago, Mark had run into a college friend who had asked him "Have you seen Leo Crane's blog?" in a way that meant *Dude, you* have *to see Leo Crane's blog*. And when Mark found the blog, he saw why. It was called *I Have Shared a Document with You,* and it was like watching a vase fall off a shelf. In places, Leo's prose had that mad true thing in it, like when people write ill-advised letters right after they get dumped. But in other places, it was just embarrassing. Mark started lifting some of the mad true stuff for his radical-creativity seminars. He didn't think it counted as plagiarism, exactly. Leo wasn't even putting his name on his stuff, and the ideas in the blog posts were pretty much public domain–type ideas. Mark just used a few of Leo's phrases. Like *fears and desires*. Leo was always going on about fears and desires in his batshit blog.

In the café of the toy museum, Mark spent ten minutes trying to compose a postcard to Leo. His pen floated over the white rectangle. What could he possibly write?

You would like this museum, he began. But no, that wasn't what mattered.

I'm sorry I put you in my stupid book? I've also been using some of your stuff in these seminars I give? Which are bullshit, by the way? I miss you? You sound crazy these days? We once had the world by the balls, you and I? I'm lonely? I'm in trouble? I'm lost, like you, but in a different way?

No. It was too late for any of that. It seemed to Mark that all of life was either *There's still time* or *It's too late*. He tore up the postcard.

He spent another hour poking paragraphs around the screen. But now he'd lost the thread he'd been pulling on. Who cares about what he remembered from his childhood? A teacher in high school once told him that until you can describe clearly what it is you mean, you don't really mean it. That was the last great thing he had been taught in a classroom.

It was time to make his way to Straw. He went back to the flat to clean up. Mark always tried to bring his A-game to these Straw sessions. Not that Straw really seemed to notice what Mark brought. And maybe

A-game didn't really describe what Mark brought. What Mark brought was a big, elaborate, flattering lie.

Mark had been James Straw's life coach for a year now. It was an easy arrangement: he was required only to find the man's rambling soliloquies compelling, pretend to see meaning in them, then offer some not too transparent but not too opaque homily or parable that confirmed what Straw already thought. Straw treated these sessions as if they were genuine therapy and vented about the stresses of being hyperwealthy. Clearly, Straw had suggested Mark's London sabbatical mainly because he, Straw, was going to be in London for a few months and didn't want to be without access to Mark.

And there was something going on other than life-coaching. After a session, Straw might take Mark to lunch or dinner at some private club or his Mayfair town house. They would cross London in Straw's armored and motorcycle-escorted Bentley. Last week, after a session and a boozy lunch, Straw brought Mark to a shirtmaker on Jermyn Street where he ordered for Mark twelve dress shirts in a chromatic range from white to cream, all with double cuffs and eyelet collars, and bought him also the little silver barbell things that joined the collar tips behind the necktie.

Cleaned up and steeled with a line of crushed Ritalin, Mark left the flat again. He liked crossing London by tube. If he was in the right mood, he could feel himself carried along on the human tide, and the experience imparted a pleasant anonymity; it made the leaf-in-the-stream stuff apparent, and he felt that he was connected to the sweaty straphangers— the adolescent transgressively sexifying her school uniform, the suave subcontinental with his head bobbing to the tinny Hindi that Mark could just make out.

But despite the Ritalin zing, Mark's mood was sour. Weaving around the abject tourists trying to work the ticket machine in the tube station, Mark resented them intensely and would have personally banished each one to the gulag for the offense of getting fatly in his way. He was not a leaf in a stream but a stone in a dark pool, sinking, and there was really no hope for humanity, because everyone's out for himself and there's no way around that.

"You were right about the Chileans, by the way," said Straw once they'd taken up their classic analytical positions—Straw supine on a couch and Mark in an Eames chair, facing some degrees away—"I mean, that I shouldn't have gone into business with that lot. An unsavory people, the Chileans." They were in Straw's double-height great hall of an office, on a fog-spangled corner of the SineCo building in Canary Wharf.

Mark could not remember formulating or articulating any opinion about Chileans or about going into business with them; he didn't know what Straw was talking about. This was always happening with Straw. In such situations, you have about thirty seconds to say to someone *I don't know what you're talking about,* before your remaining silent rather commits you to the lie of pretending to understand. Mark was committed.

Luckily, James Straw was so deferred to that he never seemed to consider the possibility that a person he was speaking to might not be following his every Straw-centric turn, so he never asked for any confirmation. He had assistants whose job it was to de- and rebrief anyone leaving a Straw meeting to make sure that the poor schmuck understood what he had just been instructed to do. But Straw's relationship with Mark was different. Straw considered Mark's ear and counsel a relief from the pressures of his day and life (no one understood him, basically). Mark definitely got the sense that a few of Straw's legion of assistants resented Mark's having cut the line, particularly the elfin Swiss named Nils. So Mark had to watch out for those guys. It worked because his sessions with Straw were private; there was no one else in the room to hear just how transparently flattery-based Mark's approach to Straw was. Straw spent their hour-long sessions complaining about inept inferiors and scheming competitors and greedy siblings and "communist" government regulators. Mark would simply listen, nod, and every few minutes say something like "Have you considered that these people might be motivated by jealousy or that they lack your grasp of the bigger picture?"

The trick was the careful and well-timed echoing-back of Straw's own ideas and phrases—*the bigger picture* came up regularly. In fact, in the year that Mark had been life-coaching Straw, he had constructed only the vaguest idea of what Straw's workday consisted of or how SineCo churned out its billions. Syndicates acquired companies, or cornered sectors, or consolidated holdings. Mark did understand that Straw was something of an objectivist, though the man had never heard of Ayn Rand (he read exclusively nautical-adventure fiction and mass-market management theory), and over time, Mark heard himself agreeing by nods and *I sees* with an ever more market-based and owner-operated notion of how the world should be run.

Since coming to London, though, Straw had begun to talk more during their sessions about the nature of his business empire. Lately, he was very excited by a new branch of SineCo he was calling the Core Vision Department. Mark assumed that such a department would churn out PR claptrap about the core vision of the company, something about how everyone should be empowered by choice and leveraging knowledge and improving access et cetera. That had been a large part of Mark's job for the biogenetics company in Cambridge: writing very abstract copy about the value of innovation.

But when Straw explained further, Mark had to wonder why he was staffing this Core Vision Department with expensive new hires from the cream of the digital-slacker class. Straw was poaching code-writing princes from computer science departments and subcontinental shantytowns and billing-software companies and failed music-downloading sites. He mentioned three hundred new hires in the past month. That was no PR department. It piqued Mark's curiosity.

Today, Straw was very excited about the Core Vision thing. But it seemed to Mark that Straw was now calling it New Alexandria. He was apparently describing some sort of Tolkienesque realm where knowledge could be stored and protected. He kept saying that what was needed was all the information in one place; then everyone with access to that information would be able to make perfect decisions.

"Imagine it, Mark," said Straw from his couch, "all those other operations, muddled by imperfect markets and stunted by the bureaucrats — they will all become obsolete. With a single stroke! And New Alexandria will stand alone. The world will never be the same."

Mark had long ago blown past the point at which he could say: *I'm sorry, what the fuck are you talking about?* But there was a limit, even for Mark, to what one could pretend to understand. What were the other operations, and how were they muddled by markets and stunted by bureaucrats? By *bureaucrats,* Straw usually meant anyone in the public sector, from the president to the postman.

"It does sound extraordinary, James," said Mark. "But, to be honest, I'm not certain I understand what you mean. You'll have to go back a bit. If you could."

At this, James Straw turned quickly on his couch and craned to face Mark. Straw was in good shape for a man his age, but this was the lithe maneuver of a much younger man. Mark found it jarring.

"No. There is no way you could understand it. Not yet. Forgive me, Mark. There is a part of this that I have had to keep even from you. I have partners in the project, great men. Men of vision and risk, like the two of us. But there are rules, procedures." He waved his hand before his face and shrugged a shoulder, as if to acknowledge the strange reality that even he, James Straw, could be bound by rules and procedures.

"I'll tell you what," he said. "Join me on board *Sine Wave* next week, will you? By then I will have secured the necessary permissions. Can you?"

Sine Wave. Straw's yacht. At last. Was Mark supposed to say that he would need to check his calendar? Some pretense that Mark was very busy with other professional and intellectual pursuits had always been part of his thing with Straw. But no, this was different; this was new waters.

"It would be my pleasure, James."

"Excellent." Straw rose from the couch and crossed to his desk, stabbed at the intercom. "Gertrude. Mark will be joining me at sea next week. Arrange for it. Let's say Tuesday."

"You will be at Bilderberg on Tuesday, sir."

"Balls," said Straw. "How long is that?"

"Two days in Aberdeen, sir. You are tentative for Thursday transfer to—"

He cut her off. "Yes, yes, fine. Arrange transport for Mark for Friday."

"Very well, sir."

Leaving the SineCo building, Mark had a veritable spring in his step. The invitation to the yacht felt like a game changer. Straw had been stingily withholding that invitation for a year, dropping lines about, like, *the passage to Majorca* in such a way as to arouse interest from Mark and saying, *I must have you aboard sometime,* but then not summoning an assistant, which was how Straw alchemized wish into reality. Mark was deeply excited simply to join the tiny subset of people who'd ever set loafer on the megayacht. He had read about *Sine Wave* in the *Wall Street Journal.* Straw was not the kind of man who allowed his yacht to be photographed or featured, so the only photos in the article were long-lens exteriors. Still, the vessel was said to have ten decks and two helipads, a tennis court, anti-pirate devices, and a crew of Italians in crisp whites. Also a driving range, an herbarium, and a surgical theater.

But hours later, the springy step was gone. It was a night with a wicked slope.

He walked home from Straw's office and dined in some fuck-off restaurant in Canary Wharf. Mark loved a good fuck-off restaurant. He loved the stuffy, expense-account places with the board-presented menus and the bread rolls swaddled in ironed napkins and the chilled butter pats brought on saucers. He loved the trendy, dismal, haute-cuisine joints with the square furniture and the pixie waitrons and the cracked mirror decor. He loved displaying to waitstaff, with his charm, his informed questions, and his swift decisions, that he was a person happy and allowed to spend a hundred pounds on dinner for himself. Eating alone in an expensive restaurant, reading a magazine or a book, he thought he must look powerful and intriguing—an important business traveler, or maybe a tragic young widower.

But that's not what happened tonight. Tonight there was something off about everything. He'd come in too early and he was nearly alone in the posh restaurant, which turned out to be a steakhouse, all brass and carpet. The staff hadn't even really finished their opening chores; he could hear a radio playing in the kitchen and he could smell a bleachy bucket behind the bar. The pretty waitress was *not* taken with him. That was clear. She saw the *Superyachts Monthly* magazine that he hadn't hidden well enough beneath his notebook, and she raised her eyebrows in a tiny, devastating way.

No, no, it's not like that, he wanted to say to her. *I'm not some schlub pressing my face to the glass. I bought this magazine because the world's fourth-richest man just invited me aboard his yacht. And they were out of* Megayachts Monthly. *The yachts in this magazine are* smaller *than the one I'm going to be on next Friday.*

But then the stern part of him yelled at the stupid part of him, the part that cared whether this waitress knew how close he was to power. *Don't you also want to tell her that the only reason you're so close to power is that someone misunderstood the one good thing you ever wrote,* the stern part yelled, *and that you're stuck in a lie that's going to bring you down or eat you up?*

And like a child running upstairs to get away from his parents' screaming, the real Mark, who was neither the stern one nor the stupid one—who was both—ordered a fifty-quid bottle of Rioja and a rare steak. He needed to work on the Blinc manuscript. He tried to write in his notebook, tried to at least look like he was writing in his notebook. But he knew what he really looked like: he looked like a man drinking quickly, alone, in the early evening.

He left that place after the bottle of wine and wandered west, into

Brick Lane eventually. It was real evening now, and the city was full of life. He found a busy pub and drank thick pints at the bar. He realized that he was bothered by something from before the yacht invitation. James Straw had been keeping things from *him?* That was unsettling. Mark knew that there was plenty he didn't know, situations he needed help with. This Blinc book situation, for example, had definitely gotten away from him. But with Straw, he had at least been certain that he knew more than the old man about what was going on between them. Now he wasn't so sure.

With a single stroke! Straw had said, and he'd chopped the air in front of him. What could that mean?

Well, in a week he would find out; he would be brought in on the Core Vision Department or New Alexandria or whatever. Most likely, it would turn out to be some vain and boondoggly tycoon project. Even Straw's worst ideas had full-time staffs. Straw was an art collector, a philanthropist, a professional nemesis to tax collectors all over the world. ("I don't have any money, Mark," he said once in a session when Mark had accidentally mentioned that Straw had a lot of money. "Money only passes through me.")

Leaving the pub, Mark misjudged his drunkenness and knocked into a pair of men smoking near the door. "Sorry," he said. Which wasn't enough for one of the men, who looked him up and down, judged him no threat, and said, "I'll crack your head, you nancy Yank shite." The accent was broad, and the man was smiling in a dangerous way when he said it, so Mark didn't understand at first. As the man leaned in closer, Mark saw a scar on his face that must have reduced his investment in it. His friend made to restrain him. "Best move on now," said the friend to Mark, "he's had a few."

So Mark moved on, quickly. It was probably a little routine of theirs, just a couple of poseur bullies, but it still dumped a bucket of fear down his spinal cord, and on the heels of that, a shame at his physical cowardice. *Nancy* meant "fag," right? How he wished he were with his long-ago friend Wallace, a bear-size homo from Wyoming and Harvard who spoke of dick-sucking in a farm-boy drawl and took pleasure in the lead-up to the barroom fights he got into and won every time.

How had the guy known Mark could be intimidated? Was it the vibrating chord of his cowardice? Charm and wiles were all Mark had; those were no good in close-quarters combat.

Once, long ago, when he was a boy playing Matchbox cars at a friend's house, he heard the friend's construction-foreman father call his dad "that ankle-grabber." The friend's mother said, "Hank, please!," in a way that Mark knew even then meant the accusation was more than idle. It had needled him ever since.

Mark was nearing the shawarma place with the attached off-license. But it was closed already. So he stopped into the pub with the doors black as polished boots. He wasn't drunk enough to sleep. And this was the bar where he'd met the guy who gave him the number of the guy who delivered drugs by bicycle. He had a pint at the bar, and then he texted the number, using the little code the guy had written on the back of the card. *Sardines* was cannabis. *Herring* was coke. *Salmon* was salt heroin. Mark had no need of herring—the Ritalin was better anyway—and despite his tough act, he was a little afraid of salmon. He ordered sardines. Twenty-one grams, because this book wasn't gonna write itself.

The walk home proved more challenging than he had anticipated. Navigational issues. That should be one of the Ten Steps to Committed Living: Take Careful Note of Route from Pub to Home. He wandered for an hour, deeply lost, probably within a quarter mile of where he was trying to be. There was Sheepshead Lane and there was Mince Pie Close, but where the fuck was his street? At one point, he found himself behind what seemed to be a Roman avenue of auto garages: impact wrenches whizzed and whined in the moonless night; fluorescent light spilled from half-open shop doors, wooden, eight feet tall. From one, men shouted in a language Mark hadn't the foggiest of. Then, later, he dead-ended at a canal and leaned over to get a better look at what was bobbing beside an oil drum in a yellow-foamed eddy on the greasy surface of the canal.

Ah. A bloated pit bull, its eyes a-bug, its swollen tongue distended.

Other men might panic. About the swollen pit bull staring at him with crazed eyes from a greasy vortex, or about the fact that he had been tripped up by vanity and then by greed. But Mark panicked about neither. He backtracked to the last recognizable point, made an executive decision, and then vectored through a smaller grid of streets and lanes. There, at the end of one, was his.

Steps One through Ten were and always would be: Never Give Up.

And then ten seconds spent on the doorstep of the flat searching his pockets for keys, a crystal-clear image in his head of the three-key ring reclining on the bar top of that last pub.

But then, *hosanna!* there they were, in the Slydini pocket that his tailor had engineered into the brown suit jacket. Interior. Lower left side. Three by four, with a horizontal flap. The keys dropped into his palm.

He unlocked, and locked behind him. But the stairwell light would not come on. Mark found his lighter and ascended the steep steps like an Egyptologist, the wan flicker of the weak Bic, his left hand feeling the rough brick and stone of the stairwell walls.

He had seen her once. His stillborn sister. His mom was holding her, and his dad was holding his mom. His dad had parked him in a plastic chair in the hospital hallway and told him to wait. But he heard a sob from his mother, and love trumped fear and he ducked into the room. In his memory, his dad was wearing a hat. Was it a trilby? A fedora? Seemed unlikely. His dad did indeed wear such hats, but surely not under those circumstances?

The baby was dry and lilac and still and had died before she was born. His dad was about to send him out again, but his mom said, *No, let him stay.* So he held her tiny hand for a moment, his mom's hand enclosing theirs both. Someone once asked him if he had ever seen a ghost. He'd said no but he could have said yes.

QUIVERING PINES

After his interview with the doctor, Leo was moved from the intake single to a more spartan, shared room in the men's wing. It looked like a room in a small, mid-price-range motel. Taupe carpet and wood laminate.

Leo's roommate was a goateed man in the drifts of his forties who looked like a melancholic devil and carried without comment the incredible name of James Dean. He did not clutter the air with clatter about which dresser was his and here's how the shower works or any of that. That first evening, Leo stayed in their little room and James stayed out of Leo's way. Leo skipped dinner out of embarrassment—he wasn't ready to explain to anyone what he was doing here. He thought he would be gone by the end of the weekend anyway. James came back from dinner with a glob of rice pudding in a plastic clamshell and gave it to Leo like a prom corsage.

"The rice pudding's good here," he said.

At nine thirty, when reading or journaling was recommended, James read from a worn paperback about the Stoics. From its cover, the alabaster bust of some stern beardo stared pupil-lessly. At ten o'clock, the onion-looking counselor walked down the long corridor of the men's wing, rapping once on each door or door frame. James didn't budge, so neither did Leo; he made no move for the light switch or the door.

"Curfew!" said the Onion on his return trip up the corridor. He stepped just over the threshold of their room, like a big shot.

"Yeah. Just one minute, Gene," said James, "this is a great paragraph right here." The Onion made a show of waiting impatiently while James did a fair impression of being just *fascinated* by a paragraph. Then the Onion went to switch off the light and James quickly held up an index finger without taking eye from page. The gesture made the Onion pause, after which he realized that he had paused, which pissed him off, which made him snap the light off. "Those are false idols, James. False idols," said the Onion as he closed the door in a too-swift way that made it clear James had won that skirmish.

Leo assumed the show was at least partly for him, and he was gratified. The one summer he was sent to camp—fourteen—his bunkmate turned out to be an overweight emotional bully who played the French horn and masturbated ceaselessly. In these situations, a good bunkmate helped a lot.

"Gene's a big Christian," said James from the shadow of the other side of the room. "Very easy to needle, I think you'll find." Moonlight came through the window, fell on the pine veneer and the taupe carpeting. Leo noticed the strange viscosity of the institutional bedding. "The good doctor is also a Christian, I think. Though if so, he is a sly one, and difficult to needle."

The *I think you'll find* part was as good a welcome to this place as Leo had yet received. It planted a seed in Leo, that maybe he might choose to stay here.

He was nowhere near sleep. The fluidity of his last thirty hours, the uncertainty of the next thirty, at least made this an exciting turn in what he now saw was his poorly led and dim-prospected life. He wanted to stick around to find out whether talking his way *into* rehab would turn out to be a good idea or just a brief detour in a longer descent.

James must have sensed that Leo, though silent, was miles from sleep, because he started talking. Just started telling his story in a nice baritone voice. It was like a rehab lullaby; a country ballad with no music.

He was a criminal defense attorney from Vancouver, Washington. He had fended off a DUI three months back. Now, concurrent complaints about him by his ex-wife, his business partner, his girlfriend, his parents, and the state's attorney had made his appearance at Quivering Pines the best of a very limited range of options. He copped to the charges immediately. More or less. That is, he admitted up-front that he couldn't seem to stop smoking crack cocaine, that he regularly lost his car, that his legal career was in tatters. And while he objected to the creepiness of the word, he conceded that he had technically, legally, *stalked* his girlfriend. "But I love her," he said. "I love terrible things." He allowed that his ex-wife could fairly be called saintly and long-suffering for putting up with his shit. But he said she was also a vindictive harpy ball squeezer who could drain the joy from a Ferris wheel. Their five-year-old son, Caleb, had been lately wreaking havoc and throwing all the antisocial he could at the Vancouver public-school system.

But the business partner was a scheming little prick and should not be credited. On that point, James was crystal clear. The two men owned a sports tavern on a busy stretch of state highway. James owned 55 percent.

"It's called Aces. Pretty grim. Lots of cardboard cutouts and hangy-down advertisements. But, you know, ten grand cash, easy, on the big nights."

James was barred from the premises of his own tavern. "All I need to do is have a drink in there every night, just to remind the staff that I'm a real person. That dickbag has turned them all against me. I could've drunk Sprite. I mean, I couldn't have. But, you know. Judge was ready to include the workplace exemption in the DUI adjudication when Dickbag gets me barred. Submits an affidavit, says staff may feel *compromised* by me. Whatever that means. And if you're working at Aces, you're pretty compromised already, to be frank. I just wonder which one of my enemies told that moron what an affidavit is. I think he may be making a play for my ex-wife. You believe that?"

Leo decided right then that he was deeply in James's corner on this; Dickbag was definitely a bad guy, and pretty much Leo's enemy also. In the dark, from his pillow, unseeable, Leo made a face that meant all this.

"So I'm having some trouble taking on board the forgiveness stuff that they're saying is in some totally undemonstrable way necessary to stay sober. Right now I see two reasons to stay alive, sober or not: to help my boy out of this patch and to take a gun down to Aces and shoot Dickbag in the face."

"Ah. Don't do that, now," said Leo, his voice raspy from underuse. "Seems self-endangering to the point of suicide. And if not death, then prison, right? Or would you escape after shooting Dickbag? No. You can't leave your son alone in the world. I mean, you will one day, I guess. But not yet you shouldn't." He thought that sounded bossy though, and he wanted to let James know that he was speaking from experience. "I know," he said. "I am an orphan."

Leo wondered whether the word was justified. He had never dropped it like that before. He was twenty-two when it happened: the fire, his escape, his parents' non-escape.

An extra beat of silence in the blue room while James absorbed that. "Yeah, I know. I can't leave Caleb," he said, and sighed, and said *fuck* while he sighed, and the sadness in the sigh gave the dull cuss real weight. "My boy may have a worse brain than I do, but he has a better heart. I should forget about Dickbag; let him rob me of that whole toxic joint. Bankruptcy's low down on my list of problems right now. I know what I'm *supposed* to do. But I just can't seem to quit devising ways of making that man suffer. I tried to say could I use that as my Higher Power—my obsessive sense of vengeance against this one guy."

"They said no, right?"

"They said no," said James. "I think I want to use Zeno of Citium. 'The passionate emotions are the result of errors in judgment.' That's Zeno.

Yep, once I get rid of those passionate emotions, the errors in judgment will just fall away."

Was that wry? Leo had always wondered about *wry*. Whatever it was, it was comforting to hear about this man's bus accident of a midlife. Compared to James's, Leo's situation didn't seem all that bad. Okay, he was a fragile-minded, careerless, privileged loser. Okay, he was alcoholically inclined and overfond of pot. And okay, so he'd let his imagination run too wild; he'd seen patterns and meaning where really there was only the ordinary world, drab and difficult for every poor sinner. He was embarrassed, deeply embarrassed. But embarrassed was related to humbled, wasn't it? And humbled was said to be a good thing.

So he was actually a little cheered as he lay in the dark. Crack cocaine? Girlfriend-stalking? Bankruptcy? He saw that he had stopped well shy of the true cliff edges.

In the morning, before breakfast, Leo followed James to the lounge-like area in the middle of the men's wing. James explained that every morning a new man led his co-recoverers on a guided meditation. It was on the chore wheel in the lounge: Snack, Library, Kitchen, Meditation, Sweep Patio. Men's names beside these duties. Leo's wasn't up there yet.

Men sat in chairs and on the floor. "You're just not allowed to lie down," said James. A few men were pushing the edge of that rule, slumped in near-sleep in the corners of couches. Most men kept their eyes closed. One show-off sat in full lotus. The meditation was led by a man in loafers and feathered hair. He took his job seriously, making his voice all Garrison Keillor-y as he drew with words a sylvan path along a quiet shore. "The water laps at the mucky shore, the pine boughs wave gently in the morning breeze," he said. But after a few minutes of that, he depleted his stock of relaxing imagery, so he brought the men out of a stand of pine to a clearing of shore, where they found a bass boat, "an Allison XB-Twenty-One Bassport Pro Two and Two," said the man. "With a hydraulic jackplate, Garmin GPS in the dash, two chargers, a Livewell pump-out, tip-up consoles, a swing trailer tongue, LED lights, disc brakes, oil-bath hubs, a Minn Kota Pro-Eighty trolling motor, and dual-rod storage racks." Gamely, Leo tried to imagine this craft.

After the bass-boat meditation, Leo tagged along with James to the smoking station, a pedestal ashtray set the state-mandated thirty feet away from the main facility. Next to the ashtray was a concrete pillar, six feet high with a dirty metal circle near its top, its function a complete mystery to Leo. Security camera? Cyclopean statue?

James put an effeminately slim menthol cigarette in his mouth, then reached a hand around the rear of the pillar and pushed a button. In seconds, the dirty metal circle glowed bright orange. James leaned his cigarette into the glowing hole.

It was an electric cigarette lighter, like the kind in a car's dashboard. Of course, butane lighters were contraband around here. And it was definitely a tobacco disincentivizer, making smokers embrace a concrete pole and stick their cigarettes in its fiery, head-high anus. It didn't seem to faze James, though, and Leo liked him even more for that.

"Sorry. You want one?" He proffered the open pack to Leo.

"No. Thank you," said Leo. The smoke coming off James's cigarette looked greasy.

"See, the Stoics, they probably wouldn't let us smoke. Maybe there's a Stoic treatment facility. If I say the Stoics are my Higher Power, they have to send me there, right?"

"Speaking of, what are their powers of sending?" Leo asked James. "And do people ever just walk out of here?" Leo was beginning to put together a plan for getting out of Quivering Pines. Clearly, the sisters would have to be appeased, as would Dr. Smugpens. He didn't want to push too hard; he was still worried about landing in a worse place, an electrodes place.

"Well, you know, it's not a locked facility."

"Yeah, why do they keep saying that?"

"I think it helps if they get a runner every now and then. It keeps things taut. We had a genuine B-list rock star here last week." James mentioned a name. Leo shrugged to indicate he had never heard of him.

"The drummer for Skinflute?" said James. Leo nodded as if that meant something. "Wore leather pants. A girl came and got him in a Jaguar after dinner. Can you imagine? How we workshopped about that one."

Another man shouted to Leo from the patio. "Hey, new guy. You smokin'?"

"Only two men at a time allowed at the smoking station," James said to Leo, and then he called back to the shouter: "Leo and I are talking, Bob."

"Smoking station's for smoking, is all I'm saying," called Bob.

"Sounds like you're harboring a resentment, Bob. Go journal about it," James called back, and he gave Leo a wicked smile, as if they were prank-calling the supermarket. "Some of these guys aren't so bad, actually. It's kinda fun, you know?"

Leo did know. Even thirty-six hours into his stay, the interesting absurdities of the place were offering relief from the self-hatred and the incessant buzz of dread that had filled the last weeks.

"It's a phantasia," said James.

Leo didn't understand the word.

"The impression left behind by sensations," said James. He did a lot of bodywork while smoking and talking: he cupped his elbow in his palm; he scratched at his goatee; he rolled the ashen tip of his cigarette carefully on the rim of the ashtray until it was a clean and rounded ember. "Even that guy Phillip, the guy with the bass boat. He's an egomaniac, but he's okay. I mean, when it comes down to it." James straightened; the light breeze dropped and the sun warmed the earth. He quoted some Stoic into the morning air: " 'I can neither be harmed by any of them, for no man will involve me in wrong, nor can I be angry with my kinsman or hate him; for we have come into the world to work together.' " He scraped his cigarette out on the little metal grate, rubbed his hands together, and then said to Leo, "Come on. Let's go make some memories."

In the cafeteria line, waiting for breakfast, Leo met a one-eyed man named Kenny; he was in his twenties, small, wearing a tracksuit, and clearly rougher than most of the other men here. Kenny said that on the outside he collected scrap metal from "unsecured" job sites; he exuded a street knowledge that made him stand out at Quivering Pines, with its pretty paths across clipped lawns and its selection of juices at breakfast. Still, Kenny must have had rich parents, thought Leo, to have ended up here.

"What's your drug of choice?" Kenny asked him. "Or are you just an alcoholic?" Leo felt cornered by the questions. The phrasing presupposed a certain on-boardness with Twelve Step precepts, and he was trying to stay noncommittal on the point. He could answer, *Dunno. I haven't tried them all,* or *Drugs aren't really my problem*. But in the context, either answer would seem snooty. Kenny was just being kind, chatting to the new guy in the cafeteria line. So he said, "Pot, I guess."

Kenny nodded, unimpressed, and said his was crystal meth. Then he said he lost his eye when he leaped from a train car while being chased by cops. Leo, who hadn't asked about the eye and had been considering eggs, opted instead for cereal, which he dispensed by turning an auger beneath a clear plastic bin.

It seemed that the men here wanted to get a read on Leo and tell him their stories. At the table, a youngish anesthesiologist volunteered that he was at Quivering Pines to keep his medical license. He said he'd been found by his hospital to have installed a hep-lock in his own ankle so he could mainline synthetic opiates between procedures. He clearly considered his drug habit to be of a higher order than the drug habits of his fellow patients, with their hidden jugs of vodka and nasty little vials of specious, tub-produced amphetamines and attention meds swiped from their children.

After breakfast, the men returned to their wing, some to pull ferociously on cigarettes at the smoking station, others to finish their homework or do crunches in their rooms before Morning Small Group.

Leo showered. In the previous weeks, his personal hygiene had slipped noticeably. Correcting this was a low-hanging fruit in the show-them-you're-better orchard. And he liked the shower in his room. It was one of those one-piece plastic-stall kinds, and it had a big soap dispenser that released a zippy, viscous, dish-detergent-type soap that Leo just slathered on. Brushed the hell out of his teeth. Combed his hair. Shaved like an ad man, leaning close to the mirror. There were men here who shook just bringing Cheerios to their moist mouths. Leo's hand was steady. *I am going to be okay,* he thought.

But James was not in Leo's Morning Small Group, and Morning Small Group was really in a very small room; Leo felt his anxiety ratchet up. His Small Group counselor was called Keith. Keith was a sharp-looking dude in jet-black jeans. He kept his lanyarded ID tucked into the breast pocket of his short-sleeved button-down shirt.

If you had to wear a lanyarded ID, that seemed to Leo to be the classy way to do it. They began with a check-in: You were supposed to say your name and ascribe to yourself a feeling word. Keith was clearly having an ongoing disagreement with Kenny, the tracksuited scrap-metal collector, who sat hunched and fidgeting in his chair. Kenny tried to use *pissed off* as his feeling word.

"*Pissed off* is not a feeling word, Kenny," said the counselor.

It's a feeling phrase, thought Leo.

Fidget-fidget hunch. "But that's how I feel."

"Can you find a less aggressive way to put it?" asked Keith. Kenny scanned the list of feeling words on the sheet taped to the back of his notebook. He chose *angry,* though it seemed to make him more pissed off to do so.

Leo chose *bewildered.* He liked the wildness in the word.

Leo was hoping that in Small Group he could start talking his way through and then right out of rehab; that he could, politely, make clear the differences between himself and the men around him. His binges were symptom, not syndrome, he reasoned. Sure, it might help to sit in circles and talk about distant fathers, about daily disappointments, about the strange tide of anger that sucked at the sands of a day. But who was going to give a shit, really? The mean world waited outside for them all, and it seemed to him that what was going on here was a willful over-simplification of the problem. He was embarrassed for these men, who were quickly able to see thirty years of estrangement from their families as evidence of their common disease. Who laid every problem at the feet of addiction. *Well, it's probably not that simple,* he wanted to say. They were shifty here on what the word *addiction* even meant. Usually, they said it was a medical disease, like diabetes, but then suddenly they'd get more abstract about it, as if it were a sinister and scheming nemesis, like a wraith from a Blake woodcut.

But he could find no opening to say any of this.

"You're awfully quiet, Leo," said Keith. "What Bob just said about how difficult it is to stay sober when there's all this alcohol being pushed at us all the time, what do you think about that?"

Bob was the one who had been annoyed by Leo's not smoking at the smoking station. He was a pilot for a major airline.

"It sounds like Bob needs to move to Mecca if he wants to stop drinking."

"Well, how about you?" said Keith. "Do you want to stop drinking, stop using drugs? Don't you see that that's what got you here?"

The *don't you see* part pissed him off. "Look," he said, addressing Keith, not all the men in the room. "Clearly I like to smoke more pot than some people do. More than most people. And all that drinking was gross, I guess. Yeah, it was gross. It could have been Windex, for all the relief it brought me. I got in way over my head. So I should probably stop all that. But that's not exactly how I ended up here."

"How'd you end up here, then?"

"My sisters were worried."

"Well, wasn't it the drinking and using that had them worried?"

"I think it was more the unreasonable elation, the no sleep, the delusions of reference and grandeur."

Keith squinted at Leo. *Great, a vocabulary guy,* Leo could pretty much see him thinking.

"But let's talk about what came after that—the alcohol and the marijuana? The not getting out of bed?"

Fine, but that seemed to Leo beside the point. Or at least, not as important as what had come before. No one had tried to intervene on him when his head was full of light and links. They told him to quit talking so fast, not to take himself so seriously. But they could find no way to arrest his ascent. Each mean tether snapped at the pull of his racing self-regard. They'd waited until he was brought low. And he thought he knew why this was: they were jealous.

Now that he was past that, he could see that he'd been, at times, obnoxious about his insights, and that he'd generally overshared. And he was willing to concede that some of his thoughts, at the end there, were straight-up paranoid. But there had been *something;* he had been onto something real. How it looked to others shouldn't really matter. And what they wanted him to do here was give all that up and aim for what they called serenity. And that would be great—water lapping at a shore, all of that—but he knew it would never be his. He tried again, addressing the whole room. "I do see that I am unwell somehow. Sometimes I feel like I've got my hands around the truth, you know? And when that feeling goes away, when it's replaced by its opposite . . . well, I feel just terrible then. The gloom gets so deep it's like I can't see. I feel like a teacup that's certain to shatter; my mind goes over and over the same terrible data. And then, so, yes, maybe I use the pot and the drinking to treat that, to escape from it. Maybe that's a bad system. But the pot and the drinking—they're not the root complaint or final cause or underlying issue or whatever."

Keith seemed to be waiting for someone to respond. No one did.

"Wallace." Keith prompted one of the men. "I know you said depression is something you've battled. Can you speak to what Leo just said?" Wallace was a heavyset black veterinarian from Tacoma with kind eyes and large hands.

"Not really," said Wallace. "That teacup-about-to-shatter thing, that sounds a little different than what I got."

"I heard you caused trouble in Small Group today," said James as they lay in their separate beds in the blue of the room.

"Yeah. That didn't go the way I was hoping."

"You have to be careful around here, you know? Tell them what they want to hear, but don't go overboard."

"I couldn't tell them what they wanted to hear. I don't think I'm supposed to be here, James."

"Couldn't that be, you know, denial?"

Coming from James, the question didn't make Leo defensive. "Could be, I suppose. But I think there's something worse going on."

"Worse?"

"Worse than the getting fucked up, you know?"

"Like you're crazy?"

"Yeah. Well, like I *was* crazy. Now I kind of want the crazy back, because it felt better than what it left behind. But I can't ever have it back, because now I know it was... well, I was the only one in that world. I was all alone. Being alone is like being dead."

"How crazy? Gimme an example."

And because Leo was certain that James was exactly who he appeared to be, he started talking, telling James all the things he couldn't tell the doctor (because there was something fishy about that doctor) and that he couldn't tell his sisters (because they loved him and couldn't help and would only worry that their little brother was a late-onset schizophrenic).

He started with the truth holes. It was the first time he had tried to explain the phenomenon to anyone. He saw that that phrase, *truth holes*, was kinda batshit. But what else would you call them? And what about for the first eight, ten years of his life, when loving parents encouraged his obsession with dragons and secret worlds and animals in vests who poured tea and drove motorcars and who gave him to read Tolkien and Susan Cooper and the Brothers Grimm and Madeleine L'Engle and C. S. Lewis? Is a boy supposed to leave his imagination on the side of the road when he boards the bus to manhood?

Truth holes: Five or ten times a day, a small zone in Leo's field of vision (about the size of a pocket watch held at arm's length) would flare and then become soaked in light and meaning. Leo would get drawn in, and within a moment, a bridge would emerge from the truth hole, a cable or cord connecting him to some other patch of knowledge or information. It actually didn't feel all that weird—it felt like some sort of communication device that might be prosaic in the twenty-second century. The knowledge and information wasn't abstruse, and it was never bossily delivered. It wasn't even *from the future* or anything stupid like that, and in those moments Leo didn't feel as though he was understanding Mayan or Martian or Kwakiutl. But he was definitely taking on information via a very broad band.

"I think I know the kind of thing you're talking about," said James. He recalled a summer's day two years earlier when the sun spangled into ribbons as his son's little feet raced across the wet sand of the wide beach at Manzanita. "My heart filled to bursting. That was love. Love for Caleb. Pure. Best drug ever, actually. Maybe that's the sort of privileged information you're talking about. Everyone's heart should fill to bursting sometimes. But ten times a day sounds clinical. Maybe you were smoking too much pot?"

"Almost certainly. Or maybe I'm not smoking enough now."

"You still seeing them?" asked James. "The truth holes?"

"Not in a while, no."

"Then, honestly, that doesn't sound that crazy."

"Well, it went on from there." At first it was great; those shining months he had come through, when sleep was just a bowl of fruit he took a plum from and everyone brought him news and it all seemed to link up somehow. He wrote without ceasing. Letters and manifestos. Sonatinas and villanelles. Household signage. Short stories. Shorter stories. Tiny little plays. Menus for banquets he would like to attend. Haikus about neighbors. Thank-you notes to people who would not expect them. Abstracts for operas. He wrote a backgammon column, a self-defense manual, and a monograph (*On Outwitting Pretend Humans on the Telephone*). He wrote letters to advice columns and to corporate headquarters and to his congresspersons and to newspapers. For his nieces in New York, *The Memoirs of Señor Skrapits, the Squirrel in 7A*. Back then, the sunlight off the hanging pots meant something; the way the worms writhed on the wet sidewalk after a rain meant something; even the newspaper news meant something. It all meant that there was a common direction, a flow, to human events. And he could see it. He put it all in his blog.

Then he told James about how the paranoia began to creep up on the beauty, and then to eclipse it.

He did at least try to keep away from the stupider wings of the Internet, where cranks peddle conspiracies. But he was constantly tempted. He would read too much about nanotechnology and then begin to see the tiny machines all around him. Or he would come across news of a huge private correctional corporation manufacturing a mobile, container-based prison system that could be delivered and installed in days and how one of the principals of that company was a higher-up at FEMA. Problem is, when you begin to talk about FEMA even possibly being nefarious, people edge away from you. So when he saw any garden-variety crackpottery in his copy, he'd scrub it out before he clicked Publish.

And then how it devolved further; how it slid below the surface of cogency and into such solipsistic nonsense that it became clear to the blog's fifty readers that Leo was in the grip of something, maybe drugs and alcohol, but probably something else as well. His output increased, and he stopped doing any sort of editing, really. There were rants about being slighted by the UPS guy; bossy warnings about leaving your computer unguarded, about the puffer machines at the airport, about nonstick pan coatings, and about the direction of the culture. There were bellicose and politically incorrect challenges to received notions and the status quo; exhortations to avoid respectability and to live by a code.

And then he told James how he had become focused on the vast and terrible conspiracy that he alone had divined.

"Okay, here we go. This is the stuff. Tell me about this," said James.

"See, I was online, right? Just poking around," Leo said. "And, well, you know that blowhard Mark Deveraux?"

"The self-help guy? *Bring Your Insides Out,* or whatever?"

"Yeah, that guy. Well, I used to know him. Ten years ago. We were best friends in college. Anyway, I found this video of him on the web, where he was talking about how you can have whatever you want, you just have to learn to control your wish-making faculties."

"Sounds like bullshit to me."

"Well, it was the way he was saying it. But here's the thing: He was lifting this stuff from *my* blog. Not word for word. But I was pretty sure it was mine."

"Motherfucker," said James.

"I know, right? He was probably making money off it. He got it wrong, is the thing. I never said you could have whatever you want. I just said you should notice that you *do* get most of what you wish for. You wish to enter the traffic stream without touching other cars; you wish to propel your sleepy body bipedally to the bathroom; you wish that the meaning of this or that moment would become more apparent to you—these are granted wishes.

"I was furious. So I started to look into my old friend Mark Deveraux. Turns out, in every talk he gives, every idiotic 'blessay' he pens, he also shills for SineCo and for this new device of theirs, the Node—"

"Oh, I saw one of those," James interrupted, "they're cool."

"No, they're not, James," said Leo, his voice gone granite. "They're totally evil. They're biometric sampling and surveillance devices that SineCo—or whoever's behind that company—is distributing."

"Hold on. They're selling them, right? Not distributing them?"

"At a steep loss. The tech press can't figure it out. They're saying that either SineCo is building these in some secret incorporated part of Asia using, like, incarcerated children, or it's the shaver-cartridge business model—you know, where they sell to us schmucks, at a loss, the thing that makes us have to buy their expensive thing forever."

"Yeah, it's true. That shaver-cartridge racket is bullshit."

"But I say that it's a much longer con. I say that they want to get this device into the hands of everyone in the whole world, where it can collect all of our movements, our vital signs, our images, our voices, our ambient audio, our DNA. All of it."

"They can collect that?"

"Oh, they do already, as much as they can. They biomonitor your sewer pipe, and they use HIPAA siphoning, and facial recognition at ATMs, and AV collection grids at major intersections. And I won't even go into airport security. But with the Node, you bring that motherfucker home. At your bedside, in your pocket, on your dashboard, to a date. You're always showing it what you're looking at."

"You ever figure out who the They is?"

"Well, no. But check it out: The TSA has this program called Clear, where if you get pre-vetted, you can skip security."

"Yeah, I saw that. But I never see the line those people are supposed to use."

"I don't think they're even in the same part of the airport as you and I. And *clear* is also a state that Scientologists are trying to achieve. And Clear is the name SineCo gave its new operating system. And Baxter-Snider, that huge pharmaceutical—they make Synapsiquell—they're giving out free contact lenses. For research, they say. The program's called Contact Lens–Enabled Astigmatism Research: C-L-E-A-R."

Blue room; James thinking. "Okay. Put that way, it's weird, I guess. But so you think SineCo and the Scientologists and the TSA and Baxter-Snider are in cahoots?"

"And my old friend Mark."

James didn't say anything.

"I know; it sounds bonkers."

But at the time it really hadn't. He'd wanted to alert the world. Once he'd decided that everything transmitted electronically was being vacuumed up into an enormous shadow-government database, he asked his friend Jake if he could use his letterpress machine, then camped out in Jake's studio for thirty hours, setting type until his hands were black.

When the first broadside clacked off the machine, he took it outside to read it in the five a.m. light. He saw the text was smudgy and poorly kerned. But reading it, he knew what he had was electrifying. He knew it could change the world, stir the people, bring them to the ramparts. The thirty-six-point banner headline was THEY ARE COLLECTING EVERY-THING (Leo could only find four thirty-six-point capital *E*s).

"How many copies do you want to print?" Jake had asked, handing his friend a mug of coffee.

"Five thousand? Ten thousand?"

"Let's start with fifty," Jake said.

But Leo omitted the goriest details from this account of his unraveling. He did not tell James about how he had bragged in the broadside of his illustrious pedigree. "Descended from the American intellectual elite," he'd said he was. And he did not tell James that he had actually threatened Mark Deveraux in the broadside. Near the end of his breathless, alarmist, offset screed, he announced that he had "incriminating footage of SineCo fraudster and pitchman Mark Deveraux." As he recalled now, that seemed appropriate, because he was exhorting everyone who wished to join the resistance to do everything in his or her power to oppose this evil plan. What was in his power to do was to trip up one of SineCo's frontmen.

But he saw now that that part was extra-weird—the public-threat-making part. Why had he failed to do any moral calculations about blackmail? At that point, it was *by any means necessary*. But nothing was *by any means,* was it? There was always context.

"You know, it's not even that far-fetched. That's not what's wrong with it," said James.

Leo did know. And he knew what James was going to say next.

"It's that . . . why would you be the only one to see it? It has that classic schizo thing, where you're at the center of it all."

There are many centers, thought Leo. *Not Jesus Christ but the Holy Ghost.*

"And, while I think the Scientologist part is tenuous," said James, "the rest is not totally implausible, I suppose."

Leo appreciated James's assessment.

"I mean, that drummer who came and left last week? He was also a sound engineer, and he said he was pretty sure these rooms were bugged."

Sunday evening. After dinner. Most of the men were sitting in deep brown and blue couches in the sunken part of the lounge, watching *When Harry Met Sally* on VHS. Leo kept half an eye on the screen while he ate a succession of mini-yogurts from the fridge in the break room, which was just the raised part of the lounge.

Actually, all the men were watching *When Harry Met Sally*, but about half were pretending not to. They were loudly shuffling their Step work assignments or conspicuously journaling. A steady rhythm of smokers nipped out into the cool summer night beyond the patio. A man wearing a football jersey was trying to make microwave popcorn, but he seemed unable to program the microwave for anything more than one second. It went *whir hum ding* and the man would harrumph and fuss with the buttons and then the microwave would go *whir hum ding* again.

"Hell, Larry," said one man from the lounge, "it's not cold fucking fusion."

"There's a popcorn button on the one I got at home," complained Larry.

Leo wanted another little yogurt, but he was embarrassed by the small fray of empties in front of him. He looked into the darkling of the sunken lounge to see if James was in there. The movie watchers had formed a horseshoe of couches and easy chairs about the TV. Stragglers—men who had started off in the pretending-not-to-watch camp but had succumbed—sat in an outer ring of springy conference chairs. A few men, the younger ones, were nested in throw pillows on the floor. It looked like a slumber party zapped by an aging gun.

Leo couldn't see James in the circle, so he walked to the patio door to see if he was at the smoking station. But the dim room only stared back at him in the glass of the patio door. A moving ember glowed like a distant buoy. The wide green world whispered to Leo. *You will be okay,* it said, *come let me hold you in my arms.*

Leo stepped outside. Down beyond a slope of benighted lawn was scrub tangle of brush and beyond that a train track. Beyond the train track was the white-lit loading bay of a commercial warehouse. Leo could just hear the buzz of those distant lights. He walked to the slate edge of the patio. It was not James smoking out there. There was no hunch in that man; he had one hand in his pocket, trying to look cool.

"You're not watching the pitcher about Harry and Sally?"

It was a voice from behind him, one he had not heard before. Leo turned and saw an old man in a plastic patio chair. It was the man who had come to Quivering Pines after Leo and who had been in the intake single all weekend. Leo had glimpsed him through the sometimes-open door of his room, sitting upright on the edge of the bed the way old men do preparatory to standing, his cane propped beside him, his hands settled on the mattress. Leo had also seen him waiting outside the nurse's office. He moved like a construction site, with a walker and a cane—he hung the cane on the walker and used it for short trips away from the walker. He also wore a sort of brace that went from his hip to his chest. It looked like a plastic ceiling fan had flung itself out of orbit and embraced him.

"I guess I was. It's pretty silly."

"I'm Al," said the man.

"I'm Leo," said Leo.

"What you in for?" said Al.

"Started going crazy; smoked and drank a lot to keep it at bay. But that may have made it worse. I can't decide."

"I done that, sometimes. How old are you?"

"Thirty-six."

Al exhaled whistily to express how ridiculous it was for someone to be that young.

"How about you?" Leo asked. "How'd you get here?"

"Interstate," said Al. Then he chuckled once and said, "Goddang kids.

Showed up outta nowhere." Al was wearing his brace and holding his cane, lightly spinning it with hands that were nimbler than the rest of him. He was without his walker. "Had an interventionist with them." He said the word slowly. "Name of Leanne."

The engine sound from a small plane came at them in the night. The smoker who was not James stubbed out his cigarette with purpose, hacked, and strode back to the patio and through the sliding doors, which made a sort of sucky spaceship sound when they were opened and closed.

"It's nice here though, anyway," said Leo. He wanted to appear to Al to be broadminded. He sat down in a patio chair.

"Yup. It's nice. But I gotta put in my brussels sprouts; shed needs a coat a' paint," said Al. "And I need a drink, so I'll be on my way here soon."

"You like drinking, huh?" said Leo.

"No one likes drinking."

"Oh, I don't know. I think I see people who do."

"They're not doing it right," said Al. He wore a checked shirt and a cardigan sweater, the straps and plastic of the ceiling-fan brace visible between the two layers. He had on a faded trucker's cap, the kind with the plastic-mesh back. The brim threw Al's face in the shadow of a shadow, but when the TV light from inside sparked brightly, Leo could see that Al's face was not cloudy, like the faces of some of the older men here.

"So how you gettin' outta here?" Leo was unconsciously flattening his speech and slowing it, trying to sound more like Al, who spoke in Desert Prairie Interstate West.

"It's not a locked facility," said Al. "*Leo* means 'lion,' right?"

"Yeah." Most people assumed Leo was short for Leonard. He liked saying, *No, just Leo, like lion*. His mother was a Leo—had been a Leo.

"Well, look, Lion, I'm a mouse, okay? And I'm gonna chew you outta this net right here."

Remember this. Remember exactly this, thought Leo. But now he was doing that thing he did when a waitress recited the specials—he was trying too hard to pay attention, so he was paying attention to paying attention, not to what was going on.

"You do exactly what they say, okay?"

"I'm trying to reserve judgment, actually."

"What? Shush. Just do what they say. They're right, but for the wrong reasons. There ain't no promised land like they say there is here, but if you keep drinking like I did, there is a hell."

"So why're you leaving?"

"You know how old I am?"

Never answer this question. "Nope."

"I'm sixty-six."

He looked twenty years older. "That's not too old. You should stay."

"Naw, they ain't got anything for me here. A Higher Power? They think I ain't thought a' that? Hell, I didn't drink the whole time Ronald Reagan ran the place."

"Maybe you can make Ronald Reagan your Higher Power," Leo suggested.

Al laughed at that a little. "I just might," he said. "I just might."

"It's been nice, though," said Leo, "these last few days, not being drunk once. I guess I tend to forget that I've been drinking for some time." Why on earth did he care whether or not Al stayed at Quivering Pines?

"Boy, I *spilled* more than you drunk," said Al. "Just stop now. Forever. It never gets back to easy, it just keeps getting worse. Everything will get worse. Let me save you thirty mother-scrubbing years here. You use alcohol to clean wounds and get chewing gum out of woodwork. It is not for internal use. You drink it, you are inviting pain and dulling the only blade you brung to this fight. You will waste your days and sully your name, and your family will live in dread of you. You got that?"

Leo nodded. He couldn't help it. His eyes had actually gone wide.

"Think you could help me inside?" Al said.

"Shit. Yeah. Of course," Leo said.

"Here, gimme that chair."

Leo manipulated a white plastic patio chair in front of Al.

"Now, take my cane."

Leo took the cane, one of those orthopedic-store jobs, with the clicktety-sprung-ball-through-the-line-of-holes system for adjusting height. Al steered the chair across the patio and Leo walked beside him, bearing Al's cane and offering him a shoulder. When they reached the patio door, they saw that there was a minor hubbub within. The credits were rolling on the movie, and the men were hopping off the couches like locusts. A man called Phil patted frantically at the pockets of his sweatpants, then began digging in various wedges of upholstery, looking for his lost cigarettes. Men who could claim not to have come down to the pit at all during the movie squared the pages of their reading and sucked from the straws of their juice boxes.

"Dang. Looks like I don't get to know what Harry done to Sally," Al said. Leo opened the sliding door for the older man. Al put his hand on Leo's shoulder and tried to step up the high threshold. But the top of his sneakered foot scraped against the metal drip edge on the door sill, and he fell back in pain. For a moment, Leo had the man's whole weight on him; he felt like a stack of plates. Leo put his hand on the small of Al's back to steady him. Through cardigan and checked shirt, he felt some of the armature of the plastic brace.

"Shit," said Al in a pained exhalation. Leo put his hand on the underside of Al's thigh and helped him to raise up his foot. Their entanglement barred the exit of the smokers, who had to give way before Leo and Al. Al told someone inside to fetch his walker, and Leo, beneath and behind him now, handled a man twice his age into another piece of scaffolding.

"I thank you, Leo," said Al. "You think on what I told you," he said as he walkered away.

Leo was thinking on what Al had told him an hour later as he lay in bed. James was flossing his teeth, wearing boxer shorts and a law-school T-shirt, as attorneys will do.

"What did you and that geezer talk about?" asked James while examining some bit of floss dross.

"His name's Al. He scared the shit outta me."

"Yeah. Man looks like he's mostly parts."

"No, it wasn't that. He just made a very concise and compelling case against ever drinking again."

"Yeah, but that was probably in the abstract." James worried up his spent floss and dropped it in the wastebasket.

"Not really," said Leo.

James flicked the light switch and got in bed. It wasn't that dark. A pale spreading light from the parking lot seeped into their room.

Leo considered again that he should stay here awhile. The tomato juice was cold. There was a little weight room beneath the cafeteria, beside the laundry room; a rough jogging track scored into the hill before the railroad tracks. (Some high-quality chain-link fence between Quivering Pines and the railroad track. "They never said it wasn't a *fenced* facility," James had pointed out.) He could eat the hell out of those mini-yogurts, *run-run-run* around that track. Just get his wits back about him. He should hear what they had to say here; give it a chance. James was here. Al was here. This might be just the place.

On Monday morning Leo was sitting in the large round room with all the men trying to pay attention to a sort of science class—the onion-looking counselor was drawing pictures of confused neurons on a whiteboard—when Keith, Leo's Small Group counselor, interrupted the class.

"Sorry, Gene," he said to the Onion. "Can I see Leo out here?"

Leo did not want to go. He was afraid, as he left the circle, that he was Leaving the Circle.

Outside, Keith told Leo that the doctor wanted to see him again, and it couldn't wait until the afternoon. Keith said that was weird.

"Listen, Leo," he said, "I really think you should try to stay here. You have to dry out, man. You're not going to be okay unless you do. There may be some, you know, comorbidity here. Like, you have mood issues. But sobriety will help you."

"I know, I know," said Leo. He truly wanted Keith to believe him. "I'm actually totally down with that." He had really lathered on the fruity soap that morning, and brushed his teeth until his mouth gleamed like a bank lobby. "I think that maybe I might stay."

"You're going to have to do better than that," said Keith. They were outside what was called the medical building, which phrase Leo could have told them was needlessly creepy. "Why'd you put down such crazy stuff on your MMPI?"

"My what?"

"The true-false questionnaire you took when you got here, the personality profile."

"Oh, the are-you-afraid-of-doorknobs thing? I thought that was a joke."

"Just tell him you didn't mean it. The doctor. Make him believe you want to be clean and sober."

"Clean and sober. Got it." Man, did Leo want to be clean and sober.

"So, Leo," said the doctor. He was in a grand mood, and wearing a lab coat today. That must be an affectation; there was no laboratory at Quivering Pines. The folder on Leo had thickened. "Do you know what it is we do here?"

Leo's heart began to race. "You treat addiction. I got that."

"Yes, we treat addiction. And you, Leo Crane, are an addict."

Leo didn't like the tone at all.

"Thing is, we don't want to waste your time"—the doctor might have smirked there—"so if you aren't receptive to certain basic assumptions, I'm afraid you'll find that we don't have that much for you here."

"No. No. I *am* receptive to those assumptions," said Leo, sipping at the stale air of the office to keep a lid on the part of him that wanted to object to this doctor, to push back, because you got the best stuff when you pushed back. "More than receptive," he said. "I am powerless over . . . in this case, I guess, alcohol and marijuana."

"Well, I'm glad to hear you say that," said the doctor. He opened and closed the folder on his desk, swiveled around in his seat a bit, made Leo wait. "The thing is, Leo, you have, oh, a sort of preexisting condition."

"You mean depression, right? I know, but I think that's related. To the drugs and alcohol. I mean it's gotta be, right?"

"Well, it may be," said the doctor. "It probably is. But I think there may be a problem with your personality."

Well, I guess there's nothing to be done about that, then, thought Leo. "What do you mean?" he asked.

"I mean that I think you suffer from a personality disorder."

"You think I'm mentally ill?"

"A personality disorder is not the same as mental illness," the doctor said. He flicked some fuzz from the cursively embroidered and over-penned breast pocket of his lab coat. "You exhibit certain clusters of symptoms," said the doctor. "The brief, intense bouts of anger, depression, anxiety; the engagement and then rapid disengagement with jobs, with women; the feelings of worthlessness. It's true that your capacity for delusional elaboration and self-centering is not usually part of the presentation. A mild form of BPD is not something that would ordinarily stand in the way of your being treated here —"

"BPD?" asked Leo.

"Borderline personality disorder." The doctor swiveled around in his chair twenty degrees. "It even occurs to me that you might be somewhat Aspergian."

Yeah, and I think you're somewhat assholian. He really shouldn't have had such fun with those tests. Why did he have no good instincts about what to take seriously and what to blow off? It had always been that way.

"Do you know what is meant by the saying 'People who live in glass houses shouldn't throw stones'?"

"Are you serious?" *You mean, when it's actually used by people who live in glass houses and throw stones for a living?*

"Yes. What do you think it means?"

"It is a maxim encouraging introspection and warning that hypocrites are liable to criticize in others faults that they themselves display."

The doctor only nodded.

"But it's really quite meaningless," continued Leo. "I mean bland. I mean, presumably it's the throwing stones at houses that should be avoided. Or maybe living in a glass house. It would be so hard to keep clean."

The doctor had already started speaking. "...mania and the paranoia that you exhibit is, I think, of such a degree—this conspiracy you saw involving the computer company and the Scientologists and the contact lenses from the drug company—that you would probably do better at a facility with a more psychiatric orientation."

Facilities have orientations? "No. I should stay here. I want to try this thing, this sobriety."

"Certainly, getting those drugs out of your system is the first step, and I imagine that that will be, ah, achieved at whatever facility we, as your care team, decide is best for you."

The first step is admitting you are powerless—even Leo knew that. *And who's we? You and that desk blotter?* "You mean my sisters?"

He ignored the question. "So here's what we're going to do." He had kept swiveling and was now actually looking out the window behind his desk, like Mr. Burns. "Tomorrow morning your sister will be here—"

"Which one?" interrupted Leo. "I got three." He was trying to sound like Al. He held up three fingers.

The doctor swiveled back around and looked in his folder. "Daisy," he said.

That made sense. Leo was somewhat less mortified that it was Daisy missing work for this shit rather than Heather or Rosemary.

"She will accompany you to a place that better suits your needs."

Where's that? A locked ward, or Amsterdam?

He thought he would attempt a straight-up approach. "So you're really convinced I shouldn't stay here?" He was going to try not to plead. This doctor seemed like someone who would take a certain pleasure in a patient's pleading. "Look, I want what you're selling."

"We're not selling anything."

"Offering, whatever. Surely you're supposed to treat people who want to be treated. I do like this sober and clearheaded thing, by the way," he said to the doctor. "And I take that all on board. I think I *will* stop smoking and drinking. I think that's just what's needed." Leo realized too late that he sounded like he was sucking up.

"But you said you were embarrassed to be here," said the doctor.

"Well, of course I am. Isn't that reasonable?"

"Oh, I don't know," said the doctor. "Many of the people who get here are relieved to get here."

"Okay, well, then I'm embarrassed *and* relieved. Those are both feeling words."

But it was pointless now. Leo saw that he was being booted from rehab. It was like that morning in Sharon's office. Too late, he saw that he wished to stay among these fallen men.

A kind of lightness was floating into his limbs. "Right, well, look, Doctor, you say I'm out of here tomorrow, right?"

"We're currently arranging a space for you in a more appropriate facility."

"Which might be called ...?"

"When your sister gets here tomorrow, we can discuss all that."

"Yes, we can." Leo stood up. "Well. I've got some journaling to do."

"You're excused from all the afternoon treatment activities, Leo. Actually, you'll be staying up here in the medical building tonight."

Really? That is un*likely to happen.* "You think my borderline thing might be contagious, huh?"

Leo made his way across the quad and back to the men's wing. It was another grand morning; the firs and aspens were shaking their green fists at the sky. He decided that he would just leave Quivering Pines. It was not a locked facility.

But it had a very long driveway, which led to the fuzzy edge of a lush outer suburb that Leo did not know at all. He would have to walk two miles to the Fred Meyer and call a taxi to get home. It would be an undignified escape. But it was weird, the way the doctor had said, *You'll be staying up here in the medical building tonight.* Was there even a bed up there?

And there was the other weird thing, Leo realized. How had the doc known about the conspiracy, the Scientologists, and the contact lenses? All that had been only in the broadside. Would Jake have given that up to his sisters?

The drummer from Skinflute thought these rooms were bugged.

No, that was the paranoia, he reminded himself. But just to be safe, Leo should get out of here today. He could meet Daisy at his house tomorrow, deal with the fallout from there. Maybe she'd let him come live with her for a few months. Go to meetings, mind his nieces. He'd impress upon her that whatever he was supposed to have taken on board here—James Dean or Al or the doctor or the cautionary sight of broken lives or the glimpses of grace and mending—he'd absorbed it already.

The men's wing was deserted; the others were still down there learning about neurons. Leo stopped in the kitchen and knocked back a couple of mini-yogurts. He went to the front desk, asked the nurse behind it to unlock the phone cabinet for him. It was a plain old desk phone inside an authentic wooden phone booth.

"I'm sorry, I can't do that. That phone is for evening use," she said in a honeyed, unkind voice. They seemed to think people here needed such explicit retraining. He got the point, but please.

"Yeah, but I think I've been eighty-sixed. So I'm really not a patient here anymore. I'm more like a guest. I just want to call my sister. She's coming to get me."

The nurse puckered her mouth a bit and scrunched up her key bracelet protectively. "Okay, well, I'm just going to have to call the doctor to see if that's okay."

"Knock yourself out." Leo loudly ho-hummed while she rang interofficially; he fingered figure eights into the Plexi top of the desk, which was really a chest-high wall of the reception enclosure, where sweatered nurses rolled in chairs and consulted lateral files. The woman sat down at her station, which featured multiple Ziggy cartoons. "Hi, Doctor. Yes, it's Brenda. Okay. Yes? I have Leo here. He says his sister's coming to get him, and he'd like to make a call to her. Yes? Okay. Thank you, Doctor.

"Leo, go ahead and call your sister," said the nurse. She handed him the key to the booth, which had as its outsize fob a child's toy plastic telephone.

He used one of his mnemonics to recall Daisy's mobile number. *Seven seven four one nine one nine.* Two giant green squids dining together in a pagoda; that was the seven seven four. Nineteen was a hot-air balloon over a lake; so two of those.

Her voice on the outgoing message comforted him. "Sis, it's Leo," he said. He couldn't say, *Don't bother coming to rehab,* in case Mata Hari out there was paying attention. He decided he would speak to Daisy's voice mail as if he were speaking to Daisy, to stall for time. "Yeah. Good, good," he said into the phone. The fake phone call was a pretty basic maneuver in the daily spycraft that Leo had had to use for a while there, back when he was trying to figure out what was real and what was random. He used it also to avoid Greenpeace canvassers on the street. He would have made a good stage actor.

"No, no, anyway, listen . . . what? Oh, probably a waffle iron. Yeah." He laughed as if at a joke.

When they were little, his sisters had a game where a certain word or phrase would negate the following word or phrase, or make it into its opposite. It was one of many coded languages they used. Leo only barely got the rules to most of the secret languages that his sisters employed. This one was simple enough, though, and when he'd played it, he'd chosen *waffle iron* as his code switch because he loved the machine, was allowed to operate it from a young age, had never burned himself on it. His sisters thought that was hilarious, since *waffle iron* was such a difficult phrase to slip into conversation. Thereby, *waffle iron* became the standard code switch between the siblings—it meant *The following is an insincere statement; it means the opposite of what it seems to mean.*

"I'm glad you're coming to get me," Leo said down the phone. "I'll be here when you arrive. I'd rather just meet at my house, but of course I'm not going to do that." He *uhm-hmm*ed a few times, said *loveya,* and hung up. He returned the phone-booth key to Nurses' Island.

Back in his room, he saw that his clothes had been packed up for him. His trifolded trousers, neat rows of T-shirts, and rock garden of balled socks had been transferred from the veneered pressboard wardrobe into the blue duffel bag that he'd come with, which lay at the foot of his bed. Unknown hands had scooped his toothbrush and comb and organic deodorant into his Dopp kit. Creepy. Who does that? He put everything carefully on the floor beside his bed. He lay down. A breeze with jasmine on it came through his open window. Leo was tired. He decided he would rest before his escape; he wanted to say good-bye to James.

HEATHROW AIRPORT

Leila had four hours before she was to meet the Ding-Dong guy and then another four hours before her flight left for LA. She was bored and ragged and underslept. She wished she hadn't agreed to the Heathrow meeting. Over the last thirty-six hours of travel, the implausibility of Ned's story had really become apparent to her. Part of what he told her was probably true; something shady had been perpetrated on her. But that's pretty much all the Burmese government did—perpetrate shit.

And yet. She couldn't throw out the little owl icon that the original Ding-Dong e-mail had deposited on her desktop. The other programs on her laptop chugged as if on thin fuel, while this one just blinked away, and twice opened itself up to reveal a message from a guy called Seymour, one saying How about coffee? and then another saying Java-Jiva? Terminal 3, 2 p.m.? They were written as if she could respond, but there was no Reply button or anything.

Maybe if her father weren't on bail and bed rest, if her brother hadn't been begging her to come home and deal with their mom—maybe then she would have had more time for the Mystery of the Security Men in the Forest. As it was, she was ready to forget the whole thing. She let

Heathrow distract her. She killed a few hours in its chutes and atria. She strolled through handbag stores and wandered through a cigar outlet, passed a waxing joint and a place called Pretzel Junction.

There had to be better ways than this to build an economy, right? If people just spent their money on less stupid stuff, wouldn't so many problems disappear? Yes, but *whose* idea of stupid, she knew was the issue. There were a few face products on which she didn't mind dropping some serious ducats, so that probably made her a hypocrite. But she'd be willing to make adjustments for the greater good. The world reflected by the stores in this airport seemed to be going the other way. There was a place that sold water, but in rhinestone-encrusted bottles and for hundreds of dollars. There was bad candy made in China and flown to London and sold to people, some of whom were flying to China. There were cheesy lingerie shops and a vitamin outlet and there were two distinct yogurt franchises. There were newsstands, which at least still sold some product that seemed related to living. But why any shelf space at all for *Abs!*, *Superyachts Monthly,* or *Model Train Enthusiast*? Actually, *Model Train Enthusiast* was fine. She picked up an armful of newspapers and some pecans.

Leila got to Java-Jiva ten minutes early. She read the *Irish Times,* because she'd never read it before and because it was one of those gigantic broadsheets you need to have upper-body strength to hold upright. She had to spread the thing out over the back of another chair to read it. She remembered how briskly her dad could fold and fold a newspaper page, until he had just the columns he wanted. He used to read to them from the papers in the morning, so Leila could recall when the embassy hostages came home and when Sadat was assassinated and when President Carter was attacked by a swamp rabbit.

"Are you Leila?" said a woman to Leila. She was in her thirties. Greek-looking. Dark-haired. Business-suity. An American accent, but what kind Leila could not tell. It sounded without place.

"Yes. I'm Leila?" said Leila, as if she were meeting herself. "Are you"—she dug in her bag for her planner—"sorry. I have it here."

"Seymour Butz? No. Seymour couldn't make it. I came instead."

Seymour Butz. That *was* the guy's name. Damn. Leila had not said it or heard it out loud and had missed the joke, if that's what it was.

"I'm Paige Turner," said the woman.

"That seems unlikely," said Leila.

"May I sit?"

"Be my guest," said Leila, who was getting intrigued at exactly the same rate as she was getting annoyed. She just wanted to confirm that this "network" was a sort of stunt, of no use to her, so she could take the whole thing off her desk. But if it was a stunt, what kind of stunt? Was it some sort of stupid viral-marketing thing, or a cult, or someone's MFA thesis? Even in the mire of her family- and job-related distresses, Leila was good at analyzing situations. She supposed that could be called compartmentalizing. When she heard people refer to this as a male trait and view it as generally a bad thing, she was uncomfortable.

There are people who will try to con a woman by banking on her politeness or by presuming that female restraint will trump her curiosity or her skepticism. Rich had once called her *blinkered,* a word choice he had quickly regretted.

But Leila hadn't run in two days. And she was tired. The sleep she had nabbed had been the airport kind. She felt, as her father used to say, not enough sandwiches for a picnic.

As soon as the alleged Paige Turner sat down, Leila said, "Why don't you tell me in less than ten minutes if you are part of some sort of opposition network, what you oppose, and how you think you can help me."

"I am. Part of a network," said Paige. "We're called Dear Diary. We do not *oppose,* exactly, but are hoping to move *past* the nation-state thing. We can help you by asking you to join us. We think you'll want to be a part of what we're working on. In the near term, though, we *are* opposing something, which is 'the Committee' "—the woman made air quotes with her slender fingers—"which is a thing where a sort of cabal of businessmen and some other bad guys are planning an electronic coup so that they will control the storage and transmission of all the information in the world. Those men you saw in Burma were part of that. You weren't supposed to see them; you certainly weren't supposed to send out e-mails about them. That's why they screwed you." She said all that without a bit of drama but with a sort of practiced enunciation, as if she were reciting the specials.

"Get the fuck outta here," said Leila. "So what are you? If 'the Committee' "—Leila made air quotes like the woman had—"is a cabal, what are you guys?"

"We're just a network. We stay in touch and keep each other up to date, share ideas."

"You mean like Friendster?" said Leila.

"If you like. Look, I'd be skeptical too, okay? But listen. The Committee has founded a secret, sovereign corporate state to achieve its ends. We want to stop them. But we can't just call the police or whatever, because they operate way above that level."

"What do you mean, way above that level?"

"They control seventy percent of the bandwidth in Asia, all the newspapers in contentious geopolitical zones, and the major pharmaceuticals. They control Sine, Skype, Facebook, all of that. They own forests and water basins and silica mines and railroads and airports. They have shareholders in the security services of most of the nations in the world. They have a very capable, committed executive tier. They recruit by convincing, co-opting, or blackmailing. They have extraction teams and attorneys and a kind of HR department. And they're planning to put it all into play. Soon, we think."

A waitress approached their table. "Can I get you anything?" she asked. Leila hadn't realized it was a table-service place; she had just chosen a chair on the periphery and camped.

"I'll have a mint tea," said Paige Turner.

"Nothing for me," said Leila.

The waitress went to clear a cup from their table, which was covered with Leila's papers and magazines.

"Oh. Sorry. Here," said Leila. She collected her stuff and shoved it into the open maw of her big bag, then put it all on the floor beneath her feet. The waitress acknowledged Leila's help, and then knelt down to push Leila's bag farther under the table. She made a watch-out signal to Leila by tapping at the corner of one eye and then indicating the rivulet of passersby in the concourse.

"Yes. Thank you," said Leila, and smiled back at the woman.

After the waitress left, Paige Turner went on. "They're simply going to start a protection racket. Like, it's going to be sold as a service, but they're going to sell you what had been free before. Some of them are Malthusians who believe that the Earth won't continue to carry us beyond about ten billion, so they want to secure their access to resources: water, genetic material, the electronic transmission of data. But then a lot of them are probably just profiteers.

"To stop them we've hacked together a broadcast platform which we think we can stand up and defend for, maybe, seventy-two hours. We're going to use it to disseminate to everyone in the world the truth of what's been going on. We'd also use that platform to offer everyone in the world a third way?" She did the rising-intonation thing, as if unsure of herself or awaiting some reassurance from Leila.

Wasn't the third way a Clinton thing? "Go on," said Leila.

"Right now, if you're born in certain places, you're just fucked, right?"

"Yes. Definitely."

"While we have the world's attention, we're going to send back to them all the information that's been collected on them. Then destroy that data and offer everyone the chance to sign up with us."

"What do you give them?"

"A number."

"Say again?"

"We give them a number. Well, we each discover our own number, really."

"Why does anyone want a number?"

"Because it's the beginning of a new way of organizing the world."

"Yeah, it's also the beginning of a way of subjugating the world."

"That's why we want to have a really good launch. But once everyone sees the scale of the data-mining the Committee's been doing and the fascist reach of their operation, they'll know we're the good guys."

"That's terrible logic," Leila couldn't help saying. "If I'm sitting at my desk or whatever and I get your big announcement, I'm going to want to evaluate your claims independently . . ."

"And how would you do that?" Paige asked.

"I guess I'd start by searching for *committee, cabal, electronic coup.*"

The waitress came back with Paige's mint tea and a little handheld payment device.

"Thank you," said Paige. She fed the payment device her credit card and keyed a PIN code into it. The device chittered out a little receipt, but when Paige tore it off, the bit of curled paper fluttered to the floor. "Sorry," said Paige to the waitress, who had knelt to pick it up.

"I told you," Paige went on, "they control all those search engines. We're working on getting paper about all of this. But the Committee is basically paperless. Maybe that's to save trees."

Leila needed a moment to see that this last part was a joke.

"When you get handed back your file and you see how much they know about you, you'll be mad enough to really do something," Paige assured Leila.

"Walgreens knows I buy Pantene? I don't care."

"Okay, but how about if a shadow government is filing away everything about you: your genetic sequence, your demographics, images of you, your social schematics, your skills, your access to wealth, your patterns of movement, your pressure points, your hopes and dreams, your fears and desires? How about if they're doing this because they have a twenty-year plan to own or control all the knowledge in the world? How about if they're betting on a breakdown of the digital infrastructure, because in that case, they'll be able to charge the whole world for data recovery? Only it's not really betting, since they can cause the breakdown; they can initiate the emergency."

A chill rode Leila's spine. A reflexive disinclination to believe in political conspiracy theories flows from two beliefs: that human incompetence makes such conspiracies untenably complicated, and that people do not allow terrible injustices to be perpetrated upon them.

But Leila had just spent six months in a totalitarian state where she had been daily reminded that the second premise was not axiomatic. *If it can happen to someone else, it can happen to me,* she remembered. Anyway, there was something plausible here—that a syndicate would cause an emergency and then sell the rescue. That's what all good mafias did, wasn't it? It was probably a totally orthodox business plan. "But how'd they get the genetic information?" she asked Paige. "I never went in for my mouth swab."

"Monitored waste streams, biosampling postage stamps. The Node. Look, I'm not from the technical side, okay? I'm a travel agent. I'm just here to deliver your tickets and documents."

"Oh yeah? Where am I going?"

"Dublin. To attend a meeting."

"No. Listen, just so we're clear: I'm on my way back to California."

"Well, look, maybe we can help you out with what's going on there. And we hardly ever divert people like this, but you're apparently a potentially valuable asset"—Paige rolled her eyes a tiny bit here, maybe bitchily, even—"so this is like some big deal. You should try to enjoy it."

That line, to Leila, was stranger than the one about the biosampling postage stamps.

"Enjoy it?"

"Yeah. Like, your ticket gets you into the fanciest lounge in this airport. There are really nice showers in there."

Her ticket? And was that a bitchy swipe, about the shower? In fairness, she could use a shower.

"And here's a phone," said Paige, sliding a phone across the table. "It works only when it has a secure path, and sometimes it only lets you text."

"I don't want your phone. If you want my help, you're going to have to make a better case."

"That's what they're going to do in Dublin." Paige Turner had disengaged. She sipped her tea. "I told you: I'm just a travel agent. I'm not Communications. Listen, I've got to meet another client." She neatened her little tea mess. "Have fun in Dublin."

Leila decided not to attempt a response to this. This lady was not making sense. So she only nodded politely when Paige stood to go.

"Okay," said Leila. "Um, I'm going to leave this phone here." She actually hadn't touched the mobile phone. It was a cheapo Nokia.

Paige was unfazed; she was slinging her chunky valise over her shoulder.

"Well, thanks for your time. I guess," said Leila.

Paige checked her outfit, nodded at Leila, and strode away, toward Security.

". . . you nutjob," added Leila quietly to herself.

It was maybe two minutes later that Leila thought of her bag. The thought came to her suddenly, and she knew before she checked that she would find something terribly amiss. She knew because her heart and lungs dropped to her belly.

Correct: Her wallet, her planner, her phone, her laptop. They were all four gone. She straightened up and looked around herself quickly, accusingly, as if a paper airplane had just bonked her in the head. But in two minutes, alone in a moving crowd, the recoverable world slips away from you at a pace. There were no waitresses here.

The laptop had been replaced with a cookie tin the approximate size and weight of a laptop. In controlled shock, Leila opened the cookie tin and saw, along with cookies, a billfold, worn loose at its spine. As if with a purloined diary, she opened the wallet carefully. Inside, she found the documents of a person called Lola Montes who, it seemed, shared some of the general outlines of Leila's life. Lola was a coastal North American with credit cards and a gym membership and business cards from restaurants. Lola had a U.S. passport, a California driver's license, and a New York Public Library card. Lola looked a lot like Leila. Lola had a lot of cash: three hundred euros, one hundred pounds, two hundred and fifty dollars. Leila poked deeper into the wallet and found a napkin with numbers written on it, the corner of a postcard from Cancun, a rubber band around a little sachet of—what, ashes?—from India or somewhere. And in the wallet's third layer, a picture of Leila's brother, Dylan, and Scratch, her long-gone cat.

It was only then that Leila returned to the photo IDs. Okay, Lola didn't look like Leila. Lola *was* Leila. Or Leila was Lola.

So. She was sitting in an airport holding a stack of high-grade forged documents, having been stripped of her own legitimate ones by an all-girl pickpocketing team.

It would be *very* hard to explain.

Still, they had given her something like a thousand dollars. Her own wallet had probably had about two hundred dollars in it. So this wasn't larceny. Maybe this was exploding money or something. Or, oh yeah, maybe she was being recruited by a global counterconspiracy that was sending her to Dublin to meet its upper officers.

A calm descended upon her, and an awareness. She could have led mountain expeditions or been a sea captain, because when things just got fubar, she generally got steely and clearheaded. When Dylan had sliced his arm open that time he fell through the coffee table, it had been the fifteen-year-old Leila who wrapped it in a towel and kept it elevated and compressed. Her dad went all ashen and unhelpful; she told him to drive. Her mom just kept wailing; Leila told her to please be quiet.

So Leila knew at once that her best move would be to go along with this until some better option opened up. The possibility existed that she had already been played. If they could pickpocket and then put-pocket her after she went through security but before the plane, they could probably have her detained or worse, if that was their aim.

The cheapo Nokia chirruped and buzzed on the plastic table like a fly caught in a web: 1 New Message, the screen said. She pressed View.

Your papers will be returned to you in Dublin, after we meet. You can walk away then, if you like. DD.

There was a problem with Mark's ticket to Rotterdam, which was where he was supposed to board *Sine Wave*. The problem with the ticket was that the SineCo representative at Heathrow didn't have it. It was this man's job to meet and see to the lounging, ground-transportation, and onward-travel needs of any of SineCo's executives, upper-level contractors, and guests who came through Heathrow.

"Mr. Deveraux, can I take you to the lounge? I'll come back for you there when I get this straightened out?" Mark asked if he could use SineCo's private Heathrow lounge, which was behind about three unmarked doors and usually satisfied even the most self-important trans-Heathrites. But that room was in use, apparently. So the rep ordered up a golf cart and he and Mark sat facing backward on the rear seat. As the cart whizzed along the polished concourses, Mark saw things recede before they had approached and was put in mind of near-death experiences he'd read about. A luggage store zipped forward from behind his head and was whisked backward into his past. A yogurt kiosk was similarly birthed and then faded and winked out. The cart beeped like a satellite. They arrived at one of the fancier first-class lounges, and the rep saw

Mark in and promised to return once the Rotterdam thing was straightened out. It was ten o'clock in the morning.

He collected three newspapers, a *Superyachts Monthly,* two bottles of water, and four croissants. He settled himself into a leather couch. He scoped out his fellow loungers, checking to see if anyone had recognized him. He ordered a cup of coffee from the steward and tried not to eat his croissants too quickly.

Mark dialed Straw's main gatekeeper, Nils. He got no answer, so he texted: Glitch in Rotterdam meeting? Waiting at Heathrow. Pls advise. He was going to stay sober today.

Mark looked at the crossword in the paper, but it was a grueling Friday puzzle, and his eyesight was kind of swimming from lack of nicotine and too much coffee. He ordered a glass of tomato juice from the steward, and then said, as if it were the first time the idea had ever occurred to him, "On second thought, why don't you make that a Bloody Mary." He moved from the crossword to the Jumble. He made sure that no one had a sight line on what he was doing. The Jumble was for precocious children and retirees.

"What the lazy aphorist needed to finish the job" was the motto over the little illustration of a man sitting stumped at a desk, huge books piled on either side of him. The cartoonist had managed to convey the fact that the man was a blocked writer; something desperate about the eyes. The answer was a three-word phrase: one letter, four letters, three letters.

With the Jumble, you unscramble jumbled words and take the circled letters from the unscrambled words and use those letters to construct the phrase that answers the riddle in the motto above the picture. The trick was to kind of blur your eyes when you first looked at the jumbled word you were trying to decipher. You had to sneak up on the letters; notice them before you read the word; you had to remember how words looked before you could read.

KWHCA.

Whack. Just like that. Mark carefully inked the letters into the little boxes and extracted the *C,* the *K,* and the *W,* which had ended up within circles.

It was like Step Three: Notice Everything Anew. Though, come to think of it, it was also a bit like Step Five: Stay Open to the Possibilities. Yeah, the steps did kind of run together, like those of a bad dancer.

SMAHUB. This one resisted Mark's eye-blurring trick. *Bumhas?* No, not a word. *Shambu?*

A beautiful girl walked into the lounge. She went to the little concierge desk, not looking entitled enough. The woman at the desk examined her ticket, a trace of disdain apparent in her manner. The girl had a rolling suitcase and was dressed like she had come from somewhere hot. She was maybe five foot four. The fittings and furniture in the lounge, which were king-size, made her look like a waif. She made straight for the bar. Parked her rolly suitcase, mounted a bar stool.

Mabshu? Oh, come on, this was ridiculous. He was a public intellectual, for Chrissake. He moved on. VARESH. *Ravesh!* No. *Sharve?* No. *Shaver.* Ha, yes. *Shaver.* Mark took the circled letters of the word *shaver*—*S* and *A*— and scribbled them at the bottom of the page. His Bloody Mary arrived, and Mark sipped, sipped, and then drained it. He tried to casually place the empty glass outside his little zone of executive kerfuffle.

It was after his second drink that he decided to start fetching his own Bloody Marys from the bar. That steward was a little too on the ball for his liking. Plus, the girl at the bar had not turned around. Mark strode up to the bar and ordered another drink. He placed himself near the girl, but not too near. "You can skip the celery stick," he told the barman, who was Indian or Pakistani or Sri Lankan or something. "The celery stick is a bit much, don't you think?" He addressed this to the girl, who had apparently barely registered his presence beside her.

"Hmm?" she said, and she met his gaze briefly. Where could she be from? Even just the *hmm* told him she spoke American, but she was something other than white. "Yeah, a bit much," she said. She returned to the notebook she was reading and writing in.

Fine, then. It was while returning to his perch that he noticed an older woman walking toward the back of the lounge with a pack of cigarettes.

What was this? Could there be . . . ? Yes, there *was* a smoking lounge attached to this lounge. The rich world was still surprising him. You could smoke . . . *inside an airport*. He put his drink down by his seat and ambled pointedly toward what turned out to be a negative-pressure conservatory-type thing labeled, romantically, *Fumoir*. Would wonders never cease? The problem now was that he had no tobacco. There was only one other lounger in the *fumoir*, the woman whom he had followed in. He bummed a smoke from her and lifted two extra from the back of the pack. She was Israeli. Mark heard all about her granddaughter in New York while he sucked the life out of a slender cigarette. The low drone of the extractor system made the lady hard to hear. Plus her accent didn't help. And it was a smoking room, the fancy name notwithstanding, and smelled like it; no amount of expensive up-dressing could disguise that.

In the silent outside beyond the frosted glass of the *fumoir*, the sun made a shimmer of things, and little trains of luggage carts snaked down painted-on tarmac-avenues. The tires on planes: Were they little or big? They looked amusingly diminutive beneath the planes but massive next to the jumpsuited men who serviced them. Maybe the sixth or seventh step could be something like Keep It in Perspective. Or better yet: Choose Your Perspective.

He returned to his spot in the lounge. Shoot, he had left the Jumble faceup on his papers. Actually, he'd left all his stuff unguarded. Is that just one of the things you can do when you are among the first class? He hoped so. But, no, there must still be a type of thief who operates within the wealth-saddled set, lifting merch from his hosts and fellow travelers: the cigarette case from the end table, the Rolex from the gym locker, the Vicodin from the medicine cabinet. He should be more careful. Step Nine: Watch Your Fucking Back.

He returned to the Jumble. LAVNI. He squinched up his eyes. Nothing.

The girl at the bar was still rabbiting away in her notebook. It was strange that she had been so cool to his opening. Not strange because he was all that or anything. But who doesn't have time for a little interaction? Sheesh. *Vilan?* No. *Laniv?* No. *Nilav?* No. *Anvil?* Wait, was *anvil* a word? Yes, that thing you just hammer away on. Ha—three words expertly unjumbled. But *anvil* yielded only an *A,* which he scribbled down next to the other letters he had netted. What would a lazy aphorist need? And what the fuck was *shambu? Hubasm?*

His phone chirruped at him. It was a message from Nils. Meeting location changed. Await instructions.

Well, excuse me, he thought. A different kind of waiting, when you don't know how long you'll be waiting. He closed his eyes, just to rest, not to sleep. As if providing a living caution against public sleeping, an overweight man snored at random intervals in the corner, drool like beetle silk strung between his slack lower lip and the fist-size knot of his iridescent purple tie.

Maybe *busham* was a kind of plant, or a unit of measurement. Hadn't he heard something like that? Like, twelve bushams to a furlong or something? He stood up and neatened his piles of papers and put on his jacket and buckled his valise and put it in his seat. He ate a breath mint. He walked to the bar.

"Make me another one of these, would you?" he said to the barman. Then, turning to the girl, he said, "Have you ever heard of the word *busham?*"

"Excuse me?" she said.

"*Busham. B-u-s-h-a-m?* Is that a word? Like a measure of something?"

"I think you mean *bushel,*" she said. She might be younger than him, but she was worn already around the eyes, or maybe just recently underslept. She was ragged but beautiful in the way that hair-gel ads were always trying to sell raggedness as beautiful.

"Ah. Yes. *Bushel.*" Mark bit his lower lip.

The girl returned to her notebook, but then seemed to reconsider. "Why do you ask?" she said. Whether this was out of patronizing politeness or genuine interest, Mark could not tell. He could work with either, for now.

"Oh, it's just this thing I have to copyedit. And I think there's a mis-print."

"It sounds like *ambush,* but swapped around," she said.

Well, hell: *ambush.* "Yeah, *ambush,*" he said. "Thanks."

"No problem."

The barman had stuck a stalk of celery in Mark's drink. "Oh, it's fine like that," Mark said, but not before the man had flung the celery stalk in the bar sink so that it suddenly seemed as if Mark was saying that the bar-man needn't make the whole drink all over again; as if he, Mark, were forgiving the celery contagion. He realized this made him look like an asshole, so he was especially grateful upon receipt of his drink and made a stupid *mmm-mmm* sound when he put the drink to his lips, standing there at the bar. That made him look like a real douchebag, so he left a ten-pound note on the bar and retreated.

Okay, so *ambush* gave up its *A* and its *H*. So he had *C, K, S, A, A, A,* and *H.*

Well, the first word was obviously just *A,* the article. Give one *A* to each of the remaining two words. *A wash cak? A cash kaw?*

Oh, how he sometimes despised himself. In his seminars, he was al-ways warning against self-pity, which everyone knows was this terrible character flaw, with its overtones of mope and sob and gripe. But what about straight-up self-despising, like, with good reason? Aren't you sup-posed to be appalled at yourself sometimes? He meant not just the confusion over the drink order just then, or the midday drinking, or the being stumped by a juvenile word game when he was under binding con-tract to deliver a book within weeks. He meant his general dishonesty, the part of him that always had to calculate his approach angle to any sit-uation. Presumably, everyone did this some of the time. You can't just blob around, all id, like a clothed baby. You had to game it. But he had gotten to the point where it was all game. How much better waking life must be for people who did not operate this way. Here was the self-pity part, he supposed, because it seemed to him that he had an invisible handicap, and if buses could kneel for wheelchairs, the world should be able to accommodate him somehow.

That girl looked like his ex, but more exotic. He had half a mind to go back and try to talk to her again. Like his ex, she had a palpable prickliness about her, but that was the kind of wall he liked breaching.

His ex. Thinking about her now made him feel shitty. He'd really messed that one up. What if you got only one chance at something like that? What if you made enough poor choices that your life was going to suck no matter what? What then, self-help guy? Five minutes of thoughts like that began to have a worrying cardiac effect—like the muscles of his heart were snapping; like his blood was becoming thinner. Surely, that was not happening? When you had anxiety attacks, the first rule was Tell No One About Them. Or at least, if you did, describe them in such a way that others were left with the impression that the condition was the result of your being a very sensitive and intelligent person. What you *did not* want to do was make the complaint so that the solution—do not smoke, do not drink—was plain.

The second rule—or the first, really—was Don't Forget to Breathe, which Mark now saw could really be Steps One through Ten.

What *was* going on in his upper chest? If he cardiac-arrested right now, would that ace steward zip over and defibrillate him? A couple of minutes of controlled breathing while looking out the window at the beautiful planes, and he became less aware of his splashing heart. There was a 747 parked—parked?—outside. *The swannish head of that plane is so graceful,* he thought. Mark let himself sink into the leather of the seat, apologized to his body, made it certain promises.

He did not need another drink. Actually, ice water was the way forward. He returned to the bar.

This time, she spoke to him.

"How's the edit?" she asked. She had a nice smile.

Step Seven: Put Yourself Forward. "Well, you know, I wasn't really copyediting anything. I was doing the Jumble. You know what the Jumble is?"

"No."

He showed her the folded page, which had gotten crinkly and shroudish from his efforts with it.

"That thing? I thought that was a cartoon."

"Well, it is, kind of. But you have to solve it." The barman had approached them and Mark asked for a glass of water. "I didn't want to tell you that before because it's not a very high-minded game, the Jumble. That's probably pretty stupid, huh? To lie to a stranger about something like that."

"I don't know that it's stupid to lie," she said. "It seems weirder to cop to the lie."

Mark smiled and nodded in a touché kind of way. Then he said: "Well, will you help me solve the Jumble?"

She smiled and said sure. He sat next to her and was pleasantly aware of her proximity. He thought at first she smelled like peanuts, but then he realized that that was the little dish of peanuts on the bar. She made short work of the Jumble answer: A Hack Saw.

He didn't like it. "What's he supposed to do with a saw? Saw those books in half?"

"No. Saw, like a saying—you know, an aphorism. A hack saw would be, like, a poorly made aphorism."

"Yeah, I get that," Mark said petulantly, "but there's supposed to be more of a . . . a linkage between the picture and the answer to the riddle thing. Like the guy should need the other kind of saw, a wood saw. Or it should have been, 'What the lazy *carpenter* aphorist needed to finish the job.' I think that's unfair."

She laughed at him and said, "Well, it's *way* down on the list of unfairnesses, you have to admit."

Fuck, another zinger. He liked her. See, he was not a vain idiot; he didn't mind being made fun of. "I'm Mark," he said, and when he asked her name, she said, "Leila, no, I mean Lola," which was really very suspicious. She was a choreographer. Where was she traveling?

"You know, I'd rather not talk about it," she said. "What about you? What do you do?"

"I'm a consultant," he said. "I have a meeting with a big client today, but I don't know whether it's canceled or what. I've been here for hours. I'm just supposed to wait to find out if the meeting's off or been rescheduled. What's the longest you think someone's waited in an airport lounge?"

"You can't just go home? Have them call you when they know where you're going?"

"Go home? No. No way. Too big a client."

They both just sat there for a few beats. Strangers at a bar.

"Do you have any cards?" she asked him.

"Business cards?" He patted his pockets in that too-elaborate way that cheap people do to convey their wallet-lessness.

"No. Playing cards. Maybe they have cards here."

Did he have playing cards? Usually at least two decks. Sometimes a Svengali deck or a forcing deck. He went back to his corner and dug in his valise. He pocketed a forcing deck and returned to the bar waving a legit one.

He let her choose the game. She liked a simple nine-card kind of rummy he hadn't played in years. She said she'd played it with her dad when she was young.

He let her win a couple of hands to suss out her game play, baited some discards to see whether she favored the knock or the hoard. She was a decent player; handled her cards with little fuss and displayed no obvious tell when he threw her a card she was after.

"I hope you don't consult on card games," she said to him, her pretty sloe eyes twinkling. So he ordered a beer and took the next three hands.

The man asleep in the corner was listing now and harrumphing pachydermishly at regular intervals.

After Mark had beaten her soundly a third time, he noticed that Lola's or Leila's eyes had gone from twinkly to annoyed.

"Want to play something else?" he asked her.

"No. It's your deal," she said. "I'm going to use the bathroom." She took her shoulder bag with her. Which might mean that he hadn't cleared sociopath yet. But her little rolly suitcase was still beneath her stool.

Mark took a card from the forcing deck in his pocket, a deck composed entirely of jacks of spades; he wrote his name and his New York mobile number across the face of the jack and slipped the card, jack out, behind the little plastic window on the top of her suitcase, the place meant to frame an ID. Once she was rolling that suitcase around again, the jack would be hard to miss.

When she came back from the bathroom, he taught her Conquian, a Mexican game from which rummy games are descended.

"Okay. You actually know a lot about cards," she said. "Were you hustling me?"

He had always liked the term *hustler,* with its confused connotations of hard work and underhandedness. "I think that would require money bets," he said. Answer and don't answer.

"Do you know any tricks?"

"I do not like the term," he said archly.

She smiled at that. "Come on. Show me what you got."

What should he give her? The Dunbury Delusion? The Chicago Opener? Or something showier, like a cascade control? The real trick he had already accomplished. That's how it always is.

He started his patter. "I mean, the thing with cards is, they all have these incredible stories behind them, you know? The numbers, the characters. Like the seven of clubs. You wouldn't want to be alone with a seven of clubs."

She gave him a *yeah, right* face, but he widened his eyes and rocked his chin slightly. "I'm serious, Lola," he said. "You don't wanna fuck with a seven of clubs. Excuse my language."

"Excused."

He riffed and riffled and shuffled and shenaniganned. He was still using the legit deck, so he let her hold and handle the cards. She was obviously confirming that these were the same cards she had just played with.

"Nines and sevens have a certain thing going on, a kind of charge," he said. "If I were a mathematician, I maybe could say why. I'm not, so I can't. But it's definitely there." He flipped a seven of diamonds and then a nine of spades rapidly out of a spread deck; not an illusion at all, just a demonstration of digital finesse. "Strangely, when suited, they seem not to like each other." He drew a nine of diamonds and held it near the seven on the bar, then popped it so it jumped from his hand. As it tried to sail off the bar, he snatched it out of the air with his other hand. Her mouth actually opened a bit; a tiny misalignment of her two front teeth caught his eye.

"How about you?" he asked her. "You have any relationship with a particular card?"

"You serious?"

He *mm-hmm*ed.

"No. I'm not really into numerology. I think that sort of thing's rather vicious, actually."

"You mean superstitions do harm and should not be indulged?"

"Yes. That's exactly what I mean."

"Fair enough. Well, how about the shape of a suit? Its color? You must have some response to those."

She considered this. "Spades," she said. "If I have to choose."

Most people chose spades. "Was it only rummy that you played when you were little?" Mark asked. "Any other games?"

"Stupid ones. War. Spit. Go Fish. My dad once tried to teach us a Persian game, but it had funny cards, and we were bored."

Of course: she was Persian. He was pretty sure that meant Iranian. "Go Fish is an honorable game, I think. Where did you play?"

"What do you mean?"

"Like, was it around a coffee table?"

"Yes. It was." She narrowed her eyes. "Is this one of those sneaky fake-mystic tricks? Like, everyone remembers a coffee table?"

He narrowed *his* eyes at *her* and appeared to consider. Then he said, "Most remember a coffee table. Some a carpet. But that doesn't make it a sneaky fake trick." He sounded a little hurt. "We're just talking here."

Saying *We're just talking here* makes your interlocutor feel aggressive.

"Yeah. It was this wagon-wheel thing. With a glass top."

He swapped the legit deck for the forcing deck. He did this quickly, beneath the cover of one of his large hands. It would have looked odd had he not spent the past ten minutes doing even slicker manipulations. "Okay," he said, "I want you to choose a card. Then look at it and do not show me. But it's important that you really think hard about the card once you've chosen it, once you've looked at it. I mean, I suppose you could try to think of a different one to mess me up, but then I might not be able to accomplish this. And what fun would that be?"

"Way to lower expectations," she said.

He fanned the deck on the bar before her.

"Turn around," she said.

If she looked at more than one card, he was cooked: there were fifty-one jacks of spades before her. But he turned his back without hesitation. At least that way he could easily prep for reswapping the decks.

"Okay," she said, "I've chosen a card."

"You thought hard about it? You put it back?" he asked, still turned away from her.

"Yep."

He swiveled around, scooped up the fan in his left hand, and then appeared to pass it to his right. In fact, the forcing deck stayed tucked in the meat of his wide left palm and then dropped soundlessly into his lap. He concentrated intently on the legit deck, now returned to the stage. So did she. He held it as delicately as a baby bird.

"Are you going to shuffle those?" she asked.

"You want me to?"

She considered. "Yeah."

He looked concerned. Then he shuffled the hell out of that deck. His riffles were as quick as machinery but as smooth as wavelets meeting on the sand. *Crak-crak* went the deck halves as he rapped their sides on each other before knitting them together like a zipper; a tiny *whir* rose from their arched congress. He stopped. "Here, I think," he said, then he held the deck delicately again. "The card you chose is on top. Go ahead and look."

She reached out to take it.

"Wait!" He said that so loud that the barman jumped a little and a man with horse-head cuff links lowered his *Financial Times*. She snatched her hand back and then looked sheepish and then annoyed. "Sorry," he said. "I think I screwed up." He shuffled the deck for another thirty seconds and then re-offered it to her.

"You sure?" she asked, all scolding.

"I'm sure."

She plucked the top card from the deck and brought it to her vision.

This is actually the hardest part: enduring the disappointment in the eyes of the mark when the wrong card is drawn. He could see in her dark eyes the hope change to something like hurt. She twirled the card between two fingers for him to see — a seven of diamonds.

"That wasn't it?" he asked lamely. She shook her head. He looked genuinely embarrassed. Once, the mark had by chance drawn the same card as he had forced, and Mark had had to act all pleased with himself when in fact he was wondering how he was going to get the force card from the woman's hatband. You could, of course, remove the force card from the legit deck before this stage in the routine, but that was one more maneuver that could be spotted. More than two or three close-up techniques was too many for a routine. The illusion lay elsewhere.

"Fucking sevens," he said under his breath.

"Try it again," she said to him quickly, as if he had just fallen off his bike.

"It's not really like that," he said grumpily. Then he brightened a bit. "Maybe it's the next one."

She was game and drew the next card. Nope. Even the air around them seemed to wilt.

"Okay, I'm going to have to actually draw the card to the top. This is kind of an advanced maneuver." He cupped the deck in front of himself at eye level, stared daggers at it.

"Okay, now draw the top card. It's yours."

She regarded him suspiciously. She drew the top card. This time, she could not even meet his gaze. She flopped the card down before him.

"I take it the king of diamonds was not your card?"

She shook her head.

"Was your card a king at least?"

She shook her head again. "You want to know what my card was?"

It is when they ask this that you can stop.

"No," he said, convincingly deflated.

"You want another drink?" she asked.

"Might as well."

She ordered a glass of wine for him and one for herself. She raised her glass to him, but he was already gulping his, so they were both embarrassed. She returned to her notebook.

"You have a stage name?" she asked him a minute later. "Maybe you need a stage name."

"A stage name? You think that's the problem?" he asked. "How about Deveraux the Baffled?"

"That's pretty good. Is Deveraux your real name? What kind of a name is that?"

"I'd rather not talk about it," he said.

"Oh, sorry."

"I'm kidding. Yeah. It's my name. It's Acadian."

"Acadian? You mean, like, Cajun?"

"Well, that makes me feel rather like a chicken dish, but yeah."

The SineCo rep approached from behind.

"Mr. Deveraux? Sorry to keep you waiting. It seems that the location of your meeting has changed. I have passage for you to Hong Kong. Will that be all right?"

Hong Kong. He'd never been. Odd, because Mark could have sworn that Straw said that *Sine Wave* had been up in the fjords last week. "Oh, that's fine. Thank you for seeing to that." So reasonable. He tried to note whether Lola had gotten any of this: Hong Kong, location changed, his unperturbedness.

Seldom is an illusionist offered an exit like this. The reveal would come in a third act. The SineCo rep hovered behind him.

"Well, look, Lola," he said to her. "Good luck, okay?"

"Oh, yeah, thank you. Mark, wasn't it?"

"Yeah, Mark." Off the high stool and back on terra shiny, Mark found his equilibrium. He wasn't as drunk as he had feared, could do a convincing imitation of a weary-for-good-reason business traveler. The fact that the SineCo rep had said *passage* and not *ticket* gave Mark reason to hope that he was going to Hong Kong on one of the Sine aircraft; the excitement of this prospect momentarily overpowered the torpor of six hours' drinking. "So maybe I'll see you again in one of these places?"

"Unlikely," she said. "Good luck with your meeting." And then, sly-like, "You'll want to work on that trick."

"Yeah, I'll do that," said Mark.

DUBLIN

Coming through the sliding glass doors of the Dublin airport with her satchel and her nom de guerre, Leila saw a man holding a piece of paper on which was written in sloppy Sharpie *L. Montes*. He was holding it in that who-gives-a-shit sort of way that taxi drivers use to show that they are not limo drivers. But he softened when he saw that L. Montes was a girl. He introduced himself as Dermot and was open-faced and bright-eyed and brisk; he led her past the taxi rank to a side lot and opened the door to the backseat of a clean but unfancy black car.

When she asked, "Where're we going?" he just said, "Stoneybatter." When she asked where that was, he just said, "Between Cabra and the quays." Was this a real taximan or an agent working on behalf of Dear Diary? He had a meter, but it wasn't running. He played talk radio—people complaining about a levy on sidewalks or something. Then there was a news bulletin, but it wasn't in English. It sounded to her like the rough forest language of a stick-waving people.

"Is that Gaelic?" she asked Dermot.

He turned it down. "Irish," he said.

"I know," said Leila. "The language. Is it Gaelic?"

He found her eyes in the rearview. "The English word for the Irish language is *Irish*." He said it kindly, but you could tell he had said it a few times before.

Leila was embarrassed. She actually knew that, or had known that once. In West Africa, she'd worked with an Irishman who sang beautifully and spoke his native tongue when he talked to his wife on the satellite phone. "We're like Navajo windtalkers," he had said to Leila, "until the guy across the train car turns out to be a Paddy."

Dermot brought her to the door of a little brick house on a street of little brick houses on a hill laddered with streets of little brick houses. She was met at the door by a man who quickly ushered her inside and into a kitchen and then said his name was Feargal and would she like a cup of tea. She nodded sure and he asked had she had a nice journey. So she said, "Fine. Except for the part where you people abducted me."

"Yeah, sorry about that," said Feargal. "We usually take things a bit slower than we have with you. We'll make our case to you as quickly as we can. There's a meeting tonight."

Leila nodded, gave him zero else.

"And, sure, while you're waiting, would you like to take our eye test and get a number?" he said.

Was he joking? Was that an Irish joke?

"No. No eye test for me. Just give me back my shit and get me to California," said Leila, tough as tacks.

But then a girl called Sarah came in, and she was kind and took Leila to a room on the third floor of the skinny brick home that had a big window in an eave and a white mattress on an iron bed and a writing desk and a plumbed hand basin and a wooden chair with a towel on it. It looked like the bedroom that Leila had been dreaming about for years.

"You should sleep for a few hours," said Sarah. "You'll want to be sharp for this next part."

"Look, Sarah, I am really here only to get my stuff back. I am not at all impressed with being shanghaied by you people, and I am not inclined to hear about your cause."

"You weren't shanghaied. You were Caracased."

"What?"

"They did a dine-and-dip on you in terminal three, didn't they? But they gave you cover and cash? Yeah, that's a Caracas, not a Shanghai. But anyway, c'mere: I know you need your devices and your documents back and I'll make sure they're returned after the meeting."

"How about the rest of my bags?"

"We pulled all those into our system. The four suitcases you had going to LA will be there tomorrow and will wait for you. We separated a fifth piece, a North Face duffel that scanned as your main traveling case. That one will be brought to wherever you spend the night."

Leila had in fact been extensively trained about how to act in the event of abduction. But none of the information that she could recall had any bearing on this situation. That had been all about crouching behind the engine block and how to keep from crying. The course materials had not addressed soft-touch abductors who gave you a nice room to nap in and rerouted your primary traveling case so you'd have it in time for bed.

"Sleep, Lola, for a few hours. There's a loo with a bath back there. And I'll make sure no one disturbs you. I'll come get you later, and I'll tell you where we're going then."

It must have been midday when Sarah and Feargal and Leila left the little brick house. They got into a small panel van with *Pat's Flowers* painted on its side. Sarah sat in the back with Leila. Feargal got in to drive but didn't turn the key. He was waiting for something.

"I'm supposed to make you wear a blindfold," said Sarah.

"Yeah, well, I'm not going to do that."

"I didn't think you would," said Sarah.

"It's just that things are getting Dicey Reilly around here," said Feargal from the front.

"If you give me my stuff back right now, I won't look out the window. How about that?" said Leila.

"Just go, Ferg," said Sarah.

He shrugged disapproval but started the van.

They drove down a hill, past a prison that looked like a church, and a church that looked like a prison. One block was pub, pub, cobbler, bookie, pub, pub, church. And then new buildings—*new* as in "unfinished," like, boom, here's some glass and steel. Feargal was giving her a little patter about the city ("There's the oldest boxing club in Dublin . . . There's the chipper where the general got shot") when Sarah, who had been looking out a tinted port in the van's rear, interrupted him:

"Ferg, what about this little white Ford here?"

He looked in his side mirror judiciously. "Yeah, that's no good," he said. "Hang on." Then he swung a very hard right into a lane. Even Leila saw the reaction from the two men in the little white Ford, watched their shoulders hunch in frustration as they drove by.

"Go to the fishmonger," said Sarah decisively. She must outrank Feargal, Leila thought, or else they knew each other very well.

Feargal nodded and sped down the narrow lane. Then their progress was blocked by a clutch of undead drinkers in tattered coats who glared wreck-faced at the van but shambled aside when they got a tougher glare back from Feargal. A minute later, the flower van was idling outside a roll-up door, and Sarah was on her phone, waiting for someone to pick up, nerves only apparent from her foot joggling on the rubber-matted floor of the van. Then a change in her face and she said simply, "We need refuge," while Feargal leaned close to the windshield—Leila realized he was showing his face to a camera she could not see. The door rolled up—more swiftly than those things usually did—and Feargal zipped in, the tires squeaking on the dry floor. The door rolled down behind them with a clatter.

They were in the back of a fish store. Feargal and Sarah got out to speak to a man, presumably the man who had answered the phone and opened the door. He was in a bloodied white smock, silver gloves and a long knife in loops on his belt. He and Sarah talked, leaning close together. The rank and briny smell of fish was rolling into the van, its progress slowed by the refrigerated chill of the room. Sarah came back. She leaned herself into the van.

"Okay, you're going on by yourself. Someone else is going to collect you on the quays."

"No. I want you to come with me." *If there's one you think you can trust, try to stick with that one*. Leila remembered that from the courses.

"I can't. It's either me or Feargal they're after. Sorry. I was certain you were safe. That house we brought you to is a week old. But I'll be where you're going. You've just got to get to the quays."

Feargal, on his phone, called back to them: "Not even the quays. She's just got to make it to the Horse Market. She can get scrubbed there."

"What do you mean, scrubbed?" said Leila. And she thought, *Eww, a horse market?* She was looking at the long knife on the fishmonger's belt.

But there was no time to object. Sarah took her by the hand and led her through the store and then hustled her out the front door and onto a deserted street.

"That way," said Sarah, and pointed down the road. "You'll be met at the market." In her voice now there was urgency instead of kindness.

Leila took off, not running, exactly, but moving quickly. She was scared. She wished she weren't alone on a deserted street in a strange city.

But then she rounded a corner and came into a long, cobbled square, and she wasn't alone anymore. It was wild, teeming with man and beast—five hundred souls, easy. And the horses, if that's really what they were, were shocking to her. A few were full-size and strong-seeming, but most of them were runted and stunted, some the size of dogs. They were being raced and prodded and kicked and brushed and preened by a strange class or type of people the likes of whom Leila had never seen, people who looked to her like white Aboriginals in gaudy leisurewear. Men in small groups were drinking from plain brown bottles, and some were staggering; boys and girls roamed in packs, flirting and fighting.

And as she stood there taking in the anachronism, two light-eyed boys galloped past her on a pair of raggedy ponies, the ponies' shoes ringing the cobbles, the boys bold as brass. Leila staggered back from the galloping boys and into the dark doorway of a pub.

"Keep going, Lola," said the man who steadied her. He was in a cap and tie and dirty shirt. "Get into the meat of it," he said, and pointed at the market square. And then he did a quick head tick, which Leila followed, and saw that half a block away, a tall man in a too-heavy coat had been startled by the same galloping boys. She saw him look for her—it was one of the men from the white Ford.

So she dove into the market. Cap and Tie followed her, and Too-Heavy Coat was quick behind; Too-Heavy Coat was talking into a phone, and he was making right for her. But a commotion engulfed him suddenly. Leila turned around to see what had happened: a clutch of men had surrounded him and were accusing him of some transgression, loudly, but in a language that made no more sense to her than stones clattering in a wave's sandy pullback. Some of the men carried heavy sticks, the nonviolent purpose of which was hard to fathom. Cap and Tie brushed past her strongly. "Keep on, girl," he said as he did. "Not far now."

It had been done for her, she saw—the entrapment of her pursuer. These people were somehow on her side. So she kept on, through the long square, past old women in multiple skirts and young men in spotless tracksuits and a little girl swinging a broken bottle at her tormentors, who ducked and darted and laughed. Leila was invisible, ignored. But if she stopped moving, someone—one person in a small task- or drink-engaged group—would catch her eye and give her a distinct *tsst* or a nod and then return to ignoring her. And at the far end of the square, the vibe was less intense—there were tourists snapping pictures and vendors selling things sweet and greasy; a spiffy streetcar clanged by. She was back in the real world.

And there, in a taxi rank by the streetcar, was Dermot, her taximan from the morning, which seemed like a week ago now. She beelined toward him and he saw her coming and opened the rear door and she slid into the black vinyl of the backseat as if it were home.

"What the fuck was that?" she asked him.

He laughed as he quickly started the taxi. "That was the Horse Market."

"They were speaking . . . that wasn't even Irish, was it?"

"No. That would be the Cant."

"The what?"

"The Cant. Gammon. Shelta." The words meant nothing to her. Dermot saw her confusion. "The Traveler language," he said.

Dimly, Leila recalled a movie that Rich had loved in which Brad Pitt played a bare-knuckled fighter who spoke unintelligibly. Leila had heard about Travelers once but assumed the whole thing—a nomadic white clan people, unassimilated by their small modern European host state?—was too bizarre to really exist. Because she had spent fifteen years helping the downtrodden, Leila sometimes forgot that she didn't know everything about downtroddenness.

Dermot steered the little taxi down a hill and across a river that was channeled into a sort of unsightly trough with two lanes of traffic down both sides, like vinyl piping. Then up a hill and past about ten churches and into a smaller web of streets dotted with butchers and newsagents, phone stores and charity shops and bakeries.

"Where are we now?" Leila asked Dermot, leaning forward in her seat.

"The Liberties," said Dermot.

They stopped outside a building with its name carved upon it: *Widows House of the Parish of St. Nicholas Without & St. Luke.* A man inside opened the front door. He was in his fifties, wearing a leather jacket.

"You're Lola Montes," he said to Leila by way of greeting.

"No, I'm not," said Leila. "What's your name?"

"Nicotine Lozenge," said the man, proud and mischievous.

Leila sighed, without rancor.

Neither was this place, apparently, their final destination; it was just another safe house. But the so-called Nicotine Lozenge offered her newspapers and a seat at his kitchen table and tea, which he served in a pot, and he did that slightly dainty thing where he held the lid of the teapot with one finger when he poured. Her dad did it that way.

"You've been very reasonable, Lola," said Nicotine. "We appreciate that."

"You've left me no choice but to be. And you people also keep implying that you're going to be able to help me somehow. Anyway, you're really burning through the amount of time and attention I have for you and your cause."

"All right, so," he said. "Milk?"

"What?"

"For your tea."

"Yes, please."

"How much?"

"Milk?"

"Time."

He was using on her some of the one-step-ahead stuff she used on people when she wanted them to feel like she was in charge.

"Three, four hours," she said.

It was a bluff, they both knew. If Leila walked and tried to get back into the ticketed world herself, she would, as Ricky Ricardo used to say ominously, *Have some 'splainin' to do.* Still, she wanted to let this man know she was not someone to be pushed around and that Dear Diary better make its pitch soon.

He took a sip of his tea and said: "For the last ten years, Lola, what have you been working for?"

"You mean, what's my employment history?"

He gave a small look-down that meant *Don't be obtuse.* But he said only, "No. More broadly."

She took a sip of her tea. So delicious, that tiny bit of nuttiness. On a plate on the table there were biscuits spilling from a torn-open packet. "I don't like it that a baby girl can get born into a place where it sucks to be a girl. Or, for that matter, where she'll be from the wrong tribe or sect, or just be dirt poor. Obviously, that's not fair, so, yeah, I've been trying to do something about that." She took a biscuit from the plate, snapped it in half. "I haven't exactly made massive headway, if that's what you're getting at."

"No one has," said Nicotine. "The problems are rather systemic, are they not?"

"Listen, Mr. Lozenge, I don't want to discuss development politics with you. I'd rather know who was trying to follow me through a horse market, how you guys think you can help me, and when is this meeting you dragged me here for."

"The man we kept from following you was one of the Committee's men. They've started to move on us in a way that we weren't expecting, and everyone around here is pretty scared. They decapitated London and New York and Berlin last week. We can't even find some of our key people. That's why we got you out of London directly. And I wouldn't say we dragged you, exactly. So there's that. As far as helping you, we might be able to clear your father. There's a man who works for the Committee's frame shop. We know a man who knows that man."

"You really just call them the Committee?"

"When they started—when they still called themselves anything— they were the Committee for Cloud Acquisition."

"But why'd they screw with me in the first place? What did I see in the forest?"

"One of their computers."

"What do you mean, *one of their computers?*"

"Their computers are very big—big as in they drive golf carts around them. And your e-mail was seriously inconvenient. A librarian at the CIA tried to unmask some imagery, and when he couldn't, he asked questions of the geospatial people, questions that other people heard him ask."

"Yeah, that would be Joel. He's dogged," said Leila, a bit proudly; they'd had the briefest of flings, years ago. Joel was a Jew from Maine, into vinyl and beer and palindromes.

"Well, then I'm sorry to tell you that Joel *was* dogged. He died two days ago."

The biscuit went dry in her mouth. "Joel is dead?"

Nicotine nodded. Then paused in a way that was meant to convey something. "Brain aneurysm," he said.

Her heart fell into her guts. "You're telling me that the Committee killed Joel. That's what you're saying, isn't it?"

"That's what I'm saying."

She kept from bursting into tears only by looking very hard at Nicotine Lozenge. He had just upped the stakes. If it turned out he was fucking with her, she wanted to recall the moment exactly. "Did I get anyone else killed?"

"No. Everyone you contacted had their scrutiny numbers turned way up. But only Joel did anything with your question, so he was the only one they intervened on. And then you, of course, and your father."

"So why didn't they just, you know, 'decapitate' me? Or my father? Isn't a frame job more expensive than killing someone?"

Nicotine did the quick, exaggerated frown that meant *fair point*. "Yes, it is. I don't know why they didn't just kill you"—he said it a bit breezily for her liking—"though, in fairness, they generally try to avoid such direct interventions—murder, frame jobs, all that. At least, they used to avoid those things. Most of their interventions are the kinds you don't know have happened. They make you sick, they get you fired, they keep you down by numbers. But ever since Parker Pope came on board, they've gotten nasty. Aggressive."

"Parker Pope, the CEO of Bluebird?"

"Indeed."

"So they can just get a middle-school principal dragged away by the FBI?"

In answer, Nicotine snapped his fingers expertly—*snap!*—as if cutting the air before him.

"So tell me what evidence they left behind so I can bring it to the police and get my dad cleared of this shit."

"It's not that easy, Lola," said Nicotine.

"Quit it with the code names, would you? My name is Leila."

At that, a young dark-black man came into the kitchen. *Dude must have been in the other room, not making a peep,* thought Leila.

"We generally do not use our real names in this organization," said the young man.

Leila didn't show her surprise at his entry. "So Lola Montes is my code name? That's a lame one."

"You pick your own," he said. "They needed to give you a temporary for the Caracas. But if you want a code name, you'll have to join us, and if you want to join us, you'll have to take the eye test."

"No, thanks. What's yours?"

"Kwame X. Nkrumah."

"That's pretty good."

"Thank you. I like it."

"You going to this meeting also?"

"I am."

"What's on the agenda?"

Kwame nodded at Nicotine. Nicotine said, "There are a few new people, like yourself. So we'll do the eye tests there. And we're trying to decide whether we can advance the launch."

Leila swam in the words—*advance the launch.* What was going on? Where was Sarah?

Nicotine saw her swimming. "Sorry. You don't know what the launch is. We hardly ever bring people in this fast. It's just that we need you up to speed very quickly."

"What for? What do you want me to do?" She could hear in her own voice the catch that meant desperation. Maybe all this nonsense intrigue was only to soften her up. But for what? And, no—they had let her nap.

"Do you know where I am from, Lola?" said Kwame.

"Ghana," she said. Leila knew some Africans and was good with accents.

He was surprised and showed it, briefly. "Yes. Bukom. In Accra. We say it is self-evident that we have the right to move about this planet. An inalienable right. So one of the things we do is help people move around outside of the legal systems they were born into."

She thought: *That just makes you traffickers.* But she held her tongue.

"After your e-mail, we analyzed you and saw that you have a very wide net. People who love and respect you are sprinkled all over."

Okay, first of all, she thought, *that last part was just some good-cop mind-fuck.* What was sprinkled all over were people hurt by her not loving them enough, hurt by her greener-pastures shtick.

"You analyzed me?"

"Don't feel all special," said Nicotine. "It takes about a minute. Anyway, we're going to need your help getting a bunch of machines to some remote parts of the world."

"What do I know about that?"

"A fair amount. But it's mainly *who* you know. Phone calls you could make to people in certain places who have a lot of time for you."

"What kind of machines do you need to get where?"

"Maybe you should limit the amount you're trying to take on board right now," said Nicotine. "At least until after the eye test."

"It's just the hardware we need to ship," said Kwame. "The software we can beam out."

"But what are you people trying to do? Your person in Heathrow said you're going to give people back their stolen information and issue them numbers."

"I wish Paige wouldn't do that," said Nicotine to Kwame. "It's really not her remit."

"We are a horizontal organization, no?" Kwame said to Nicotine.

"You get assigned to be a travel agent, you should be a travel agent," said Nicotine grouchily.

Kwame turned back to Leila. "We don't know exactly what we're going to do with what we've built. Some of us wish to wait some more before announcing ourselves. But others say we must become something known so that everyone can decide if our way would be better. And okay, with all this violence from the Committee, we have been forced to move ahead. There is a chance they will destroy us before we let every-one know what is going on."

"And tell me again what is going on?"

Nicotine leaned in. "A secret oligarchy has rigged the system past the point of its being correctable by legal political means. The world might tip the wrong way right now—toward the oligarchs. We probably have the technology to stop them—they don't know how much we know; they don't know what we have."

"What do you have?"

"The eye test and something else that I can't go into right here. Also, we've tapped their lines. Though we're losing that too. A year ago we had thousands of access points, but now we're down to . . . Kwame, you know the current number?"

"No, but Sarah knows. She spoke with Engineering this morning."

"Did she get out of that fish store okay?" asked Leila.

From the next room came the sound of a door being double-locked. And then Sarah's voice. "We had eight hundred twenty open portals yes-terday," she said, coming into the room carrying a heavy, clacketing trash bag over her shoulder. "But we're losing them fast."

Leila didn't like the cavalier entrance; she had been worried. "So that's why you're kidnapping people before you can even explain your poli-tics?" she asked all of them. "Because you're afraid you're about to lose a strategic advantage?"

"We *can* explain our politics," said Kwame with confidence.

"Then why don't I understand what's going to be so different when you run the place?"

No one answered her.

Then Sarah: "You're going to have to take the eye test."

When they left, they left in a hurry, and Dermot was outside in the idling black car. They sat all squished together. Leila was pressed up against Sarah. Leila had diagnosed in herself a minicrush on Sarah, which was ridiculous and inappropriate and probably Stockholm-y.

Dermot drove swiftly through the city, like Pac-Man ahead of the ghosts. They went back down a long hill and across the river again. It was a warm summer evening in a city made of stone, and the people were out—peddlers yelled about oranges, girls in heels clacked out of taxis, and men swelled from the doors of brass-heavy pubs. Outside of one place, a crowd in powdered wigs was drinking raucously.

"Hey, Sarah?" said Leila, not whispering, but quiet. "You still promise you'll get me my stuff back, and you'll get me home after this meeting?"

"I do," she said.

"How'd you guys do all this? What did Nicotine mean when he said you analyze people? And how did you swap my papers like that—the passport, the tickets? You did that in a food court."

"We've tapped the Committee's tap lines. So we can access as much data as they can. But we run different queries than they do. And we're read-only. And the passports and tickets? They're just basically bar codes and magnetic strips now anyway. That's all just ones and zeros. We have very good people at the ones and zeros, and an excellent art department."

The meeting was maybe sixty people in a long wooden library. For an hour, everyone just milled about and murmured; there were water bottles on a table, cans from a fridge. People spoke in hushed tones but looked excited, as if they were attending a surprise wake. Someone brought in long trays of empanadas and cake. Leila ate both, forklessly, from a plastic plate. She realized she was famished. At some signal, Sarah steered her into an anteroom, where she met a light-skinned black man in a sharp gray suit, gray like the breast of proud city pigeon. The man was in his forties and on the delicate end of handsome.

"You must be Lola Montes," said the man. "I'm Roman Shades."

Great. More suavery and pseudonyms. When would these people come clean? "Are you in charge here?" she said.

"We don't do it that way."

"Well, will you please tell me what the fuck is going on?"

"We need your help, Lola," said Roman Shades. "We'll do what we can for your father. You have my word."

"What do you want me to do?" she said.

"Will you look at this screen?"

Leila hesitated one more moment, then nodded a tiny assent, and Roman put before her a normal-seeming laptop, the black-plastic-binder-size kind that had gone from exotic to ubiquitous in the ten years that Leila was an adolescent in America. By now there must be piles of these—mountains of them—lying junked and dying all over the world. Leila had seen shrink-wrapped pallets of laptops like these loaded into the bellies of planes. Actually, technically, and reluctantly, she'd been responsible for some of those pallets—outdated computer equipment being "donated" by first-world transnationals back to Africa to avoid the expense of recycling and to get the tax write-off.

But when Roman unfolded this laptop, there was no booting up or opening of anything. Just a luminous blue rectangle with numbers in rows and columns, plus a few symbols Leila couldn't identify interspersed betwixt the numbers. The rows and columns weren't exactly staying still—they were shimmering—and the screen was rolling up; not zippily, like in *The Matrix*, but slowly, as if there were a monkey turning a wooden crank handle behind the computer.

"Okay, what do I do here?" Leila asked the small scrum around her.

"You just did it," said Sarah, who was receiving a little oblong sticker chittering out of a handheld printing device. Sarah and Roman and Feargal were quickly bent over it. "Do you want to know your number?" Sarah asked Leila.

"I know my number," said Leila. "Eight five one four six one one three two six two two five." She said it more easily than you could recite the rhymes your parents taught you.

"Yeah. But isn't that brilliant?" said Sarah, tearing off and then handing Leila the little sticker with the same number printed clearly upon it. "It's a fairly good number, actually."

*   *   *

And as Leila moved back into the main room, she tried to pinpoint what was different about the world, or her place in it. It wasn't much, actually. Or the effect wasn't cognitively intrusive. But there *was* something. Like a flush; like when you come downstairs after a thrilling sexual experience with a secret all through your body. But this wasn't fuzzy and sensual, like that feeling was. This was crisp and cerebral . . . and shared. Everyone in the long library was in on it. An open secret. These were the same strangers that had been in the room before she'd looked at that shimmering screen, but now they were known to her. Not in any intimate way. What's the opposite of intimate? But not the opposite of intimate as in estranged; the opposite as in abstract, as in broad. That's the way in which they were known to her, and she to them. So much information is conveyed by glance and stance; so much can pass between us. She trusted everyone here.

Some of her faculties seemed sharpened. Her eyesight was definitely better. She could dart her gaze around the room, hawklike, and take in a lot; she could read titles off spines at ten feet. Her sense of smell was unchanged, but that had already been excellent. Maybe her taste had ticked up, or maybe the empanadas were just very good and she was hungry.

When Sarah returned, Leila was in an alcove of atlases, traveling the world, an empanada pressed to her forehead.

"Are you all right?" said Sarah.

"Never better," said Leila.

"You're probably just getting used to the effect."

"The effect?"

"Don't worry—the trippy feeling will wear off soon. Then it's just a new way of being."

"I wasn't really worried," said Leila.

"Fair enough. Some people don't really like the connectivity part. You'll see that you can make as much or as little use of it as you need to. It's going to feel like you can speak a new language—but it's not a language you speak; you just kind of transmit it and receive it. It's dormant in all of us, though it comes out stronger in some people than in others.

We call it the Common Language, but no one has a clue how to use it yet, really, or what to do with it. You'd better eat hamburgers while you still can, though, because the Talk to the Animals people are fierce excited about the Common Language."

"But can I go back to the way I was before?"

"No"—Leila had known this would be Sarah's answer—"you can never go back. But Lola, I'm saying to you right now, hand on heart, that I've never wanted to go back. Not once. I've never wished for that smaller world. I lost nothing of myself when I joined with others. In a weird way, I see now that I always wanted this, that I'd always known it was possible. Anyway, get your skates on, missus. We need to get you to the airport."

Back in Dermot's car, lunging through Phibsborough, Leila asked Sarah, "Don't you need me to get machines to remote parts of the world or whatever?"

"Yeah, don't be worrying about that," said Sarah. Her window-side hair was getting severely tousled by the late, dark summer air. "We're generating a new task for you."

"But we're still doing a deal, right? You'll clear my dad if I do something for you?"

"We'll do our best," said Sarah. "But does it still feel to you like we're doing a deal here? Because it shouldn't feel like that anymore."

It didn't feel like that anymore. They were offering her a chance to be part of something grander than herself. These were her people now. She would put her shoulder to the wheel.

"You should have asked me straight out, though," Leila said. "About the eye test. You should have said there's no going back."

"There's no going back from anything, Lola. You learn something true, it sticks with you."

They were stopped at a light, Dermot's black car puttering. Leila noticed precisely the way traffic signals were mounted over Dublin intersections. This information belonged to her forever, as if she were storing it on an external hard drive. Was this another part of what Sarah called the effect?

"That's Bertie Ahern's boozer," said Dermot, from the front. He was pointing at a pub off their left flank. He drove like a jockey, his left hand rarely off the stick. Her dad drove that way. Cyrus Majnoun's number-one favorite thing about America? Drive-in restaurants. The man nearly wet his pants at the prospect. Had their father been in charge of meal planning in the Majnoun household, Roxana and Dylan and Leila would all have grown obese. "Look: we are kings and queens," he would say to his children as they sat in the family Tercel beneath ten thousand lumens, burgers on trays cantilevered from their rolled-down windows.

"But when will I know what it is I'm supposed to do?" she said to Sarah.

"Roman's working out the details. I'll get onto him now." She slipped her phone against her Leila-side ear.

A few minutes later, they rolled down a steep driveway and were admitted via another swiftly operated mechanical door into a bright warehouse arrayed with neat aisles of metal shelving twenty feet tall. Like the last scene in *Raiders of the Lost Ark*. Dermot rolled to a stop beside what appeared to be a staged living room: a cardboard TV before a coffee table and a leather sofa.

Leila got out of the car. "Are we in Ikea?"

"It's a new arrangement," said Sarah. "At night, Ikeas are Dear Diary dormitories."

"Whatever," said Leila.

"They're ideal. They're right beside the airport, they can sleep eighty comfortably, and if you're hungry, there's the meatballs. Kidding. Don't eat those meatballs. They come in on pallets."

"Absolutely. It's a good idea. It's just—you know—not widely known."

Sarah led Leila upstairs and through the circuitous showroom; they took the shortcut between Media Storage and Children's, walked against the arrows toward Bedroom. Leila shrugged a *Hey-there* at a trio of pajama-clad, toothbrush-holding Asian dudes. They *Hey-there*-shrugged back.

Sarah brought her to one of those little pretend apartments meant to show how an untethered urbanite might live in five hundred square feet: all you needed was squared magazines, three shirts, and a colander. Leila knew that that was a marketing deceit; she was relatively untethered, and she had more crap than would fit in this place. Plus, she and Rich had broken up in an Ikea—the one in Elizabeth, New Jersey—so the environment was not emotionally unladen for her.

But there was something funny about this demo apartment. She looked closer. It was real! The sink was plumbed—she turned on the cold tap and splashed herself—and there were sheets on the bed. She tugged at the string of the blinds and found behind them a real window, a view of a grimy annex of the airport beyond it. She turned and saw her green North Face duffel at the foot of the Malm bed with the Kvist bedding. Sarah stood at the door to the real pretend apartment.

"Are you staying here with me?" said Leila.

"No. Feargal and I have to clean down the Parish house."

Leila opened her duffel, put her hands on her own things. Her bag had not been tampered with—she always rigged a tube of moisturizer in a way that would tell her if it had been. (Once, in Sierra Leone, she had faced a skinny customs man who was *wearing her sunglasses* while examining her passport.) "That sounds dangerous. What if those dudes come back? What if they do here what they did in London and Berlin?"

"Don't mind that. It's different here."

"Here Ireland? What's Ireland got?"

"Twisty roads and an abhorrence of tyranny," said Sarah.

"So you guys will just melt back into the countryside?"

"Pretty much. Feargal and I just have to make sure no one leaves any hardware lying around."

"Like those eye-test machines?"

Sarah nodded.

"What *was* that, Sarah?"

Sarah sat down at the little table in the little kitchen. "Here, I know it's a lot to take in. Come here to me and I'll tell you what I know about the eye test."

Leila stopped fussing with her bag and sat beside Sarah.

"First of all, you know that sensate keenness you're probably still feeling? Well, that's more of a secondary effect; it's not actually what the eye test was designed to do. The eye test was designed to give a secure unique identifier to each human subject looking at that screen."

"It gave me a number."

"Or maybe it made up a number to represent some immutable and unique quality of you. But either way, everyone gets fifteen digits, and no two Diarists have come out with the same number. Not yet, anyways."

Leila counted in her head, looking up the way you do. "Mine's not fifteen digits."

"Sorry, it's fifteen *places*. There are two zeros that precede your thirteen numbers. They're silent. I've got four silent zeros. Don't worry about it."

"Who designed it? Was there a Dear Diary before the eye test?"

"Oh, there was, yeah. Dear Diary's been around for twenty years, I think, though it's been called by various names. The eye test is newer. It was made by a Diarist called Dr. Hugo Cranium. He was a sixteen-year-old who did biometrics work for the Defense Advanced Research Projects Agency in America. He wrote remote lie-detection software. And—well, to cut a long story short, he walked away from the place with the whole state of their art. That's why the machine's called a Cranium's Enumerator."

"What happened to him?"

"The Committee put a bomb under his Segway."

Leila laughed.

"I know, it sounds mental. But I'm serious."

"Oh."

"The first Enumerators were big clunky machines; they were like planetarium projectors. We had to use a totally dark room and play space music and it worked on only the ten percent who were really, really relaxable. Anyway, we got better at administering the bloody thing now, and once our genomics people were able to move the technology from, you know, electronic computers to the kind we can grow—"

Leila made a little *whachutalkinabout?* face.

"No one told you about how we grow our computers?"

"Yeah, no."

"Crap. Well, I don't really understand it. I'm Operations. But our computers don't need to be plugged in, although they do need to be watered and given sunlight, and they can talk to each other without, you know, the Internet. About a year ago, the IT people got Cranium's machine shrunk down to where they could put it in one of our computers, which look totally innocuous. That allowed us to distribute them more widely than we could before. We're trying to make it possible to put the eye test on the ordinary Internet, but the risk there is that the Committee will get ahold of it, reverse-engineer it.

"After even just a few months with the new laptop machines, there were enough people, with enough numbers, that some clever clogs noticed that the numbers generated for each subject could be considered mathematically."

Leila made a *whaddya-mean?* face.

"So, nine is not just nine—it's also three squared. Your number is *related* to you. Deeply. That's why the first thing everyone knows after the test is his or her number. And you probably know eight to thirteen digits of any other Diarist the moment you meet him or her. Sometimes, with the real sphinxes, it might be only six or seven. But in general, like. Anyway, it's a new science, or a new art, or whatever you'd call it, these numbers. Some Diarists are a bit spooked by it and try not to look too closely at their own. I see their point. But the numbers do mean something. And we really still understand nothing about our minds and how they work, the electro-limbic-chemistry part, right? We're preNewtonian when it comes to that. So why should this mystery stand out among the others? Maybe this is just the next gravity or something. A new age, and us at its birth. I can't really explain why, but when I saw your number, I knew that the logistics job wouldn't be the right one for you. Roman agreed. We asked some number people to put your number against what we need done now and come up with something that would suit you better. And I told them that you needed to be home within forty-eight hours."

"Thank you."

"So here's what we need you to do. You remember that guy who was working his moves on you in the Heathrow lounge? You didn't recognize him, but he's a bit famous. His name's Mark Deveraux. He's this life-change specialist lad; he wrote a book that loads of people loved."

"The card-trick guy?" Leila had found the jack of spades while she was putting her carry-on in the overhead bin. That was a damn good trick. "How do you know about that?"

"The bartender in the first-class lounge. He's a Diarist. And a Dubliner. Look, Lola, mostly, the Committee is a closed shop. It's a South Korean who doesn't leave his armored skyscraper; a Belorussian with food tasters and no photos on record; a pair of German twins in their seventies who manufacture seventy percent of all the pharmaceuticals outside of Asia. But SineCo is pretty much the Committee in North America; it's the front for all its operations. And the SineCo CEO — he's called Straw — he's not as isolated as these other fellows; he needs a certain amount of attention. He has that basketball team, and he's always endowing business schools and that sort of malarkey. And all that carry on makes SineCo one of the Committee's most exposed flanks. Right now, Straw is devoted to Deveraux. Deveraux has influence. We need to get to Deveraux."

"Yeah, but just because he played some card trick on me..."

Sarah shook her head. "You're not going to Deveraux. You're going to Portland, Oregon, to find a lad by the name of Leo Crane. Leo Crane went to college with your man Deveraux, and a few weeks ago he printed this odd broadside that more or less describes what's going on,

219

and in the broadside he claims to have 'incriminating footage' of Deveraux." She handed Leila a crinkly piece of paper folded four times. "Read it before you get there. We want you to find out what he's talking about."

"Why don't you just ask him? Sounds like he'd be glad to hear from you."

"You are us, Lola. But we don't want a full-recruit on Leo Crane. He might just be unwell, or fragile. He added some flourishes to his description of the Committee's plot that make it a little silly. Scientologists and the like. We don't administer the eye test to people whose grasp may be slipping.

"Lola, right now there are hundreds of Diarists working angles on how to get to someone in the SineCo organization. It's hard. The Committee runs a tight ship. Deveraux holds promise. We got started on the Leo Crane thing only when someone passed us this broadside he'd printed. But it may have become urgent. The Committee turned Crane's scrutiny numbers way up; he's currently under observation at a Committee-affiliated facility, which also makes it hard to extract him. So we're sending you to him, just to talk, to find out if he really has something useful on Deveraux or if he's just a pot cripple with a grudge and a good imagination. Plus, it's pretty much on your way home. Will you try?"

She would be home in forty-eight hours. Would she talk to some guy on her way home? Leila nodded.

"Okay. So listen. You're going via JFK. You're ticketed through, so there'll be no funny business or swaps, I promise. You'll be traveling as Lola Montes. When you get to Portland, your phone will direct you to Leo Crane. We'll try to route your civilian calls to the Diary phone also. Your own devices are in the duffel. But they won't work until you're back in LA."

Leila was bothered by something. "If it's the Committee that's doing all the evil spying and data collection, how is it that we know so much?"

"You said *we*," said Sarah, and smiled. "But yes. We made a compromise. The Committee spies on everything. We tap their lines. So yes, we are spying too. But we're spying on their spying. And when we come out in the open, we're going to stop doing that. And to come out in the open, we need to organize—and to organize, we need the data they're collecting. At least until our transmission network is up and running. But we're losing access to their data. They're moving their whole operation—probably because people like you keep running across their facilities. We think maybe they're bunkerizing, going underground. Or maybe they're putting it all in orbit. Anyway, there are fewer and fewer trunk lines to tap. That's why we need someone high up in this SineCo thing they're calling New Alexandria: to tell us where they're keeping the data."

Sarah's phone buzzed. She looked at the screen. "Shite, okay, I have to head out. Listen, Lola, when you get your computer back, or with any computer or smartphone you might use in the future, put a piece of black electrical tape over the webcam."

Leila scrunched her face, like *Are you serious?*

Sarah's phone buzzed again, and this time she stood up. "Okay. You know what, Lola? Don't look directly at any nonhuman lens, okay? The Committee doesn't have anything like the eye test; it's not clear that any of them even understand what the Enumerator does. But we fear they're trying to make something like it. So just never look directly at something that might have a camera in it. *Ar eagla na heagla.*"

"Air oggla na hoggla?"

"It's Irish. 'In the fear of the fear.' It means 'just to be on the safe side.'" She was backing out of the little Ikea home. "Let me know when your father's safe, will you?"

"Yeah. How do I do that?"

Sarah waggled her phone. "You have my number."

"I do?"

"Don't you?"

Leila looked hard at Sarah. She *did* know Sarah's number. And knowing it, she knew some things about Sarah. The little crush wasn't for nothing. Sarah was a good woman, kind and fair and fun. Impatient, though, and ill at ease with children. All this Leila knew as if she'd known Sarah for years.

"If the phone won't let you call, find me through the Dear Diary homepage," said Sarah, walking away quickly.

"What homepage?" Leila called after her. But Sarah had her phone to her ear again and was talking urgently into it, moving swiftly through a sea of furniture.

IN TRANSIT

How long is the flight to Hong Kong?" Mark asked the SineCo rep.

"Twelve hours," said the man. "Patel will meet you in Hong Kong and handle you forward."

Ooh, he was getting handled forward. Maybe *Sine Wave* was plying the South China Sea. He'd be putting his seat way back and sleeping off that lounge experience. What did she say her name was? Lola Montes, like the dancer. What a fantastic name.

The aircraft they pulled up beside didn't look to Mark like it *could* be privately owned. White as dice, without a mark on it save the call letters on its tail. It was an Airbus, he saw as he climbed the stairs that came out of the cylinder of the plane like a lemon wedge. He paused midstairs and looked out at the airport, busy with little trucks.

When Mark was a boy, after his dad left and his world had been halved, his mom bought him a remote-controlled car. Not one of those shitty, plug-in RadioShack ones but a gas-powered racer from a hobby store, with inflatable rubber wheels and a roll cage. For a month of Sundays, she took him to the parking lot of the mall that had been made obsolete by the newer mall, and he ran the crap out of that racer. His mom had to mix the fuel, and she spilled a lot, which made her curse, which she hardly ever did. What fun he had with her on those days. How had she known just what joy the racer would bring? She brought hard-boiled eggs and fruit leather for him, lithium for herself. She set up obstacle courses for his racer with sodden, cast-off sweatshirts and derelict shopping carts. But when he came home one day and, through tears, told her that a ganglet of older boys at school had jacked that gorgeous racer, she just said:

"The world is not a fair place."

She said it like that, she who always stuck up for him. He was shocked. "You make it fair!" he yelled at her, furious. And she to him: "No, Mark. I can't. It just isn't." And that is how she'd raised him: she'd been doting and fierce, but never promised what she could not deliver. She stepped back from the voids that he saw other mothers race to fill.

Well, maybe it wasn't fair, thought Mark, but it was sometimes retributive. Those monkey-bar thugs who'd taken his racer were lucky if they could even fly commercial these days. They were probably bent over rented desks or fryolators in parts of America with high cancer rates. Mark knew his mother relished his success, though she had made little comment on *Bringing the Inside Out*. She stuck his postcards on the door frame and bragged about him in the checkout line; she left magazines folded to his image in the break room at the tire store. And whenever he went home to see her, she'd always say the same thing to him when he left. "Make me proud," she would say.

He wished she were boarding this plane with him now. Wouldn't she be proud of him? Wouldn't she be impressed?

He handed his jacket to the hostess at the top of the stairs and stepped into the cabin. There was room to stand unstooped, and there was a walnut conference table and there were brandy snifters arrayed and secured behind more walnut carpentry. All the seating was in smoky brown leather. And what's this? He would not be needing to put his seat back, he saw when he walked ten steps aft; there was a *bedroom* on this airplane.

Mark could have pumped a fist, but a hostess was already at his side with a glass of ice water.

"The captain asked me to tell you that we're just waiting for one more passenger."

"Very well. Thank you," he said. *Oh, farts*. He would not have the place to himself. There might be awkward maneuvering about who got the aft cabin. If it was one of Straw's main henchmen, Mark would have to be down dog.

He settled himself into one of the single seats, a swiveling leather behemoth; it was like sitting in a gorilla's lap. He fussed with his satchel and pockets again, tried to hide the fact that he was totally psyched to be on this amazing plane. He wanted to perform a complete reconnaissance — what was the lavatory like? What about the galley? And he had gotten only a peek in that aft cabin. Could you lie down and look out the window?

A guy younger than Mark stepped into the cabin. He was dressed down, but expensive down. He nodded and grunted at Mark as he walked by and made straight for the back of the plane. *Shit*, thought Mark, but then the guy stopped short of the aft cabin and instead settled in another one of the singles. Mark swiveled in his chair, which allowed him to keep the guy not entirely behind his back. The guy did all the following things in quick succession: removed his shoes and put on fat socks; buckled his seat belt; squidged foam plugs into his ears; slipped a sleep mask over his eyes and noise-canceling headphones over his ears. Then, in seconds, his shoulders went slack and his lower jaw dropped a bit. One of the hostesses collected his shoes from beneath him. The other one was retracting the lemon-wedge stairs.

Mark committed himself to some conscious relaxation; he slowed his breathing and heavied his limbs. Tried to feel his muscles and his bones, the working machine of him. The jet rolled forward into the little dance line of Heathrow. He wondered whether driving a plane on the ground was like driving a car. It was probably not at all like driving a car. When the roar happened and the aircraft sprang forward as if to escape its own

225

metal self, Mark was at the lip of sleep. He let himself be tucked in by the g-force, pushed firmly into the huge seat and into a dream.

He woke because someone had slipped a woolen sock in his mouth. *No. No woolen sock. Terrible thirst. Dry mouth.* He smacked his lips and reached for the ceiling nozzle dousing him with cold dry air. But someone was holding him down, pinning him in the seat. *No, that's a seat belt. And the seat is reclined.* A hostess was quickly at his side. Wordlessly, she directed his hand to the controls hidden in the armrest beneath a flap of upholstered leather. With the buttons, she sphinctered down the cold-air nozzle and began to unrecline his seat.

"Thank you," he said. "May I have a glass of water?" His voice came out all dry and reedy.

She brought it to him, and when his throat was unparched, he looked around again. The guy behind him was awake. He was working on a tablet and eating from china at the conference table.

The guy raised his head from his tablet. "Lamb?" he said. He held up a meat-laden fork.

Mark extracted himself from his seat, took his water, and walked aft, jingling the ice cubes in his heavy glass. He put his game face on.

"You with Bluebird?" said the guy.

"I work for Straw."

"Sure. Yeah. So do I, I guess," said the guy. Then: "I'm Seamus Cole." He put his fork down and held out his hand. Mark took it as he noticed the guy's earplugs on his plate, squidged like tiny wax-smeared penises beside a half-eaten bread roll. This guy did not know he was Mark Deveraux. Is there a polite way to inform someone that he should be aware of you? Surely Bill Clinton and Sean Connery never found themselves in this situation.

"I'm the executive engineer and information architect of New Alexandria," said Cole. "We're going to launch my new serve-whales tomorrow. I thought I should be on board for that." He took a big slug of viscous brown fluid from a snifter.

"Mark Deveraux," said Mark.

"No shit? You're the guru guy. I thought you were Bluebird."

Bluebird? thought Mark. *The security contractor? What the fuck?*

"I'm just one of Straw's advisers, really," said Mark modestly.

"Sure. Like Kissinger was just an adviser."

Mark couldn't tell what Cole meant by that. Perhaps being compared to Kissinger was a compliment. Plus, Mark couldn't figure out how to ask what a serve-whale was without betraying his own cluelessness, so he stood.

"I just have to put my eyes to this thing I'm writing," he said.

"Sure," said Cole.

Mark asked the attendant—super-politely, to distinguish himself from Cole—whether he might use the aft cabin to get some rest. She said of course but wouldn't he like anything to eat? He asked her name and she said Monica and he said, "No, thank you, Monica, but could I please see the galley?" And she showed him the galley. It was all little metal trays and tools that slotted or secured into the wall, like a much cooler version of the kitchenette in the VW van his mom had borrowed from some hippie friends one summer when she and Mark drove to Texas to see about a man. The man turned out to be a disappointment, but the trip was a hoot.

The aft cabin was a bedroom, truly, lit with tiny little spots ensconced in burled walnut. Monica showed him where the buttons to work everything were. Then Mark stripped to his underwear and lay down between real sheets. The pillow wasn't quite right; it was too springy. So he looked out the little window into a cloudscape like a Maxfield Parrish painting, and soon he slept.

In Hong Kong, Mark and Seamus deplaned and were met at the bottom step by Patel, who was all business. He swept them into another white sedan and then sat up front, beside the silent driver. Their bags were transferred from plane to car.

"You will have another forty-five minutes of travel time," said Patel.

"There is some hurry. There is weather coming in, and the helicopter has its tolerances. Mr. Deveraux, Mr. Straw expects you for dinner."

Dinner, thought Mark, a word now drained of meaning by jet travel. Dinner could mean anything.

They drove for fifteen minutes, at a decent clip, through two security barriers, and then they stopped at a third. Patel got out and conducted some business in the office beside the barrier. Cole didn't look good. His face was puffy and he held his hands as if they'd just been given to him. His eyes were glazed. But then he seemed to surface from his daze and become suddenly aware of himself. He focused on Mark.

"You sleep okay?" he asked. There was maybe resentment in his voice.

It was the first time Mark had ever been on a helicopter. The inside was like a very nice van. Two three-man bench seats, but facing each other, and upholstered for potentates. A sort of a coffee table in the middle. More walnut. Walnut trees must live in fear of private aviation. Cole had put Dramamine patches behind both ears and kept his eyes fixed on some point outside the helicopter. Patel was immediately into a legal pad with an expensive pen.

Mark tried to channel his helicopter excitement. The sleep on the jet had done him good, but now he was too keyed up, and no one was going to offer him a drink here. He would pay attention only to the flight, to the sea out the window, to his body in the seat. All the worrying he could expend on the job/money/debt issues or the addiction question or the lack of book progress or what he might be heading into on this yacht—he would not expend it. He would ask his brain, politely but firmly, to refrain from the distressing thoughts and attend only to the clouds and the incredible fact that he was choppering through the sky toward a megayacht.

It worked, mostly. In fact, riding in a helicopter was much more exciting, ergono-aeronautically, than riding in a plane. As they lifted off, Mark felt his body describing a ridiculous straight-up-in-the-air line. He thought of T.C., the chopper pilot on *Magnum, P.I.*, a show that Mark had watched religiously. Was it Thursday night? TV had been so important to him, stoking his little head with stupid fantasies. Now he pretended T.C. was piloting him.

But he couldn't keep the aggressor thoughts at bay: there was something wrong with his heart; the path he was on was not a good one; his mother was not proud of him; his luck would turn again; he would die alone and unloved.

He kept returning to the scene out the window. Helicopters let you see more than planes did. No plate-size portholes, but broad rectangular windows. They were flying below the clouds, over a scudding sea without indications of scale save for little white paisleys on the blue-green that could have been whitecaps or mile-long reefs.

He checked again on his co-passengers. Cole was looking pretty wretched. He was taking shallow sips of air. People really do get a green cast when they're motion-sick. Patel was making notes in the margin of some widely spaced document — or pretending to, anyway, a trick Mark knew well. It began to rain and the chopper ducked lower. Mark could see the white combs breaking on the gray sea.

When they flew lower, he could tell that they were really eating up the distance. Then their forward motion ceased. They were above some tanker-type ship. Mark scanned his section of horizon for a sign of *Sine Wave* but could see none. Were they stopping to refuel?

Landing a helicopter on a ship did seem to be rather tricky. The craft hovered just above the deck for what felt like too long and then dropped the last bit suddenly. Cole's eyes fluttered at that final jolt, and then his face filled with the obvious relief that he had not puked. Someone outside the helicopter scuttled around its skids, and someone else opened the door from the outside.

This is *Sine Wave*? wondered Mark as he followed Patel out of the helicopter and set foot on the stamped metal of the vast foredeck of what appeared to be a freighter. Some distance away — like, two or three blocks away, Mark judged it — the flat face of the ship's superstructure rose, the windows made to sparkle and bling by the setting sun before them. Cole followed Mark, and the three men walked toward the office-building-size pilothouse. It was a fair walk too; no little white car to take them.

Where were the raked decks and sunny lounges? Where the gleaming brightwork and snapping pennants? The teak and walnut? This was a serious fucking ship, all rivets and cranes and cabling, heavy portals secured with massive mechanical locks, NO SMOKING stenciled hugely onto many surfaces. Mark saw someone emerge from a bulkhead hatch on the pilothouse. It was a crew member, but not a hottie in crisp whites. He was a South Asian in a blue jumpsuit, wearing a pistol on his thigh. He held the door open for them, looking down as he did so.

"Mr. Patel," said Mark before he stepped over the raised threshold, "we're not aboard *Sine Wave,* are we?"

And here Mr. Patel gave his first smile. "No, Mr. Deveraux," he said. "Indeed we are not. We are aboard *Sine Wave Two.*"

A steward, unarmed, met them just inside the bulkhead. "I am Mr. Singh," he said to Mark. "Please follow me." A different steward came for Cole and led him off in a different direction. Patel went with Mark and the steward.

From the deck, the pilothouse had looked maritime-functional. But once inside, Mark saw that it had yacht-grade surfaces and appointments (again with the walnut paneling and the subdued lighting; Mark spotted a piano, an orchid in a vase, a painting on the wall that was maybe a Rothko), and there was a zing in the air, the kind produced when subjugated staff members move swiftly through corridors.

They arrived at the door to a cabin. Mark's cabin, apparently. Singh said, "You are to dine with Mr. Straw in forty-five minutes. I will return just prior to that. You will please not leave your room before then."

"Where would I go? The Lido deck?" Neither Singh nor Patel laughed. "Well. Thank you, gentlemen." He nodded gravely at Singh. "Mr. Patel, thank you for seeing me here."

"It was Mr. Straw's wish," said Patel. The man had probably been in service for decades and had learned how to deliver a brush-off so that the sting was delayed a few beats.

Right. Okay. This guy wouldn't extinguish me if I were on fire. Mark's charm was flattery-based and so only traveled up. Employees hardly ever liked him. Well, fine, whatever. He didn't need Patel's blessing or friendship.

Alone, Mark checked out the cabin. It was plain, close to spartan. But the expensive kind of plain: wood with twelve coats of varnish, drawers on smooth metal bearings, only a few moving objects in the whole room. There was a berth he would need to climb into; there was a porthole; there was a little writing desk with twelve blank legal pads and a fist of sharpened pencils in the pencil well. There was a tiny and ingenious bathroom, a bar of soap engraved *SW2* in the soap well. Mark looked out of the porthole at the empty sea in the last light and tried to feel like Jack London.

Dinner was crown roast—Straw liked showy food—and lots of claret, poured by a gloved table man who held a folded square of napkin at the neck of the bottle to blot any errant drops. The third person at dinner was a man whom Straw had always referred to as "my boon friend Parker." This turned out to be Parker Pope, CEO of Bluebird, the security company that had recently changed its name to Blu Solutions/Logistics. He was twenty years younger than Straw but looked like he was made from the same stuff. Mostly, the two men carried on a contentious discussion about whether the Cape buffalo or the southern white rhinoceros was more difficult game. Straw said, "Rhinoceros. It's megafauna."

"It's a small-brained ungulate is what it is," said Pope. "Whereas with the *mbogo,* you never know what they're going to do. They despise men."

Mark tried to see both sides of it ("I'm not much of a hunter myself"), but in the end, he went with the rhinoceros, because of the armored hide. Pope seemed to set himself against Mark right then.

"You came in with the new head of engineering, I believe," Straw said to Mark. "Seamus Cole?"

Mark said that he had.

"Cole says he can mend the new drift net," said Pope to Straw although he was looking at Mark.

Mark bit. "Cole mends nets?" he asked Pope. "He's a net mender?" Then, turning to Straw and adopting the intimate tone he used with him during their sessions, he asked: "Is that why we're on such a huge vessel? Is that what we're doing here, James? Fishing?"

"Of a sort," said Pope, quick as an eel. "Cole is a fisher of men. One of the best. But they like to be called data hydrologists—"

Straw cut him off. "Mark hasn't been belowdecks yet, Parker. And I think the phrase we went with was information architect."

Pope raised his hands, a sarcastic *jeez Louise, sorry*. "I just assumed that since you're offering Marcus here the, uh, position, you would have been over the outlines of the project."

"I was going to do that tomorrow. But I may as well do it now, I guess." Straw sounded angry, like a kid whose party had been ruined. "Mark, how would you like to be SineCo's storyteller-in-chief?"

Mark sat before his unfinished sherbet cup. He hated sherbet. Was that a title? What would be the compensation? If he was going to play this right, he had to quit letting Pope rattle Straw. He had to get Straw away from Pope. "I'm intrigued, James," Mark said. "But I'm also exhausted. Let's discuss it tomorrow, you and I together."

Then a quick rap at the bulkhead, and a hot, butchy woman stepped into the dining room. "Excuse the interruption," she said. "Mr. Pope, you'll need to be on the next call. The prince is irate."

"That fucking cum-guzzler," Mark definitely heard Pope mutter, presumably of the irate prince. "Thank you, Tessa. I'll be right there." The woman stepped back but remained nearby. She was waiting for Pope in a way that made it clear to Mark that she was his first assistant. Pope pushed back his chair. "James: Until tomorrow. Marcus: Congratulations on the storyteller thing." Then he looked straight at Mark and said evenly: "It's the last job you'll ever take."

That night, Mark woke like a shot from a dream of a cigarette. His plan had been to get by with nicotine patches—he didn't want Straw to know he smoked. But the patches made him feel thin-blooded and their effect lingered, making sleep into a briar patch. He paced the cabin. His porthole laughed at him. All he wanted were a few smoke-moderated breaths in the night air.

He decided to chance it. He found the two cigarettes he'd nicked from the Israeli grandma in the *fumoir,* and he slipped out into the hallway. He just had to find some access to a deck or gangway. But he was immediately confused by the labyrinth of the giant ship. It was like being in the gut of something. His first many steps took him *away* from the porthole in his cabin; then he made a right and then a right and then went up a flight of metal stairs. And then he could swear he was in the same place he'd been in thirty seconds ago. His heart began to beat faster. Singh the steward hadn't exactly ordered him to stay in his room when he'd escorted Mark back there after dinner, but there was definitely a stay-in-your-room, Agatha Christie–type vibe on this ship, like dinner was the last scheduled event of the day, and then it was curfew.

So when Mark heard very intentional steps heading down the corridor intersection he was approaching, he slipped quickly through a nearby doorway. The move would have been superslick and graceful but for the fact that it landed him in a cabin that belonged to Pope's assistant, the woman who had interrupted dinner. She was standing at a desk, leaning over a computer, wearing what he believed was called a camisole.

"You did *not* just sneak into my room," she said.

There are times you go straight to the truth. "No. You are correct. I did not," said Mark. "I was trying to get outside, on deck or whatever. I want to smoke this cigarette"—he held up a thin cigarette as proof—"but I got lost. This boat is nuts. And then I was kind of ducking to hide somewhere, because someone was coming, and I'm afraid of that creepy steward, and I know that's stupid . . ." She wasn't buying it; her expression said, Un*interested in the particulars.* "Look, sorry, please excuse me," Mark said, and he stepped into the corridor, out of her space. But she did not move to shut the door behind him. He looked left and then right. Then he turned around to her again and said, "Any chance you could help me out here?"

Tessa's room was more of a stateroom than a cabin. It was twice the size of his. But it looked like she spent a lot of time in it. There were four laptops and a dozen other assorted technological devices blinking away in corners, paperwork in legal-type binders piled on two desks, empty cups and glasses marooned on ledges, and three huge duffel bags stacked in an open wardrobe.

But the salient feature of Tessa's room was its balcony, or whatever it was called on a ship. That's where they sat and smoked, listening to the slap and slosh of ocean ten decks below. Tessa smoked a Lucky Strike. Mark suffered through one of the Israeli woman's fey cigarettes.

"I guess it was pretty dumb of me to sneak around," said Mark, his mind having been made still and clear by the nicotine. "I mean, we're guests here, right?"

"Well, yes and no," she said. Some light fell on them from her state-room, but the dark sea and moonless sky beat it back; he couldn't see her face well enough to read any information that it might have held.

"Let's talk about the no part, shall we?" he said.

That amused her. And then: "You really don't know what's going on, do you?"

"Well, I guess not about this, no. But maybe there's stuff I know that you don't know."

"What I don't know is how you even got this far," she said. But then she must have thought that too harsh, because she leaned a bit toward him and said, "I mean, you must have skills; Straw is mad about you. You want a less silly cigarette?" And she offered him one of her Luckies.

He took the cigarette. "He's a close reader. He told me that my book inspired him to begin this big project of his, the thing he's calling New Alexandria."

"But you don't know what he meant by that?"

"James and I don't really discuss operational specifics, just goals. Ab-stractly, more or less."

"Oh, you're the kind of therapist I want," said Tessa.

She had a point. In one of their recent sessions, when Straw had im-plied that New Alexandria involved data collection on an unprecedented scale, Mark had only agreed that it was a good idea to collect knowledge. When Straw veered off on a rant about how after the correction, there wouldn't be so many damn people braying about their information rights, Mark didn't say, *Wait. What correction are you talking about?* He just tried to steer Straw back to the stuff about how we all benefit by making our interactions more transparent.

"I guess tomorrow you'll get more of the operational specifics," said Tessa. "Though as our new SIC, you'll want to go light on that part."

"Ess-Eye what now?"

"Storyteller-in-chief."

"Yeah, that. Listen, I haven't actually said I'll take the job yet. James and I are going to talk about it tomorrow."

"Your thing with him looks pretty complicated."

Mark thought that was very perceptive of her. Complicated it certainly was, at least for him: he had to act like a dutiful son but one who gave counsel to the father; manage Straw's egomania; say enough to display his mind's agility but not too much, lest he betray the sizable gaps in his knowledge.

"Have you always gone in for older men?"

Mark snapped to. "Pardon?"

"I just mean, you know, the age difference between you. I was once in a relationship like that. I found it challenging."

"I'm James Straw's counselor," said Mark slowly. "I counsel him. That's all."

She leaned forward and into a bit of light. She looked sincerely confused. "Really?"

Mark nodded.

"Oh," said Tessa. "Huh. You're not his . . . partner?"

Shit. Who else thought this? "I'm straight. You know that, right?"

She made a tiny big-deal sign with her eyes. "Well, I guess I do now. Do you know that I'm queer?"

"I couldn't decide," he said. "What, exactly, made you think *I* was gay?"

"Pope said Straw was bringing his boy into the operation. And since you're not his son, I thought he meant the other kind of boy."

This was terrible. People thought he was Straw's boy. There came to his mind a fleeting image of what it would be like to service Straw, to be pressed against his skinny, limp flanks, hold his mottled hand.

"It's strange, though, you know?" said Tessa. "Because I read your book, and I must have missed the part where you advocate for the construction of a diffuse remote network of offshore data vaults."

Diffuse remote network of offshore data vaults? "Well, I believe I did go on about preparedness," said Mark. "You know, as a generality. I suppose remote whatever offshore data vaults kind of fit in with that."

She definitely thought he was funny. He tried to get more out of her about the scope and nature of what the ship was engaged in, but she would say no more about it. A bit desperately, he tried the direct approach—"But there's nothing illegal about New Alexandria, is there?"—and the way she immediately clamped down told him all he needed to know.

And then she said, "Listen, I actually have loads more work to do tonight. So I guess I'll see you tomorrow. Hopefully, after you've taken the tour." It seemed likely that when this woman pleaded work, she actually meant she had to work. Various of her devices had *bloop*ed repeatedly with incoming messages, and the binders on her desk were too big to be for show. She saw him to the door of her stateroom and used her long-fingered hands to scribble for him in the air a route back to his cabin.

There was a klaxon splitting the air. Mark leaped from his bunk, forgetting how elevated it was, and one ankle buckled beneath him and he yelped in pain and ran to the door of his cabin in his underwear. Opening it, he found Singh standing outside, as still as a queen's guard.

"Good morning, Mr. Deveraux," Singh said rather loudly, because the klaxon was as deafening in the corridor as it was in the cabin.

"Where's the emergency?" yelled Mark, but even before he'd finished the question, the klaxon quit klaxoning, and his yelling was suddenly strange.

"There is no emergency, Mr. Deveraux," said Singh. "That was the morning bell. It is six thirty. Breakfast will be in half an hour."

Breakfast was smoothies and sardines on toast, served in a sort of officers' mess, not the wood-paneled dining room of the night before. Straw was there and was very excited. Pope was there too, slathering sardines on his toast. Hovering nearby him was an attractive female assistant twenty years his junior, but it wasn't Tessa, who Mark figured was probably above hovering.

"We'll join you again just as soon as you've seen the ship," Straw said to Mark. "I thought that you and I could take the afternoon to relax."

The first half hour of the tour was docented by a bearded and barrel-chested Greek who clearly didn't want to talk about anything other than life rafts and bow thrusters and nautical miles and who kept correcting Mark whenever he failed to use a feminine pronoun for *Sine Wave 2*. Anyway, Mark was too boggled by the size of the ship to do any good ferreting. From a cornice high on the pilothouse, looking out over the length and breadth of the vessel, the thin line of the horizon strung across its distant bow, Mark felt that *Sine Wave 2* was the center of the universe, that it could bend things into itself. Or into herself.

"So what does it carry?" asked Mark in some exasperation, indicating the quarter mile of mysterious volume that extended from the ship's superstructure like a titanic boner. The Greek simply shrugged his shoulders.

"You don't know what this ship carries?" Mark asked the Greek's back. He was docenting the tour at a fair clip now.

"Not my department," he said with such blank-wallness that Mark understood he was done talking about this.

Luckily, the guy who the Greek handed Mark off to was chattier.

"Mark Deveraux. It's an honor. Big fan. Big fan," said Tony, pointing two thumbs at his own chest.

*　　*　　*

They stepped into a room that Mark could have mistaken for the bridge—it ran the width of the ship and had windows on three sides and was buzzing with people and bristling with screens and devices; serpents of bundled data cables snaked the allées between the workstations. But Mark had *begun* his tour on the ship's bridge, at least four decks up, where he'd seen a dozen handsome officers in uniforms sharp with pleats and insignia. Most of those guys were looking at radar screens and gauges and the actual ocean, binoculars in leather cases on the walls behind them.

The people in this room weren't part of the ship's crew, though there was something tight, controlled, synchronous about them. Near silence, just the low buggish background of plastic keyboards. Near stillness, just dudes (they were all men) intent in Aeron chairs, oblivious to the sea.

The room looked as serious and data-heavy as Mission Control at NASA, but the techies weren't middle-aged guys with too many pens. They were Asian guys and white guys and a few black guys, all under thirty-five, wearing Gap jeans and oxford shirts. Their stations showed those minimal attempts at cubicle decoration usually seen in all-male IT departments: snapshots from epic weekends, ironically offered action figures, pinups from windsurfing magazines.

Mark and Tony stood at the center of the large room near a well-stocked deli tray set up on a folding table: a shiny coffee urn; Danish; little ramekins of Splenda. Mark was boggled and back-footed. Was this New Alexandria? There was a tiny, keen ringing in his ears. To cover his distress, he poured himself a coffee. Tony was talking.

"The feed comes in from the computer"—he gestured forward vaguely—"and in this room, we do four things." Tony indicated each of the four corners of the vast room as he spoke: "You got your gatherers, your bundlers, your amalgamators, and your gleaners. Once the gleaners do their thing, we move the data, in tranches, over to Processing and Encryption, and that's when it gets written on the whales and launched."

"The whales?" said Mark. If you repeat the last thing your interlocutor said with a rising lilt in your voice, it's like politely saying, *What did you just say?*, and the sayer usually then feels obligated to offer more clarity. Mark centrifuged a sugar packet. He didn't take sweetener in his coffee, but *fwap*ping those little envelopes made a man look unconcerned and in control.

"The serve-whales," Tony resumed brightly. "Well, I guess, technically, they're remote seabed servers, or whatever we're supposed to call them. But when you see one launched, it's just hard not to think of a whale. The way they spin and dive, that sound they make.

"There's Mr. Cole," said Tony. The airsick net mender was coming toward them. Tony began to introduce Mark to Cole, but Cole outranked Tony and so flattened him. The SineCo culture intensified the male penchant for hierarchy; every interaction had a top and a bottom, and everything, even the air in the room, was zero-sum, get-your-own. Anyone who liked getting ahead had to like seeing people behind him.

"Sure. Sure. The writer," said Cole, as though *writer* were a funny antique job, like falconer. "We met coming in."

"Of course," said Mark, like it was some historical event instead of yesterday.

"Come with me," said Cole. "Pope wanted you to see what the gleaners do."

Cole walked Mark down a line of workstations. He moved like a teacher seeking his pet, and when he stopped behind the desk of an overweight guy in a Liverpool jersey, the guy sat up a little straighter in his netted chair. He had about ten screens before him, keyboards like snare drums in the orbit of his left hand, and his right hand stroked a postmouse input device that Mark had never seen before. Two of the screens really were just running code, but at a clip so fast it was barely discernible, so the effect was like one of those little plug-in Zen fountains from the SkyMall catalog. The guy was wearing a flip-down visor across his eyes that looked like it could be used for telesurgery. He seemed to be selecting items on the screen and moving them around—dragging and dropping—but at a speed that Mark had never conceived of. It was like watching a dervish.

"Do you know what he's doing?" Cole asked Mark.

Not really. Mining data? "I do. But you're the information architect. Why don't you tell me?"

Cole nodded, as if to say *Fair enough.* "So the material these guys are working with has already been enriched. This isn't Sears cards and DMV photos. This is the cream of the cream that rises to the top of the ten exabytes per day." He said the *exabytes* part like Mark should know what that meant. Mark nodded.

Cole went on. "So you're talking deep financials, all the way back to birth; full medical, obviously, HIPAA data and biosampling; kinship; relational; ownership; political. Then we do hopes and dreams, fears and desires, stills and video, voice and text..." He did this and-on-and-on motion with one hand.

"Voice and text?" said Mark, just choosing at random.

"Everything the subject's ever said or written over a digital line."

"How everything?"

Cole just shrugged. "Everything everything. Capturing it's easy. Well, not easy, but...you know, achievable. It's just always been a question of jurisdiction, interpretation, organization, and storage. Once we beat those, it was a cinch. Here, put these on." He handed Mark a visor with a flip-down screen, like the one the gleaner was wearing.

Mark donned the visor. One large screen was plain before his eyes; ten little ones encircled it, as in a kaleidoscope. He could still see the room they were in, though; he could still see his hand before his face.

"Say a name," said Cole. "Any name."

The name came instantly, unbidden. The Lost Girlfriend. Five years ago was the last time he'd seen her. He gave the name. "I think she lives in New York. She works for—"

But Cole wasn't listening. The gleaner sitting beside them swiveled and stroked his devices. And in seconds, she was there, on the large screen before his right eye. And it wasn't some mug shot, DMV photo, or surveillance still.

One of the smaller screens blossomed for a moment. Skype call with mother. T-16 days, it said on the screen. Another small screen showed the mother.

Margaret, still beautiful, at a kitchen table with a little girl. The girl looked like Margaret. So she had gotten the baby she wanted. And then Margaret stood and beamed and showed her rounded belly to her mother, to Mark and Cole and the fat guy in the Liverpool jersey.

"We're not saying the names yet to anyone, but I'll tell you. If it's a boy, we're going to name him Hershel." Hershel was her dad's name. Her dad had died of a heart attack while running with Margaret when she was a teenager. That had screwed her up for years.

"Now bring it forward and extract fears and relevance," said Cole to the gleaner.

And from a bud in his ear came scratchy audio, hissing like old tape. One screen in the corona blossomed again: baby monitor, daughter, husband, T-3 days.

A man was singing a lullaby:

... *speed bonny boat, like a bird on the wing* ...

"Where's Mommy?" asked a small girl's voice.

"Mommy's sad right now, bug."

"Why is Mommy sad?"

"She's sad because your little brother's not coming," said the man's voice. "But it's okay, bug, we're going to try to make you another little brother or sister."

"But I want *that* little bruddah," whined the girl.

And the man said, "I did too, bug. I did too." And then he was sobbing and stifling his sobs and Mark tore the screened visor off his head.

Seamus Cole was staring at him evenly, like *How now, guru guy?*

"Why the hell would you be collecting shit like this?" Mark said, looking straight at Cole.

"It's public. It's over our network. We call dibs on it."

Dibs? They were calling *dibs?*

"But it's illegal, to spy on people like this."

"Information is free. Storage is unlimited," said Cole, totally unbothered. "Our privacy policy is reviewed regularly, and our mandate to collect is spelled out in the implied-consent decree of 2001. We're just keeping this stuff safe, anyway. The other server giants have terrible vulnerabilities; they could be erased so easily." Did he just *smirk?* "But that's not really my department."

"What *is* your department?"

He brought Mark to a little elevator, and the two men rode four decks down and then walked through two negative-pressure rooms with sticky floors. There were men coming the other way, peeling off paper gowns as they walked, as the handsome surgeons on the hospital shows do. Now the passageways were tubular, striated with cabling and cancerous with little blinking boxes. Mark and Cole arrived at a sort of viewing platform, a room with a glass wall. Mark had to get right up close to the glass before his eyes could make any sense of what was on the other side.

It was a machine. But what kind? A death ray? They were standing at one end of it, and it appeared to extend the length of the ship. On the other side of the glass, men in paper gowns were walking alongside the machine on little scaffolds. It hummed at some primordial frequency. Mark's fillings were ringing.

"What is it?" he asked.

"It's a beast," said Cole. "A beast that's all brain. We feed it information—all electronically transmitted information, all the time, over any line we claim—then it builds models: predictive, algorithmic. Ten moves out, twenty, but the pieces aren't chess pieces, they're people pieces. And then it extracts anything of value and makes a copy of both those files—the everything file and the anything-of-value file—and writes those files onto solid-state atomic drives and launches the drives down to the ocean floor."

There was no way Mark could continue to hide his surprise. "Well, fuck me," he said, a little under his breath.

"Yeah. I think what Straw wants from you, at least until we unveil, is more like a cover story."

*   *   *

The "relaxing" that Straw had mentioned was, as Mark had feared it would be, entirely *un*relaxing. It took place beside a swimming pool in a little stone-tiled terrazzo cloister that was carved into the middle of the top deck of the pilothouse of *Sine Wave 2*. By means of a remote control that seemed to both dazzle and baffle him, Straw fought with a vast louvered-glass roof that opened and closed across the cloister. Mark kept getting scorched and blinded by shafts of equatorial sun that flooded the poolside whenever Straw accidentally commenced a louver retraction.

"Damn it," said Straw. "You ask for one thing to be done right..." Then he buzzed thrice and angrily a little buzzer that sat beside his iced tea; a crew member hustled out from one of the glass walls of the cloister, wearing a sort of waiter's jacket and shorts. "Close this stupid ceiling," Straw barked at the guy.

Shorts were the thing around here. On this upper deck of the ship, the maritime vibe was replaced with a Mediterranean villa vibe, and the male crew were all in snug shorts. Mark had tried *Sorry, I forgot my suit,* in an attempt to avoid time poolside with Straw, but to his horror, Straw said, *No worries, I have one here,* and whipped out a particularly abbreviated pair.

So Mark had to stay reclined in a lounge chair beside Straw's lounge chair while he tried to get some specifics on the job that Straw seemed to have no doubt he would accept.

Having spent a year allowing Straw to be vague about SineCo business, Mark was having a hard time determining the nature and extent of what was really going on here. Straw moved from half-formed notion to ill-formed conclusion via cloudy and self-serving thought processes.

"But you told me that New Alexandria was going to be like a library," said Mark, "that it would serve the public."

"It will. And a library can ask you to obey its rules; it can ask you to apply for a library card, pay late fines, and, yes—if it is the best library the world has ever known—pay a nominal fee for membership."

"But if the books that the library, um, collects are already the property of the people the library wants to loan the books to . . . if you take something and then 'loan' it back to its original owner for a fee . . ." He left the rest of the sentence unsaid, but Straw seemed totally unbothered by the implication, so Mark had to recalibrate. "James, can you see why this"— he made a little sweeping gesture meant to take in the ship and its mission—"would be a hard story to tell?"

"Mark, let me ask you this," said Straw. "Can you tell me where the nearest black hole is?"

"What?"

"A black hole. The nearest one to us," prompted Straw.

"I don't know. A trillion miles away?"

"No. Right in your face." And here Straw reached out and touched Mark's face, lightly. "Your eyes. They are black holes. They take in light; they absorb information." His fingers lingered on Mark's cheek as he waited for Mark to appreciate the depth of the observation. "The machine you saw today is like that. Not just some computer you dump data into, but an organ that needs to make sense of the world. That's not really something you'd want to stand in the way of, is it?" He didn't wait for Mark's answer. "So, I suppose you tell the part that you can tell, which, yes, until we really unveil the product, is not the whole story. And I know it's going to be hard—that's why I want you. You're the best."

"And what is the product, exactly?" asked Mark, a little desperately.

"It's a product *and* a service," said Straw proudly. "It's *order*. It's the safeguarding of all of our clients' personal information and assets. But it may be a while before our clients discover that they are our clients. So you'll have some time to work on that part.

"And there have lately been some information breaches, Mark. We've had some close calls. I don't know much about that. That's Parker's department. He says his people are dealing with that, rolling that up. If exposure should begin before our planned unveiling, we may need you to generate some interim explanations for what we're doing. If we can stay discreet, as we are now, then we need you to keep telling the story of the Node. We're getting excellent results with the Node, but we need one hundred times the saturation we have now. In five years, I want every non-impoverished *Homo sapiens* to be carrying a Node. Also, SineLife, the new socialverse we're rolling out. You know how the youth today won't make a move without consulting their little circles online?"—he didn't wait for a nod from Mark—"We need you to get everyone doing that."

He sat up in his lounge chair, a little man, too tan, tufts of springy white hair on his shoulders. "We need you to do what you do so well: Don't sell them on it, convince them of it. Something like 'SineLife sets you free—to concentrate on what's really important.' But say it in that way you do."

Clients who do not yet know they are clients? Mark saw the twisted beauty of it: in this plan there were no victims, only indentured clients.

And then Straw named for Mark a starting salary. It was the kind of money that Mark had actually *stopped* thinking he was ever going to see; the kind of money that really does simplify the moral calculus of a thing. He could trade in Dumbo for Tribeca, browse the Argentine estancias listed for sale in the back of *Superyachts Monthly*.

And yet. That terrible spying. "But is it legal? What did Cole mean, the implied-consent decree of 2001?"

"It's not only perfectly legal under ICD 2001," said Straw, "but also right and moral under natural law, which, I think we can all agree, allows me to pick up and use something that another man has thrown away. And as long as we operate from within one of our sovereign parallel platforms"—Straw gestured with a flourish of his fingers at the ship they were on—"we need obey only the laws we acknowledge. You taught me that."

"I taught you that?" Mark asked, his voice squeaking a bit.

"'Build the world you want to be a part of.' That's you. Page seventy-seven."

Oh fuck. What hideous project was using his stupid banalities as cover? He had even objected, at the time, to the *world you want to be a part of* line, thinking it was too obviously lifted from Gandhi, or from the Internet Gandhi at least. But he had not considered the risk that something benign like that might give comfort and encouragement to a fascist consortium declaring itself free of all laws and building a data sink on a leviathan freighter.

Up here, poolside, it was faint, but there was still that high whine somewhere, a ringing. Not like a mosquito. Like a distant alarm.

"Does the ringing sound bother you?" asked Straw suddenly.

"What? Yes. You hear that?"

"No. Not anymore. Here, try these contact lenses. They make the ringing go away." He handed Mark a clear vial, the size of a film canister, with lenses on a little wand inside.

All Mark could do was claim seasickness. "I think I need to lie down before dinner," he said. A lithe pool boy brought him belowdecks, and Singh escorted him the rest of the way to his cabin.

In his berth, horizontal, he heard the ringing more keenly than he had on the terrazzo. He was closer to the beast. There was a tiny cycle to the ringing, and a regular modulation in amplitude or whatever. Mark folded his pillow around his head like a helmet, but he could still hear it inside him.

He had no trouble indulging megalomania. Obviously. He was a writer, so the egotists always saw him as their ethnographer, like he was Margaret Mead or whatever. But this was something else; this involved intimate surveillance of everyone in the world, and a computer with scaffolding, a computer like an engorged penis that ejaculated other little computers that swam away with stolen data.

He didn't know what to do. He willed himself into a stuporous nap; he had the shirker's hope that somehow, something about the thing he had to do would be easier tomorrow or next week or when he woke up. Sometimes that hope is rewarded.

Dinner was lobster. Mark thought lobster sickening. All that rich tissue, and the cracking sounds. Pope, sitting next to him, was sloppy with his melted butter and splashed some on Mark's cheek. He also turned out to like telling racist and unfunny jokes in what he thought was a comical Indian accent.

"Where can I find your assistant Tessa?" Mark asked Pope when dinner was finally over.

"She's not my assistant. She's an attorney. And she is lesbacean"—this part he said in his "Indian" accent—"so you can forget about it."

"Actually, there are some legal issues I'd like to speak to her about," said Mark. "If I'm to be the SIC here, I'd better make sure I'm clear on what it is we do." This despite the fact that he had written copy for a biogenetics company for six years without knowing the difference between a gene and an allele.

"If?" said Pope, a fork erect in his fat fist. "James, I thought you said your boy here was on board."

"He is. He is," Straw assured Pope. "He's just doing due diligence." Straw handed Mark a little card that looked like a magnetic key card— no text on it, just a pattern of colored bars, with a little clip to clip it to your pocket. "That lets you go anywhere on the ship," said Straw, "you talk to anyone you want to talk to."

Mark knew that his cleverness wouldn't help him too much here, so when Tessa came to the door of her stateroom, he just said, "I have some pretty basic questions."

"I thought you might," she said.

She led him through some maze work of ship to a room that looked like a staff canteen; maybe ten people in the room, eating off plastic trays, and three dudes playing cards. Tessa nodded at some of them.

"You want anything to eat?" she asked Mark.

He said no but changed his mind when he saw the little plastic clamshell of rice pudding in one of the fridge cases along the tray course. Tessa chose an egg salad sandwich and a piece of pie, and they sat down together at one of the Formica tables.

"How can it possibly work?" he asked her.

"It's working right now," she said.

"But, I mean, you guys are going to get busted."

She didn't look scared. "By who?" she said, expressing a sachet of bright yellow mustard into her sandwich. "There's nothing to bust, is our position. We've been going for years, anyway."

"Captain Konstantin told me this ship is a year old," said Mark.

"Who?"

"Konstantin? Konstantinos? Constantinople? The captain guy."

"Oh, yeah. A year sounds right. Before the ships, we were land-based. I think we still have some of those terrestrial facilities in Burma and North Korea."

"I guess I don't understand the payoff, though. I mean, how is this ever going to be worth the expense?"

She put down her sandwich and looked at him. "You don't understand because you still live in a time when you can access analog knowledge. But that won't last much longer. Soon you won't be able to do much of anything if it's not online. You're skeptical, I can see, but that's because you think being online means being in front of a screen, using a keyboard. Because your imagination is limited, and because most computers still look like typewriters. But we're on the edge of some technologies that will change all that—"

His imagination was limited, was it? He interrupted her. "Everyone around here sounds so fucking ominous. What technologies *will change all that?* Because I remember hearing an awful lot about virtual reality and how I'd never have to go to a real beach again."

Tessa did a beckoning thing toward the table where three dudes were playing cards. One of the dudes, handsome, sauntered over. "Mark, this is Chris," Tessa said.

"Ryan," said the dude.

"Sorry. Ryan," said Tessa. "You were working in Inputs back in California, weren't you?"

"I worked Inputs for six years. Biosampling, mainly."

"Tell Mark here about some of the best stuff you've gotten to work on."

Ryan did this raised-eyebrow thing and ticked his head at Mark.

"It's okay," said Tessa. She nodded at Mark's little colored-bars card. Ryan straightened up.

"Pharmaceuticals that transmit, I guess," he said. "That was pretty cool. But then the nano people kinda robbed us of that one." He thought. "This wired contacts, though. I'm part of that shop, and we're doing amazing things." His pride was sincere and evident.

Tessa did a very subtle closure gesture and Ryan cleared his throat, nodded, and went back to his card game.

"Wired contacts?" said Mark. "What? That dude invented LinkedIn or EliteNet or whatever?"

"Contact *lenses,* Mark. It's called visual-channel-collection technology, and we're five years into it."

"Who would wear such things?"

"I'm wearing them right now," she said and looked him right in the eye. He could see no contacts in her eyes, only the brown, with a hazel fleck in the left. "It's like nothing you've ever known before," she said.

He was adrift. They were serving egg salad sandwiches and building a secret world around him, around everybody.

"We're early adopters; we're stakeholders, Mark," said Tessa. "We want to be part of what's next. Don't you? Or do you want to be one of those people who would have been, like, *Thanks, no, Industrial Revolution, I'll stick with my loom and my gaslight?* You want to be left behind?"

She was eating her pie now. "These ships are just a small part of what's next. And yes, right now this part runs up against something called the 'right to privacy'"—she made air quotes—"which is a no-tion that hasn't really meant much in thirty years and means less every day. You may as well defend people's right to own steamboats. *Some-one's* going to control access to all the data and all the knowledge. All of it. Everything that every government, every company, and every poor schmuck needs to get through the day. You want that to be the other guys? Once everyone's on our network, the old, unwired world will be worthless.

"And that's how you guys will make a lot of money out of this," said Mark, trying to be all bottom-line-y.

"*Money* does not come close to describing what we'll make a lot of," said Tessa.

When sleep finally came for him that night, Mark was tossed deep into a grandly staged drama where his mom told him not to take this job. *Do not take this job,* she said, pulling away from *Sine Wave 2* in her old lavender Dodge Dart, which was now also a helicopter. And he went back inside the ship, which was no longer the ship but had become his childhood home, and he grappled with Tessa beneath his Luke Skywalker bedspread, the sweetness of the grappling cut with anxiety that James Straw would walk in on them.

QUIVERING PINES

Leo," said James. "Leo."

Leo woke. The jasmine was still in the air. He had fallen asleep with his shoes on, which made him feel dangerous.

"Your sister's here."

"What? No."

"Yes. At the smoking station."

Leo clawed at the light in the room. He'd been asleep for less than an hour, he was certain. Unless he had been asleep for twenty-four hours. "That's not possible. I mean it's highly unlikely."

"Ah. Okay. Someone pretending to be your sister is here, then," said James.

Leo got upright and started moving out of the room and down the hall, still napped-out and confused. James was right behind him and they moved briskly. A woman at the men's smoking station would be a level-one breach of Quivering Pines' gender-segregation policy and would probably set in motion some sort of regime response. They were racing the clock.

"I left her out there, but I couldn't keep Clive from talking to her," said

James. "He thinks he just won the lottery. Hurry. He'll bore her sideways."

The small knot of men in the lounge were also aware of Leo's alleged sister outside. But they had gone into prison-yard mode, and no one wanted to be called a snitch. Leo realized that they liked him, that they didn't want him booted from their midst. He passed through the lounge and stepped out to the patio, and as he did, one man posted himself along the corridor to keep a lookout for counselors, and another clutch of men arranged themselves in front of the patio doors and busily scribbled in raggedy notebooks to distract from and obscure the transgression taking place outside.

Leo saw a girl there and in the bright sun was a little dazzled. Clive was talking to her. She was dark like Leo. No, darker. Very pretty. But too small to be a Crane. Cranes leaned back on the air behind them; this girl leaned in. He stopped at the edge of the patio. James stopped beside him.

"Yeah. That's not my sister," he said.

"Really?" said James. "You sure about that? This is important."

"I'm serious. That's not my sister. Look at her."

The woman turned around just then and looked at Leo.

"Shit. I guess you're right," said James. "Well, she said she was your sister. I'd better come out there with you."

They walked to the smoking station. "Clive," said James when he and Leo had reached the smoking station, "come back in with me. I want to talk to you about something."

"In a minute," said Clive.

"No, Clive. This can't wait," said James.

Clive copped on. He quickly dug a business card from the breast pocket of his fleece top and handed it to the woman. James gave Leo two of his menthol cigarettes and then escorted Clive back to the facility.

Leo gave the girl one of James's cigarettes. "Here," he said, "look like you're smoking this." He demonstrated by taking a fake drag. "So you're my sister," he said.

"Yeah. No," said Leila.

"You're not my sister?" It came out like a question.

"No, I'm not."

"I know. I know you're not. Why'd you tell James you were?"

"The lady at the front desk kind of supplied me with that one. It seems that your sister was expected. I needed to see you."

"Do I know you?"

"No."

This was a relief. "What can I do for you?"

"I'm here because of your broadside. I'm with the people resisting the thing you warned about, and we want to know what you have on Deveraux." She held her cigarette like she'd seen them held in the movies, but she took a passable fake drag, and then did a good fake exhale.

"You read my broadside?"

"I did."

Leo noticed that the eye of the stanchioned cigarette lighter was glowing orange. Behind the girl was the medical building; a slender telescoping satellite antenna had sprouted from its roof.

"Did you drive here?" he asked her.

"Yes."

"Are you in the lot?"

"Yes. It's a little black Toyota. Two doors. Beneath the basketball hoop."

"How about I meet you there in four minutes?"

"Copy that," said Leila.

Leo turned and walked quickly back to the patio. The summer buzzed in his ears. He was elated. More. New. Information. James fell in with him when he strode into the lounge. The onion-shaped counselor had come down the corridor and was sniffing at the frisson in the room. He looked perturbed. Leo motored back to the dorm room, James right behind.

"What's up?" said James when the door was closed.

"Couldn't rightly say," said Leo.

"You packed?" said James.

"No. They packed for me," said Leo. He dropped the Dopp kit into the duffel and slung the whole thing over his shoulder, like a sailor. He stepped up on the windowsill. "James, I'm going to leap out of this window now," he said.

He leaped, and landed twenty-four inches below the window in the loamy softness of the Quivering Pines bark-mulch moat. A ceanothus scratched at his legs. "I'll see you on the outside," he said to James, through the window.

"Go with God," said James Dean.

Leo made his way across the landscaped *zona* that surrounded the residential wing. He bobbed and weaved a bit between the bark-mulch inner ring and the hedgerow before the parking lot. He saw the girl in a Toyota where she said she'd be. He dashed over to it and tried to get in on the passenger side. But the handle lifted, clickless and impotent. He rapped on the window. She looked at him. He saw that she was beautiful, eyes full of intent.

A clunk came from the door. But Leo was impatient and tried the handle again before it had finished and the door had fully unlocked. He saw the onion-shaped counselor come out of the front door of the main building and look his way. Leo dropped to a crouch on the ground. The girl opened the door from the inside, and it bonked into his head.

"Ow," said Leo.

"What?" she said. "Where are you?"

Leo slithered around the car door and slunk into the passenger seat. He sat spinelessly and below window level, like an adolescent not wanting to be seen in a car with his mom.

"What are you doing?" she asked him.

"Is there a man coming toward us from the main building?" he asked her.

"What man?"

"Guy looks like an onion."

"Um, yeah, actually."

"Okay, we gotta go."

"Who is that guy?" the girl asked.

"No, I mean, right now."

"Are you allowed to leave?"

"It's not a locked facility. Go-go-go."

So she did. She reversed zippily from the spot and then saw the man from the building quicken his stride. Briefly, she choked and forgot she was in neutral, and the engine roared unengaged. The onion man broke into a trot. "Shit," she said. Then she found her gear and the little car leaped, and they flew down the leafy drive and walloped over a speed bump. Leo unslumped himself and tried to catch mirror glimpses of Quivering Pines receding.

"Okay, what's that up ahead?" asked the girl, alarmed suddenly.

Leo looked. Something was happening to the next speed bump. It was rising from the surface of the drive, like a mechanical maw. The girl braked hard and skidded a bit and ended up stopped a yard from its solid jaw.

"You said this wasn't a locked facility."

"That was my understanding," said Leo. In the rearview, he saw the Onion crest a hillock on a speeding Segway.

The girl reversed rapidly down the drive, looking for a break in the deep gutters that lined the sides of the road. Finding one, she shifted, and they left the road sharply. She was trying to go around the embassy-anti-car-bomb pie wedge. But once off the road, Leo saw that the potted cacti beside the drive were positioned in a pattern that prevented a direct path through the field beside the road. The girl had to slalom around the cacti at low speed. When they passed very close to one of them, Leo could see the large planters for what they were: steel and concrete vehicle blockers. The Segway was getting closer.

The girl managed to drive them between the planters. She got the Toyota back on the road beyond the raised pie wedge. Then she sped down the rest of the driveway and over the little railroad crossing that marked the boundary of Quivering Pines.

*　　*　　*

They came into the city on I-5, from the south, up over the long upper-deck stretch of the Marquam Bridge and down its poorly cambered and vertiginous far side. Mount Hood was clear in the distance, sharp and faceted, like the mountains on beer labels. The girl's car smelled hotly of new and petroleum-based upholstery. He rolled down his window. A tumult of summer air whooshed through the car and buffeted his head, cooling the prickle of sweat that had broken on his brow.

He was visited by a sharp memory from childhood: Coming down the Henry Hudson Parkway in the backseat of a Volvo on a summer Sunday night. His dad steered a sirocco beside sheer walls of Manhattan schist, beneath the massive arched feet of the George Washington Bridge. The hot city air met the cooled layer of the river over the green verge of Riverside Park, smelling of Dominican barbecues and backed by an elm-ish funk.

Returning to the present, Leo tried to steady his mind. He had to rule out the possibility that this girl was a figment. If she was, then he had met the requirement for suicide; that was the deal he'd made with himself.

And yet—still. Here again was the world he had imagined; here was life. There was evil afoot and he was being asked to oppose it. Why had he been chosen for this counterintervention? Would Quivering Pines give chase?

They slipped along the concrete channels of the freeway like they were riding a log flume at a water park and exited onto a street of car dealerships—tubular wind-sock men and Mylar glitter bunting dazzling drivers-by. They passed the hospital and the derelict Wonder Bread factory, slated for demolition, backhoes and breakers waiting dinosaurishly in its fenced-off yard.

"I never introduced myself," said the girl at a red light, the first they'd come to. "My name is Lola Montes."

That was odd, he thought, she didn't look Latin, and she'd paused between the first and last names.

"Leo Crane. Would you get in the left lane here?" he said. What would a sane person do now? "Bring me home and I'll make us some coffee and we can talk."

But when they rolled up to his house, he saw someone standing on his porch, so he didn't tell Lola to stop there. When they'd gone a block, he asked her to pull over. Then he adjusted his side mirror until it reflected his porch.

"Something wrong?" asked Lola.

"That was my house back there. But the letter carrier's lingering."

Lola adjusted her rearview, and they both surveilled.

"Is that not your regular mailman?"

"I got a few. I must be on a crappy route. Sometimes it's this very fit, too-tan lady. Sometimes it's a Sikh dude who wears the whole outfit, you know? The cape and what I think may be a postal-issue turban. Sometimes it's a slacker in, like, a Slayer T-shirt. But I don't think I've seen this guy before."

They both discreetly observed him as he left Leo's porch and walked across the street to a little USPS minivan. He popped the lift gate at its back. It looked to Leo like he was sorting large envelopes back there and scanning bar codes, as mailmen sometimes did midroute. Then the guy got in the driver's seat, but he didn't start the van. He unwrapped a sandwich and started to eat it.

Sure. Could be lunch, Leo thought. "Would you tell me more about your people," he asked Lola, "the ones you said are resisting the thing?"

Lola seemed to collect her thoughts. "We're called Dear Diary. Though I think that's supposed to be ironic or something. I'm very new. Anyway, that's just a sort of a placeholder, you know, as a name. We're in a state of flux."

"And there are lots of you?"

"There are tens of thousands. Hundreds of thousands."

"And the other side? The ones you're resisting?"

"They're called the Committee, and they're building an extralegal, nation-replacing, wealth-protecting, fee-based data-rights system."

"A system?"

"Yeah, like, 'Hey, sign up now, richest point-zero-zero-zero-five per-cent of the world, for our data-protection plan. That way, when we cripple the electronic infrastructure, your shit is safe and everyone else is a fucking peasant.'"

"So is it as I described?"

"You embellished. The Scientologists aren't involved. And it has noth-ing to do with your illustrious ancestors."

Yes. He had bragged about his illustrious ancestors, written that he was descended from the American intellectual elite. How mortifying.

"But you were right about SineCo," she said encouragingly, as if sens-ing his embarrassment. "Straw is using that search-and-storage empire of his for something very bad indeed."

The search-and-storage empire. Yup, that's what had first aroused Leo's suspicions. "We'll Keep It Safe" was the tagline for SineCo's new, unwired socialverse. And Lola was telling him that SineCo was only the part you could see.

"It's like a network or a club. The Committee owns some companies outright. Not just SineCo, but Bluebird—the private-army people—and General Systems, that company that makes thermostats and break-fast cereal and airplanes. And then there are hundreds of other assets that they just control—the word they use is *claim*. Dams and mines and airports and pharmaceutical companies and TV networks and hospital corporations and a couple of the big NGOs."

"It's a cabal," said Leo.

"Yeah, a cabal, I guess."

"A shadow government."

"Well, if they're not that yet, that's what they aim to become."

Whipsawed. That's how he felt. Where was the flatline? How he longed for a quiet brain, trusty, like a pony. He would need days with this Lola Montes stuff. To let it sink in, to untangle the real from the imagined. But she was clearly in a hurry. And even bipolars receive star-tling emotional news, right?

*   *   *

Leo tried to channel James Dean the way James had been when he helped Leo work through the plot the other night. Leo turned his attention from the passionate emotions to the reasoning faculties. *Follow the plot, don't drive it.*

"But there's lots of law enforcement monitoring all that, and there are spies sitting in office parks in Virginia looking at screens, aren't there? Isn't their main job now to keep North Korea or al-Qaeda or whoever from crippling anything? Or there's, like, investigative journalists and honest public servants. Someone would have seen this and blown the whistle on it."

"Well, as far as the Committee getting caught by crusading journalists or whatever, that ship has sailed," said Lola. "And a lot of the guys sitting in office parks in Virginia *are* the Committee."

The mailman finished his sandwich, started the minivan, and pulled away.

"And you were right about your old friend Deveraux," said Lola. "He's a way to Straw, to SineCo. That's why we want to know about your incriminating evidence.

"Leo?"

"What? Sorry. I guess I was considering something else."

"What were you considering?"

"Whether or not you're real."

She turned in her seat, took his hand, put his palm on her chest, and pressed it firmly against her breastbone. There was no sex in the gesture, but it whisked them both somewhere farther along the line of their story. He could feel her heart beat and smell a mild funk from her.

"I am real," she said.

And he knew that she was. No figment would have done that. She let go of his hand. "But I am also in a hurry," she said.

Yeah. She sure was. It was chop-fucking-chop with this girl. "And I want to help you," he said. "Problem is . . ."

She waited a few seconds. "What's the problem, Leo?"

"The incriminating thing I have on Mark Deveraux..."

"You don't have it? You made that part up?"

He could tell her he'd made it up, that he didn't have it. But those lies would only confuse a confusing situation. The world sends you a Lola Montes at a critical juncture, you do not shy away from truth-telling. You take one careful true step at a time.

"No. I have it," he said.

But how was he to say this? Straight out, the way she was talking to him. "But it's a piece of film, Lola. A silent movie. Super-Eight. From college. It's Mark beating off while pretending to be crazy and retarded," he said. "It's not really a movie. It's one shot. Three minutes long. But it is a *long* three minutes."

He could see her take this in.

"Is that really what you people do?" he asked her. "This kind of black-mail? Isn't that the other guys?"

Damn, thought Leila, that wasn't at all the kind of incriminating she had been anticipating. The look he gave her was right on: this did change the landscape. Every time the word *blackmail* had crossed her thoughts as she was crossing an ocean and a continent, she'd managed to brush it aside. This was a pitched battle, after all, everything at stake. Besides, Leo's broadside had made it sound like what he had on Deveraux was incriminating because it would expose the Committee somehow, like it was evidence of a crime. This was different. This was a guy beating off twenty years ago.

"Let's go inside," Leo said. "The mailman's gone."

She needed to pee, and she needed to devise a next step. She'd come all the way here and boosted this strange man from a rehab facility or something worse. The incriminating film did sound unusable. But was she supposed to just leave? Or get new instructions from Dear Diary? Or get the film from Leo and take it back to Dear Diary and let them make the call? Her little Nokia hadn't issued her any instructions since she'd landed this morning, when it had directed her to Quivering Pines. What about Leo Crane? Had their escape put him in danger? If he wouldn't give up the film, was she supposed to just leave? Let him in on a secret and then take off?

He had her pull around the block and go down the narrow, green-bursting alley behind his house. She nosed the front half of the Toyota beneath a tumble of blackberry vines so they both had to get out on the driver's side. They hopped a fallen cedar fence into his overgrown back-yard. At his back door, he took a spare key from the mouth of a little metal frog and let them into his kitchen.

She went to pee. Walking through his house, she thought Leo must be rich, or comfortable, anyway. He was a single man with lots of furni-ture. There was well-matted art on the walls. And there was expensive product in his bathroom—German skin tonics and organic soaps and a wooden toothbrush. If he was rich, Leo might not be well disposed to Dear Diary politics. Then again, it wasn't like Dear Diary wanted to take away his German skin tonics, was it? For that matter, Leila was a big fat Western consumer herself, and if it was that kind of revolution coming, she'd be in trouble pretty soon after Leo.

Sitting on the toilet, she took her little Nokia from her pocket and composed a text to Sarah. Had to boost Crane from the facility you sent me to. Incriminating thing he has on Deveraux not really incriminating, just embarrassing. Pls advise. Lola

When she came back into the kitchen, Leo was arranging cookies on a plate. There was coffee burbling in a moka pot on the stove.

"You like apple?" he asked her.

She did like apple.

He cored and sectioned an apple and then pulled a jar of almond butter from the fridge. He added the apple boats to the cookie plate, put a schmear of almond butter beside them, and placed a little spreading knife beside the schmear. He was swift at his kitchen coun-ters. In her family, the men were lost in the kitchen. Certainly her dad, who had some generational excuse, but also her brother, Dylan, who did not.

Leo took the moka pot from the stove, then racked a plastic tray of ice cubes into a heavy Pyrex pitcher and poured the hot coffee over the cubes, which cracked and popped dramatically.

"Listen," he said. "About that movie I mentioned. I wanted to explain. I mean, about why I even have it still."

"That's none of my business," she told him.

"Yeah, but I mean, I don't want you to think that I still have it for any repressed homosexual reasons."

Oh, great, she thought. *That's what he's worried about.* "I don't care why you have it," she said. But that came out too sharp. And he had made her this nice snack, and, yeah, it was a rather volatile thing to have and to keep—footage like that, of an old friend.

"So why do you have it?" she asked him, snapping a cookie in half.

He poured their iced coffees. "Milk?" he asked her.

"Not when it's iced, no," she said.

"That's how I do it too!" he said, apparently pleased with this small commonality.

He sat down across from her at the kitchen table and started talking.

"When we were in college, Mark signed up with one of those sperm-donor agencies—it was called Cryogenetics or something—that trawled the Ivies for semen with good SAT scores. I always thought the idea was weird. It seemed to me unfair and unwise to scatter your seed far and wide. Men are supposed to want that, you know? Men are supposed to take pride in their genes. Like: Lucky you, world, here's more of me. But I didn't have that. I still don't. Sometimes, I've even arrived at the opposite conclusion: that maybe my line is best stamped out. I thought Mark might feel the same way, and I asked him about it once. We didn't really disagree about much back in those days. I asked him if he was bothered by the idea of being father to a child he would never see. And he said, 'No, on the contrary, it seems to me like a good deal.'

"But I knew he'd had some fun with the Cryogenetics profile—he added three inches to his height, said he was planning to be a marine bi-ologist. That sort of thing. So I said he should at least let purchasers of his seed know that he was actually a depressively inclined binge drinker whose cracker magician father had abandoned his family and probably committed suicide.

"Mark must have changed since those days, because back then he was never inflated or hypocritical; he was always willing to consider a thing. So he said that he was smart, white, and skinny, and that that was mainly what these people were looking for. But then he said, 'You're right, I should give them a better picture of myself,' and he started doing this loony pantomime, like a silent-film actor. He tied a Harvard scarf in an idiotic bow around his head, like a guy with a toothache in a cartoon, and he grinned goonily and pretended to be masturbating. I started filming because I filmed everything that year, and because it was so funny. We also were probably stoned. We were usually stoned. And then he picked up a *Wall Street Journal* and fastened his eyes on it as though it were the most forbidden erotica. That made it even funnier. So when he took his actual dick out of his actual corduroys and started actually masturbating, what am I gonna do, be the prude who yells, *Cut?*"

She saw his point. The whole thing was honestly arrived at. Leo wanted her to know he was not a creep who'd secretly filmed his friend's dick. Fair enough.

"But I know what it looks like," he continued. "It looks like it was made by crazy idiot people mocking their own privilege and celebrating their own leisure and just generally being wildly unaware. And it looks like it was shot by a repressed gay best friend. It is nothing I want to be associated with. But that's not even really the reason I can't give it to you, that's not the reason we can't use it against Mark."

"I know," said Leila, seeing where he was headed. "Just because something is embarrassing doesn't mean it's wrong."

"Yeah. Exactly. We'd be not just blackmailers but creepy, prurient judgers."

"Yeah, and you'd be the backstabbing old friend who kept the creepy footage," she said.

"The only reason I still have it is that I have all the film I shot that year and most of the tape I shot in the years after I gave up film. To discard a reel of film because my old friend's semi-hard dick appears in three minutes of it, *that* would be weird, wouldn't it? Like, methinks he doth be a bit too repulsed by penises."

"But then why did you threaten him with it? *You* called it incriminating. That's why I'm here."

He deflated a bit. "I was so mad at him, Lola," he said. She was getting used to the name. "He dumped me. Like, as a friend. And in one of the so-called parables in that idiotic book of his, he made up this character based on me. I'm clearly the 'spoiled son of a toy tycoon.' Apparently, my insulation from the rigors of the market has kept me spiritually scrawny. 'Like a hatchery fish.' He actually wrote this shit. *He* still owes *me* eight hundred bucks.

"Then a few months back, I guess I just started having a hard time. I mean, at first it was great and then it got harder and harder, you know. And I ended up making some terrible decisions . . . or just, you know, forgetting to keep remembering that I'm not the center of things."

"I don't understand," said Leila. This was how Rich used to talk sometimes. She'd learned to steer paragraphs toward a conclusion. "Do you mean you went crazy? Like, actually psychotic?"

It worked here. "Not psychotic, no," he said. He spread almond butter on an apple boat. She waited. "My mind jumped the rails just before that happened. Or maybe I made that decision. It was like: Keep going up on this ride—which you're going to have to get off eventually, inevitably, by the way—or jump off now. Anyway, my mind and I chose to jump off, which was the right decision, I think. But we landed in a terrible place. I wrote that broadside just before I jumped off."

But here's the thing, thought Leila. *He doesn't look crazy.* Quite the contrary, with his apple boats and his well-matted art. And his eyes were soft and deep and they didn't even seem that troubled. She had seen troubled. Refugees. They had reason to be troubled.

"But that was a rehab facility I picked you up at, right?"

He nodded, like he knew where she was going. "Yeah. Yeah. It was. And I know, maybe I'm not really crazy. Or anyway, I probably fall within the functional types, the shouldn't-complainers. Probably the drinking and the marijuana made it worse, you know, tipped me over? And that was dumb. So I'm going to remove those from the equation and see if I'm still a fucking teacup, see how hard life is then."

This too reminded her of certain Rich conversations. Too many. Rich was a man of broken resolutions. People like that will waste your time.

"That's great. I mean it. I mean, if what you just said is that you plan to get sober," said Leila, tamping out the little fire her heart had started to build for him. "But I'm not your sponsor or anything. I came here to see if you would give us the thing against Deveraux." This was a kind of war; the Committee had done worse things to her dad than blackmail him. She would ask again. "Will you give me that movie?"

Leo walked to the open back door. A mild breeze, honeysuckle-sweetened, was coming in, enough to stir the dish towels hung on the handle of the stove.

"No. I've been up and down the question, Lola. I see no way around the moral prohibition against blackmail."

"But the thing we're trying to bring down is just terrible, Leo," she said, exasperation creeping into her voice. "Who cares about Deveraux's dick, or your feelings about it?" He winced. "They want to enslave us all. We have to stop them." She didn't want to go into her family troubles.

"I believe you. Please tell me what else I can do." He had raised his voice. "There's gotta be something else. Maybe your asking me to do this is some sort of test question, like a test from Dear Diary."

She hadn't thought of that. "No, this is not a test question. This is just a request for a thing."

"Or maybe you were sent by my judges."

"What do you mean, *judges?*"

"You know: God, Higher Power, angels, Santa, Elvis. Whatever."

"And in your case?"

"Dead parents."

"Your parents are dead? I'm sorry." Her heart blew on the little embers of the fire.

"Not your fault," he said.

"But you think I was *sent* by them?" She leaned on the interrogative there a little bit, to make a point.

"Well, whether you were sent by my dead parents or by a global on-line underground trying to stop the nefarious plot that I made out more or less correctly when I went near-psychotic, my decision is the same: you're asking me to do something that you know I should not do, that *I* know I should not do."

That's why he was turning her head. He let her see his confusion, but he would not budge from the place his conscience had told him to stand. It was usually the other way around: people pretended to be so certain of things, but they were just guessing at what they thought was right, and they could be swayed easily. Also, he smelled like coffee, and beneath that a very mild dank, like a barn. Also, he had nice hands.

He asked if she would like to take a shower or a rest or anything. Both sounded nice. She hadn't had a real night's sleep or a run in seventy-two hours, and she still needed to drive to LA tonight. That was fifteen hours at the wheel. It sounded brutal. *Vehicle accidents still danger number one in conflict zones,* she'd learned on those courses. People make poor decisions when they're pushed, when they're ragged. And she hadn't yet heard back from Sarah or Dear Diary. She looked at her watch. Three hours, maybe. If she had three hours' sleep, maybe she could take stock, at least.

He showed her to a room upstairs. It was very clean: a mattress on the floor, stacks of books arranged in some organizational system around all the walls. There were blinds on the windows that cut the light into bars.

"Listen," he said, "that guy we saw was probably just the mailman. But keep the blinds the way they are, I guess, and stay away from the windows. Right? I mean, until we know what's going on and have a plan. It's pretty hot in here. But that little plastic fan kicks ass."

It would do just fine. "Knock on my door at six, will you?" she said. "If I'm not awake."

"You got it," said Leo, and closed the door.

She sat down on the mattress. There were nice sheets on it. *I bet these sheets do not come in plastic envelopes,* she thought, *I bet you have to buy these in a linens store.* Her shirt stank. She stripped to her bra and lay down. She set the alarm on her Dear Diary phone for 6:03 and put it on the floor beside her. A fat fly bumped against the bright window behind the slats of the blinds, which rattled in counterpoint. She fell into a vat of sleep.

The door swung open a bit and squeaked.

"Lola. Lola Montes," he said. He was standing in the doorway, backlit. She shuffled her feet beneath the sheets as her eyes adjusted to the gloom of the room. Behind the slatted blinds, there was still daylight. Three hours hadn't been nearly enough; the sleep held her like vines. "What time is it?" she asked.

"It's six o'clock," said Leo.

Her phone began its reveille; she sat up to quash it, and the tawny cotton bedspread fell from her shoulders to her lap. Her near nakedness lit up the room. She covered herself swiftly. Leo launched himself out the door. She should have been embarrassed—she was a principal's daughter, after all—but she was too tired for embarrassed.

"I got your duffel from the car. It's here outside your door," he said from the hallway. "Okay, well, I'm going to go make dinner. Come down whenever."

She took a long, North American shower. After studying the ingredients, she used some of Leo's German skin tonics and his hippie body wash.

Dressing, she checked her phone. 1 New Message.

What diff btwn incriminating / embarrassing? If CRANE no use leave him. We'll keep an eye on him. Proceed to LA.

When she went downstairs, there were two fish on the kitchen counter, headless and frozen. A pot of water on the stove. Leo had begun some sort of rustic preparation around the fish — there were lemons and garlic and some peppercorns that had spilled from their fancy tin and rolled themselves away. It looked like Ernest Hemingway was trying to make dinner.

"You want a drink or something?" he asked her. "Though it would appear I have been relieved of all my ethyl alcohol."

"Water, please."

"You sure? I may have some Grey Goose in the toilet tank."

She didn't laugh.

"That was a joke," he said.

"Oh," she said.

He handed her a glass of water. "So I was thinking," he said.

"Were you?" she said. "A dangerous pastime."

"Indeed, Lola."

She almost told him then that her name was Leila, not Lola. Because now they were actually bantering, and the fake name seemed unfair and unnecessary. But she held back. She had to leave tonight.

"I was thinking that you never told me how you hooked up with Dear Diary. You said you were new. Is this really just about keeping us from all being enslaved by our digital overlords? Or are you in it for some other reason?"

Stall. "Why do you ask?"

"I don't know. Because of the urgency, I guess. There's something in your eyes. Like a part of your life is being threatened even as we speak."

Her phone rang and vibrated in her pocket. ROXANA, announced the little screen.

"I gotta take this," she said. She moved to a sofa in the far corner of the big living room.

Before Leila could finish saying, *Hello, big sister,* Roxana was yelling down the phone: "This number's been going to voice mail for, like, two days," she said.

"I'm sorry. I've been traveling. You have me now." Big-sister outrage was sometimes best tabled, ducked, averted.

"Where the hell are you?"

Could she say? Yeah. The Diary phone was secure. "I'm in Portland."

"Oregon? Why?"

"I'll explain when I get home."

"When's that?"

"Tomorrow."

"Okay, well, it better fucking be tomorrow is all I gotta say."

"Back off, okay? I'm trying to help here."

"How? By mysteriously delaying your arrival home?"

"It's complicated."

"It always is, with you."

Ignore. "How's Dad?"

"Suffering through Dressler's syndrome," said Roxana. "Usually follows a myocardial infarction: Pleuritic chest pain, tachycardia, fever, fatigue, malaise, anxiety. You'll be home tomorrow?"

"Yeah."

"Okay. Well, I need to talk to you before you see Dad. And you need to talk to Dylan about the lawyers. They're saying it's not the slam dunk you sold them, and suddenly they want to be paid up-front. Call me at work when you land. You have the number?"

"Not the one at that new place. I'll call your mobile."

"My mobile doesn't work in that building. The number there is—"

She said ten numbers.

"Got it," said Leila.

"Say it back."

This was just big-sister bossy. Roxana could recall long series of digits or words or random code. She could call up whole conversations and repeat them verbatim. It was one of the freak capabilities that had emerged early and made her parents know that she was something else, along with being severely disabled. A phone number was easy-peasy for either sister, though.

Leila said the phone number back to Roxana.

"Okay, I gotta go. Dad came home yesterday. But I want him moved downstairs. We got a hospital bed for the den. The bed guys are outside. I'll see you tomorrow."

Only after Roxana had quit the line did Leila really let it all sink in. Her throat thickened with grief. She began to cry.

"My big sister was super-pissed at me too," said Leo, from the doorway.

"What?"

"My big sister. Well, one of them. The one they thought you were at Quivering Pines. She's flying back up here to talk to me. Very sternly, I bet."

"Sorry if I got you in trouble," said Leila, and sniffled a little.

Leo made a *pish* gesture. "You got me *out of* trouble. Anyway, I just need to convince Daisy that I'm done being crazy and that I'll stay sober now. This one actually believes in me, though. So I have some ideas about how to convince her I'm serious. I think I'll *not* go into the part about the online underground."

"It's my family I'm doing this for, Leo," she said. "You asked about my being in it for any other reason. That's the only reason, really."

And when she said the word *family,* she started crying again, and he came and sat near her on the couch. He gave her his dish towel. It smelled a little grungy, but she found a clean corner of it to wipe her nose and eyes.

She told him most of it then. About how she'd seen something in Burma, and the e-mail she sent out, and then the guys who started following her, and then the other guys who started following her, and then how her father had been arrested for something he could not have, would never have, done, and about the heart attack. And she told him about Ned from the university saying it was worse than she thought, and about Ding-Dong.com and Heathrow and Dublin and the white Ford and the Horse Market and Ikea. She left out the eye test, though. And she still didn't tell him her name.

He listened carefully to all of it.

"Motherfuckers," he said when she was finished.

"I know, right?"

"I'm going to figure out a way to help. You want some dinner? The fish is gross. It was in the freezer way too long, I think. But the rice is good."

"No. I gotta drive home."

"To LA?"

"Yeah."

"Lola, that's, like, fifteen hours."

"I know."

"You can't drive that now. You're wrecked. Stay here. Leave in the morning." He said it plainly.

He was right. So they ate rice for dinner and she told him more about Burma and he told her about a bookstore he once owned. It seemed like he could talk all night, and though she liked him, she couldn't keep away from thoughts of the nightmare waiting for her at home: Her father accused of child predation. Dressler's syndrome. A fucking bed in the den, like for a dying man. How was she going to beat these evil fuckers? How was she going to save her dad?

Before the light had even left the sky all the way, she said she had to go to bed.

"Let's both think on it, Lola," he said to her as she climbed the stairs. "Maybe there's some other way I can help you. There's gotta be. I'd do anything to help you save your family."

She woke before dawn, packed quietly, and crept downstairs. In the kitchen, there was only the refrigerator hum and the daylight beginning to spread from the windows. She found a notepad by the phone.

Leo—she wrote—*you are fun and smart and kind, but you have your own problems right now. I mean, I have my own problems and they're different from yours and I don't see how we can help each other. Though we did try, didn't we? That's definitely something. Good luck with convincing your sister you're okay now. I'd vouch for you. But that wouldn't help, would it?*

She wanted to say more, but the thing about making a clean getaway was that you really had to commit, so she signed it: *Thanks, L. PS: to keep us both safe, you shouldn't try to contact me.* She snuck out the back door and across the new blue dawn light of the backyard and into the alley behind.

He had shifted the blackberry vines so that they nearly covered the car; she had to part brambly strands to open the driver-side door. But the car slipped easily out of its hiding place, and she crept out of the alley and quickly found the on-ramp for I-5, only blocks away.

BROOKLYN

These dreams Mark was having, in the three days since he'd choppered away from *Sine Wave 2*.

It was as if every night he clumped into a basement theater to watch a cycle of dark, allegorical one-acts, but he was the actor as well as the audience. Once he dreamed that he was sputtering up a dead-end street in a dying car and came to a brick wall on which was tagged—beautiful and sparkling, like on a New York City subway car before Giuliani—*Who You Kiddin?* Another dream had him as a human squirrel who re-alized too late that he was supposed to have been gathering nuts. Most every night there was one in which he was given some simple task that turned out to be totally beyond his abilities.

Last night it had been a very realistically shot one in which sunglassed agents were walking up to his front door, which was made of papier-mâché.

Mark had returned from London to find that his general contractor—a suave Quebecois named Maurice who had a two-year waiting list—had made zero progress on the loft. Maurice had somehow sensed the dwindlement of Mark's available funds and gone on to greener pastures. So Mark camped out in his gutted one-bedroom with its plywood subfloors and electrical wire curling from junction boxes.

When he'd gutted the place, it had never occurred to him that he might lack the funds to put it back together again. He thought seventy-five grand and nine months were totally reasonable figures.

Blown and blown. What an idiot. He'd spent twice that. He'd paid Maurice for materials that never materialized, for subcontractors who never got paid. He still owed ten grand to the Croatian for stonework in the bathroom. He seemed like a very nice guy, the Croatian. But the last time he came to ask Mark for his money, he'd brought his son, who was six foot eight and just stood there in the doorway the whole time.

It had been a perfectly good apartment too before Mark had torn it apart. But back then he'd wanted steam showers and wine cellars and pocket doors. Now he'd settle for floors and plumbing fixtures and five thousand dollars' worth of Ikea whatever.

Lying there clammily on furniture blankets, Mark decided to run through his options. Again.

Option one was to take Straw's job and become SineCo's storyteller-in-chief. Advise Straw while he and a faceless consortium "secured" all the information in the world. Abet the crime and provide cover for it. Continue to plug and evangelize the Node but now also be a "pioneer" of the new socialverse, SineLife.

Say yes, and his money troubles would vanish. Poof. And Straw definitely implied that if Mark became SineCo's SIC, the Blinc book—or at least its looming deadline—would also vanish. When Straw had pressed him for a firm decision as he left *Sine Wave 2,* Mark had tried to buy a few weeks by reminding Straw that he had to "finish that thing for Marjorie." He had to shout these words. They were standing near the helipad at the bow. "Don't worry about that, Mark. I'll talk to her," shouted Straw. And then his last words to Mark: "You know, Mark, that I assured the principals that you would take the job. That's why we let you come aboard before your commission."

Maybe he even *should* take this job, morally speaking. So that he might influence it for the good. Seemed unlikely, but still.

Option two: Don't take Straw's job. Disappoint and piss off his Croesus-rich patron. Finish—well, start and finish—the book he owed Blinc in two weeks, its deadline twice extended. The book would be crap, most likely. His shtick would be laid bare. He would run out of money, owe still more; he would have to find a real job again. This last part might be difficult, as he had few skills and had pretty much told his last employer to eat shit, and anyone interviewing him for a job would probably be unable to resist saying, *Wait, aren't you the guy who wrote that book about how you would never have to work again?*

Who was he kidding? It was like being between a rock and a feather bed. Unless he personally had to drown puppies or whatever, this was a job he was likely to take.

But just in case some new information arrived in time to stop him from taking Straw's job, in case he did indeed have to deliver the Blinc book, Mark was working on it as hard as he ever had.

"I am a writer," he said aloud to himself, and he rose from the dingy pallet, wandered past his six-burner French cast-iron stove—marooned and plastic-enshrouded in the middle of the living room—and went into his bathroom, the floor gritty with mortar spatter.

There were moments—high and drunk moments, let's be clear—in which he saw that there might be a third way. The book was so late now that maybe they would have to publish whatever he submitted. A great work could be hidden in that inane title. It was *conceivable* that he could write something very, very good in a couple of weeks, his reaching mind told him. Didn't Jack Kerouac or whoever just put a *scroll* of paper in his typewriter?

It would have to be good enough to make up for the crap that already bore his name. But if it was good enough, maybe he'd be allowed to write more. Not for Blinc, obviously, but for a real publisher. He knew he didn't need as much money as Straw had offered him. There was the slim relief in this, in finding a limit to his own greed.

He filled the coffeemaker from the bathroom tap, then called the deli around the corner and ordered an egg and bacon sandwich. He did his sit-ups and push-ups, proudly, on the dirty floor.

Now that he was back in Brooklyn, he had access to the weed he liked. Clean, hydroponic, fairly traded. He got good and stoned and got down to work.

After an hour, he had to get stoned again and take a brisk walk around his incredible city. He was trying to skip his record, open his heart, see through time. Or possibly he was trying to shirk work, hide from the truth, and find in the gabble of his stupid, teeming brain some way out of his current bind.

He wound up in Prospect Park in front of a bronze statue of Abraham Lincoln. Mark didn't like it at all. In this rendering, Lincoln was too richly robed—he was wearing a cloak, for Chrissake; the man was born in a log cabin—and pointing like a know-it-all to a bronze Emancipation Proclamation in his bronze hand.

Mark had a thing for Abraham Lincoln. Always had, since his dad had taken him to the Lincoln Memorial when he was a boy. Probably the same year he left. *Look. See how he wants to get out of that chair?* said Mark's dad, leaning close to his son. *See how his attention is focused on the thing that he had to do? That was a man charged with a great and difficult task.* And even at twelve, in a beloved windbreaker, shorts, and tube socks pulled up high and tight, holding a huge eraser from the White House gift shop, Mark understood that his father, whose mother's people were Louisiana from early times, was saying something important. So he had listened closely and he came away with the hope that one day he would be charged with a great task.

But Mark's dad's great and difficult task, apparently, was to abandon his wife and son, to go off and be gay somewhere. So why should Mark honor anything the man said?

When they came back from DC, Mark couldn't stop talking about the Reflecting Pool and White House tour and, especially, the Lincoln Memorial. His mom was annoyed. They probably didn't have the money to be taking vacations, even Amtrak ones. That was probably it. And one night, before she clicked the light off, she said, *You know, Mark, sometimes we have to do the right thing even when nobody's looking. Everybody's got to help. There's lots and lots of great people — and women too, remember, not just men — who don't get statues, who live faithfully a hidden life, and rest in unvisited tombs.*

Somehow that bedtime speech found footing in the coral of his little-boy brain, and in college, when Mark got to the end of *Middlemarch*, he really thought for a minute that George Eliot had somehow cribbed from his mom, but then he realized that it was just her sneaking the literary canon into his head, the way she liked to do. His charm was his dad's, but if he was smart, it was because of her. She would not want him anywhere near this SineCo shit, he thought as he wandered stoned through the park on a Tuesday at noon.

There *had* to be another way. Straw wanted him to catch people in a net. Being a hack was one thing; being a criminal propagandist quite another. For his mom. For his mom, he had to say no to the job.

But the money. The money his mom might need.

Maybe, for his mom, he had to say yes to the job.

Two years ago, when he'd first come into what seemed at the time like totally bankable fame, when he had been certain that the universe was telling him, Here, Mark, you can take care of your mother, who took such good care of you, he had made certain promises to her: a less toxic house, with a little yard; a car that didn't break down; a real doctor whenever she needed one.

But unless some rich gigs were forthcoming or some new source of income came into play, next month he should really tell her to give back the car, because that was money that should be put toward her health insurance. (*Toward!* It cost two grand a month to be on hold with these people.) The insurance was called Healthy Choices, which made it sound like a cereal, but it should have been called Abstract Obligations — he couldn't understand a word of the literature they sent him, even though *Don't worry, Ma, just have them send that stuff to me* was what he'd said to her a year ago.

Health insurance trumped car right now, definitely. Her brain might be going coralline, according to some of the very initial tests they run on you if you can't remember how to drive to the tire dealership at which you've worked for fifteen years, and if your home appliances start to menace and stump you, and if your bridge partner dumps you (and if you have a fully paid up Healthy Choices Gold Shield plan). And who knew how much money he'd need if it turned out she was slipping down the banks of Make Sense into the River Dementia?

Okay, so maybe *this* day, the brisk walk had led not to writing but rather to more of the morose and desperate outlook and hours of aimless walking and a few more terrible minutes at the typewriter and a few gorgeous minutes (those immediately following the five o'clock whistle and the untwisting of the gin cap) that he spent at his window looking at New York Harbor and Lower Manhattan, imagining how it would be when his stupid self-help book turned out to actually be a work of truth and power, of forgiveness and rebirth. Old friends would get back in touch; they'd say, *I always knew you had it in you, Mark.* His home would become a salon, with smart and worldly people who cared about ideas and distant struggles and good food and him.

And the stupid little fantasy buoyed him, and he found that a glorious evening waited outside. He walked east, the sun throwing his shadow long. His neighborhood was teeming with prosperous liberals and the harmless homeless, and he steered himself into a restaurant to find food and to douse again—with Thai beer, it turned out to be that night—the worry and fear that had stolen another day.

The next day, Blinc's office called. Not with a reprieve on the book (*I'm sorry to inform you that Marjorie Blinc was mauled to death by her vizslas* was what he'd secretly hoped to hear when he answered), but at least with a paying gig, the very next day. An overnight to Chicago, at Conch's expense, to lead a morning seminar for...it wasn't clear to him for whom. But anyway, it would be a break from the writing, and he'd probably get ten grand for it. That's what he'd gotten last month for a similar-sounding gig. That would keep a few hounds from the door. He could hold off the Croatian with the threatening son, keep his mom's car lease a few more months, find an electrician to bring his apartment into compliance, and the rest would go toward the worst of the credit cards.

Mark hadn't actually spoken to Blinc since that unfortunate dinner in East London. She was conveying her displeasure and impatience with him by communicating only via underlings. Her chief assistant called him with the news of the Chicago trip, but it was a lesser assistant who waited until the next morning to send through the itinerary-and-engagement-specifics letter.

It could hardly be worse. He was to be on a "moderated panel" in a bookstore. It wasn't clear even that he was the headliner. And then the really bad news: the whole thing was considered a promotional event, to which he was obligated by contract. There would be no honorarium. Hotel, airfare, and probably some fucking bagels. That was it.

The bookstore wasn't even in Chicago. It turned out be in a suburb the name of which Mark did not recognize. Transport from airport to hotel was by shuttle van. The hotel belonged to a sub-brand of a better hotel and was only a few steps above the kind in which they shove the flight-bumped. It had a lot of frosted glass; the lobby plants needed dusting; in the elevators and even in Mark's chill, dank room, there was an abundance of cheap advertising for local attractions and services—skydiving, a cheese museum, a steakhouse called El Primo.

The next morning was worse. Mark shared the courtesy van with one of his co-panelists, a handsome weatherman whose first book had been holding in the middle of the lists for a month now. The weatherman pressed a copy on Mark immediately. *Sunmakers: How Effective Leaders Use Bright Ideas to Get Through Dark Times*. It had generous margins. The shuttle van rolled through exurb after exurb.

"I really loved *Bringing the Inside Out*," said the weatherman. "You working on anything?"

Mark nodded and breathed out in a way that was supposed to convey he was so hard at work lately that he barely had time to answer the question.

When they came to the right exurb and arrived at the system of parking lots that served the mall that housed the bookstore, Mark and the weatherman were met by a teenager and brought to a dingy break room. There were bisected croissants and small pucks of cream cheese on a plastic tray by the door; the water bottles were off-brand and room temp. There were two other co-panelists already waiting: a Quit Your Job and Start Your Own Business guy and a Make Your Fortune Through Distressed Properties guy. Only the weatherman seemed not to realize that this was a dog of a gig. A techie with a greasy ponytail fitted Mark and the others with lavalier mikes. Twenty minutes ticked by before the teenager came back and led them into the MegaBooks! proper — as big as a hangar — to a dais beside Blender's, the in-house café.

There were easily two hundred people in folding chairs before the dais, plus maybe another fifty standing, plus some spillover from the Blender's crowd.

Who the hell, thought Mark, chooses to drive out to the local book barn on a beautiful Saturday to hear people like himself and the weatherman opine on self-betterment?

But when Mark saw who came in next, the crowd was a little more explicable. That was Diane What's-Her-Face, the single mother who had calmly lifted a small car off her son's leg (sincerely unaware, it seems, of the steady-handed neighbor lady with the flip camera getting the whole thing). After that thirty seconds of footage had been viewed ten zillion times, Diane Carlifter wrote what Mark had to admit was a very good little book about the experience.

I Didn't Do It Alone: Why a Connected World Is a Better World was one hundred and fifty pages and clear as a bell: "I discovered that I have so much more strength in me than I believed I had. And even as I felt Jimmy slip out from beneath the bumper of the car, I knew that I must never forget that it is my *belief* in my limitations that hobbles me more than my limitations ever will." Also, it didn't hurt that she was hot.

The moderator was the MegaBooks! founder and CEO. His own memoir—*How to Build Something from Nothing*—he had written five years ago without professional assistance and had published himself. It was such a deeply and essentially bad book and so roundly mocked by everyone who read it (*Holy Shit, Look at All This Money I Have!* was an alternative title suggested by one reviewer) that the CEO had attempted to buy back and pulp every extant copy, and had nearly succeeded. That, in turn, had made the book a *very* rare volume and given it a weird cachet among a tiny cult of book collectors.

They were on that dais for an hour, and for Mark it was a very long hour. The crowd really just wanted to hear from Diane Carlifter, and Mr. MegaBooks! did a crappy job of moderating. The Distressed Properties guy, having sat there unconsulted for forty-five minutes, actually got up to use the bathroom.

Mark mainly just sat there, an engaged and I-see look playing on his face. When the attention finally fell on him, he used one of his go-tos. A musing, Buddhist-ish parable he called Mistakes You Should Try to Avoid Making.

It was his ability to appear to be searching his soul that made Mark remarkable; that was probably what Blinc saw in him, way back when. It was easy for him. But now he felt like the guy who'd written one good jingle or whatever.

"Assuming that you're smarter than the other guy," he told the crowd, "that's the mistake you should avoid making." He said he used to make that mistake all the time, until he'd met a homeless man named Cecil.

"This was years ago. Every day, on my way to work, there was Cecil, sometimes asking for change, sometimes too plagued by his own demons even for that. I started spending so much energy trying *not* to give him any of my attention, because of the guilt he caused in me just by being there, you know? He was not easy to look at—he'd lost one foot to diabetes and the other was looking dodgy. He had this wet-wool-and-rough-sleeping-human funk around him like weather. After months of seeing him every day and trying not to, I just . . . well, I don't know what

I just, exactly, but it was bitterly cold that day, I remember, and I bought Cecil a cup of coffee. Pretty soon we were sharing a cup of coffee every morning. I'd pay a buck for the coffee and a quarter for the extra paper cup. And we'd take our coffee together there, outside the subway station." Mark looked just as you would look if you were casting your mind back to the memory of a lost friend. "Cecil taught me so much," he said meaningfully. "He taught me about eye contact. How to use it to protect yourself *and* to assert yourself. He had to do both, Cecil. He lived by his wits on the streets." Pause. "Though in the end he also died by his wits, I guess."

At the book-signing after the event, Mark regained some ground. He was an expert at the signing. Though the protect/assert stuff was bullshit, eye contact *was* important somehow, and Mark was naturally good at it. He might give a brotherly nod or a kind elbow touch in the handshake. Three times in the last year, a woman presenting his book to him had been broadcasting on a certain frequency, and he'd signed her book and then, with eye contact established, Sharpied his cell number onto the reverse of the dust-jacket flap. That method was two for three.

Which is why he got a special thrill when he saw that Diane Carlifter had written *her* cell phone number in *his* copy of her book. This depressing junket might have a consolation prize.

He met her that evening in a passable and nearly empty Italian place in the lobby of her hotel, which was nicer than his. He thought he was showing up for a date or an assignation, if that word meant what he thought it did. But a few minutes in, it started to feel like something else.

When they sat down, Diane Carlifter just drained a vodka tonic, which back-footed Mark a bit. He was going to try to keep to two drinks tonight. If the assignation thing happened, he wanted to be able to perform. He'd not actually gone there—like, with a real person—in months, and he had some concerns.

"You're going to have to stop using the Cecil story," she said after they had ordered.

"Is this professional advice? Because I'm open to that. I've been having a hard time coming up with new stuff lately. I loved *I Didn't Do It Alone,* by the way."

Oh, you little idiot, she pretty much said with her eyes. "I suppose it is advice, yes. Coffee hasn't cost a dollar since 1989, and people named Cecil do not end up homeless. You should've called him Joe or something." Damn. Mark had actually considered Joe. "But you don't have to come up with new stuff, Deveraux. They provide the content; we're just the platform. They certainly don't want any more of that homeless-sage thing. Unless you can throw Synapsiquell in there somehow."

"They?" asked Mark, signaling the waiter for another drink.

"Well, in our case, *they* is Straw, I guess, or the Conch Group. That's who you'll be under, I assume."

"You know about..." About what? What should he ask her if she knew about? His deadline? Serve-whales?

"I know all I need to know, Mark, about you and this situation right here. You're stalling; you've had four days to signal your intentions clearly, four days to pick up the phone and say yes, please, and, thank you, yes." She made four days sound like an eternity. "Let me assure you that without Straw behind you, you would have been given zero time to mull things over. You don't want people thinking that you think you're too good for them."

A teenage waiter arrived with their mains. When he'd retreated, Mark said to Diane, "Okay, Pope sent you, didn't he?"

"Pope? If Pope wanted to convey his concern about you, he would do it more directly." Then she softened a bit. "Tessa sent me."

He just looked at her. How many masks?

"She said you should give up the menthols?"

Okay. Diane was from Tessa. Tessa was a friend, he was certain.

"Tessa said to tell you you're on thin ice. You may have hurt Straw's feelings." Then Diane leaned in and loud-whispered the next part: "Take the fucking job, Deveraux. What's the holdup?"

What's the holdup? Now he leaned in and whispered loudly, "The holdup? You serious? How about the massive undersea vaults of stolen information? That beast just gorging itself with every minute detail of our lives so that one day the *computer* can tell the *person* what kind of day he had? We're just supposed to look the other way on that?"

Diane sat back. "You're supposed to change your perspective. Isn't that one of your saws?"

Actually, it was Tell Yourself a Better Story, but he got her point. "That's in the abstract," he said. "Like, you apply that shit case by case." It felt good to be the one at the table pointing out what was wrong with this model.

Maybe Diane saw him puff a bit, up on his (only slightly elevated) moral ground, because she sounded tough again when she said, "You must know by now that there are carrots *and* sticks in this game, right? Those computers have been gorging on every minute detail of *your* life. Don't you want to keep that safe?" Only the tiniest lilt of sarcasm on *safe*.

He had no answer to that.

"They moved up your next presentation. The Nike thing you were going to do next month? You're doing that next weekend instead."

He'd done something at Nike a year ago; he'd knocked it out of the park, actually. Digging Deep and Finding Killer App.

"I'm not prepared for Nike," he said.

"I told you—you'll be supplied the content. But Mark?"

"Yeah?"

"You better bring your A-game. They'll want to see that you can dance."

"The Nike people?"

"No, you moron. Our people. You need to commit. You get a few of those Nike pooh-bahs behind SineLife and you will have earned your first paycheck. You phone it in, like you've been doing, you may just run out of rope."

And as if she were on Diane's team, a waitress who had snuck up behind Mark said, "Would you like me to wrap that up for you?" Mark hadn't touched his food.

"Yeah, Mark," said Diane, "you could bring yours to your nice home-less friend." The waitress cleared their plates and retreated. Diane wrote a phone number on a piece of paper. "This is Tessa's direct line. About nine people have it. She said you should call her if you need any more help making this decision." She gave him the piece of paper. "But Mark?"

"Yeah?"

"You do *not* need any more help making this decision." And then she was gathering her purse and getting up.

That was it? He was supposed to walk back across eight lanes of traffic to his shittier hotel? There was only one chance at relief here. So as she stood up, and without giving himself time to consider it, he said to her, "Invite me up." He looked at her hard, but with his mouth a little open, his eyes saying *Please* but also *Come on, you know you want it.* "You can tell me more about the thin ice."

She smiled. Some encouragement in the smile.

But she was digging in her purse. "Wow," she said, "I've only ever heard about people like you." She put three twenties neatly on the table-cloth and walked away.

And so he was sitting alone in Fontana di Trevi in Creekville or Rockville or Rocky Creek, Illinois. He looked around to see if anyone was witness. Only a busboy, bringing him his boxed Alfredo on a tray the size of a shield.

His hotel room did turn out to have a minibar and Mark made maxi use of it. There was a *Law & Order* marathon on. If he stayed in the middle of his bed, sucking from the little bottles and clicking up and down during the commercials, he was able to avoid thinking about the situation.

Then, in the opening segment of the next *Law & Order,* a fruit ven-dor was found dead in his store, prone over produce, and, Lenny, the older detective, delivered his zinger: *If this is the carrot, I'd hate to see the stick.*

You must know by now that there are carrots and *sticks in this game,* Diane had said. Mark was filled with dread and panic again. He clicked around. *Shane* was playing on a high-up channel. His dad loved this movie. He switched from dark liquor to clear. He opened a seven-dollar box of Junior Mints.

Later, when the alcohol had smoothed the turbid seas and blurred his vision, he had an idea. It came to him in the bright light of the plastic bathroom. *You know who would love this shit?* he thought to himself, focusing hard on a far tile. *Leo Crane would love this shit.* Leo was always the first to see the patterns beneath the surface. He was always talking about *sifting data.* That summer they pretty much lived together on Mass. Ave. They shared that motorbike. There was a beautiful girl who worked at the deli. Leo came over every day after his shift at Widener. Widener still had that little rabbit-hole door to the stacks. Leo would come in and he'd say, *Data sets, Deveraux! Great data sets today.*

Yeah, Leo would love this shit. Leo was in Portland. Nike was in Portland. Of course!

This was such an excellent idea that Mark had to begin executing it at once. He stood, but forgot (1) that his underpants were still around his ankles, and (2) that he was holding a box of Junior Mints. Falling, he scattered the minty rounds about the bathroom in a wide arc. His humerus made hard contact with a corner of the plastic bathtub. The pain was so sharp he could only yell, *Gah!*

Then, recovering on the cool tile, he remembered that he had insulted Leo Crane in his stupid book and then totally dumped him and then *stolen* material from *his* weird blog, which had gotten weirder, until, when last Mark looked at it, it seemed like Leo was headed toward the Crane curse. In that big kitchen on the garden level of the Riverside Drive place, Leo's mom used to tell tales about her husband's "eccentric" brothers. Barking mad, they sounded.

But you never know. Whose genotype is without booby traps? And maybe Leo would let him borrow some material, for old times' sake.

He erected himself and left the bathroom, stepping on the scattered Junior Mints and mashing them into minty brown squidges. He found his computer. Using one hand to cover one eye, and one finger to carefully depress keys, he navigated his SineMail and composed the following:

Leo, old friend. It's been so long and that's all my fault. I will be in your city this weekend. Let's have dinner. friday or saturday or brunch. If brunch too gay then drinking.

CALIFORNIA

So what's the deal with your being two days late?" Dylan asked her as he took her bag out of the car. It was midnight. Dylan had been waiting for her on the street, smoking by the garage, when she pulled up.

He embraced her before he said anything. The sweet stink of his cigarette was overpowering, but she was so glad to see him that she found it delicious.

"And whose car is this?" he asked, checking out the vehicle.

"It's kind of a rental, I guess."

He gave her a *bullshit* look. "From where? Planned Parenthood?" Leila saw what he meant: the faded and peeling pro-choice stickers on its rear bumper.

"Yeah, well, I guess I kind of borrowed it from some friends, then," said Leila.

"Intriguing," said Dylan.

"Oh, yeah, brother. Most intriguing. But maybe pointless, after all. So I don't want to get into it tonight." She saw that Dylan was even looking a tiny bit old, like the ledge of his shoulders was less straight than it had been a year ago. She saw it then for the first time: he looked like their father.

"Is Dad up?"

"Probably not. He's pretty checked-out at night, actually. I don't see why he has to be on that much stuff. But Roxana says it's okay."

"Is she pretending she's a doctor?"

Dylan smiled. "No, the actual doctors put a stop to that pretty quickly. But she's liaising with that half of the situation."

"And you're legal?"

Dylan gave the faintest nod. "That's the idea."

"But then what do I get to do?"

"Just do some of your magic."

"Right. My magic."

"Well, you can help me with the legal stuff. Or you can take it over, actually. It's not going great on that front. The FBI is just canvassing everybody who ever came through that school to find any dirt on Dad. And, you know, even Dad has enemies. Someone's gonna make something up soon. Yesterday, one of the lawyers said maybe we should see what kind of deal they're offering. I didn't even tell that to Dad. If this sticks to him . . ." Dylan was at a loss for words. "We can't let that happen." He dropped her bag by the front door and hugged her again, but the other kind of hug, the kind where the hugger lets go of his own strength for an instant and sort of hangs off the huggee.

"How about Mom?" said Leila, partly to bring the hug to a conclusion.

"Yeah, that's what you can do, actually."

"Is she totally wigging out?"

"Well. No. I mean, she's wigging out. But not about the right things. She tore into a checker at Safeway the other day, for double-bagging or not double-bagging or something. But she's pretty much ignoring the actual situation. She hardly noticed when I got back from the airport two days ago and you weren't with me. I told her you were hung up in London, and Roxana told her you had to stop in New York. She never investigated either claim."

Shit, thought Leila. "Is she up now?"

"She's not home. She's out with Peggy."

"Peggy Pillbottle? Hasn't that old wagon tripped over a golf tee yet?"

"You know that Peggy quit drinking ten years ago, right?"

"Yeah, I know." Peggy Pilkerson was one of the few non-Persians in the small crew of friends Leila's mom had run with since she arrived in America. But Leila was forgetting that Peggy Pilkerson was also Bobby Pilkerson's mother, and Bobby Pilkerson had been Dylan's best friend growing up and then had died, presumably accidentally, by autoerotic asphyxiation at seventeen, which tragedy had a few extra layers of pain on it and had been six months' worth of local gossip and had led to Peggy's divorce and then to her spectacular collapse. "Maybe Peggy's a great one to handle Mom, under the circumstances," said Leila.

"Yeah, maybe," said Dylan, in a way that meant "probably not." "I think they're playing blackjack right now."

"What's blackjack?" said Leila.

"The card game," said Dylan. "Like, they're at a casino. That's where they end up when they go out. Last week they drove to Vegas."

"Mom can't play cards." This was a known fact. She was always calling jacks jokers and folding when it turned out she had a killer hand.

"Well, then let's assume she's losing," said Dylan.

"Or maybe she's been hustling us all these years."

"That would be a very long con, sister."

Leila slept in the little room off the kitchen, beneath the stairs. It had once been Dylan's room. But now their mom used it to stack cases of President's Choice diet cola and to hide all the real-life things that housewives need to hide in order to make their houses look spotless. But there was still a narrow bed in there. Dressing in the tiny space, Leila was put in mind of Cinderella or Anne Frank. But then she remembered that one of those was a fairy tale and the other a girl murdered by Nazis.

In the morning, sitting on the toilet, she looked between her knees and was comforted when her eye landed on the little hexagonal floor tile that had cracked to look like an old woman talking to a butterfly. Dylan had once said to her, *No, not an old woman talking to a butterfly. That's a fish about to eat a piece of fish food.*

But, lifting her gaze from the cracked tile, Leila noticed that the bathroom wasn't as clean as it should have been. This was strange. Mariam Majnoun considered herself the personal enemy of any scuzz, dust, film, fliff, grime, or splodge that tried to breach her walls.

After a long shower, she dressed and then knocked lightly at the door of the den. Then a little less lightly.

"Come," said her father.

Leila had prepared herself—she thought—for the sight of her dad as a cardiac patient. But no, she hadn't, it turned out. When she was home a year ago, he was just a guy nearing retirement—a bit stooped, and squinting at labels—but you could be that way for twenty good years. Whereas the Cyrus Majnoun in the hospital bed in the den looked to be near the lip of the canyon. The skin around his eyes. Leila must have displayed her shock, because her dad winced before he smiled. But his smile was a true thing and he said her name in a still-strong voice and as she ran toward him, he zizzed up his adjustable bed with dispatch.

She hugged him as best as you could hug someone who was sitting up in bed.

"So was it London or New York you were stuck in?" he asked her.

"New York," she decided. "I had to debrief with Helping Hand."

"Ah, yes, the employer with the dumb name. Are they going to straighten out your problems with the unreasonable Burmese?"

"It's unclear."

"Well, anyway, I get to see you, which brings me joy."

There was a ten-second stretch of not saying anything, and then Leila thought she would cry, so instead she said, "This bed fits in the den just fine."

"Yes, it does," said her father, nodding and surveying the room, as if Leila had flown home from Burma to evaluate the feasibility of putting a hospital bed in the den. Another ten seconds or two weeks ticked by and then her father said, "Leila, I have not yet said to you that this thing they say I did . . . these charges. I want you to know——"

"Dad, I know." Leila cut him off. "I know that. And not just because it's you, but also . . ." She stopped. What would be gained by telling her dad about Dear Diary? Would it help in any way to say that she *knew* that he had been set up? Not by the maladjusted math teacher he'd fired two years ago (as Dylan reported he suspected) but by a cloaked and tentacular super-mafia? And that this had been done to him because of *her* nosiness and *her* whole pursuit-of-truth thing? And that she knew this because the nameless agency's antagonist network had semi-abducted and mind-melded her?

"I just know it, Dad. Don't ever have a sliver of doubt that I know that, okay?"

"Not a sliver," he said, and then *he* looked like he might start to cry, but then he saw, through the large den window, that his wife had arrived home.

Mariam Majnoun was getting out of Peggy Pilkerson's (actually, her ex-husband Pete Pilkerson's) sparkly brown Corvette, which was of an era when Corvettes had ludicrously long and potent hoods. Wafting from the Corvette, across the tiny garden and through the window, came the tinkle of her mom's pretty laugh, unrestrained, and a guffaw from Peggy, deep in the penile car. Mariam swung the big car door closed— she was almost unbalanced by the force she had to summon for the task—and crossed the lawn to the front door, with the extra-intentional gait of the still slightly drunk.

It wasn't until her mother had come inside and *click-click-click*ed straight upstairs and Leila had turned to watch Peggy's Corvette growl away that she noticed that her Dear Diary loaner car was gone.

"So, you left with the impression that these Dear Diary people could, like, unframe Dad?" said Dylan. He was skateboarding beside her as she ran. It was the second morning since she'd returned. She wanted to do at least five miles, but after two she was hurting and was considering a tighter loop; if she cut over behind the place that used to be the Noodle House but was now Cell Phone Depot, she could pick up Valley Drive and go back home that way. That might also be a way to lose Dylan, whose pointed questions over the first two miles had caused her to realize that she didn't know enough about Dear Diary's aims and methods.

"Yeah. That's what they said." Leila was not a talk-while-you-run type, so she did not expand on the answer.

"But you didn't get from the rehab guy what they wanted you to get from him, right?"

"I did not." They were on a slight downhill incline here, so Dylan was cutting the pretty, slacker-y arcs of the expert skateboarder. Leila liked that part of skateboarding, but the noise of the wheels she found grating. "I'm just saying," he said over the noise, "you got a big song and dance from these people who claim they can ignore borders and hack the state and rescue Dad"—he carved a lacy arc—"but that also just makes them hackers and human traffickers, and I haven't seen any letup in the pressure on Dad. You say they whisked you around Dublin and lavished all this hot spy attention on you"—another lacy arc—"but they could have been guerrilla theater, for all you know. All you got out of it was a broken Nokia." He terminated another lacy arc in front of his sister. She was retying her laces and shifting the Dear Diary phone, which was an annoying lump beneath her sweaty waistband.

The phone hadn't pipped since Portland, since it told her to leave Leo behind. She had tried to send messages to Sarah asking for updates, instructions. But No secure path available was all that displayed on its little visage.

"Though I guess the fake-documents thing takes them out of the class of theater," Dylan allowed. He did that scrape-kick-catch move that skateboarders do to come to an unbothered and indolent stop.

And the eye test, thought Leila. But she hadn't told Dylan about the eye test. "You should take better care of your board," she said.

Dylan looked at her like she was thick. "No, I shouldn't. It's a skateboard. You NGO people are such dorks."

This would be a good time to ask him. She'd have the rest of the run to think on his answer.

"Hey, D, did you go with Kramer and his forensics guy when they examined Dad's computer?" Kramer was one of the lawyers. Dylan said he seemed to be the one most behind them.

"Oh hell, yeah. We had to report to a creepy, bunkerized office building in Long Beach. The Regional Interagency Technical Services Facility. But those guys are so juiced on power, they insist on calling it the RITSerF. And I thought our forensics guy was going to be able to examine Dad's computer. But he didn't actually get to touch or even see the computer or the hard drive. They gave him access to what they call a *mirror image* of the hard drive. I know, right? In America. It's like the state says to the defendant, No, you can't see the evidence we have against you, but here, we'll draw you a nice picture of it."

"That sounds like bullshit."

"Well, that's how it is now. And yes, we sat there and looked at all this nasty porn that was allegedly on the so-called mirror image of Dad's hard drive."

"Was it that nasty?"

"You want to know this?"

Leila nodded.

Dylan shrugged. "I've seen worse. It was mainly pictures, static images. Nothing violent. But the girls were totally girls. I mean, they were *young*." Dylan dropped his eyes to the ground. "And then there were also these PowerPoint presentations. Shitty porn, no alleged minors evident, but with heads cropped from pictures of students from the school. It was revolting, especially because whoever did it didn't scale the heads right."

Leila exhaled. "Students from the school?"

"Yeah. See, that's why it's so bad, Leila. If they have any chance to get this before a jury, you just know they could select the kind of jury that would take one look at Dad and see a principal cutting and pasting their daughters' faces into porn collages."

Fuck. He was right, she thought. "But couldn't they have shown you anything? Come on. I mean, the mirror image of the hard drive?"

"I agree with you, sister, but read your Patriot Act. I told you that you shoulda voted for Nader."

"He was a spoiler."

"Well. We're supposed to accept this mirror-image business because all the metadata on all the images is consistent with their having been downloaded to that computer, that ISP, on dates between eighteen months ago and four weeks ago. You know what metadata is?"

"I think so. Time stamps and stuff."

"Yeah. And then there's this elaborately attested to chain-of-custody protocol—a big sheaf of papers tied in a folder, with affidavits and thumbprints that swear, *Here are the technicians who handled the evidence; here is the date at which it was moved from the middle school to the RITSerF.* You even get to see a little photograph of the computer itself, sitting on a shelf in a room in the building you are in. But you cannot go to that room."

"Motherfuckers," said Leila.

"Indeedium, sisbag."

"I'm gonna cut up here," said Leila, indicating a long flight of cracked steps. Dylan wouldn't want to take her shortcut. It would mean scrabbling across a scrub lot, and unlike his skateboard, his sneakers were precious to him; his shoe-care regimen was a family joke. She started up the stairs at a rapid clip, with taut fists, like Rocky.

Dylan called after her. "I hope you didn't give those Diary people anything. What if they were a cult? Or an Armenian ID thievery ring?" It was annoying that Dylan was getting to be the sensible one here, he who had once styled himself a didgeridoo musician.

But why had her phone gone comatose? And the way the Toyota had been repoed. That felt like evidence disappearing. She still had her Lola Montes papers. Was she supposed to destroy them? Or would they self-destruct? She moved them from beneath her mattress, lest she be engulfed in flames, and put them into a plastic envelope and then under the large pot of the struggling lemon tree on the tiny back patio.

That afternoon in Costco, Leila had a fight with her mom about the type of T-shirt they would buy for Cyrus. Mariam had selected for her husband another five-pack of white V-necks, the same shirt she had been buying for her husband for thirty years.

"How about some of these, Mom?" said Leila, holding a couple of alternatives above the rowboat-size shopping cart. Two crew necks, brown and light blue.

Mariam did not disguise her disdain for her daughter's suggestion. She made a waving motion with her hand at the idea. In the back of her throat, Leila could feel a fight coming on.

"You think if you came home with shirts other than those broken-man shirts, he would somehow not be all right with it, right?" said Leila, a little too loudly. "You're going to imply that *he's* the one who has trouble with change. But that's you, Ma. Just let the man try a blue shirt." Leila thought she saw the surprise in her mom's face; she thought she saw her almost engage on the point. Things had been brittle between them in the three days since Leila had returned. Her family was like the American Midwest—storms brewed for days before cracking open. But the middle of a Costco aisle was not the place, in Mariam's view.

"Leila. Show a little respect." She cast her own eyes down quickly, as if to teach her daughter how submission was properly expressed.

"Mom," said Leila, trying a deep breath, "I do show you respect. But I'm a grown-up. Let's try a little co-respect, can we?"

Mariam rolled her eyes in a brief and minuscule fashion. "Leila," she said, "I really don't know what you want from me. Your father likes these shirts. I should ignore what I know to be true? You say I make him into a broken man. Why would a daughter say that? It is not respectful. Your father needs routine right now. Those shirts you would bring to him . . ." She stopped and silently contemplated the medical risk posed by the T-shirts that Leila had chosen.

"They would cause his death. I know, Mom. That's why I want to get them for him," said Leila, fuming.

Mariam poked her chin high to avoid crying, and then she started crying and wheeled the cart away from her daughter. It was a grand wheeling-away, swift and dramatic. Leila looked like the asshole who had made her mom cry. She had swung too wildly, using that word *death*. *What is it with the brutal lights in these hangar stores?* she thought. *It's like living under a different sun.*

A fat man in a Lakers jersey and cap, munching a sample burrito, stopped to stare.

"Fuck off, clown," Leila said to him.

Leila bought the two T-shirts and met her mother at the car. Silently, they co-loaded the groceries into the Camry.

Only when they were both sitting in the still car did Leila say, "Mom, I'm sorry. I didn't mean to upset you in there."

Mariam was in the passenger seat; her eyes were smudgy with run makeup. But her voice was soft when she said, "Yes, you did, Leila. You are so good at it. But you should refrain from doing that, at least in public. There were people in there watching us."

Leila pounced. "What do you mean?"

Her mother caught the pounce. "People. People who know your father, who are probably looking at us for some sign. What people did you think I meant?"

Leila ignored the question. "Mom, you've been totally oppositional since I got back. You're finding every fault in me."

Mariam came right back. "You are always mocking me. The others don't make fun of me or of how I've spent my life. Then you get home and I am the big joke."

There was some truth in that—Leila was the lead plaintiff in the family. "Yeah. Maybe a little. I'm sorry. But you know what, Mom? You can't very well tell me I'm letting down the side by causing a scene in Costco when you're out whoring around with Peggy Pilkerson every night." Mariam pretended to be offended by the verb. "Oh, come on. You know what I mean. Gallivanting. Whatever."

"For years now you have been saying I should loosen up and get my own life. Now I should stop having a little fun in the midst of a dark time. Which is it?"

"How about you can take up gambling and gin but only after Dad's out of these woods?"

"So we're negotiating now? How long are you home for this time?"

"That's not what we're talking about here."

"Certainly not. We're never allowed to talk about that."

Deep breath. "Mom, it's not that we're not allowed to talk about it. It's just that that's not what we're talking about *right now*."

"Then what are we talking about right now?"

That could have been a rhetorical maneuver—put the agenda-making on the other guy's shoulders—but here it seemed a sincere offer of armistice, like when you admit that you are adrift on the sea of your argument. Leila tried to see her mom in full. Not just as her mom but as all the things she was: a woman who had given up a career, an exile who had never stopped missing home.

"I guess we're talking about why we've been so mad at each other since I got back. I think our sniping at each other is making it harder for everyone else, you know?" Leila started the car and eased out of the spot.

"Okay," said Mariam. "I'll tell you why I'm mad. You always treat your father more kindly than you treat me." That was all she said, and she even said it without rancor.

Leila was pierced with contrition. Of course, now, with his being laid up in that bed, marooned in the den, Leila was being extra kind to him. But her mom was right: Leila had always been a little nicer to her dad. That's just the thing she had with him: more distance, more kindness. "I'm sorry," she said. They were waiting to take a right.

"Now, you go," said her mom.

"What?"

"Why you're mad."

Fine. "Because I'm doing what you told me to do. *You* said I should be independent. *You* gave me all those lady-doctor coloring books and *you* said study study study. I am *really* good at my job," Leila said. She didn't want to go into the situation with Helping Hand, about how maybe she hadn't been as good at that job. Point was that she was accomplished and well thought of in her field. "You never ever say anything about that. And now you just want me to make babies." She joined a slow chute of traffic and was looking to get three lanes left in a block and a half.

"Leila, you *will* want children. Please don't wait too late. The study study study was just so that you would have your pick of men. I wanted you to have the smartest and kindest and handsomest."

Of course. Mariam was mad at the NGO sector for making her marriageable daughter into a global houseguest, willing to live in a second-tier megalopolis for eight months in aid of toilets or something, but unwilling to do the work that leads to a family. Now Leila had waited too long, turned down too many good men; she would end an unclaimed treasure, a clog-shod saddo, a terminated branch of the Majnoun tree.

But for Leila, her mom's endorsement of marriage and children had come too late. Mariam had done a fine job raising her children, but she'd looked mildly aggrieved throughout. Little Dylan once asked her, "Mommy, are your shoes too tight?" It was not recorded as a funny family anecdote.

"Well, also so that you would be smart," Mariam hastened to add. "So that no one would be able to fool you. But it was *not* so that you could be alone, giving all your youth to these . . . bureaucracies."

How Leila wished to refute the charge. But lately it did feel as though her impressive career was adding up to nothing behind her. Allie, her best friend growing up, had two children and a successful bakery business, with a fleet of vans and a twenty-foot-wide oven. Leila had lots of good stories, and was prized at dinner parties. But the stories people wanted to hear were not the ones she wanted to tell. She still carried school debt and still had cardboard boxes in her parents' tiny attic.

They rode most of the rest of the way home in silence, though not the frosty kind that had stretched between them at breakfast or the taut kind that had snapped in the Costco. It was kinder; a détente. Nearing home, they passed Peggy Pilkerson's place, with its plaster lions rampant before six feet of driveway. Leila tried to bring up again the subject of the nights out till all hours with Peggy. What she wanted to say but couldn't quite was: *Why are you choosing right now to quit being the Good Wife? Don't you know he's innocent?*

"I think *you* could stand to go out, Leila," said her mother as they neared the house. "You're helping neither yourself nor your father by just sitting in that little room and looking at that Tubeface."

Unfair. Leila had been reading her dad the newspapers, trying to help with the house when and where her mother left an opening. She wasn't online more than a few hours a day, and then certainly not on Facebook. She worked in the little room under the stairs because she was sleuthing; she needed to concentrate, and she didn't want to explain every page, or the black electrical tape over her webcam.

There was nothing on the Internet about Dear Diary. Finding nothing on the Internet about something is suspicious. Like, *yeah,* too *quiet.* There was a scrapbooking website called Dear Diary and some wry hunter's blog called Deer Diary. But there was no whiff of Dear Diary the secret resistance and people-smuggling network with postnationalist aims and a neurotransformative eye test, nor of its pitched battle with a fascist consortium of data miners. Was there another Internet besides the one she knew about? Were there secret domains? She scoured her computer for the little owl icon that had let her contact Dear Diary in the first place, but it was gone. She went over and over the Heathrow meeting and the day in Dublin, but she could think of no way back in.

"I'm helping Dylan with the legal stuff, Mom."

"How? Dylan's taking all those meetings. *He* updates *you.* And what's with that other phone you carry around and look at but never use?" Her mom was like this—oblivious, oblivious, oblivious, and then—*bam*—a noticer.

Then Mariam's phone rang. She dug it from her purse. "Hello, Dylan," she said. Her voice always brightened for him. As long as we're talking about who's nicer to whom, thought Leila, Dylan had better be getting this hard sell on grandchildren also.

Then Mariam sat up straight in the passenger seat. "What?" Her voice was hard with disbelief. Leila stepped on the accelerator. "But I don't understand," she said. Leila slowed a little; if the news were bad and medical, she wouldn't have said that.

"What is it?" she asked her mom. "Can you put him on speaker?"

Mariam waved her away, annoyed. "How can you be sure?" Nod. Squint. *Hmmm-mmm.* "Okay." She hung up, and even then she didn't start sharing. She was savoring knowing something Leila didn't. And when Mariam did speak, it was strange, because instead of sounding ecstatic and relieved, she sounded puzzled.

"That was Dylan," she said needlessly. "They're going to drop the charges against your father."

"He didn't tell you his name? He didn't have some funny name? Did he mention me or Dear Diary?" Leila asked Dylan. They were outside the house, Leila breathing hard. She had run the last half a mile at three-quarters intensity. Before going out to run, she had left a note on her brother, who was asleep on the couch. *Can you meet me outside 8:30?* it said. When she pulled up at 8:35, he was outside, smoking a cigarette, drinking slurpily from a Winchell's cup. He was definitely looking un-young these days, but that was probably the hours he was keeping. He worked full-time at Whole Foods, went to law school at night, a school much less fancy than the one he'd dropped out of.

"No. I told you. I was just eating a hot dog, on a bench, like a schmuck—"

"This was yesterday?" she interrupted.

"Yes." And he punished her for the interruption by taking an especially languid drag from his cigarette. It was going to be hard for Dylan to quit smoking; he smoked so expertly, his eyes bright behind the noxious veil. "And this guy walks right up to me. Too fast, you know? Like I kinda thought I was about to get knifed. But he just hands me this folded manila envelope, like I should know what it's about. So I said, Excuse me, but what the fuck?"

"Is that what you actually said?"

Dylan thought. "Yeah."

"And what did he say?"

"Wow, you're really helping me tell this story, sis."

"Sorry."

"He said, *Show that to your solicitor.* And then he walked away."

Leila made her eyes wide to indicate *That's all?*

Dylan made his wider to indicate *Yeah, that's all.*

"Dylan. What was in the envelope?"

"A thumb drive. I was about to poke it into my own computer right there on the bench. But then I got spooked and thought it should go straight to Kramer. Which was prudent on my part, because it turned out to have this thing where it could make only one copy of itself before it died. And at Kramer's office they brought it straight to their forensic electronics guy—who marks like four hundred and fifty dollars an hour, by the way, and sits in a room called a SCIF—a sensitive compartmented information facility. He took the one file that the drive had on it, and he immediately copied that file about a hundred times to their special offline servers. When I saw what the file was—like, on the screen—I didn't understand it at all. It was code, computer code. It could have been anything."

"Did the forensics guy have any idea what it was?"

"Well, first he says, 'Oh, this is useless, it's just a bunch of corrupt scraps.' He said it was like someone had emptied the shredder bins at IBM and then glued everything together to look like a document. But twenty minutes later, he actually stood up from his chair and sort of started hopping around. I have never seen a tech guy so excited. He's saying, 'It's written on the back, it's written on the back.'" Dylan took another drag of his cigarette, squinted through an exhale. "And it turns out that if you turn the code over, there are legible files on the other side. See, Mystery Dude gave us both the encrypted file and the decrypted file. The tech guy said that the code he thought was junk is actually the first nontheoretical use of quantum encryption he's ever seen. He said it was like someone had just FedExed us the Rosetta stone."

Leila stretched her calves against the little concrete wall that enclosed the tiny garden. Her dad had another olive tree failing to thrive in a terra-cotta pot. She felt the taut line up the back of her.

"It's a work order, Leila. Or an invoice. It's an internal document, anyway. From a company called TMI Data Solutions, in Roanoke, Virginia. It details the work this outfit did on Dad's hard drive. The file is called C. Majnoun Minor Porn. The work is broken down, itemized: Flick-Burst Transmission, and Evidence Custody Chain Repair—they did twelve units of that—and then there's one line item that just says Collage Fabrication. And there are these things that I guess are chat windows within the working document. Like, where people scribble notes, you know, on a document that has to go through an office. And beside Collage Fabrication, some professional framer has written to another professional framer, like at shift change or something, *Pull images of the blonde with the bangs in the folder JV Volleyball '06. That's the one I'd want to fuck if I was this guy.*"

The run had gotten her mind ticking right. Leila sucked down the news. What Dear Diary said about the Committee's reach was true.

"And it's enough?" she asked Dylan. "It's enough to make the prosecutor back down?"

"Well, so, by last night, our forensic guy had spoken with their forensic guy. And when we show up to the RITSerF, you could tell that the prosecutor was pretty shaken, actually. Kramer thinks that the man had no idea. They built that facility a year ago and it cost a billion dollars and it's supposed to be the safest place in the world, and we've just given him proof that the evidence in a high-profile case is being written like a storybook by some black-helicopter-contractor outfit in Virginia with apparently free access to his shop. Dude went white."

"And he said he's going to drop the charges?"

Dylan made a little grimace. "All but one. He wants us to plead to one count possession of unauthorized material. It wouldn't be a felony conviction. The sentence would be that Dad would have to sign a legal instrument saying he would never speak or write about the events."

"Dad's not going to do that. And if the prosecutor concedes that the evidence is fabricated, where's the unauthorized material?"

"When the FBI interrogated him, Dad admitted to having installed on his personal laptop a copy of, I think it was, Adobe Creative Suite. That was software licensed for use by the school only."

"You're fucking joking with me, right? They can do that? They can ream a guy like they reamed Dad and then turn around and compel his silence?"

Dylan, who took care when speaking and who saw no reason to add to the scope of the trouble they were facing, said, "Let's not worry about the *them* here, Leila. Or not at this moment, anyway. Let's just worry about Dad, and what's happening right now. Shouldn't we take this offer? Plead to the bullshit count, and Dad walks away?"

A car went by. Jim Brenton and his severely autistic son from three houses down. Leila waved, and Jim gave her two honks, like you do when you're supporting picketers. Dylan had told her that some neighbors were already keeping their distance and that an unknown man had yelled vile things at the house soon after the arrest. So the two honks made Leila want to weep with gratitude. Behind Jim Brenton's car came one of those cute USPS mail jeeps with the right-hand drive. The mailman inside was better-looking than your average mailman. Leila waited until both vehicles were well past.

"You think he should take it, I know," she said. "But, Dylan, he can't walk back into that school without it being perfectly clear to everyone that he was completely exonerated, cleared of all charges. The gag-order part of this would kill him."

"Maybe, Leila." They were standing close to each other now, like conspirators, like siblings. "But the risk of the other course is we fight this and lose. Or it could be months or years, and then we have to take the same deal, or a worse one. So maybe Dad won't be able to walk back into that school. I just want him walking."

Leila began to object.

"I know. I know. I know. It's a travesty of a mockery of a sham," said Dylan. "But imagine. The case would be us saying, No, it's not that a pedophile principal was making sicko collages out of the volleyball-trip pictures; it's that a shadow-government frame shop is persecuting innocent Americans. It would be a tough sell, sis. The drive that Mystery Dude gave us is enough to beat this. I say let's thank our stars and go home, because I don't know that it's enough to convince twelve content civilians that they're living under a tyranny. Maybe that's for another day, you know? Who knows, maybe that prosecutor will do the right thing and ferret this out."

"You're saying we should eat this? Let them get away with it?" She was checking his math, though, and saw that he was right, just in risk-to-Dad terms.

Dylan shrugged his shoulders, exhaled a thin stream of smoke. "Unless . . ." And he did this cool little rapping of the air, with his smoking knuckle.

"Unless what?" she said.

"Unless you can get your Dear Diary friends to hook us up with some more of the good shit."

PORTLAND, OREGON

Leo slept soundly, and ludicrously late, happy to be in his own bed again, certain in his dreaming head that the world had sent him word. A girl in a Toyota. So when he finally roused himself—ten fifteen!—and raced downstairs and found Lola's note and her absence, his world spun again. What utter bullshit. Leo was a *light* sleeper. *The universe sends you a Lola Montes, and you let her creep out of your house while you snooze like a fool?*

He sat very still in his kitchen, wondering what to do. For an hour. Then he made some coffee and thought about getting stoned. He pushed that thought away and thought some more about Lola, about why she had come, why she had left. And when a car he did not recognize pulled up to his house, Leo didn't know whether to run toward it or away from it. But the footfall on his porch was no threat, nor was the knock at his door. It was Daisy.

"You wanna tell me what the fuck?" she said to him.

The next morning. Daisy woke him very early, barging into his room and saying, "Let's go to that diner I saw by the freeway. We can write your contract there." She shook him hard. His sisters had always been physical and

307

executive with Leo. He didn't mind. Big brothers hold your head underwater and drive their knees into your solar plexus and throw your turtle out the window; big sisters just dress you up and order you around a lot.

They walked to the Overlook Diner and sat at a vinyl-and-Formica four-top by the window. *The freeway. That's what it overlooks,* Leo thought. He had wondered for years about the eponymous claim.

Daisy waited until they had coffees before them, and then she turned over her paper placemat and slid it across to him. She pushed over a pen and said, "Here. I'll dictate it to you."

Leo gave her a *seriously?* look. But his sister stone-faced him, so he took up the pen.

"'I, Leo Crane,'" she said, "'will not drink alcohol or smoke weed, starting now until forever, or at least until all my sisters are dead.'"

"Oh, come on, Daisy," said Leo, lifting pen from placemat. Daisy only made a *don't interrupt* gesture.

"'I will attend an AA or an NA meeting every day. I will meet with Alice Waters twice a week—'"

"The chef?"

"No, not the chef, you asshole. She's a therapist and an LCSW and she's good people and she's smart. Keep writing. 'And I will see Larry Davis, prescribing psychiatrist, once a week. My sister Daisy is old friends with Alice and Larry both, from PA school, and she will totally check up on me, and with them, whether or not that's ethical or whatever. I will speak by phone or Skype to at least one of my sisters every day, and I will accept every single call I receive from them.'"

"What if I'm in the shower or something?"

"'Unless I am in the shower or something, in which case I will return the call promptly. I will not sit in my house by myself. I can journal but I cannot blog. I will keep away from conspiracists.' That one's important, Leo. Also this one: 'I will find a job—'"

"Can you give me a few weeks on that?"

"'—within three weeks, maybe with that nice friend of mine the carpenter who fired me six months ago.'"

"Gabriel? I don't know. He was pretty pissed."

"I talked to him. He said he's willing to do it."

Leo nodded okay. "What's in this contract for me?" he asked.

"'In return, my sisters will not make me go back to Quivering Pines or any other inpatient rehab facility——'"

"Or nuthouse of any kind."

"'——or nuthouse of any kind. Though, of course, if I go crazy again or can't stay off the weed or the booze, my sister Daisy will be unable to plead my case anymore, and without Daisy advocating for me, I will be screwed.' Because Rosemary totally thinks we should have brought you straight to a serious psych facility back east."

"Wait. Is this part of the contract?" he asked.

"You don't have to write that bit down," she said. "But you get my point, right, Leo? This is the last bit of slack you get."

He did get her point. From where his sister stood, he probably appeared to be loitering at that fork in the road between eccentric wanderer and mentally ill loser. Daisy was just trying to call to him from down the road she had chosen.

That being the case, Leo knew at once that he must concede at least some of the claims he had made earlier were delusional—like that Marilyn and Brand-New Day and the people hanging warning signs by the light-rail tracks had been acting in concert and against him, because of his greatness. He knew that that was all nonsense, all bullshit; that was just bad genetic code; that was uncles.

But he also knew not to tell her the *and yet* part. *And yet* it turns out that he *had* been right about a lot of it; that there *was* a terrible plan afoot to collect and commoditize all our information; that SineCo *was* bad and *was* in cahoots with other bad guys, including his old friend Mark Deveraux; that not all facilities and institutions were what they seemed; that many were not, in fact, what they seemed.

He wanted his sister to see that he knew that he was lucky to be relieved of the self-spangled connectivity, the elation, the certainty. He didn't even want them back. Truly. The plain old world was strange enough, turns out. What he wanted back was that girl. But when he imagined trying to convince Daisy of Lola's role here, he saw that she'd probably end up saying something like *I believe that you believe it, Leo*.

No, the kinder thing here was not to make his sister worry any more than she was already legitimately worrying about his sanity and grip. She had enough on her plate. Everybody did. Groaning plates, all around.

He knew that Lola was real. He remembered putting his hand on her breastbone, remembered how little space she had occupied in the driver's seat and on the mattress. And when the blanket had fallen: chin and neck and swale of clavicle and rise of breast and fall of rib. Anyway, he had kept her note. And she left a hair elastic on the white cliffs of his sink. He was wearing it on his wrist.

So he signed the contract. Daisy booked a flight home for three days later. She said she wanted to stick around to see that Leo still had what she called a basic set of life skills.

She woke him for seven a.m. walks and light breakfasts. She made checklists for him and taped them to his fridge beside his placemat contract. *Walk. Breakfast. Meds. Meeting. Look for work. Clean big stupid house. Walk. Dinner. Sleep.*

Daisy was keeping a very close eye on him, and she was bossy. But she was not unreasonable. Leo liked having her around, and he was allowed to give her a hard time in his way. "On the walks, I don't have to carry those stupid little pink weights you carry, do I?"

And she to him. "No, you'll probably get a workout cleaning this Richie Rich house of yours."

Zinger. It wasn't a Richie Rich house, though. She meant it was too big for one person. He had bought when the neighborhood was still rough.

Daisy drove him to his first session with Alice Waters, who turned out to be a totally uncreepy blue-spectacled Buddhist social worker. The next day Daisy drove him to his first session with Larry Davis, a bearded and besweatered old hippie who explained to Leo without condescension the pharmacology of and current theory on a drug called lamotrigine. He gave Leo his home and mobile numbers to use in the event of an adverse reaction.

Daisy didn't have to drive him to his first AA meeting, because there was one a few blocks from his house, in a dingy building in a still-ungentrified patch of his neighborhood. The building announced itself as Promises—the word painted brightly across the pocked masonry of its facade. Leo had always assumed it was some sort of evangelical outlet, or maybe a bar for black people or for the kind of white people who felt able to walk into black bars. So he was embarrassed to discover, when he consulted his little meeting guide, that Promises was the opposite of a bar—it was a sober club—and that the addictions and afflictions that brought people in there were highly democratic. This was no Quivering Pines. This was folding tables with that sticker of wood grain—that, but peeling—and tubes of powdered creamer made from hooves, and all types of people. It skewed a bit rough, but it was as mixed a room as Leo had ever seen in Portland.

After his first meeting, he drank thin coffee with Len, a grizzled electrician who had appointed himself Leo's sponsor. Len said Leo was clearly white-knuckling it and that he should Let Go and Let God.

Such meaningless advice. Not even noise, really. Leo wanted a new sponsor. Maybe he could break James out of Quivering Pines. Len said that Leo should try sharing in the meeting or talking to some people afterward; that he should try to tell the others what he was going through.

"You have to trust that there is some knowledge in the room," said Len, pulling from a Pall Mall. "Knowledge that could benefit you. Like, you ain't the first one been through this shit."

Leo tried to take that on board. But as beautiful and strange as the stories here were, as real as the suffering was, these people's predicaments were deeply unlike his own. This objection is said to be a form of denial called *terminal uniqueness*. The phrase was supposed to mean it was a false position. But a secret global network had sent a beautiful girl to involve him in a worldwide counterconspiracy. And then she'd asked him to blackmail an old friend, and when he'd said no, she'd left in the night and broke his heart. *You* tell that to the room.

He thought it could work—the meetings and the sit-ups and the attempts at prayer. The checklists and the granola and the lamotrigine.

But oh, how he wanted her back. The way she had made him feel; the way she had asked him straight, and told him straight; the way she had walked up the stairs.

He should forget about her, her wild claims of a secret world, her half nakedness, her having asked for his help. Yeah, *right,* he should forget about her, her wild claims of a secret world, her half nakedness, her having asked for his help.

Leo liked his sister's regimen. Her lots-of-leafy-greens diet; her bed-before-eleven, rise-at-seven policy. And he had to agree that the morning walk was a good idea. It gave his brain a baseline for the day. Or maybe that was the lamotrigine. So the day after Daisy left, he called his friend Louis, the guy whose wife was a public defender, early in the morning and asked would he like to take a walk in the woods.

Louis picked him up in his ratty Mazda truck, his old dog Cola on the bench seat beside him. Leo squashed in beside the musty brown dog and the trio drove to Forest Park, across the river, up over the arched back of the Fremont Bridge.

"Hey, do me a favor," said Leo, as they debouched at the trailhead. There were only a few other cars parked on the verge. "Leave your phone here, will you?"

"This more of your Gene Hackman conspiracy thing?" Louis asked him.

"Sure. We can call it that."

Louis was a city government reporter at the best alt-weekly in Portland. Leo knew that his job required being discreet and dogged at the same time. He thought Louis might be a good resource for how a non-schizophrenic person would go about confirming the existence of a secret cyberplot and the online underground opposing it.

Louis let the dog off leash and she shed five years, dashed away into the green brush beside the trail. The two men walked behind her.

While Leo talked, Louis kept his hands in his pockets and his eyes on the trail ahead. He asked only a few questions. He was pushing the pace. Leo was breathing hard as he spoke. Cola coursed around them, a house dog returned to her element.

After a mile, Louis said, "I thought you decided all that stuff was delusional."

Leo stopped there, where the trail offered a particularly nice view of distant industry. A heavily used bank of the Willamette was far below them, far enough below to look like it was from a storybook: train cars and brightly colored tanks and stacks, their grimy, carbon-economy purpose obscured by the distance, the view softened and Fenimore-Coopered by the trailside conifers in the foreground.

"Some of it was, some of it wasn't," said Leo.

"That's convenient."

"No, Louis, it's very *in*convenient, actually."

Louis regarded the view, and then his friend. "Well, I can look into what you said about SineCo, I guess. I know a guy who does that kind of reporting."

Yes. Someone to help him with this.

"You lost a dog?" called a man from the bank ten yards above them.

Louis turned quickly. "She's not lost," he said. "I'm right here." He whistled for his dog. Cola sprang to go to him, but the man had her tight by the scruff of her neck and he yanked her back in midair. Cola yelped in pain and surprise.

"She's got no collar," said the man evenly. "Could be a stray."

Louis moved toward his dog, and the man clamped down harder on her neck, pushing her into the ground. Louis stopped moving forward. He held up one hand to display leash and collar. "Easy now," he said.

"That's okay," said the man brightly. "They got microchips, now, in these dogs." He took what looked like a Node from the pocket of his too-heavy coat and held it scanner-style against Cola's shaking shoulder blades.

"Yeah. Here it is. You Louis Hanson? Live on Northeast Twenty-Fifth Street? Two little girls in day care at Sunflower's, on Killingsworth?"

Louis said nothing. Leo said nothing. The man gripped the dog.

Then Louis said carefully, "Yeah, that's me." The man let go of Cola. She raced to Louis, who slipped her collar on her and began walking quickly downhill. Leo stood rooted to the trail, looking at the man.

"Let's go," Leo heard Louis say, his voice weird with fear and urgency.

The man on the hill nodded at him, knowing, dismissive. "Yeah. Best be on your way, Crane."

Louis was ashen and shaking on the drive back across town. Cola licked Leo wetly on the ear. Getting out of the little Mazda at his house, Leo said to Louis, "You forget about what I said, okay?"

"Yeah, that's exactly what I'm going to do, Leo," said Louis, looking out the windshield. Then turning to look at his friend, he said, "You can understand that, right, Leo? My girls."

"Perfectly."

After that, Leo was more careful. He acted exactly like a man who was *not* trying to get to the bottom of something. Walk. Breakfast. Meds. Meeting. Look for work. Clean too-big house. Walk. Dinner. Sleep.

The watchers seemed to be everywhere. Or were those just random men, thick-coated and alone, nearby? They could be dads on the way home from work, guys heading back from the gym, a legitimate telephone repairman in a cherry picker across the intersection from Leo's house.

The man buying one loaf of bread and a quart of milk behind him in line at the New Seasons could have been just that. But why wasn't he using the express lane in the busy store? Maybe because this checker was hot. So after she rang him up, Leo said loudly, "Damn. Forgot something. Be right back." He left one heavy bag of purchased groceries at the end of the station to attest to his return. He grabbed the other bag and walked back into the store's aisles. Then he ducked quickly through Bulk and into Produce. He slipped on a squished grape, lost his balance, and felt the twenty lemons in his bag rumble weightless and almost spill. He caught himself and ducked through a portal made of hanging plastic strips, into the store's offstage. Busy employees took little notice of him. He found an exit by the loading dock.

If that bread-and-milk buyer had been following him, he wasn't anymore, Leo was certain. So he went to his local library and found a public computer in a carrel at the back. He spent an hour online.

That night Leo squeezed twenty lemons and soaked sheets of raggy paper in their juice.

He'd tried this once, at Brand-New Day. Well, not this, exactly. He'd let the children paint with lemon juice on a big roll of white butcher paper; they'd used fat ink brushes. The lemon juice dried to nothing, and he rolled up the work again. Then he brought the paper outside and unrolled it in a bright sunny corner of the OPZ. In minutes, the sunlight exposed the lemon-juice figures on the long roll: hand turkeys and love hearts and dinosaurs in proud, confident strokes; misspelled names a foot tall. The children cheered wildly.

This was a more delicate operation. But after a few hours of experimenting with types of paper, length of soak, and drying time, Leo had produced the result he needed. Then he had to figure out how to increase the impression force on the little electric Smith Corona that he'd picked up at a yard sale. He found the knob that adjusted that. Then he slipped one of his lemon papers into the typewriter's platen, sandwiched it between two plain white sheets, and wrote a letter to Lola Montes.

LOS ANGELES

Leila was driving downtown to have dinner with Roxana at her office. She was late, because the 405 was crawling. A huge white box van — *Stan's Sewerscopes: We Look Down There* — had been behind her since at least Balboa. Was it the van that was making her nervous? Or was she nervous because she had decided to ask for Roxana's help?

Roxana was still frosty about Leila's unexplained delay in getting home. Big sisters like to be kept in the loop. Leila hadn't wanted to get into the whole thing with Roxana, because where Dylan was skeptical, Roxana would be scathing. Plus, Leila hadn't gotten her alone yet. Roxana lived in a spare and highly modified Echo Park bungalow. She mostly went between home and whatever office, driven by her mobility assistant and body man, a now-old Pole named Eddie who had been at her side for seventeen years.

Roxana was born a phocomelus. That is, she was born with phocomelia syndrome. That is, Roxana had no arms. Her first years, in Iran, she was a travesty. Take the arms off a baby and what's left looks so much like a fish that Mariam's friends started avoiding her — most were saddened and secretly disgusted by the daughter. The market is the grown

316

woman's school yard, and Mariam found herself alone buying dates, buying butter, sipping tea.

When the Majnouns escaped to America, it got better. There were programs for Roxana; there was help. Iranian refugees were cool for a while there, in academia. Cyrus earned a master's degree in education, and the Majnouns met people eager to show support for the exiled family. Grants and loans paid for home modifications; other costs were defrayed or subsidized in kind, mysterious ways.

And when Roxana's staggering linguistic and computational skills began to emerge, the people who had helped felt vindicated, and they helped more. The circle of benefactors grew. Now Roxana was a prodigy, not a travesty. There were all sorts of scholarships for an armless girl who at eleven had learned to speak fluent Ojibwa from a documentary on PBS. Magazines and TV news shows even called, and Mariam and Cyrus said, *Yes, of course, run a profile, but we're sorry, no photos,* which made most of the magazines and all of the TV news shows go away.

Leila hadn't even noticed her sister's missing arms until around age seven. Then one day at the corner store, Roxana balanced on one leg like a shorebird and used her toes to count her change at the candy rack. *Gross, Dad, look!* said a boy. And his dad yanked his hand, and in a flash Leila understood that Roxana's armlessness was a *problem*. It was grotesque. Leila had four stuffed unicorns, but all her dolls had arms. Her sister was the *only one*. Leila glared daggers at the boy, then went home and cut the arms off her dolls.

Roxana did a steely job of ignoring the gapes and gasps, and she also ignored the limitations it was assumed she had. At eighteen, a junior at Cal, she announced that it was her intention to become a doctor. No one had the balls to say to her, *But you have no arms,* so she pursued that for a few years. As it turned out, Roxana's lack of interpersonal skills posed more of a problem than her lack of arms. When an MD career was ruled out ("Well, you can't really lay hands on people, now, can you?" said Dylan one Thanksgiving), Roxana moved to research genetics, and then to research oncology. In these labs and faculties, she was generally ten years younger than her closest-in-age colleague. From oncology, Roxana moved into some sort of mathematical-linguistic crossover research that Leila had never been able to grasp. The last time Leila had visited Roxana at work, she'd been at some laid-back cubicle-based research facility in Pasadena—Leila remembered a golden retriever wandering the halls and a lunch bag in the break-room fridge that said *I am Jim's sandwich. If you are not Jim, don't eat me.*

Roxana had a new job now, and Leila assumed from the company's name that it was in some kind of astronomy facility. As it turned out, though, it was in a huge, windowless building that Leila could see minutes before she found a way to reach it. It looked like it was *right there,* but then the exit to it was suddenly four lanes over, and you'd have to be a test pilot to cross them in time. Leila pulled all the way around in a tedious loop and made another pass, this time making the exit. The maneuver also allowed her to shake Stan's Sewerscopes, which was a relief.

She parked beside a freeway pier, in the thick shadow of its rumbling deck, and spent ten minutes looking for a front door to the mammoth building. She walked by it twice before she noticed a small sign beside an otherwise unmarked door that read *LA County Large Array Facility Visitors Must Wear ID at All Times.*

Leila waited at the front desk for Roxana to collect her. There was only one wooden bench in the lobby. Nothing else. Not a magazine or a potted palm or a wastebasket. Leila sat on the bench, the pleasing heft of a white deli bag on her lap: chicken salad sandwiches and pickles, Roxana's favorite. It was quiet in the desolate lobby, so quiet that Leila could hear the small hydraulic hiss of the receptionist adjusting her desk chair.

Her sister arrived wearing what looked like a desk lamp with a huge whisk on the end of it, secured to her trunk with straps. It was one of the beta-version prosthetics she sometimes wore, test-driving them for a prosthetics-inventing friend. She did it as a favor: no robotic arm would ever give Roxana anything close to the grace and functionality she achieved with her dexterous legs and feet.

"These came for you, Dr. Majnoun," said the receptionist, and she held up a worn manila interoffice envelope as well as a USPS Express envelope. She handed these to Roxana's robotic-whisk-clamper thing without clumsiness or embarrassment.

"What's with the no-signage and why'd they take my phone?" Leila asked Roxana as they walked to a bank of elevators.

"There's a fifty-tesla magnet on the third floor of this building," said Roxana. "For the Plasma Working Group. And I think they get a lot of Pentagon money, so the whole building has to be secured."

"Wow, a fifty-tesla magnet, huh?" said Leila. She was imagining a gigantic horseshoe-shaped magnet in a vaulted laboratory, little lightning bolts zapping from its feet, attracting distant paper clips.

Leila hadn't understood Roxana's work in twenty years and knew only that Roxana now worked in a field called control and dynamical systems and that she'd spent the past five years "modeling language" and that two years ago she'd won a lucrative prize that nonscientists have never even heard of and that three Czech mathematicians in their sixties were totally supposed to win that year. Since then, Roxana had been operating in extremely-smart-people world, a world in which her severe physical handicap was no professional impediment. Her colleagues were in far-flung learning capitals, screens away, married to desks and number clusters like she was. Her job required neither arms nor tact.

And so the girl whom the neighbors told the parents to throw out when she was born now worked in the upper atmosphere of the world's best research institutions.

They ate their sandwiches in Roxana's little office, which was all screens and tablets and specialized furniture. Also a lot of cacti. No photographs. Roxana didn't eat in front of anyone but her family and a few lifelong friends. Even the well-meaning and well-trained couldn't help but stare, and once or twice people in restaurants had asked loudly to be sat well away from her.

But in fact Roxana was so graceful that Leila, in her sister's presence, felt her own arms were excess appendages, that Roxana was a swan and she was a spider.

"I wanted to say thank you, Leila," said Roxana a few bites into her sandwich.

What was this? Roxana didn't exactly rain *thank-you*s. Leila couldn't remember the last one.

"For what?"

"Dylan said you know the people who got us the proof that Dad's computer had been tampered with. So thank you for that. If that's why you were delayed coming home, I'm sorry I was a jerk about it."

"That's actually what I need to talk to you about. Not about your being a jerk. I'm used to that"—a smile, to show that this was just play—"but about the people who got us the proof. Rox, I need your help finding them again."

"What do you mean?"

Leila's plan was *not* to get into the politics with her sister. Politically, Roxana was well to the right of Leila. Always had been. When Leila, at ten, had sat behind a cardboard box soliciting donations for Save the Whales, Roxana had really grilled her: *Do you even know what they do with the money you send them?*

So when Leila told Roxana the story, she told a truncated version. She told Roxana about Ned and Ding-Dong.com, how the owl icon had appeared on and vanished from her desktop. She said she'd been "diverted" to Dublin, and that she'd met some people there who had told her that they had proof that their dad was framed by a totally evil cabal. She said the Dublin people had asked her to meet with someone in Oregon to find something out for them, and that, in return, they would provide this proof that might clear her father.

Stumbling through it, Leila saw that she was leaving sizable gaps in the story, gaps that Roxana would probably want filled in before she'd help. Leila kept talking, hoping to race past the gaps. "So if there were, like, a hidden Internet—like, hidden inside the real one—would you know how it could be accessed? Or would you know someone who knows?

Weren't you doing that kind of work for a while, at PARC, that place in Pasadena? Because this woman in Dublin definitely said I could find her through the Dear Diary homepage."

Roxana didn't ask about how Leila had been diverted, and she didn't ask about the people in Dublin, and she didn't ask about what they wanted Leila to ask the guy in Portland about. Roxana asked only one question.

"So this is your fault?"

Leila sat there, stomach-punched.

"Isn't that what you said Ned said? That the evil cabal people did this to Dad because *you* went snooping around where you didn't have any business being, like you do?"

"Like I *do?* What the fuck, Roxana? Do not choose right now to pick me apart. Why would you do that?"

Leila had wanted to slug her sister one thousand times in her life. She had succumbed only once, at her own eleventh birthday party, when Roxana had stolen the love and pity and admiration of the room yet again, and on purpose. She'd learned then that slugging the armless is considered very poor form.

"If Dad gets hurt by this—" Leila said, after catching her breath.

"*If?*"

"—if Dad gets *more* hurt by this, I will never forgive myself, okay? I will hate myself, actually. Every day. I promise. Please, Rox. Right now, just help me find these people."

Roxana's face was set hard, but something gave in her eyes, and she spun in her netted chair. There was a mouse and a joystick below her desk; she worked them swiftly with her toes.

"You said 'Dear Diary'?" she asked.

Leila nodded confirmation.

Roxana entered the words in a search field, using an eye-line entry device, flitting her gaze over a keyboard on a screen.

"I already put the name into all the search engines," said Leila.

"Yeah. These aren't really search engines," said Roxana snootily.

As Roxana searched she asked Leila more about Dear Diary. Leila tried not to sound like a jabbering nutjob when describing it. But Roxana used a stay-silent trick that made Leila blab to fill the void, until Roxana said, "Leila. This totally evil cabal thing—you sure that's not just...is it possible that you, you know, went native a bit when you were in Burma?"

Roxana, with her pretending not to know that the neocolonialist language bugged the shit out of Leila.

"Went native?" said Leila, ticking her head to the side.

"Just be sure these people aren't playing you. Sometimes you want to do good so bad that you forget to be careful."

Ah, the Roxanian condescension. The big sister's knowing know-it-all-ness. "Well, they obviously didn't play me, Roxana, because I didn't get them what they wanted and they still helped us out."

"Yeah. Dylan told me what their 'help' amounts to. Dad pleads to some dinky shit, and everyone still thinks he's a pedophile. You said they use fifteen-digit identifiers?"

Leila nodded. She had decided to go with *they,* not *we;* she had omitted mention of the eye test, just as she had with Dylan.

"Okay, did she say *the* Dear Diary homepage or *a* Dear Diary homepage?" asked Roxana.

" 'The.' "

"I just don't want you mixing with the wrong side," said Roxana. She was really pressing her advantage here, the fact that Leila had asked for her help and had to just sit there and take this.

"The wrong side?" said Leila. "You serious? You looked outside of your bubble recently? Shit is going down out there."

"Look, Leila," said Roxana, "did a squeegee man give you a particularly pathetic look today? I know you're always out there swinging for the dispossessed, but remember that it's only because we got here that you can swing for anyone. Only because they let us in." This was the line she was always returning to. "You think I would have done okay under Ahmadinejad?"

"Once he realized you could calculate rocket trajectories, I bet you would've done fine."

"I would have been dead or behind some dumb wall before that. You know it."

Leila rolled her eyes. She wanted to stamp her feet. "Look. Yes. You're right. I do not think you — or any of us, actually — would have done okay under Ahmadinejad." Roxana didn't look appeased. "Rox. I'm proud to be an American. Okay?"

"Are you really, though? Aren't you one of those apologetic Americans? That's kind of what you do professionally, isn't it?"

"Screw you, Roxana. I'm not out there apologizing for the Bill of Rights. And just so you know? Every year, wealth and power are becoming more concentrated in a smaller mafia. Five hundred men, fifty multinationals. The way to get really rich is still — *still,* Rox, and we're well into the new millennium — to take advantage of all the poor schmucks beneath you. The way we have it set up now, there have to be thousands of poor people to offset each rich person. You think I apologize too much? Maybe you should be apologizing to some girl who has to shit in a canal while you have people building you prosthetics."

"Okay. Okay," said Roxana. Leila's burst of anger had worked. "I'm sorry I said that about your job. I actually think that what you do is admirable," Roxana conceded, shrugging her pear-like shoulders. "But you're wrong about how we have it set up now. All those poor people are welcome up here, with us. I love this country, Leila. And I think anyone talking about its overthrow is misguided. And I think that so-called radicals are dangerous, because they move too quickly, like children. And, like children, they fall off walls. They usually end up bringing about something other than what they intended."

"I'm not trying to *overthrow* America. Have you considered that it's the *other* guys who are doing that, that *they're* the ones subverting and co-opting and rigging things? We've got to push back before it's too late to push back. We've got to at least be ready."

"But you said it's a *postnationalist* organization," said Roxana. "That sounds to me like a bunch of affluent anarchists. Turtleneck types with tiny glasses of red wine."

"Okay. *You're* affluent now," said Leila, moving in. "You know that, right? Like, more affluent than I am; more than Mom and Dad are. Any idea or politics you have is, by definition, *affluent.*"

"I'm just saying. Either your new friends have pull or they don't. They can help us or they can't."

"They definitely have pull, Roxana. I saw things."

"Mysterious much?" prompted Roxana.

"Just, you know, the way they switched my papers in Heathrow, the way they kept me safe in Dublin. They have a robust network. But I can't access it since I got back here. They gave me this weird phone, Roxana." Leila reached into the white deli bag and pulled the little Nokia from the extra mayonnaise sachets and napkins and sugar packets (for bulk) and creamer pucks (for the signal confusion said to be caused by the reflective racket of the foil lids).

"You aren't supposed to have that in here," said Roxana. This pleased Leila because it laid bare for a moment the brown-nosey quality in Roxana, which the magazine profilers never mentioned since they were generally there for the overcame-adversity angle. "It won't work, anyway. The whole building's shielded."

"Fine. But just look at it. When you called me when I was in Portland, your call rang through to this one. I also used it to exchange text messages with the woman from Dublin. But it hasn't made a peep since I left Portland. Now when you call me, your call comes to my BlackBerry, the BlackBerry I left at the front desk. This one, the Nokia, the Dear Diary—its little green light stays on always. The clock knows the time zone. It's not a smartphone. Like, there are no apps. I can compose a message, but when I try to send it the screen just reads, No secure path available."

"When I said you aren't supposed to have that in here," said Roxana, "I meant you aren't supposed *to be able* to get transmitting electronics—

any type or kind of transmitting electronic device—past the sally port in the lobby. This is a hardened, unwired facility."

"Well, they didn't look between the chicken salad sandwiches, okay?" said Leila, waggling the phone.

"Let me see that."

Leila handed the phone to Roxana. Usually—all their lives—this had meant that the object would pass from Leila's hands to Roxana's feet. But since she was wearing the tester prosthetic, Roxana put out her graspy-whisk-on-a-desk-lamp thing. Leila, who had never once expressed discomfort with Roxana's armlessness, shuddered a little as she handed the phone into her sister's bionic prosthetic.

"Yeah, I know, it looks weird," said Roxana. "The final product will be covered in fake skin or whatever. This is the mechanics."

Leila was embarrassed to have been caught shuddering, and she saw now that the whisk thing was more like an ingenious paddle, with nesting, Teflon-coated wires forming a sort of cupped paw. Roxana could hold the little phone securely and even manipulate it more precisely than a human hand might.

But after a minute of close scrutiny, Roxana dropped the phone from her bionic paw and caught it with her feet. She felt the phone with her naked feet, the way you might feel a piece of fruit before eating it.

"I think I see how this phone got in the building," she said. "It's not electronic. There's no signature. You sure this isn't just, like, a gum dispenser?"

Despite the crack, Leila could see that Roxana was intrigued by the Nokia, and she kept it before her on her tall desk as she started back in on her screens.

"Okay, all I'm seeing is a strange deficit in the frequency that the words *Dear Diary* appear in Speechwave."

"What's speech wave?"

"Cool new software we got with foundation money. It samples daily human speech from all over the world, in real time."

In real time? "Samples it from whom, Rox?"

"Everybody. You and me, probably. Whenever we pass through a collection point."

Leila's mouth must have dropped open a bit, because Roxana continued, "Oh, no. It's not like that, Leila. There's no risk to privacy. It's deeply blinded; the data is completely severed from its source."

Wow, and you're supposed to be the genius in this family? thought Leila. But she said only, "So what's so strange about the deficit?"

"It's just strange. Statistically significant. Why are those and related words being used less frequently in the last five days? There's also been less crying and more laughing. That's correlated with anticipation."

Wait. Since when are astronomy facilities in hardened, unwired buildings? thought Leila, suddenly looking around Roxana's office. The door was four inches thick.

Then Roxana was consulting another screen. "Let me ask you this, sis," she said. "Did these Dear Diary people *do* anything to you? Like, did they administer a test, or a substance? Were you disoriented at any point?"

"What are you working on here, Roxana?" asked Leila, partly to dodge the question, but also because it suddenly seemed germane. "I mean, in the LA County Large Array Facility? I thought you were working on something about content-free static grammars. You're not an astronomer now, are you?"

"No. But I don't think there's even a telescope left in this building. Most of it's leased to New Solutions. That's who has the money for these nice computers. I get to use the computers to work on my thing, and I'm just expected to put in a few hours a week on one of their projects."

"What's that project?"

"Sorry. I'm not supposed to tell you."

Leila made a *really?* face.

"I'm not. I signed papers about this."

"What's New Solutions?"

"They're a pretty big IT contractor. I think they used to be called Blu Solutions/Logistics."

"That's a *defense* contractor, Roxana." Leila was scolding her sister and had grounds to do so. Roxana had always kept on the other side of that line. She had turned down lots of money before. She wouldn't work for the hackers either, though. She used to say it had to be real research; it had to be public. Everything she did, she wanted to go right in the public library.

"Okay, maybe," conceded Roxana, suddenly defensive. "There is a lot of that around here. And you're right — it's not my scene. I don't like not being able to talk about what I do. But it's not like anyone ever understood me before. Of course I liked SNARC better. I'll probably go back there. I was at SNARC, not PARC, by the way. PARC is in Palo Alto, not Pasadena. And my thing, the thing I'm working on like forty hours a week, is context-free *stochastic* grammars. You never pay attention to my career either."

Fair point, thought Leila. SNARC, the *I am Jim's sandwich* place.

Roxana was doing more justifying and rationalizing: "This is a one-year fellowship. The money is . . . good. I can pull more data here than I can anywhere else. Anyway, the thing they want me to help them with is totally good."

"The thing you can't talk about?"

"Well, the software is classified. But the application, Leila . . ."

Leila waited. She just knew her sister was going to blab.

"It's a gaze-capture device," said Roxana proudly. "A screen you work with your eyes."

"You've been typing on one of those for years."

"Yeah. *Typing.* Big whoop. This thing helps thoughts *come out.*"

Leila looked blankly at her sister.

"Leila, I may be like this" — she straightened up in her chair, to display her disability — "but I feel lucky when I think of the people locked in. Cord injury, Parkinson's, the myelin-sheath disorders. This machine could give those people a new way out."

"There are other things that machine could do, Roxana," said Leila. "How far along are you guys?"

"We're there, pretty much. We've built one. But it draws a ridiculous amount of energy. I think maybe that's why the fifty-tesla magnet on the third floor, actually. But the people working on that part say they may have found a way. They have a device they've been trying to reverse-engineer for months. They want my help with that too, but they're super-cloak-and-dagger about it—like, I would have to sign still more papers. I told them to find someone else."

Then both women jumped in their chairs, because the Dear Diary phone rang, loudly, with one of those skeuomorphic old-timey rings, and vibrated too, and scattled across the broad laminate surface of Roxana's desk. Roxana picked up the phone with her foot.

"Who is it?" asked Leila.

Roxana brought the phone to her face, squinted at the little screen. "Sarah Tonin?" she said.

Leila grabbed the phone from her sister's left foot, pressed ACCEPT.

"Sarah?" she said into it.

"Yes. Lola?"

"Yeah."

"Can you talk?"

Annoying to be asked that when *you've* been trying to get in touch with *them* for days.

"Um, yes. Hold on." She put the phone to her chest. "Roxana, do you mind?"

It took Roxana a moment to understand. "You want me to leave my own office?"

"Do you mind? Five minutes. Please."

Roxana got up and left, huffily.

When she'd gone, Leila said, "What the fuck, Sarah? Why'd you guys go quiet on me. I have a lot of questions."

"It's not just *on you,* Lola. When the network can't carry signals securely, it won't carry them. That's just protocol. You're in LA. It's pretty wired up there. Not a lot of green space. Sometimes you get only about an hour a day of secure transmission out there, usually late at night. The equipment we use . . . it cycles, you know? Like breezes do; like tides. What happened with Crane in Portland?"

"The thing he had was Super-Eight film of Deveraux beating off, back in college."

"Eww," said Sarah.

Leila felt the need to defend Leo. "I don't think it was like that. It was supposed to be funny. Deveraux was a sperm donor. It was some joke about that. I think he was making fun of himself."

"Well, anyway, you can forget about Deveraux. After you met him in that airport lounge, he went aboard *Sine Wave*. That's Straw's yacht. He's probably wearing their contacts by now, and out of our reach. He was a good lead, though."

"But Sarah?"

"Yeah?"

"I was right, right? I mean, we wouldn't engage in that kind of black-mail?"

There was a longish pause. "I think you made the right call under the circumstances. That's not really the kind of incriminating we were look-ing for. But, I suppose, if it were important enough . . . Leave that aside though, Lola," said Sarah. "I'm calling about Rusty Trombones."

"Who?"

"Rusty Trombones. Our man who passed you the stuff with your dad's hard drive—"

"Yeah, thank you so much, Sarah," interrupted Leila.

"No. That was mishandled. Rusty was supposed to get that to the prosecutor; it was supposed to look like it came from a whistle-blower, not from someone associated with your dad's case. That it came through your brother complicates things. It gives the Committee reason to believe that you've had contact with us. We kept you clean from Heathrow to Dublin to Portland to LA. But when Dylan walked into the RITSerF with that drive, there was a line drawn connecting you to us."

"Well, fuck 'em. I don't care that they know that. The hard drive worked. They're going to drop the charges against my dad. Most of them, anyway."

"You do care. Trust me. You don't want to be a known Diarist right now. Not in a large American city. And they're not dropping the charges against your dad."

"No. They are." She said it too loud. "I spoke to our attorney this morning. He said the prosecutor signed off on it."

"Yeah, well, today a stove exploded in that prosecutor's face. There's a new prosecutor. And the SCIF in Kramer's office was seized, and Rusty Trombones has vanished. He's probably in a six-by-six at Fort Meade."

Leila went cold.

"Look, Lola," said Sarah. "Don't worry. If things really go pear-shaped, we have a contingency for all the Majnouns. Sit tight. The Committee still may not have realized you're connected to us. Until they do, there's no reason to believe they'll make things any worse for you."

Until? Any worse? "How long? How long do I *sit tight?*"

"Give it a week. Things will probably be going one way or another within a week."

"What's the contingency plan?"

"We can probably get you all out of here. An emergency exfiltration."

"I don't like this plan, Sarah. Just wait around? I want a better assignment."

"Well, actually, there is something else we need from you."

"Yeah?"

"We need to talk to your sister."

When Leila called her sister back in and handed her the phone, Roxana made a thing of asking Leila to step out into the hallway. Minutes ticked by. Leila walked up and down the bland corridor, but it was spookily blank: nine other office doors, each identical to Roxana's, the elevator bank, fire stairs at the end, a water fountain.

She was trying to super-compartmentalize, to take the problem apart. The stove that exploded in the prosecutor's face. A line between herself and Dear Diary. Could they really *un*drop the charges against her father? What had happened to the free country the Majnouns had fled to?

She sat down on the floor outside her sister's door, anger, panic, and despair thumping through her heart. She got up and paced the hallway again, tried the door to the fire stairs, just to see that it opened.

She did this for twenty minutes: sit down — anger, panic, despair; stand up and pace — rack your brain for some new angle on the thing.

Leila heard a strange sound from behind her sister's four-inch-thick door. She stood, pushed the door open, and stepped back into Roxana's small office. Her big sister was weeping. This was the third time in Leila's life that she had seen her sister weep; Roxana's disability had hardened her. And when the armless weep, it is worse than when the rest of us do. Roxana was wiping her nose and eyes with a wadded napkin held in her left foot.

"What is it, Rox?" Leila said at once, and moved to her quickly.

A sob rose through Roxana and convulsed her, and Leila hugged her sister for the first time since she'd been home. It's gonna be okay, she whispered in Farsi. And when Roxana could speak again, she whispered to her sister:

"*They* did this."

"I know, Rox," said Leila.

Sniffle. "No. *This,*" said Roxana, and she touched Leila with her clavicle.

Leila didn't understand. Then Roxana spun on her chair and nodded Leila toward the largest of the many screens on, above, and around her desk. Onscreen were displayed two documents: an interoffice e-mail thing and what seemed to Leila to be a high-res photo of a paper document.

The interoffice e-mail thing was sent from one twenty-five-character alphanumeric code to another twenty-five-character alphanumeric code. The subject line read: A two-fer!

Dude. You know the drama that the Ruiners dropped on the principal in Cal because of that hot, nosy NGO girl? shit is double useful. My sleuths got old-fashioned on the background, went into the archives. Attached find doc from trial of a drug Prodigium. 1970! It was supposed to make geniuses. Made lots dead babies instead. The few geniuses it did make are mostly in full-time care by now. (wouldn't that suck? being a genius vegetable) But check it out. One of the Prodigium betas that didn't die now working at the LA facility. Roxana Majnoun. Hot name, but she has no arms (If she wore a hijab, she'd look like an anorexic ghost lol). Shes not commissioned. Shes there under pretense. Shes working on the gaze sink stuff. They were hoping to bring her in nice—the political department rated her amenable. But shes not playing ball. She won't take the project to the next level. So legal should keep all options open on the principal, because they want traction on the armless sister too. Since we have the father, may as well use him.

did you see the prosecutor job? nice, right? First exploding stove I ever ordered.

Leila leaned close to the screen to examine the high-res photo of the paper document. Damn, it was in Farsi. Leila's reading comprehension of Farsi had been deteriorating in her adulthood. This was troubling. Plus, Roxana wrote beautiful Nasta'liq script with her feet, so Leila didn't want to admit that she was losing what was, technically, their mother tongue.

But when she began reading the document, Leila found that her Farsi comprehension had come back; it was better than it had been in years. She was reading a formal letter of understanding between Baxter-Snider Pharmaceuticals and the Iranian Ministry of Health. It had clearly been drafted in English and then translated into Farsi, and that plus the mix of Western legal obliquity and Eastern pomposity made it sound stilted.

Permission had been granted by the ministry for public-health research, and researches into—

"What does that word mean, Rox?" asked Leila, pointing at the screen.

Roxana sniffled and tilted her head. "Mind science," she said.

—mind science that would bring glory to the nation and make Iran once again the seat of medicine and learning. Baxter-Snider was free to conduct any and all discreet population-based longitudinal chemical trials of promising compounds. The ministry gave Baxter-Snider full but unnamed partnership with itself. The ministry agreed to provide Baxter-Snider unlimited access to all its current and future epidemiological research, monitoring, and outreach operations, and would temporarily cede full management and control of the nation's prenatal and maternal programs, medical and social.

What the fuck? thought Leila. "Rox, what do they mean when they say you won't take the project to the next level?"

Roxana had collected herself. "You know those SineLenses, the contacts that permit computer interface?" Leila did, but she had found the idea creepy even before all this started. "Well, these guys are working on a similar platform, but one that can actually implant devices for the purpose of data collection. See, they can do retinography from the surface of the eye just fine. But that's still like standing on the viewing deck at the Grand Canyon, you know?" Leila did know. Not about retinography, but about that August driving vacation in—was it 1982? One of Cyrus Majnoun's Honor America tours. "Now they're sort of able to stash the retinography equipment in the back of the eye via these contacts."

"What retinography equipment?"

"Tiny camera, tiny light, tiny transmitter."

"Christ, Roxana."

"There are great uses for that technology! For research. To find out about how information *comes in,* Leila. It is a *very* important field. There would need to be years of lab trials, obviously, and then animal trials."

Leila was shaking her head at her sister, disappointment clear in the set of her eyes and mouth.

"I know," said Roxana. "I guess I was stupid to believe them. Vain, maybe. But they wanted me to write something that allows instructions to be *sent* to the back of the eye. That's the one I said I wouldn't work on. I've told them no three times, but they still send me new data every day."

"Well, what are you gonna do?"

"What the fuck do you mean, what am I gonna do? You think I would let these people use me? That I could allow this to happen while I'm around?"

Leila shook her head. "No. Not that. I meant operationally. I mean how do we stop them?"

Roxana softened. "Well, I'm putting my shoulder to the wheel, anyway." Was that a *pun* from Roxana? About her condition? Unheard-of. "Your friend Sarah Tonin has a job for me." Pause. "They want me to make them something." Pause.

Roxana, like their mother, was a fan of these pauses. "What, Rox?"

"A piece of terrible jewelry to pin right on the chest of their whole network."

Since she had started writing code, at thirteen, Roxana had always called her programs jewelry; it annoyed the exclusively male cohort she'd had to endure in that particular swath of her arc upward. *Terrible jewelry* meant a computer virus.

This was like the old times, when Leila would help Roxana execute the teasing defense strategies she needed to endure an armless adolescence. Old times, but with everything at stake.

"What's going to make it so terrible?"

"One hundred percent circuit collapse on their network," said Roxana, all ho-hum. "You want to make malware, you copy the guys making biomalware; they're a few years ahead of the curve. Hand me that big manila, would you?" Roxana meant the big interoffice envelope she had carried in from the front desk. "And the Express envelope too."

Roxana drew from the envelope a sheaf of papers and started to leaf through them. It wasn't just papers. It was photos and X-rays and metered waves chittered out on thermal graph scrolls and pages dense with numbers.

But Sarah had told Leila that Dear Diary couldn't get anything on their network, because it was solid-state or something. "Even if you can make this virus for us, how are we supposed to get it on their network?"

"I dunno. Apparently, some guy you met in a bar was their best shot at that," said Roxana. "Sarah said they're working up another way." When Roxana came to the end of the sheaf, she turned her attention to the other envelope. "Uh, Leila. You know a Lola Montes?"

Leila snatched the envelope from her sister and examined it. "Recipient: Lola Montes, c/o Roxana Majnoun, LACLAF, Los Angeles, CA." The handwriting was tiny. There was also a zip + 4. Leila pulled the cardboard ripcord on the envelope and removed a single sheet of paper from within. It was brittle, blank. She turned it over and over. Was this from Dear Diary? No, she had just been on the phone with them. Was there a return address? She looked for the envelope, but Roxana had already retrieved it from Leila's lap with her left foot and was examining it closely.

"Who's the sender, Roxana?" she asked impatiently.

Roxana seemed to be peering at the tiny script, or else she was pausing for effect again.

"Leo's Lightbulbs and Lemon Juice?"

Leila waited until she was home and in the small room beneath the stairs. She took the tacky lampshade off the little lamp on the Ikea bedside table. She held the paper close to the light, passing it over the 60-watt bulb delicately, as a careful plumber is delicate with the blue of the torch flame on the copper pipe. She began in one corner, and as the typewritten words started to appear, she could tell up from down, right from left; she warmed the page again, this time from the upper left. The words appeared, embrowning on the raggy paper:

Dear Lola or whatever your name is, I have this way of remembering numbers. I guess it's a mnemonic: the numbers suggest little pictures to me, and I remember the pictures. Sometimes, that's more confusing than it is helpful. But in this case, it may get me back to you.

In the dining car of an underwater bullet train, two tree surgeons are playing pinochle. That was the picture I saw when you rattled off that phone number when you were on the phone with your sister the other night. Sorry for eavesdropping. But not really. That phone number only got me the LA County Large Array Facility, though. Is your sister an astronomer?

I know you were trying to keep me from the specifics of your situation, but there's this Internet they got now, and "middle-school principal" + "FBI" + "Los Angeles," and I saw the news about your father. I saw what it is they're doing to him. And so I know your surname is Majnoun. The LA Times mentioned your sister because I guess she's some kind of prodigy. Maybe your real name's not that important. Lola suits you fine.

Did you ever hear the joke about the guy who goes to his shrink? Guy says, Doc, sometimes I think I'm a teepee and sometimes I think I'm a wigwam. Doc says, The problem is, you're two tents.

Now, I know that this joke is nominally about the double homophone. Or maybe the joke is supposed to be funny because it's so lame, like a hardy-har-har kind of joke. But see, what I like about it, the poor schmuck just went cycling back and forth between two ideas of himself. He's the guy, in the whole canon, who gives clearest voice to a common problem — the problem where your mind runs back and forth, binarily, between two opposite notions of itself while all the time your mind somehow also knows — because why else would the guy go to a shrink if he didn't? — that the two poles of that endless back-and-forth cycle are probably not useful reference points anyway. Teepee? Wigwam? Were those ever really even the right words to denote distinct styles of Native American housing? And then you have the capper, where the health-care provider mocks and dismisses the patient and his complaint, which I think is pretty biting. That's how I feel: I'm a teepee, I'm a wigwam; I'm a genius, I'm a loser. I am connected, I am alone. Yes, I concede: the drink and weed pulled that out of me more. So I've stopped all that. For my sisters. And for myself.

I fear, though, that beneath my bad habits, there is still the teepee/wigwam problem. It's always been there, it'll always be there; it's like the water table or something. It's just a condition I'll have to manage my whole life, I guess. Lots of people have those, right?

I know — I had you at binarily. Act fast, Lola. How long do you think a weak-minded addict will stay on the shelf? Because that day you walked in? That day I saw you? I swear, my heart slowed and my breath came easier. All that rabbiting I do — it just stopped. Not stopped by like magic, but stopped with reason. You are as strange and amazing as anything my stupid little brain has ever come up with, and you are from outside of it. You have no idea what great news that is. And I'm going to lift some copy here, but there is a time for everything, that day and night here you were the still point of the turning world, and I knew for sure that I had a place in it. That place is next to you.

The Argentines have a phrase: my media naranja, they say — my half-orange.

But listen. Even if you're not interested in the above, know that I am furious at these people who have harmed your family. Let me help you stop them. I am highly qualified to oppose secret nefarious cabals, and I have an idea, a new angle on the thing.

Guess who got in touch yesterday, Lola? Mark Deveraux. He wrote to me. I think he wants to apologize or something. He's going to be in Portland this weekend.

We never considered just asking him for his help. Why didn't we consider that? Your people must have decided he would never go willingly. But I think he might. Mark may be a self-centered bullshitter, but he's no evil genius. And he got me out of a few ditches. When my parents died, I was kind of ghosting around, seeing flames everywhere, and my sisters had me going to this vulture-y trauma counselor. Then Mark showed up in some girl's

Saab and took me up to Maine, where the girl's parents had this pretend farm on a private island, and he installed me in one of their converted barn guesthouses, and for about a month he brought me magazines and pot and soup. Then there was this other time, when I bought the bookstore and totally failed at that, and when I had to sell it, he came and helped me pack it all up. I leaned on him hard then too.

Point is, I think he's a good man, at heart. Maybe he's gotten caught up with these people without meaning to, and all he needs is to be offered a way out. That's how it's been with me sometimes. Like when you came to get me.

But I want you there with me when I see him, Lola. I need you there. You'll do a better job explaining the situation than I would. Come up here. I'm supposed to see him on Friday.

I understand that there is some danger here, and haste. I will not waste your time, and I'm taking precautions. I will mail this care of your sister, at her workplace. And you figured out the ink thing. I knew you would. Let me know that you're coming, and when. Leave a message on my landline saying you're at the dentist's office or something, and leave a callback number that is actually the date and time of your arrival. I'll be here.

I really am quite sure that there is something we're supposed to do together, that there is more that is supposed to go on between us. Aren't you? Isn't there a held breath in your life right now? I've missed a few boats already, and I really don't want to miss this one too. I realize that in that metaphor or analogy or whatever, you are a boat. That doesn't really quite get what I mean, because I am also a boat. We are both boats and we are both passengers. We should not miss each other.

Leo Crane

Years ago, a boyfriend who was trying to make up for some bad behavior had written hundreds of little notes to her and left them around the apartment they shared in DC. He was the drinker, that one, a poet and a plate smasher. Those notes bought him six more months with

Leila. But, finally, the affair had left her with a mild distrust of love letters.

Not this one. She recalled what Leo looked like; how his voice had sounded. A key in her was turning. She realized how unfair it was of her to leap into his life like that, demanding something and then vanishing. She hadn't even given him her name.

NEWARK AIRPORT

Mark had a Friday-morning flight out of Newark, and when the car dropped him at Terminal C two hours before departure, he was in a sharp suit, with a charged laptop and his wits about him. He was nervous about seeing Leo that evening and about the Nike thing the next day.

The security line had stalled. The guy in front of Mark cursed under his breath, gathered his plastic bin, and moved—shoeless, beltless—to the next line over. Mark saw the problem. The TSA agent in Mark's line was getting stern with some poor schmuck who apparently had no boarding pass. "Sir, without a boarding pass, I cannot let you through," the meaty agent was saying. "Sir, you will have to step out of the line, sir. I'm not going to tell you again, sir."

Mark thought, *Jeez, this guy hasn't been in an airport in ten years?* But then he looked closer and started listening. The man was speaking Spanish; a chewy, Central American kind of Spanish. He was trying to make himself understood. Mark's Spanish was poor, but even he understood what was going on. The man's wife and daughter were through security, twenty feet away from him. The daughter clung to the wife while another agent swabbed the daughter's wheelchair with one of those dainty

340

little wands. It wasn't an airport-issue wheelchair, but a more specialized job. The daughter had matchstick legs and a severely torqued spine; her face was bent with worry and pain.

Some muscle at Mark's core flexed, and without deliberation, he said to the TSA agent, "This man just wants to walk his wife and daughter to the gate." The agent ignored him. But the Central American man gave Mark a *thank-you* look, so Mark, who still had his shoes on, stepped closer. "He just wants to stay with his daughter a little longer," said Mark to the agent, "Look at her. It's no big deal. Just let him through."

"You have no input, sir. Step back in line." The agent was about Mark's age, though smoosh-faced and small-eyed. He had a shit job, but it had one perk, and that was being able to tell anyone—any civilian—to Step Back in Line.

Mark felt his breath go thin. Some line about the Gestapo came to him. But he wanted to get to Portland this morning, and though you could make a point—probably *should* make a point, actually—you were not going to beat Homeland Security while standing in Security Check-point C-3, even if you still had your shoes on. So Mark stepped back in line, though he did not drop his eyes while he did so.

Their little fuss had attracted two more agents, one of whom hovered near Mark while the other tried to get the Latino dad to leave the line. People behind Mark were shifting to other lines. The supervisor interacting with the Latino dad wanted him to return to the ticket agent and get something called an escort pass. The Latino dad was saying he had tried to do that; that the ticket agent had told him to ask the TSA. But none of the gloved and badged men in the huddle spoke Spanish.

"Look, he tried that," said Mark, from behind his little minder, a mousy dude who didn't even really fill out the royal blue of his TSA uniform. "They obviously told him you people make this kind of call. He got the runaround. Why not just let the man walk his family to the fucking gate?"

"I'm going to need you to stay out of this. Choose a new line now," said the supervisor, a handsome, mustachioed black man.

Then a few things happened quickly. Mark waved his hand before his face, rolled his eyes, and curled his lips; the international sign for *Oh, whatever*—the same maneuver a six-year-old uses to infuriate a reprimanding parent.

But the mousy agent who was standing near Mark took the wave as an aggressive act and grabbed Mark's wrist and twisted it about an axis it did not possess. Mark yelled. The girl on the far side of security half collapsed, and her dad made a break for his daughter. A clutch of agents, who had been doing nothing but poke through bathroom kits for years, sprang into action, tackling the dad. Mark, who had two self-defensive maneuvers—the head-butt and the run-away—automatically employed the former on the agent who was trying to bring him down. This did in fact get Mark's wrist released, as the agent put his hand to his own cracked brow. But then the handsome mustachioed supervisor was on Mark in an instant, and Mark's arms were wrenched behind him and he could hear the plastic cuffs being zizzed tight.

So this is what it feels like, he thought to himself as they hoisted him painfully to his feet. The other travelers averted their eyes as he was led away. *Yeah, wait till they come for you,* he thought.

Two hours later, he was still sitting in some behind-the-curtain security office, the plastic cuffs replaced by a single metal bracelet that chained him to a chair. His shoulder felt wobbly and his nose was swollen from its meeting with the floor. But otherwise, he felt fine. Better than fine, because he had successfully resisted the state when it mattered, had walked tall when he was led away. There was blood on his white shirt but not on his gray suit.

His jailer was the black supervisor who had taken him down and who now sat at the desk near him trying to fill out the online forms you apparently need to fill out when you've hauled someone backstage at Newark. But it was clear to Mark, even from the wrong side of the screen, that the guy was having a hard time with it.

"Filling out those things is annoying, isn't it?" he said.

"What?"

"Those forms. It's like, if you miss one field, they make you start all the way back at the beginning."

"Yeah, actually, that's exactly what's annoying about it."

"You guys never let that man walk his daughter to the gate, did you?"

"Don't worry about that, Mr."—he looked at his screen—"Deveraux."

"It's just, you know, if you think you're making us safer by doing stuff like that... Well, you're not."

He stopped typing. He actually looked kind of hurt. "You really don't think we're making it harder for the terrorists?"

"Harder?" said Mark. "I suppose so. I mean, if there really is a team called the Terrorists. But that line you guard so valiantly? You know there's a Cheese Louise and a Sunglass Barn just on the other side, right? If I wanted to get my bomb or whatever into Newark Airport—sorry, Liberty Airport—I wouldn't be trying to get it past you guys. I'd put it in a sack of frappuccino mix and deliver it to my friend's Java cart. Or, even better, I'd become a TSA agent."

"We take vendor screening very seriously. And what makes you think we'd have you?" Then the agent used a line he'd clearly used many times before. "There's a lot of this you don't see." He went back to his typing, but they were alone in the office, and Mark had gotten under his skin. He quit typing. "And you know what? It's not a team, but there *are* terrorists," he said. "And when they get close enough to you, you're going to want us."

"Yeah, but when the threat level goes to green, *you're* going to want *us* back," said Mark. Then he saw the TSA guy almost say something. "I know, right?" he said, divining what the man wouldn't say aloud. "It's never going to go to green"—and he shrugged, even with one cuffed wrist the picture of equanimity—"don't worry, we all know that."

He could talk like this because he knew something that his jailer did not. If the phone call he'd made two hours ago had the effect he felt certain it would have, he could continue in this line of argument without risk of serious sanction.

The supervisor was steaming. "Well, I'll tell you one thing, prickface. You made a real mistake when you told me how you'd get a bomb into Newark Liberty International." He smiled at Mark and started typing again, with feeling now.

Hmm, Mark thought, *dude might have a point.* "That was hypothetical," he said. "The bomb-in-the-frappuccino thing, I mean."

"I'll be sure to note that," said the supervisor.

Fuck. What if he had overestimated the effect, or the immediacy of the effect, of the call he'd made? What if the black sheriff here could just add his name to all the no-fly lists?

Tessa had just said, *I'll take care of it.* Then she'd hung up. How long does it take the first assistant to Parker Pope to extract an associate from an already initiated Apprehension protocol within a subsidiary agency?

There was a knock at the door of the office, and then immediately two men came through it. One was a silver-haired fox in civilian clothes with a laminated tag on his lapel that Mark saw was like the one he'd used as a hall pass on *Sine Wave 2.* The second man was plainer, and subordinate. He was in a TSA uniform and carrying Mark's valise.

"Cancel that page, Officer Aldridge," said Silver Fox to the Black Sheriff.

The Black Sheriff looked confused at first, but, after scanning Fox's ID badge, he stiffened.

"These pages you can't cancel once you open them . . . sir," he said.

The Silver Fox took a Node from his pocket and thumbed multiple buttons. The computer to which the Black Sheriff had been tediously feeding data for an hour shut down in an instant, and the screen winked and went blank. There was left just the tiny whir of the fans cooling the hard drives. "Take the rest of the day off, Aldridge," he said. "Actually, you never came in today at all. Okay? How's that sound?"

The TSA guy who'd come in with Silver Fox unlocked the bracelet tying Mark to the little chair. Mark stood and rubbed his wrist the way he'd seen the recently de-cuffed do on TV. The TSA man handed Mark a white dress shirt, still in its crinkly plastic envelope. Mark unwrapped and unfolded the shirt and quickly swapped it for his bloodied one, which he grandly chucked in the office wastebasket.

And then he couldn't resist. As he tucked in his shirt and buttoned his cuffs, he turned to the Black Sheriff and said, "There's a lot of this you don't see."

"You keep your mouth shut," Silver Fox said to Mark. "I don't know whose boy you are, but this is *not* what I do. You trip over your dick again, we will let you swing. No matter who calls me. You understand?"

Mark nodded.

"Okay, there's a Portland flight in five hours. Until then, you sit in a Presidents Club and do sudokus or something." The TSA man opened the door to the office and Mark was ushered out into a chute-like hallway that reminded him of the secret warren behind every food court in every mall, which he knew about because of that year before Harvard when his mom lost her job and started dating that asshole and they all moved to his shitty little city and Mark had to work at a Grill Ride in Two Lakes Mall for a meth-head manager and minimum wage. ("Welcome to Grill Ride. How can I be fresh with you?") It was while working that job that he decided he would climb out of America's bottom nine-tenths and never fucking look back.

Mark had no interest in the sudoku—he was embarrassed by the arithmetic deficit in him that the game laid bare. But he did have two phone calls to make, so he ordered a double rye whiskey.

First Leo. Mark was supposed to meet Leo that evening. But his flight wouldn't land until late, so that was out. He really should keep tomorrow night for schmoozing with the Nike people. That left Sunday morning, which was kind of obviously a consolation slot for a weekend visit. Blowing people off on the day of the thing was just the kind of behavior that had left Mark light on friends. Looking behind him, he saw twenty years of not calling people back, of figuring he'd have another chance to correct an impression (or, if not, there were plenty of other people, anyway, people with whom he could start from scratch). So the message he left on Leo's phone he tried to make super-sincere. *I have a really good excuse,* he said, and *Leo, please don't think I'm blowing you off. I'm not. Not this time.*

Then he had to call Tessa to thank her for what she'd done. And the scolding Silver Fox had given him made him keenly aware of his debt to her. But when he rang her number, it was Parker Pope who answered.

"Marcus, you old so-and-so."

"Mr. Pope. Pardon me, I was trying to reach Tessa Bright, your assistant."

"She doesn't go in for what you got, Mark." Then he did his fake Indian—"I thought you were understanding that"—and roared down the phone.

Mark cringed but laughed. "Right you are, sir. No, but I just wanted to uh . . . well, anyway, no matter, I'll drop her an e-mail."

"Did you just want to *uh . . . well* say, 'Thank you, Tessa, for bailing my ass outta TSA jail'?"

Shit. "Yes. Yes, actually that is exactly what I wanted to say to her, sir."

"Well, then, you can say it to me, boy"—fake Indian—"because it is I who am making it happen."

"Then thank you, Mr. Pope. I am very happy to be out of that spot. Your man is very . . . competent."

"That he is, Marcus. That he is. Hey look, don't mention it. No problem. That's the kind of help friends offer each other, you know?"

Mark used the beat to take a huge swig of whiskey.

"Just, tell me this, Marcus," Pope demanded, "why, why, why have you not come to work beside my good friend James?"

Mark swallowed. Too much rye in one go; it rather steamed his head with its sugary rank. His eyes watered.

"Marcus?"

"You mean, sir, why haven't I started as SineCo's storyteller-in-chief?"

"Nyyyuhhhhh-huh."

"James—I mean, Mr. Straw—and I were just still trying to, you know, tweak the position's, um, scope of work, so that I can be my most effective, you know, self . . ." Mark should be able to bullshit Pope. Why was he getting all wobbly? "And, you know, we're just not sure we have it where it needs to be."

Pope leaped: "Scope's not where it needs to be? Is that about it?"

See, it was the cheeriness that made Pope present as a psychopath, thought Mark. "Yes. I think that's a fair assessment."

"Okay, look, you little shitbag." Now it was like his voice was crawling out of the holes on the phone—ants from a rotten log. "James Straw wants you to take this job. He is going to pay you lots of money. Now, you apparently think that you deserve more than what's on the table—"

"It's not like that, Mr. Pope. We're not negotiating about money—"

"Oh, *it's not about the money?* Is that it? Yeah, it never is with you people." Mark was lost; what people did Pope think he was? "Whatever the problem is, then, get over it. Immediately. This is a good job, and we want you to take it."

Mark gathered what courage he had. "Why?"

"What?" barked Pope.

"Why do you want me to take this job?"

"Oh, don't big yourself up. We're gonna have a thousand of you. We want you now because Straw wants you near him. As far as I'm concerned, your book is grade-A bunk. But that man thinks you shit cotton candy, and whatever you do in your little sessions, it works. I haven't seen him this focused in twenty years. And I need him to stay focused. So it is most certainly in my interest to see that he gets what he wants. And right now, what he wants is you behind some glass desk no more than a thousand yards from him. So that whenever he gets the shakes, you'll be there to fan him with a hat or show him your dick or tell him a riddle or whatever the hell it is you do."

"Right. Well. I'll tell you what I'll do, Mr. Pope. As soon as I see James—"

"No, Marcus." Pope sounded almost kind here. "*I'll* tell you what you'll do. You will call Mr. Straw today or tomorrow or maaaaybe the day after that, and you will tell him, *Yes, thank you, please, I would love to be the SIC of SineCo under the generous terms you outlined, and I can start immediately.*"

Mark drained his glass. He cradled his phone in the crook of his shoulder.

"We clear?" asked Pope.

"Yeah. We're clear," Mark heard himself say.

Given a minute to think about it, Mark would probably have allowed that in Newark Airport that afternoon, his neuro-slurry was maybe looking for trouble. What with the Leo-meeting anxiety and the high stakes of the Nike presentation and the thrill of the TSA tangle and the ticktock of the SineCo ultimatum.

But by the time Mark even thought to have these thoughts, the ride had started. The one banana he'd eaten at seven a.m. fought bravely against the double whiskey, the two chardonnays, and the Xanax. Or what he'd thought was a Xanax. But when he didn't fall into a dry-mouthed slumber, he'd realized that, in his stupid drunk, he had fished out the wrong pill — a Nuvigil — from the bottom of his Dopp kit, and he went into a kind of fugue, and his mind kept running, and he kept drinking (the Nuvigil in valiant neurochemical conflict with airplane whiskey) until the flight attendant cut him off, and then he and the ghoul driving his body deplaned together, and the turquoise carpet in the Portland airport nearly made him ill, and the beach-themed restaurant in the concourse had quit serving so his ghoul got them a taxi and got them to the hotel and there was a fridge in the room and more pills in Mark's Dopp kit and then they went out together, his ghoul and he, Mark as blank as a bodhisattva, but also gross and reeling.

He woke — if that was the word — in a dark hallway of his hotel. A tiny Latina chambermaid was whispering, *You okay? You need help?* Trying to stand up, he almost pulled her housekeeping cart down on himself. She

348

steadied him and let him into his room with the key that he held in his hand. He thanked her, his voice a surprise to him, then leaned his head against the cool metal of the door frame. He took some breaths. In three minutes, he would vomit. On the upside, he seemed without injury, save for a mild carpet rash. He tried to savor his relief that his body had once again delivered itself home and apparently avoided the most basic disasters.

No idea. He had no idea about last night. Zero. A movie he never saw. In two minutes he would vomit.

He searched his pockets: wadded cash, a menthol cigarette, a swizzle stick, and...come on, come on, come on... *yesssss,* his passport and Node. Relief.

But then he checked his Node screen.

14 Missed Calls. 7 New Messages.

And the time! With a clench, he realized that he had been due seven minutes ago at Nike World Headquarters, where he was to address a passel of HR supervisors about Fostering a Prideful Environment and about the cross-platform-lifestyle delivery potential of SineLife. In one minute he would vomit.

The red light on his bedside phone was pumping. He dialed the front desk.

"Mr. Deveraux," chirped the desk. "There's a gentleman here from Nike. He's very anxious that you come downstairs."

"Of course. Tell him I'll be down in ten minutes."

Then Mark vomited.

Twenty minutes later, he had assembled himself into a functioning replica of a human. He would claim food poisoning, he would apologize, he would handle this somehow—Never Give Up!—he would come through it.

And at first it seemed he would. He shut off most of his higher-order cognition and concentrated on his breathing and the very immediate environment. In this way, he managed the tense drive to Beaverton with his Nike minder, a guy called Dave. Dave said, "You sure you're okay?" Mark said, "It'll pass." But he rolled his window all the way down, which kept conversation to a minimum and cool air storming around his sour, pounding head.

But once they got to Nike and he had to get out of the car, Mark found that his condition was dire. At a grueling clip, Dave led him into an absolutely enormous building and then into a room where fifteen people had been waiting an hour for him. A big bank of windows looked out onto the fields beyond and the gorgeous late-summer Saturday morning he was keeping them from.

Mark plowed right into his presentation he had crammed for. But he missed all his punch lines, and he was sweating. It was soon clear to him that he was not going to be all right. After half an hour he called a break. In the bathroom he did an obscenely malodorous thing, then stood before the mirror blotting his clammy flesh with the linty eco-towels stingily dispensed by the wall unit. Strip clubs. That's what it had been last night. Then to a bar with one of the dancers. But then maybe some ulterior task or destination. He remembered counting out hundreds.

"So it is only by being ready for opportunity that we are ready to seize it," he tried. Some of his audience had not returned after the break. He became aware of the smell of himself, sweet and dank. The sun through the wall of windows was brutal. "But of course, you can never be ready, because being ready means you're expecting something, and expecting something means that you will be disappointed when you don't get it." He tried to take a swig out of his bottle of water but found that it was empty, so he was caught suckling from a plastic bottle, which crinkle-crackled loudly. "But you can be ready to be ready . . ."

"Bullshit," he heard a lady mutter from the front row.

Never a good sign. He persevered. There was a point here that had worked before. "As long as you wake up each day, saying to yourself:

This is another day I will be able to...um...you need to skip your record...Now, I'd like half of you—let's say, the half of the room to my right, your left—I'd like you to write down five fears. The other half of the room—your left, my right—write down your desires. Got it?" Mark's head felt shrunken. He may have been swaying.

"Can I have a pen?" said a man in the front row. "That's one of my desires."

Mark gave the man his pen.

"I need one too," said another man.

"Yeah, mine ran outta ink," said a third.

"Why don't I go look for some more," said Mark, and he fled the room.

He was in a tremendous, carpeted corridor that receded fore and aft like a gyroscopic dream. Some people at a great distance, small as mice, crossed the corridor. He wobbled a bit; he thought he might come unstuck from the floor and pinwheel down the length of the building, like the dude in *Titanic* who bangs off the propeller and into the ocean. He obeyed instinct and made for a distant door and the green world beyond. Outside, a light breeze blew the stink off him. The panic and dizziness and queasiness receded a bit.

Okay, he definitely didn't want to interact with Dave the minder again. He needed to get out of there. He would call Leo Crane. If he said, *Please come get me, I'll explain when you do,* wouldn't Leo come through? Closing one eye, he thumbed his Node until it gave him Leo's number.

BEAVERTON, OREGON

Leila and Leo were sitting in a deep green Toyota Corolla, ten years old, a bike rack on the roof, in a vast parking lot on the Nike campus. Leo thought it felt like a stakeout on an old cop show. There was even a bag of nuts on the tray of the little console between them. Leila ate a few, absently. She was so concentrated. When did this girl relax?

"Were the walnuts in the car too?" he asked her. She had explained that the car was waiting for her in the short-term lot at the airport, keys on the right rear tire. The Dear Diary Travel Agency, she called it.

"No. They're mine. They're pecans, though," said Leila. Then, almost suspiciously, "You don't know your nuts?"

"I don't really like nuts."

"Seriously?"

She looked so disappointed that he backpedaled. "I mean, you know, in moderation; almond flour in a crust, some peanuts in your pad thai." To show how reasonable he was, he popped a couple of pecans in his mouth, but then he couldn't hide his distaste. The mealiness, the tang, the granularity.

She laughed at him. "You don't have to like nuts."

They'd been sitting there for an hour. They knew that Mark was somewhere in the enormous complex before them. Their Nike source—Leo's friend Ted, who had also provided them cover at the security booth by claiming them as his guests—said that the seminar Mark was leading for the tier-one executives was scheduled to finish at noon. The idea was to swoop down on Mark when he left the building. If they could get him in the car, Leila was going to message a local Diarist who would bring them in, give Mark the real pitch, hopefully the eye test. Leo was also looking for a way to bring up the love-letterish part of his lemon-juice letter. They had so far avoided the topic.

But Leila kept returning to Mark and what would make him come with them. "Everyone has a way in," she said. "There's something we can say to him that will make him see. What's he like, really?"

"Well," said Leo. "His dad fucked off when he was, like, eleven. He really loves his mom. They're pretty close. He's very smart. Loves to do drugs, or did anyway. According to his book, he's *moved past all that*. But if that's true, I'll smoke my hat."

"Yeah, he was drinking hard in the lounge that time."

Leo wasn't thrilled that Mark and Leila had already met, nor that Mark had apparently performed one of his magic tricks on her. He decided to remake a point.

"You know, with that trick, there was only one card you could've picked, Leila. He probably had that jack hidden before the thing even started."

"I didn't say he was actually magic," said Leila. "I just said it was a good illusion; I don't know how he pulled it off."

Nerves. Balls. Chutzpah, thought Leo. Whatever it was, Mark had plenty of it. Back when they ran together, anyway. Mark was your man for capers, for finding the fire stairs to the roof, for rapping on the windows of closing pizzerias and asking earnestly, through the glass, *You got any slices? Cold is fine.* He charmed, and bluffed, and talked his way into places. Leo looked out at the green sneaker campus. These people were engaged in a trick also, weren't they? Pay an Indonesian four bucks a day;

pay a PR machine a hundred million a year. Shazam, you can mark your shit up 500 percent and no one's gonna say boo. Of course Mark was delivering a "seminar" to the upper executives. If you were willing to lie for money, you could probably go very far.

Leo's cell phone rang: a 917 area code. Rosemary? Heather?

"Hello?"

"Leo?"

"Mark?"

"Yeah. Listen. I'm really sorry I couldn't make it last night. I was ill. But I'm free now. I'm in Beavertown."

Leo covered the receiver part of his phone and mouthed to Leila, *It's Mark.* But she was pointing through the windshield at a man thirty paces away and mouthing to Leo, *There's Mark.*

"Mark," said Leo, "hold on a sec." Then he put the phone against his chest. "You ready for this, Leila?" he said.

She clutched his forearm, like a damsel in a nickelodeon. "Leo, we *have* to be able to convince him. If Straw brought him to the yacht, then he's, like, a made man. Turn him and we can strike back at them. There's no other way."

"I know. I really think we can."

"You think? Leo, if we tell him about Dear Diary, then he's got to come with us, one way or another. We can't let him go blabbing back to the Committee."

The *we can't let him go* part tightened the air in the car, as a bolt is tightened by the clever lever of a wrench.

Leo was being asked to vouch for the good-heartedness of his old friend. They had been like brothers once. He could have vouched for Mark then. Do people change at heart?

"Right," he said. Then he gave Leila a look that said *Here we go,* and he opened his door, stood up.

"Mark," he called.

Mark looked at Leo, looked at his own phone, then really squinted at Leo. He walked over to the car. "That was quick," he said.

"I'll explain later. Get in," said Leo. Without really meaning to, he had used a tough-guy, brook-no-argument voice. He opened the back door for Mark. But Mark either ignored or misunderstood Leo's body language; he folded himself swiftly into the front seat. Leo couldn't very well make a point of it. But Mark was always pulling shit like that.

"Lola Montes?" Mark said, as if he were running across her in some context that was only mildly unexpected, like at the tennis club. "Mark Deveraux. You helped me with the Jumble. We played cards."

Oh, no, no, no, thought Leo. *Not this time, pal.*

"Mark, you don't look very well," said Leila.

Ha, thought Leo. Mark really didn't look very well. He was the color of lunch meat.

"Wait, you two know each other?" Mark asked.

Neither Leo nor Leila answered that one. Instead, Leo asked, "You finished with your seminar in there?"

Mark nodded and said, "I believe so. You guys were waiting for me, weren't you?"

"We were," said Leila. "I need your help, and Leo said you'd help me."

"You want to get out of here?" said Leo.

"More than anything," said Mark.

They crested the hill that was the city's natural western boundary and approached the dark mouth of the tunnel. Leo imagined what this place would have been like long ago for, like, a Clatsop Indian coming in from the coast to trade with the strange new foreigners. Probably there would have been no REMOVE SUNGLASSES sign, as there was now, before the tunnel entrance. What a world, thought Leo, in which a municipality or highway department or whatever made a huge sign about such a thing.

Concentrate, you idiot, he thought. Why was he such a muddy thinker? His thoughts splayed like roots, spreading outward, forking and subforking. Was that the pot? It had to be the pot, right? Years of it.

But no. He'd always been like this. Long before the pot. He'd always looked for ways to alter his outlook. As a boy he would spin around in the front hall until he fell over, and he loved the upside-down rides clamped in his dad's strong hands; he could still recall how the chandeliers sprouted like mushrooms from the floor. Also at that age he could achieve a sort of glycemic state of grace by eating four or six mini-Snickers bars, a bag of which was on top of the refrigerator. So, no, he had always been a bit like this. Or upside-down rides are a gateway drug.

"Which one?" Leila asked Leo. He surfaced from his thoughts.

"Get in the far left lane." There was an important trifurcation on Highway 26, just as you came through the tunnel. The one highway flayed itself into three and you had to choose your lane without hesitation. You had to beware of late-choosers who might slice across your lane. Leo had once seen an accident in this place, when a too-late-chooser miscalculated his vectors and hit the orange-coned apex that cleaved one lane from another. That point was called the *gore point,* for reasons having nothing to do with gore. And the water-filled things that he'd seen the car plow into were called impact attenuators. He could have used an impact attenuator that morning fifteen years ago when he woke in his smoke-filled bedroom and stood and saw greasy gray streams, wraithlike, slipping beneath his bedroom door and staggered down three marble flights of the town house calling for his mom and his dad while smoke curled around corners and the wallpaper popped into flame. Orange and amber and black lizard tongues lapped up the walls, like an upside-down ride gone fiendishly awry.

It would have been easier if that impact had been attenuated over the course of many years instead of being delivered within about five minutes — the two minutes it took to get outside onto the sidewalk and the three minutes he thought about going back inside to find his mom and dad or the dogs; those three minutes that he waited, a grown man afraid of fire, until the windows on the third story cracked like a shot and black smoke billowed out through the fissures.

There is a club for these people, the people who have waited outside the burning houses knowing that they will not go back in and knowing that the not-going-back-in will ruin them.

Hell, you could use impact attenuators for all levels of trauma—for getting dumped, getting fired. Or could you use a similar device to sort of extend life's joys? Could you stretch out the moments in which you knew you were safe and loved? Were joy and trauma really the same thing, just positive and negative values of the same ordinals?

Fuck. Concentrate, he told himself. He said that part aloud, actually, but he was in the backseat and the other two didn't hear him. They were chatting. Chatting! She was telling him about the jack of spades, about when she'd found it on her suitcase. Mark was smoking a mashed-looking cigarette, keeping its lit tip at the crack of the window. Leila was smiling. Why was she smiling for him? Leo worried that girls, despite all the feminist dogma they'd been taught to espouse, liked jerks. Or, more precisely, that they responded to jerk behavior. He knew this was unfair, to lump girls into one class like this, but he'd been burned before by a girl he loved, who'd left him for an incurious dimwit with a steely gaze and a big, swinging dick.

"Leo." He came back. Leila's eyes in the rearview, with meaning meant for him. "Can you do me a favor? Can you text those guys for me?" Maybe this was strategic, her acting all charmed by Mark; she needed to keep him occupied. That would be fine. She handed her funny phone back to Leo. Then she rattled off a number. It was like no phone number he'd ever heard.

He took a moment composing the text message; he didn't quite understand what Leila had told her Dear Diary contact they were doing. So he went with: *Package collected. Where can u meet us?* He thought that was pretty slick.

"Take me back to my hotel, would you?" said Mark. "It's downtown." He named the hotel.

Leila found Leo's eyes in the rearview again. There was a question in them. Leo understood: Should they even let Mark out of the car? Should they tell him now that they wanted him to betray his employer and join their side? What was the segue to that? Mark's hotel was five minutes away. To stall for time, Leo started to issue driving directions that bent their trajectory, as a plane circles the airport. They went back across the Fremont Bridge and slipped onto I-5 South, where it scarred the east bank of the Willamette and separated river from city. Then up over the shitty old Marquam Bridge and back down onto the 405. If Mark noticed that they had crossed the same river twice, he didn't let on. But he was sure to notice if they crossed it a third time on that same loop, so Leo told Leila to peel left off the 405 and drop down to the 30. That put them in a patch of tattered warehouses. As they waited at a red light, a forklift crossed their path moving a mammoth coil of steel.

"This really the way to downtown?" asked Mark, the penny wobbling on a ledge.

"Yeah, well, Leila should've turned left back there," said Leo. "It's my fault. I wasn't clear. We're not far now, though."

"Who's Leila?" said Mark. "She's Lola."

Fuck. He had forgotten to use her code name.

Leila took it in stride. "No. I'm Leila," said Leila.

"You told me Lola," said Mark.

"I did. I was traveling under an assumed name."

"No shit?"

The little Nokia luminesced in Leo's hand. We'll meet you dwntwn. Come now was the message on the screen. "Take a right here, Leila," said Leo. They were on Front Avenue, beneath the bridges. The phone started to issue driving directions, which Leo relayed to Leila. They drove toward the heart of the city.

When they were on Sixteenth, driving south, the phone told them Get Gas Here. Leila had just enough time to turn left into the Radio Cab garage, a brick two-story, inside of which was a gas station that not many people knew was open to the public.

"Ten dollars regular. Cash," said Leila, to the pump jockey, a hipster with a waxed mustache.

"Do we *really* need gas?" Leo asked Leila, leaning forward.

"What's going on?" said Mark.

"Not really," said Leila, "but look," and she pointed through the wind-shield to the car in front of them, at the other pump. A deep green Toyota Corolla, ten years old, a bike rack on the roof.

A doppel-car. And looking through the back windshield, Leo could see three people in it. A woman driving, a man in the passenger seat, a man in the backseat leaning forward.

"What's going on?" said Mark again.

The pump ahead of them finished with a thunk, and the mustachioed pump jockey retracted pump's nozzle, spun the gas cap, and took two bills from the driver. The car eased out the Kearney Street exit.

Wait three minutes. Then proceed eleventh couch instructed the phone.

"What's the eleventh couch?" Leila asked Leo.

"That means Eleventh and Couch Streets. We pronounce it 'Cooch' here, for the street. I don't know why."

She was smiling at the word. *God, she has a nice smile,* thought Leo.

They crept out of Radio Cab.

"Are you guys taking me somewhere? I mean, other than my hotel?" Mark was getting nervous. Now Leo was glad to be in the back, directly behind him.

"I just want you to meet someone," said Leila.

Leo thought he saw Mark glance at the door handle. He slid across the backseat to be able look his old friend in the eye.

"You have to quit working for the people you're working for, Mark," he said.

"What?" Mark tried to sound annoyed, but not before some little breath betrayed that he knew what Leo meant. He recovered quickly, though, and said, "You suggesting I take career advice from you?"

The real meaning hid in the few extra grams of weight Mark had put on the word *you.* He was calling Leo a failure; he was saying that Leo had made a hash of a luck-filled life.

Maybe he had. But in the moment, Leo's grasp on life was better than

Mark's, and both men knew it. "Come on, Mark. You don't even *want* to climb to the top of that heap. You wouldn't like anyone up there."

"What do you know about it?" said Mark.

"Are you asking me what right I have to tell you what to do, or are you asking how much I know about the evil shit that your employers are perpetrating?" Then he looked at the phone again and said, "It says we're being followed."

"Fuck off," said Mark.

"I'm serious," said Leo.

Leila sped up again. "But the thing at the gas station. That was to shake whoever, right?"

"Maybe it didn't work," he said. "Take a left on Ninth."

"Left on Ninth," she repeated.

"Okay, how about *What do you know about it* meaning how much do you know about the evil shit that my employers are perpetrating?"

"Not right now, Mark," said Leo. "Look behind us. Who's following us?"

Mark at first gave him a scrunchy, *what the fuck?* look. But Leo ignored it. "Seriously, Mark. This matters to you too."

Mark scanned the street behind them.

"And a right on Couch," said Leo.

"A right on Cooch," repeated Leila, smiling again at the word.

"Any suspicious vehicles back there, Mark?" he asked.

"Negative. No suspicious vehicles," said Mark. "Or they're all suspicious. There's a maroon Subaru and a Jeep Wagoneer that have both been there for the last two or three turns."

Leo held the Nokia delicately, like a divining rod. He figured they were probably being directed to Burnside, from where they could access a knot of highway options. I-5 in two directions was five blocks away. Or a straight shot down Burnside and then cut to I-84. The phone luminesced again.

"Left here. Left here," Leo said.

That left put them into crawling traffic. Greenpeace canvassers and smoothie carts clogged the sidewalks.

360

"Okay, and now a left into here," Leo said. "Mark, you spotted him?"

"The Subaru is a lady with an Akita," said Mark. "I don't think it's her."

"What is this place?" said Leila.

"It's the parking garage for Powell's. The bookstore." Leo hadn't tried to use this garage in years. It had a too-tight corkscrew ramp and stingy spaces. Leila slowed to interact with the guy in the pay booth, but the crossbar lifted in front of her before she could roll down her window.

"Go," said Leo, without prompting from the phone. "You kinda gotta gun it to get up this ramp."

Leila gunned it up the ramp.

"Okay, it's the Wagoneer," said Mark. "But the bar didn't go up for him."

Just when they'd reached the top of the first full screw, the phone said to stop the car and engage the handbrake.

"Stop the car," said Leo. "Engage the handbrake. It says to get out here."

They all three moved swiftly from the car to a metal door in the concrete wall of the garage. They heard the Wagoneer begin its roar up the ramp. But when its big chrome nose edged around the central pillar and encountered the rear of Leila's Toyota it stopped short, then they heard the ratcheting sound of a handbrake being levered. The Wagoneer was blocked on the ramp, at a severe incline, the kind of incline seen in disaster movies and presumably no longer allowed for parking-garage ramps. The driver was talking on a cell phone, but talking into it like a walkie-talkie. Then he released the handbrake and started to reverse the huge vehicle down the ramp. He had to do it in herky little jerks.

Leila had the Nokia now. "It just says *Go through door,*" she said. But the door before them had no handle or lever, it was some sort of fire door, and it was flush to the wall it breached. But then Leo noticed that there was a paperback book wedged into the top corner of the frame. He tried to get his fingers into the crack around the door but couldn't. He spotted a pen in Mark's breast pocket. "You mind?" he said, snatching it swiftly. "Hey" was all Mark managed before Leo had jammed the clearly expensive pen into the crack of the door and used it as a tiny lever. Leila got a few fingers behind the door and then Leo could too. The door opened. The wedged book fell from the top corner: An old *Mad* magazine paperback: "Spy Versus Spy."

They were somewhere inside the huge bookstore. "Where are we?" asked Leila.

"We're in the Red Room," said Leo. "Travel guides, atlases, other religions. Coffee-table erotica over there."

"You work here or something?" asked Leila.

"No. But I wanted to. I cased it for weeks before my interview."

"They didn't want you?" said Mark. He sounded perturbed on Leo's behalf. "But you know all about books. You owned a fucking bookstore."

"Ran it into the ground, as I believe you'll recall," said Leo. "What do we do now?" Leo asked Leila.

She consulted the phone, but it must have been mute on the point. "I don't know," she said. "Browse?"

"Where are the magazines?" asked Mark.

"Follow me," said Leo, and he led them through the huge and busy store to the bright corner room with its racks and racks of magazines. When Mark made for the magazines, Leila conferred with Leo.

"You think he's with us?"

"He's not running," said Leo. "He could, I suppose."

"Do you think they want to meet us in this store? Dear Diary, I mean?"

"I think they were the ones following us."

Leila squinted her eyes. Her thinking-hard look.

"The phone just said *You're being followed,*" said Leo. "It didn't say by whom."

"But why? We're on their side."

"I'm not in Dear Diary. He's not in Dear Diary. From what you told me, this isn't even really an HQ-approved operation. They may be worried that Mark is some sort of bait. Or maybe you're like the rogue agent who goes off the reservation and they have to treat you as potentially compromised. They got you to give up your car."

"You're right," she said. "My overnight bag's in that car."

The phone luminesced again, like kryptonite.

"They're outside," said Leila. "Let's go."

"You go ahead. We'll be right there." He gave Mark a small urgent wave.

PORTLAND, OREGON

Mark wasn't even into the meat of his hangover yet. That would come in the afternoon. He was going to feel like barf on a day that mattered. Leo Crane and the Mysterious Girl knew something about the Committee's nefariousness and wanted him to quit working for Straw? *Me too,* he could happily, easily reply to Leo, *but there's a little more at play here.*

"Where'd your partner go?" he asked Leo. But then through the big plate-glass window behind the magazines, they could both see Leila, leaning in the driver's-side window of the big Wagoneer, the vehicle they had supposedly been trying to lose.

"Okay, Leo," said Mark. "What the fuck is going on?"

"You're getting a chance to redeem yourself."

"Redeem myself?"

"This is what you've been waiting for, Mark."

That such a chance *was* just what Mark had been waiting for was beside the point. The point was that you shouldn't let people *talk you into* anything. So he just said evenly, "Actually, I meant more like, what's this little scheme you and Scheherazade have cooked up?"

"Big scheme, Mark, big scheme. Just come with us. You'll understand soon."

"Tell me I'm in no danger, then. That dude in the Jeep looks serious."

Leo looked out the window to where Leila was still conferring with the driver. He did look tough, the Wagoneer guy. "I guess I can't do that," he said.

"Jesus, Leo! Promise me something."

"I promise you that if you don't come with us now, you'll have missed your last chance to be on the right side of history. And you'll regret it."

History? Mark was just wondering how to get himself out of a bad spot.

Leila came back in the bookstore to summon them. She was buzzing. Still he hesitated. "Come on, Mark," she said. "Please? I helped you with the Jumble."

Outside, the Wagoneer was idling in a loading zone.

"Let me see the driver," said Mark.

As if he had heard that, the driver zizzed down his window.

"What's your name?" Mark said to the man.

"Trip Hazards," said the man.

"Sure. Is it just you in there?"

"Yup."

Mark did a once-over of the vehicle. It was a dinosaur, a Grand Wagoneer from maybe the early 1980s, deep green with plastic wood paneling down the side and a roof rack on top. There was a rich kid at Mark's high school who'd shown up in one of these senior year. All the windows on this one were tinted, but only slightly. It wasn't really a tint, he saw when he looked closer. It was a kind of smearing effect.

"Where're we going?" he said.

"To a meeting," said the guy.

Mark made a show of considering his options. He looked toward his hotel; scruffed some fingers around his chin; checked his watch. Then he crossed in front of the big car and got in on the passenger side.

Trip Hazards tapped at a phone Velcroed to the dash, then he nosed the Jeep back out into traffic. He was paying keen attention to the streets around him and checking three mirrors constantly. A bicycle messenger slotted in on his right flank, outside Mark's window. The messenger kept even with them for a block, then fell back. But then Mark saw the same bike messenger slip up on their far side, and another one assume the wingman position on his side. He torqued around. Yeah, they were sort of boxed in by bicycle messengers.

"What up with the bicycles?" he asked Hazards.

"It's okay. They're mine." They made three lefts and they were now headed downhill, toward the river and the Burnside Bridge. The bikes stayed with them in the thickening traffic. Once they were nearly over the bridge, the bikes fell behind and slowed. They were throwing some sort of interference, tying up the lanes behind them. Trip took a hard right, gunned it for a block, and then took another hard right, then another. He pulled the Wagoneer into a scrub lot two stories below the bridge they'd just come over, right beside a sort of construction around which teenagers were gathered in a *Mad Max*–like fashion. The scrape and grind wafted into the car. What place was this?

"It's a skate park. The Burnside Skate Park," said Leo, who must have sensed Mark's curiosity.

Trip zizzed up Mark's window from his driver's armrest, which lifted Mark's forearm with it.

"Hey, hey, hey," said Mark.

"Listen," said Trip to all of them. "I need your full attention."

But Mark couldn't provide it, because a trio of skateboarders had climbed down from the undulating concrete moonscape of the park and were coming toward the car, with intention. They were dragging a machine behind them.

"...I have no idea what's so important that they had us come into the city to get you, but we scrambled a lot of resources for you, quickly. So do me the favor of cooperating—and go easy on the chat—while I get you to the meeting."

The favor of cooperating? thought Mark. "Um, Mr. Hazards," he said. "Skaters want a word."

Dressed in layers of frayed T-shirts, the three dudes outside were arrayed around the car in a sort of menacing flanking fashion. Trip zizzed down his window and spoke to the Chief Skater. "Skin us down," he said. "Take the rack and switch the plates."

"You got it," said the dude.

Trip zizzed his window back up. The three skaters outside went to work. The plastic wood panels came off first. The machine they'd been dragging turned out to be a pressure washer. One of them switched it on and began swiping the powerful spray across the hide of the car. It growled over the metal and roared on the glass. Mark could see that the green of the car he was in was sluicing off the roof and hood and washing down into the nearby storm drain. Their car was shedding a skin; it was changing color. It was gunmetal gray beneath the green.

"We need to take certain precautions with you," Trip was saying. One of the skaters was working on the roof of the Wagoneer with an impact driver.

"I'm not wearing a blindfold," said Leila.

"You don't have to. You're a Diarist. These guys, though."

"Look, can't we just have this meeting at a Starbucks?" asked Mark.

Trip ignored him. "It's got to be a blindfold"—he indicated some sleep masks hanging from the rearview—"or one of these pills," and he lifted a little enamel pillbox from a concavity of the Wagoneer's wide dash.

"I'm in recovery," said Leo.

Trip handed him a sleep mask.

"What's the pill?" asked Mark.

"It's like a benzodiazepine," said Trip, as if he were saying *lemon–poppy seed.*

"I'll take the pill," said Mark. "Actually, fuck it. I'll take the pill and the sleep mask." He liked benzos. He popped the little capsule in his mouth and made that head-throwing-back motion of the pro pill taker. "You're on point, Leila or Lola or whatever. You and Nancy Reagan here are responsible for me." He rolled his seat back.

"You really want to do this?" Leo asked Leila.

"Yeah. I do," she said.

"As you wish," said Leo and slipped his mask over his eyes.

The skaters had finished and were dragging the power washer back to the skate park. Trip handed the chief skater an amount of cash and a thumb drive. Three of the bike messengers pulled up beside them; one of them had Leila's bag, and he tossed it into the back of the Wagoneer.

Dripping wet, and now gunmetal gray, with no roof rack and new plates, the Wagoneer crept out from beneath the grotto under the bridge.

Mark slipped on his own little sleep mask; it was the kind you get in business class. "This is really a very niii . . ." he began, but then found he couldn't say anything else.

Leo's blindfold let in a tiny bit of information—he could just make out large shapes, and patches of light and dark. He should try to figure out where they were headed. There was a *3-2-1-Contact* with a similar setup, he dimly recalled—the Bloodhound Gang was trapped in the back of a windowless van, but they determined their location by listening to something? Or timing something? Or fashioning a periscope?

Okay. Plot device of long-ago PBS children's drama not important at this moment, Leo reminded himself.

Trip Hazards must have been confident of the vehicle's new costume, because he drove at a normal speed, and in more or less straight lines; no more lane-cleaving rights. They were headed north on MLK. When they took a right on what felt like Columbia, Leo figured they were headed to the airport, but by the back way. Trip must know Portland, because a stranger to the city would have taken 84 to 205, which on a bad day might be jammed-up. They drove east on Columbia; past the Humane Society and the heavy-machinery rental yards. Then Leo felt them take the left that was almost certainly into the dinky golf course; the whine of a nearby golf cart confirmed it. They would take a left now. They did.

Then there would be the *bump-bump* of crossing the MAX tracks. There was. Now a wide left onto the terminal approach? Yes.

But then they pulled right, shy of the terminal building. They were leaving the main trail. Leo began to worry. What if this guy was not who he claimed to be? Or would that be *whom?*

"What did you say your name was?" Leo asked.

"Trip Hazards."

"And you're from Dear Diary?"

"That is correct."

Are you sure? Leo mouthed the words at Leila, or at the shape and smell of Leila.

"Trip, I'm taking this stupid mask off Leo," said Leila, and she put her hands on the back of his head. It was the second time she'd touched him.

"Don't do that, Lola," said Trip sharply. The Jeep swerved as he twisted in the driver's seat.

But it was too late. She'd taken off the mask, made him see. They were in the business-aviation part of the airport, approaching a huge hangar.

"You don't have to worry about Leo," said Leila, tough as tacks. "Anyway, he's with me."

At first it seemed like Trip was going to call bullshit on that; his shoulders looked pissed off. But then he surveyed them both in the rearview, exhaled in a way that conceded the point, and said, "Very well. This was a pretty unorthodox extraction anyway. Leo, can you move your friend?"

Leila found a luggage dolly while Leo lifted the slack Mark from the front seat of the Wagoneer. Awkwardly, they lay Mark down on it. He hmmphed and stirred, but did not wake. They wheeled him across the vast hall of the hangar to the small airplane that Trip seemed to be prepping for flight. In a distant corner, a jumpsuited mechanic was tinkering in the wheel well of a gleaming business jet. Otherwise, they were alone. Over in the main terminal, thought Leila, grandmothers were taking off their belts for the TSA, but here she could wheel an inert human from a Jeep to a tiny plane, no problem.

Leo strapped Mark across the two rear seats of the plane and then sat beside Leila on strict and narrow seats, vinyl-upholstered, facing their slumped abductee.

"Either one of you know how to take a carotid pulse?" Trip asked them from the front seat when they were all in the plane and the doors were closed.

Leo nodded yes and knelt out of his seat to press two fingers to Mark's neck. He looked at his watch and then cast his eyes down in concentration, counting the beats of Mark's heart. Leila stirred for Leo. When she'd first seen him, she'd thought he was scattered and lost-seeming, but now this fearlessness on her behalf. Why was he here? Was it love? If love, could she return it? Did she want to? He did cause in her some excitement. That letter of his. Was it his orphanhood? And why was that appealing?

"Seventy-five and strong," Leo reported. "Breathing steady and clear."

Jumpsuit Guy left the jet he had been tending and walked over to the plane they were in. By means of a little tugging wagon attached to their front tire, he towed them outside, through wide hangar doors. Trip showed Leila and Leo how to use the headphones. Leila crowned Mark with a pair, and set the little knob to Noise Cancel. Outside, in the August dazzle, their plane seemed even smaller than it had inside the hangar. Jumpsuit Guy stripped out of his jumpsuit. He was a heavyset Native American–looking man with a ponytail, wearing a faded ball cap and a T-shirt that said *Gun Control Means Using Two Hands*. He got in on the left side of the plane, beside Trip, and donned a sharp pair of aviators.

"Lola, Leo," said Trip, "this is Mild Max. He'll be our pilot today. I'll be the copilot, third officer, purser, and head steward. Here, have some nuts." He twisted around and offered Leila and Leo foil envelopes of cocktail nuts.

Driving across the tarmac, the little plane felt spindly. But then Mild Max made a tight one-eighty at the top of the runway. There was a pause, as if for breath, and then the engines started to bellow. Leila, in a rear-facing seat, felt herself pressed against her four-point belt. They went from *brrrr* to *bzzzz* and then the wheels lifted free, and then there was no going back.

They climbed steeply. A thrum ran through the whole metal body of the plane and into her chest. Soon, Leila could see the cobra curves of the Columbia River far below. She leaned across Leo to look through the window on his side. He smelled a little like toast. Plus that nice mild dank, like a handful of mushrooms.

SOUTHERN OREGON

When Mark woke—if that was the word—he figured he was dead and going to heaven. There was no sound at all but a pleasant wash. And what were those? Clouds? Really? It was clouds after all?

But, no, he was not dead. He was in a plane, a very small twin-engine plane. There was Leo Crane. And there was the girl from the Heathrow lounge—Lola or Leila or whatever. The time before was coming back to him. They'd collected him from Nike...No, they'd been waiting there for him. Then the pursuit and rescue by the same vehicle. The skate park and the power washer and the pill.

His head felt like a bag of crabs. Same as when he'd woken in the under-lit hallway of that hipster-kitsch hotel this morning. The dude who'd given him that hog roofie was up there in the cockpit, beside the pilot. The pilot looked like a fat, Indian George Clooney.

The little cabin was filthy with sunlight. He caught Leo's eye, and Leo nodded at him and even gave him the faintest thumbs-up. Was that to reassure him? Maybe it was because the girl looking out her window at the spun clouds beyond was, although not exactly curled against Leo, in a position that looked promising. Mark pressed his own hot face to the cool plastic of his window. Far below, blinking along the folded green hills of a still-wild land, he could see the shadow of their craft. He closed his eyes.

The plane dropped precipitously, and Mark's lip was painfully squeegeed over the window it had dried to. Then suddenly they were climbing hard—really leaning into the sky—and then they topped out and started another descent that made them all momentarily weightless in the cabin. Mark felt his gold cigarette case float free in the pocket of his corduroy jacket. They banked hard and he saw a scrub green ridge of mountains beneath the plane. Then the turn ended but the descent continued and they were headed toward a swiftly less distant mass of green and gray. Mark sat straight up and looked down the short tube of plane, through what he guessed you could still call the windshield. It seemed that they were going to fly into the side of a mountain. But then a landing strip appeared ahead of them. A long, straight, clay-red stripe showed itself in the green scrub, and the plane dropped toward it quickly.

The plane skounced off the ground—once, twice—before connecting for good. The plane's tail swished a bit, but then settled; the engines roared, and the plane slowed and then stopped beneath the cover of something. The sunlight that reached them was chopped up, as if the light were falling in flakes. Were they inside or outside? The pilot cut the engines quickly.

It wasn't until Mark had unfolded himself from the rear of the airplane that he understood: there was camouflage netting high above them, strung across the end of the airstrip between tall stands of trees. He thought he might be beneath the *palapa* roof of an enormous beachside bar.

The pilot—Mild Max, the others called him—wandered off and came back with a pony. A chestnut pony with flicking ears, wearing a leather bridle and panniers. Mark thought, *What a handsome little beast,* and wanted to take a picture of it. He patted his pockets—wallet, cig case, shades, but no Node.

"Hey, Leo," said Mark. "Did that guy take my Node?"

"Your phone? Yeah."

"Think I can get it back?"

"I doubt it," said Leo. "But look. A pony was waiting for our flight. Aren't you glad you came?"

Trip Hazards started to unload bundled laptop computers from a strapped-down pallet in the rear of the plane; he transferred them to panniers on the pony. It was a motley mix of laptops: some were new and candy-colored and wafer-thin, but most were old-looking MacBooks and scuffed black PCs; a few were covered in bumper stickers.

Mark had just lit a squashed cigarette when Hazards said, "Listen up, you guys. We're going to walk in a little ways now, but it's mostly down-hill, so it shouldn't be too difficult. If you need to stop or slow down, just let me know." And with that, he turned and started walking, leading the pony by her bridle.

They moved in single file, and in silence. There was the swish and zip of pant legs, the two-four time of the pony's hoof steps, the wing-battering of a flown bird. They stayed on a ridge and came in and out of the trees. A bird of prey made a lazy arc in the sky far away and let out a sharp caw that echoed and re-echoed. They heard their airplane take off, and Mark saw it climb gracefully and buzz away into a bright speck.

After twenty minutes, they crossed a wide marshy meadow and slipped into forest. Then the forest thickened and the trail got thready. At times it seemed to disappear completely, and they were following only the vegetal wake of Hazards and the pony. Twice, the pony had to tramp off-piste to go around fallen logs that the rest of them scrambled over. When Hazards was well ahead of them, Mark asked Leila, "When are you going to tell me who I'm meeting?"

"Whom," said Leo.

"Fuck off," said Mark.

"I don't know," said Leila.

"Seriously?" said Mark.

"Seriously," said Leila. "But it must be somebody important."

Mark wasn't so sure about that. It seemed just as likely that this could all end with the harvesting of his organs. No, Leo wouldn't do that. Not an evil bone in that boy's body. Mark's story about Cecil the Magical Homeless Sage had as its seed of truth Leo's friendship with a semi-homeless and semi-psychotic Vietnam vet and paperback merchant in Cambridge. For a week in the bitter cold of a New England winter, Leo had let the man sleep on his couch.

They descended into a burned patch of forest where juvenile conifers were dotted around the husks of their blackened ancestors, all in a green broth of ferns pocked with tiny, gaudy wildflowers. Coolness pooled and pocketed in the small folds of the mountain. Mosses and lichens lashed themselves to the nubbly seats of rock and the crisp ends of dead branches.

Mark was having fun. He liked tramping farther and farther away from the shitshow of his own life, down there somewhere far below him now. Maybe they were walking to heaven, or Shangri-la, or someplace where he would be forgiven for all his miscalculations about how life worked and rescued from the trap that his vanity and greed had landed him in.

The headache had more or less vanished. The air up here was delicious. But he had a shoe issue. He'd soaked one walking across a shallow streamlet; now every other step was a squelchy one. The shoes were new monks of stiff English leather, with a hefty buckle; not really sylvan-escape footwear.

They entered what Mark thought you could call a glen. They walked through a stand of sequoia trees. Between the sequoias there were flowering rhododendrons—crooked and skinny little trees holding lavender teacups to the bark flanks of their enormous patrons. Mark, who liked nature just fine, was battered by the beauty of it all.

Hazards called a halt and offered them all water from a canteen—an actual round metal canteen. There was a rushing stream near them; Mark could hear it through the green. "We can't be far now?" he queried Hazards, though they could be miles, hours, days away.

"It's just across this creek and up that little brink," said Hazards. He was pointing through the trees.

Mark just saw more trees and landforms in the near, middle, and far ground. Did he mean ten blocks? Fifty? "What is?"

"The farm," said Hazards.

They reached the creek via a series of tight switchbacks. The pony slowed and took extra care at the hairpins.

Ah. This would be more of a river, thought Mark, who had an East Coast notion of *creek.* This one was swift and wide, and a coolness came off it like from a freezer case. The pony was leery of fording it. Hazards said she needed rest and water; he told them all to take a few minutes. Mark wandered half a block downriver. He slung his corduroy jacket across a leaning tree limb and found a flattish rock to sit on, then unbuckled his stupid shoes, which were ruined. His feet felt like burritos. He dunked them in the river. The cold brought the world into sharp focus: the trees on the banks, the needles on the trees. He remembered something his dad used to say after work: *My dogs are barking,* he'd announce, and he'd put his feet on the coffee table and pour a fist-size drink into any available vessel. But Mark had no sense of what his dad had done for work. For that matter, sometimes "after work" was early afternoon, when *Super Friends* was on.

Lola or Leila approached. She didn't look half as tattered by the walk as he felt. She stood on two tricky rocks at the edge of the river and leaned down to bring water to her face in cupped hands.

"So is it Lola or Leila?" he asked her, lighting his last cigarette.

"You can call me Leila," she said.

"You guys ready to tell me what it is you want from me?"

"I don't know exactly. I assume it's something that only you can do because you can get so close to Straw."

"What makes you so sure I'll agree to do it?"

"Leo said you have a good heart."

They crossed the rushing creek and climbed the little brink. They were standing at the edge of something far below them that looked to Mark like a dull green lake but that turned out to be a small and oddly uniform forest in a perfectly round, sunken declivity.

"What is it?" asked Leo.

"A caldera," said Hazards.

Leo looked blank, saving Mark the trouble of looking blank.

"A subsidence of land due to volcanic activity," said Hazards.

"A crater?" said Leo.

"The geology is different," said Hazards. "But sure." He led the pony down broad steps carved into the steep rock walls and through a narrow path that ran straight between the...trees? Plants? But what plants? They were growing in neat rows, like corn, and like corn, the stalks were strong and fibrous and columnar. But these plants were taller than any corn, and lithe like bamboo. Mark looked up. A dozen feet above him, the path was covered in the green arch of the plants, a jungle allée. The plants had palmate leaves starting midway up their stalks, leaves fringed at their edges in a deep green fuzz. Mark had always been an end user; he'd never been near a pot farm in his life. If that's what this was. But just from reggae album covers and the like, he thought that the plant around him was not marijuana. But what else do you grow acres of in the backcountry?

They came to the end of the plant alley and walked out into a meadow. One hundred yards away, Mark saw a shingled farmhouse in a small stand of trees, with a blanched and listing barn nearby.

As they came closer to the house, he heard the *skkrring* of a sprung screen door and saw a woman come out of the little house and onto its wide-brimmed porch.

"Baby. You're back!" she called. There was love and relief in her voice, and she even gave a little whoop, which carried well across the wide meadow.

Leo was sitting in the kitchen of the little cabin with the woman who had hollered to Trip Hazards as they arrived. She said her name was Constance Nozzikins. Leo was helping her, he was shelling peas. He thought the cabin was about the coolest thing ever, hand-hewn and hobbity. There was a kitchen, a common room, a bedroom, and a sleeping loft.

She swished some potatoes around in a bucket of water and then started slicing them. Her knife looked sharp.

"What are those plants outside?" Leo asked. He was working by the window. "Is the whole crater filled with them?"

"It's a caldera, not a crater, but yeah, the whole thing: four hundred sixty acres. That's the latest crop," said Constance.

She was hunting in the tangle of pots and pans that hung from the timber lintel over the sink. "This is one of our best sites. The altitude, I think, and the silica in the soil. And the remote location, of course. No one else gets yield like we do," she said boastfully. He was about to say *But crop of what?* when she asked, "How many you got?" She meant peas. He tipped the bowl he was shelling into to show her. "Do twice that.

We're six tonight." Leo, manually dexterous and comforted by piece-work, grabbed more peas from the bowl. The sun was twenty degrees above the far lip of the walls that ringed them, and sunlight was streaming through the kitchen's western windows; the line of evening advanced slowly across a broad field of mystery plants.

Constance had moved on to mushrooms. Her knife looked sharp. She did that *tap-tap-tap* thing with the point of her knife, and a mushroom fell down in tatters on the board.

"Is it pot?" asked Leo. He had never really been up close to marijuana plants before and knew what they looked like only from reggae album covers and the like.

She stopped chopping. "Leo, look at me," she said, turning around.

He looked at her, open and easily.

Three seconds went by. Constance looked worried.

"Is this not enough peas?" he asked.

"Would you come out here with me for a sec?" she said.

They walked through the swinging door and into the common room.

Leila, Mark, Trip, and another guy who had been here when they'd arrived were sitting around a wooden table. The new guy had introduced himself as Roman Shades; Leila said she knew him from Dublin. At the table, it was clearly Mark against the rest of them.

"Look. I'll help you," Mark was saying, "but I'm not taking your weirdo test."

"Roman?" Constance interrupted them. "I thought we had only one test to administer here?"

"That is correct," said Roman Shades.

"But what about this guy? I thought he was"—she paused—"but then I looked closer, and I don't think he is. I think Leo Crane is his real name." Leo thought she was being rude, all this talking about him while standing beside him. "Montes," said Constance sharply, "you vouching for both these guys?"

"I'm vouching for Leo. Leo's vouching for Mark."

"I was wondering about him too," said Trip. "The extraction manifest had him as straight, but then on the way in here he seemed tuned in. I assumed they'd done him Portland."

Then Roman spoke directly to Leo: "You're not a Diarist?"

"What would make me a Diarist?" asked Leo.

"An eye test, apparently," said Mark, sarcastic. In his swollen, ruined shoes, he looked like a vanquished musketeer.

"This is no good, having them here," said Constance, talking to her boyfriend and Roman Shades only. "I want them both tested." She was still holding her knife.

Leo felt the current of peril in the room.

"Oh, I'll take your test," he said brightly, sitting down in a chair at the table. "I like tests."

Constance put a janky-looking laptop computer on the table. She tapped and clicked and then laid it open before Leo.

On the screen was a grid of numbers and symbols. To Leo, it looked like something between Arabic script and Masonic hieroglyphs.

"Wait. Don't look yet," snapped Constance.

Jeez. Leo looked away. How calm he felt. All this strangeness around him, and it seemed to him just like a summer evening, playing board games with his sisters on the still-warm flagstones around the pool.

Leila was sitting near him. He looked at her. She gave him a nod and a smile. Oh yeah, that's why he was calm. He smiled back at her.

"Okay, look now," said Constance.

Leo looked. His eyes swam a little bit, like they're supposed to when you look at an eye-tripping postcard. "Which way do I read it?"

"Any way. Just take it in."

"I did. Is that a fish?"

"You're not supposed to ask questions," said Constance, put out.

"You're not supposed to even want to ask questions," said Roman.

Leo thought that was unfair. He looked at Leila. She gave him another nod.

"Are you looking at it?" Constance asked him.

"I am. I did."

"It's not giving you a number," said Constance.

"That's not my problem," said Leo.

"Can you look at it differently?"

Leo looked at the screen again, differently this time, and he saw the screen behind the screen, which was another set of symbols, or the same set reordered. He felt a surge of connections fire in his brain. Like a truth hole, but this time it was coming from inside of him. He rocked forward a bit. Was this a seizure? No, it was not unpleasant. All reports of seizures had them as unpleasant. But there was a gluey slowing of time that he recalled from febrile night terrors he'd had when he was sick as a little boy. He was an often-sick child, out of school for weeks at a time, weeks when it was just he and his mom in that big town house. She'd stir the bubbles out of ginger ale, put her cool hand on his burning brow, and together they'd watch game shows. Not so bad. But at night, running a temp of 104, his hearing went too-acute and the closets throbbed with a dark knowledge. This eye test was like that, except that the knowledge was good news, or at least unthreatening. The table spilled tableness out of its being. Light and wonder poured through the windows. Faces dappled on bodies, luminous, open.

"Leo?"

He swam through his own mind, toward her voice, and broke the surface.

"Aaaaand you're back in the room," said Mark, from across the table.

Leo laughed at the joke.

"Leo?" Leila asked. "You okay?"

"Yeah, yeah." And he was. "That's a real kick in the pants," he said. Though, coming out of it, he also saw that it wasn't unlike a good bong hit, or a gust of wind off a river, or going steeply downhill on a bike.

"You like your number?" Leila asked him.

"I do." It was the phone number of the Riverside Drive place. The fire had gutted the building. Its innards had been rebuilt, its facade remade of cheaper materials. His home was a dermatology clinic now, with a hypnosis-cult thing on the top two floors. Leo had never been in.

"Why does he get only seven digits?" Leila asked Roman.

"He's got an eight-zero lead-in, I guess. It's also the thirty-fifth Fibonacci number, though," said Roman.

"And a Markov number," said Trip. "I've never seen a number as low as that. That's a lot of white space."

"Maybe Leo's just a very . . . flexible person," said Constance.

That's what I am, thought Leo.

Fuckin' *Leo,* thought Mark. Just sits right down for an eye test like that. Had he not been listening when they said there was no way back? You get only one set of eyes; you should guard them, thought Mark, who would concede, though, that he wasn't the strictest guardian of his own temple. Leo was doing it for the girl, probably. He had been that way in college also; he wooed with too much ardor. Girls had gotten cheesy dorm-room deliveries of flowers and cupcakes and poems. Had he never learned that the good ones liked to do some of the work themselves? Now that Leo was eye-tested, Mrs. Red Brigades over there was really going to lean in on him, Mark feared.

"Now you, Deveraux," said Constance, giving a chair a little scrape on the floor to make the point.

He stayed seated, reclined, even. "What if I won't do it?" he asked her. "Now that I've been here, to the Little House in the Satellite-Cloaked Alpine Crater, I mean. How would you mitigate the . . . liability I represent?" Step Eight: Make Them Say What They Mean.

After a pause, Hazards seemed to concede that the question had fallen to him. "In that event—I mean, if you were threatening to compromise us, or if we couldn't be certain that you wouldn't, we would render you unbelievable."

"Render me unbelievable?" echoed Mark.

"Certain compounds could be gotten into you that would make it so that no one would believe what you were saying," said Hazards. "Plant-based compounds. Self-limiting. Pretty benign."

Mark looked at him. The passive voice, the *could be gotten into you;* the way Hazards had looked straight at him when he'd answered. How would he deal with Trip Hazards and his plant-based compounds? Someone like that was probably always on the lookout for the head-butt. And the run-away? It was just those Dr. Seuss trees and the moonlight out there, a steep ridge and piney mountains beyond that. A twisted ankle, a pack of wolves.

"Just tell me what you want me to do. I don't need to take that test."

"No way," said Constance. Roman shook his head also.

"Why won't you take it, Mark?" said Leo, unhelpfully. "You should take it."

"Because I don't want to be *you,*" he said in a raised voice, losing some cool. He didn't mean just Leo. He meant all of them, and he used his hands to include the whole table. "No offense intended. You can keep your connectivity. I want to be me. Just me."

"But you are such a shit," said Constance. "You only want to keep your money, your privilege."

"I worked for that money," said Mark.

"Please. That's not work. That's cheating. Have you ever really worked?"

What about Grill Ride? Or what about at Harvard, where he'd faced daily the mean fact that he would never have half the money that most of those kids already knew they would have. He had worked like a fucking beaver then, deep in the passages of Widener, to prove that prep school had been a waste of their parents' money. How about when the financial aid had dwindled, and Mark had to take a leave of absence and work full-time? What friends he had drank their junior years away in Barcelona and

Prague while he took a subdignified job as a chiropractic-office manager. Who had had to open the office at a moment's notice, on a Saturday, to see that the wind chimes were switched on and that there was plenty of oolong tea on the little drinks table? Mark, that's who.

Never worked hard, indeed. How about the fifteen years of work of keeping a dream alive, of just knowing somewhere deep inside that you are smarter than most people and that there must one day be a chance to leverage this fact? How about the work of holding it all together? The work of making sure your mom gets the best care there is? The work of keeping your story straight? Besides, there is the scrape of luck in everything, from the missed bus, to the dinged chromosome, to the hurtling asteroid.

"If by *worked* you mean the book you wrote, that smug nonsense about how everyone can be more effective and richer and more self-centered, no one here's buying it."

This too stung. "Yeah, I didn't really write that one. They did. My next book will address some of those complaints, I think. I hope you'll read it. Well, not my next one, actually. You should skip that one. But the one after that. I'm going to call it *Try Again Tomorrow*." He was so proud of the title.

"See, there's your problem right there," she said. "Why wouldn't you call it *Try Again Right Now*?"

Shit. It was like a tiny missile landing on division headquarters. She was precisely right. *Try Again Tomorrow* was an excuse in the guise of exhortation. But *Right Now*? Like, *Right Now* right now?

"You really find it so unbelievable, Mark," said Roman, "that people could get along and share what's here? That we could finally see the common good, instead of all of us toiling away to buy ourselves the same stuff? Didn't you go to first grade? Haven't you ridden a city bus, or even waited in line for a movie?"

Mark had done all those things. But he hoped to never ride a city bus again, actually. "We might get there, I suppose. But I can't be sure that you know what the common good is. And I bet you've all benefited from the system you say you oppose. You people are clearly top-of-the-heap types. You really want this great redistribution to go down? You ready to toil at the bottom? Mine that mineral they need for cell phones? Cell-phonium or whatever?"

"I'm not a top-of-the-heap type," said Constance. "I'm down here in the thick of it."

Mark ignored her. "You talk about how it's going to be like a chore wheel, everyone just stepping up to do his part. You know who else thought highly of the chore wheel? The Khmer Rouge, that's who. Oh, and Stalin and Mao, and probably some of those crazy African mother-fuckers too. Idi Amin and What's-His-Nuts, the guy who's not dead yet—Mugabe."

"You're just making a lot of noise here, you do realize?" said Constance. "You're only invested in seeing things not change because of who your bosses are. No one here is going to buy any of your excellence-of-the-individual shit."

Well, it seemed that Constance Nozzikins had watched at least one of his most popular webinars.

"Look," Mark said, "you want to redistribute your way to a better world? The distributors always become the assholes. You've just got to let everyone scrabble it out, even if some people are always going to end up with more."

"You just called yourself an asshole, right?"

"No. I'm a scrabbler. I was saying you guys are gonna be the assholes." Mark turned to Leila. "You took this thing? This eye test?"

Leila nodded. "It was after we met in Heathrow, Mark. I'm new like you. Come in. The water's fine."

Creepy. Kinda hot, but creepy.

But Leila wasn't the bossable or suggestible type. He knew that from playing cards with her in Heathrow, and from today, when they'd fled Nike and tramped through the forest. How would they have gotten her to do this?

"How'd they get you to do this?" he asked her.

Leila glanced at Roman Shades. He nodded a tiny assent.

"They said they would help me if I joined them. And they did."

"How?"

"Your people fucked with my family. Framed my dad, gave him a heart attack—"

"*My* people?" Mark interrupted. "Look, if you mean Straw, SineCo, the Node, all that...I know it's data mining, and it's no damn good. But we're not giving anyone a heart attack. Or I'm not, anyway."

"Yeah. Data mining, Deveraux. Sure. That's what it is," said Constance, sarcastic as a teen. "They just want to sell your address to *Sunset* magazine."

Mark had no immediate reply.

"*Information insurance?*" said Constance. "Is that what Straw told you they're at?"

That *was* the euphemism Mark recalled was most often applied to the activity taking place on *Sine Wave 2*. She was right, *information insurance* didn't really capture it.

"Because that's not the plan at all," said Constance.

"Oh yeah? What's the plan, Nozzikins?" Mark tried to say her name sarcastically.

"They intend to influence the thought and language and culture and the social order by controlling the means by which we communicate with one another. First they're going to get us used to the idea of giving up to their systems all of the information in our lives—"

"No one will do that," objected Mark. "People guard their secrets. Or if some people want to do that, I suppose that's their thing, and they deserve what they get."

Constance waved his objection aside. "Really? What about that new SineLife app where you activate the video feed on your SineLenses and record for a day, and your Sine 'writes' an account of your day: They have people clamoring to beta-test it."

The Screenplay: You app; yes, Mark knew of it. That was part of what he was supposed to have been cross-promoting at Nike.

"And once they have all this, this book on us, there are lots of bad things they can do with it. Maybe it'll be a plain old pyramid scheme, where one cent on every dollar in the world flows to them. Maybe they'll pretend to be North Korea or Ukrainian cyberthieves, and they'll collapse everything and then sell back to you your master password, the one you didn't know you had, the one that it turns out you'll need if you want to recover your bank balance, your birth certificate, the title to your house, your right to your genetics. Whatever it is, it'll be pay-to-play, across the board. Maybe they'll just go the bleed-us-dry route. Like, make the world into a rubber plantation, with Committee principals safe in their armored superyachts and private continents."

What she described *did* sound like Straw and Pope scheming over their snifters in buttoned club chairs. He wished she would stop talking, give him a minute.

"But that's not what I think they're planning," she went on. "Or I think maybe they'll do that first, but the real plan, their final solution, is a targeted genocide. I think the Committee principals are like those Georgia Guidestones people. At the top, anyway. I think they'll need about ten years to collect enough biological and genetic material on us before they can ask their big computers which five percent of the human population should live so that they may begin the world again with their new project, which they call Enhanced Humanity, by the way. One of their writers came up with that. That's the kinda shit you'll be doing."

He had to get out of here. "Does anyone here have any weed?" he asked the table. No one responded. He asked again. "Weed? Pot? Ganj? The chron? . . . Trip, you look like a man who knows his way around the business end of a bong. You holding?"

Hazards gave him a long look, then said, "Zip-lock in the terra-cotta pot on the porch, to the left of the door."

"Thank you," said Mark, standing up from the table in a manner that he hoped conveyed affront and impatience. He didn't want to look like a scared, tired, confused man jonesing for a fix.

On the porch, he found the bag of pot, more than he was expecting—not a crinkly little baggie, but a folded freezer bag the size and heft of a dead pigeon. And what was this? A little tin of tobacco also. Yahtzee! He rolled a spliff and sparked it. He sat there in the night. The dark ring of the crater around him in the distance, a pink moon in an indigo sky. He could smell wet meadow and wood smoke.

A minute later, the screen door *skkrring*ed open and it was Leo, coming out alone. Leo approached, and Mark spun the spliff around, smooth as a sailor on watch, to offer it to his old friend. Leo made the faintest declining gesture.

"Oh yeah. You're in recovery," said Mark. "Though I see you still allow yourself neurotransformative eye tests."

"It's not like that, Mark."

"What's it like?" He was really asking.

"It's like—you know how sometimes you wake up and you know just what to do? And you're not baffled, and you're not afraid of being found out, and you have no secrets, and you forgive the trespasses and are forgiven for your own?"

"Ah, yes. The mythical Huey Lewis drug," said Mark.

But, yes, Mark did know those times. When he was with that last, lost love of his; for a while in college; some earlier times, back in the mists of his easy, humble childhood. Easy? Sure, the coop-flown dad. But we all have our things. There was the safety of his home, his mom, and Monopoly. Maybe that's why all the drugs. Maybe he was just trying to get back to that.

"Really?" he said, squinting at the lit tip of his spliff. "They scan my retina and I am found?"

"It's not a scan; you just look at this screen," said Leo, trying hard to explain. "You know, like on a pachinko board, how the little ball drops randomly on one side or the other of all those little pegs? It's like that. The way your eyes traverse the field makes a unique identifier, and you get a number. The test doesn't *take* anything from you or leave anything behind."

"Like a pachinko board?"

"Yeah, except much, much bigger. And instead of pegs, your eyes bounce off ideas. Actually, I guess I don't necessarily know what pachinko is. And the screen looks back at you."

"How can a screen *look back?*"

"I don't know. But this one does," said Leo. "Maybe it's the Second Coming."

"Say again?"

"Well, why wouldn't it happen that way? You know? Online, I mean. They wouldn't try another guy-in-slippers thing, I don't think."

"Who are *they,* Leo?" asked Mark. "And don't you mean sandals?"

"Yeah, sandals. You know: They. Our judges. You're the one who taught me to think of them as judges, Mark. Don't you remember?"

Vaguely. In those months after Leo's parents died, when he was flailing. The sisters were all older when it went down. For Leo—not a child, not really a grown-up—it hit hard. So Mark took him off to Maine, out of view, away from the sisters and the lawyers and that creepy grief counselor. On the drive up, they'd divined this whole cosmology in which there *were* angel-y spirit things that looked down on the poor earth, but they were not omnipotent or even omniscient; they were just way older than the corporeal people, and they had some pull in the world. These were the judges. You picked your judges specific to the situation, was the loophole. That made it a forgiving cosmology.

"Speaking of," said Leo. "You fire all your judges?"

"What?"

"That book you wrote. The inside-out one."

Here was his chance to do this, at least. "Leo, I'm sorry. The toy heir in the book wasn't supposed to be you. Your family makes games, not toys, right?" Leo gave him a scrunched-lip *bullshit* face. Mark stopped. "I'm sorry. I really am. My bad."

"Thanks. I'm over it," said Leo, and he really did seem to be. "But I'm kinda baffled by the part where you wrote something really good and then sold it and yourself to that creepy outfit. Your book was absolute crap. How much money did they give you?"

"Not enough," said Mark.

"Would any amount be enough?"

That pissed him off, the pious tone. "Oh yeah. I can think of some amounts," Mark said. "You have a price too, my friend, everyone does. Yours is just distorted by a trust fund."

He thought that would sting—Leo was super-touchy about the trust thing. But all Leo said was "Probably." Then he seemed to inhale the whole night before him. His chest swelled.

"But I don't know, Mark. If I had written something as good as you did in that little essay, I can't imagine letting anyone turn it into shit like you let them do."

"Yeah, well, thanks for the input," said Mark. But he knew that Leo was right. He finished the spliff and rolled off its ember in the little ashtray beside the terra-cotta pot. "But just go easy on the revolutionary stuff, okay? It's a bit rich to see you playing Che Guevara in there."

"I think Che was just some bourgeois kid, actually."

"You grew up in a *town house,* Leo. Now you're sober for a week and you get tangled up with this United Front of Whatever, these anarchists, and you think you know why the caged bird sings."

"Oh, we're not anarchists," Leo said.

Oh, yeah. It was *we* now. Mark snorted.

"But I'm damn sure on the side of the bird, not the cage, you know?" said Leo, wandering off the porch.

"Where are you going?" asked Mark.

"Over to the barn. I wanna see what that pony's all about."

A moment later, the door *skkrring*ed again, and it was Constance, come out to give her five hundred cents once more.

To head her off, Mark said, "This is good pot your man has." It was. Its effect was clean and rapid, like they make smoking pot look on TV. He offered her the spliff. Constance did a wavy dismissive thing that made her distaste clear. *Fine.*

"You want some to take home? We have plenty," she said, and she gestured to the odd forest that ringed them.

"Those are pot plants?"

"Not primarily, no. They're a novophylum. But the pollen—that green fringe on the leaves? That's a kind of cannabinoid, apparently. That characteristic has proved useful on the rare occasions that our farms have been discovered by the police-front agencies. They think we're pot farmers with advanced botanical skills. They burn or destroy the plants without looking to see what they really are."

"What are they really?"

"Well, I guess someone like you would call them computers."

"Someone like me?"

"Straight. Untested."

"How about you? What do you call them?"

"Well, they're just plants, you know? They live in a parallel world right beside us. But these ones we can communicate with."

Mark didn't understand. A plant computer? A computer plant?

"Look," said Constance. "We came down out of the trees, we made up a language, we learned to write it down, then we learned to encode it electronically as ones and zeros and store it on tiny devices."

"You're talking about, like, from the Stone Age to the 1970s, right?"

"More or less. Okay, but what we have here is something different. Turns out there was already a language that we've been sharing all along. Maybe we knew it better when we were still in the trees. It's in the air, the soil, the water. They won't be able to take it away from us. It's all around us all the time. The other guys are still writing everything down with circuits; they're still using hard drives, essentially. They call it the cloud, but that's wrong, isn't it? Their cloud is heavy and metal and whirring."

"So if your thing is so much more advanced than theirs, why are you playing defense? You and your plants should be able to bring these guys down."

"Mark, we need years to figure out what to do with this knowledge. It's so new. The eye test is still a mystery to us. These laptops we make here are very, very basic. And since that motherfucker Pope came on board, the Committee has started coming after us hard. They may even have found a way of cheating on the eye test. Some bad apples have been let through, and we've had security and intelligence breaches like we've never had before. There's not that much time, Mark. There just isn't. The Bluebirds are coming after us. They're hunting us down and taking us out one by one. It's getting more dangerous every day. And if they get us, they'll take all this—our plant science, our brain science. They'll classify it, monetize it. Corporate seizure, civil forfeiture, the spoils of the War on Terror."

Mark looked into the blue night. "You probably aren't supposed to be saying this to an untested, are you? Though I suppose you could always render me unbelievable. Or feed me to your plants."

"I can tell you this because you're going to join us." She leaned into him. "Isn't that true? Isn't that why you came out here alone? To get high and screw up the courage to do it?"

Mark took another languid drag in the night. "But Leo said I'll have no more secrets. I don't want that to happen."

"Yeah. Crane is a strange one. That's a very low number he has. It's almost like he was already one of us. Anyway, I don't agree with him on the secrets stuff. There's a whole load of shit in my life I'd rather not share. I think Crane's response tonight has more to do with the, you know, organic nature of the situation."

Mark shook his head to make her explain.

"He's in love with that girl," she said, like Mark shouldn't have needed that explained. "It's scary, Mark, I know that, to join with others. And I've been giving you a hard time tonight, but I actually like that you're a skeptic. I was. I am. We need people like you. Don't worry about your precious self. He'll stagger on. This just adds a dimension. The test makes the too-sure hesitate and the torn know what to do. It makes the strivers reflect and the slackers react; the cynics more forgiving and the hopers more careful. It helps you to see what you're supposed to be doing here, in this life. And it will give you a number. We'll know who you are and that you're with us. We can't ask you to do what we need you to do if there's any chance you'll chicken out and turn back."

"What if it gives me a bad number? Says I'm a bad apple?"

"I don't think you are, Mark. Do you?"

No, he didn't. *Well, look at that.*

Back inside. The big wooden table. "What's this going to feel like?" Mark asked Roman.

"Most Diarists report that the experience is intense, pleasant, brief. There's a spike in connectivity that comes right after the test usually. But it will recede — the grand feelings will, I mean. What matters is what's left behind."

Mark knew a bit about grand feelings, and their receding. "I can handle the high. I just want to make sure I'm not going to end up some stupid jihadi in your project."

"I promise you that won't happen," Constance said to him. For a moment, Constance looked and sounded like his mom twenty years ago, his mom when he was a boy.

Mark looked at the screen.

He felt he was taking in an enormous breath . . . and then it was over. He was just sitting at a table again. Wait, again? Wow. It could have been a night and a day, but all the evidence — everyone else in exactly the same place — indicated that it had been about a second. Like that hallway craze back in junior high where you hyperventilated and then got hit hard in the chest and fainted. He tried a check-in: he was in some Cascadian Brigadoon with a band of hackers and spies. He still wanted another drink and a hot shower; he still thought that command economies were a bad idea. Excellent, no pinwheels.

Constance read out to him his number. Even as she read it to him he was anticipating it. There were three- and four-digit sequences inside it that made images for him that were components of the larger image that the whole number made. He knew his number forward and backward; knew it like he knew his own name.

"Can I have a drink?"

Trip Hazards poured some whiskey in a jam jar for him.

"So that's it?" he said to Constance and Roman. "I'm a Diarist now?"

"With all the rights and responsibilities thereof," said Roman.

"The benefit and the burden both," said Constance.

He thought he was going to say, *I get to choose a stupid code name now,* but in the event, he left out the *stupid* part, because he already knew what he wanted to be called. He wanted to be called Dixon Ticonderoga.

Roman started to explain to Mark exactly what Dear Diary wanted him to do. The eye test had deffo shifted something in him, but he couldn't yet say what, and he didn't know how long the effect might last. Mark had had years of practice studying drug reactions through his body and mind, so that's what he did in this case. He *was* feeling articulate and rapid-fire-y, as if under the influence of a stimulant. But there was none of that fake-bulletproof, ignore-everyone-else thing that coke does. He was listening and seeing clearly, and not as if through the too-clean windowpane of amphetamines. What it felt like, physically, was like he had access to some new, shared channel. Like he was just putting his hand in a swift cold stream.

They wanted him to mule a pathogen; they wanted Mark to be a disease vector.

"But a computer virus?" he said skeptically. "Is that really going to be enough? I mean, I imagine these guys have pretty good antivirus software."

"They actually don't," said Roman. "What they have is a closed system. There are only six servers, six entry points. Two subterranean, two orbiting, one on an offshore derrick in the South China Sea. The master drive is on Straw's yacht, *Sine Wave*. That's where you come in."

Wait. "You mean *Sine Wave*, the two-hundred-eighty-foot Italian sloop with the five decks, carbon fiber sails, surgical theater, and herbarium?" asked Mark.

Constance and Roman nodded. They must have read the same article in *Superyachts Monthly*. "That's where your asset said you would find this master drive?" Constance and Roman nodded again. "And the digital pathogen I'm to deliver to there—that wouldn't happen to have, like, any Dear Diary technology that could perhaps be reverse-engineered?"

Constance stopped him. "You're wrong, Mark. The asset is ours. She's been eye-tested. She's one of Straw's close counselors. She's in real danger, by the way, doing what she's doing."

She? "Oh, you really do need me," said Mark, and he tipped a splish of whiskey from the jam jar down his throat. "There are no females close to Straw. Well, a few secretaries and stewardesses; the girl who pushes the sandwich cart around the executive lounge. He generally refers to women as 'conniving cunts.' Sounds to me like you got an eye-test cheater sending you the wrong way."

"No," said Constance, but Mark could see she was wavering. "Straw has something on that yacht that he considers *very* valuable. We keep *Sine Wave* under near-constant surveillance. It's in the North Sea now. That's where we'll need to get you."

"The valuable thing on *Sine Wave* is probably Straw's collection of erotic statuary," said Mark. "And while you were keeping *Sine Wave* under near-constant surveillance, was anyone keeping an eye on *Sine Wave Two?*"

Constance and Roman and Trip each leaned forward five degrees.

"You want to get these guys, I'll help you do it," Mark said. "But I won't help you walk into a trap."

It was Constance who asked, after a few seconds, "What's *Sine Wave Two?*"

"A seven-hundred-thousand-ton tanker? Death Star of the high seas? Floating cage for a computer they call the Beast, clamps on to undersea data cables and glugs until it's engorged with our stuff and then ejaculates solid-state atomic drives into deep ocean trenches? I guess it's the computer you were just telling me is planning our annihilation. You sure you people were *totally* unaware of this?"

Neither Roman nor Constance nor Trip had an answer.

"So I'll get this pathogen of yours onto *Sine Wave Two*. But I hope Dear Diary has submarines. Because we'll need to take care of their backup drives, to be safe. Hazards, do we have submarines?"

"A few. We'll need to make them offensive, though."

"Well, put some people on that. And reverse direction on that asset of yours. She's feeding you *misinformation* and probably providing the Committee with target lists. Forget about *Sine Wave*. I need to get back to *Sine Wave Two*. That's where I'll upload this pathogen of yours," said Mark, "the one with the silly name."

"It's not a silly name," said Leila, who had been quiet since Mark had come back in. "My sister named it, and she made it for us. It's called Prodigium Two: This Time It's Personal." Now she showed Mark a Node, his Node. "It's loaded onto your phone. Just get it close to that computer. It may require some sleight of hand, Mark. You're good at that." Then she said, "Where'd Leo go?"

"He was headed toward the barn," said Mark.

Leila excused herself.

"But listen," said Mark to the three left. "I fucked up in Portland. At Nike. Apparently, I was on thin ice already, with Pope, at least. He and I don't get along."

"Yeah," said Hazards. "We know. His guys have been on you like stink on shit. They were on you last night at the strip clubs, and then at that lingerie-modeling place on Columbia."

Lingerie-modeling place on Columbia? Eww, gross. He was disgusting. He was glad Leila hadn't heard that.

"They still are, actually."

"Whaddya mean?"

"We doppeled you guys in Radio Cab. And the doppels are still live— two of them, anyway. There are Bluebirds sitting on your hotel and on Leo's house. Bluebirds never made Lola, so her doppel slipped them again. But there was something else. Very strange. There was someone else following you."

"Yeah. You," said Mark.

"No. Someone *else* else," said Hazards. "That's why we had to do the Olympia beneath the Burnside Bridge."

"It's gotta be the mailman," said Roman to Constance and Trip.

"The mailman?" said Mark.

"There's said to be an uncorrupted U.S. government intelligence agency inside the U.S. Post Office," said Roman.

"It's the fucking tooth fairy," said Constance.

"Constance is a doubter," said Roman.

"This has happened before, though," she said. "An allegedly uncorrupted police front or intelligence agency gets near us, sends a signal that they're after the Committee also, that we have common cause. They pretend to be soliciting our help. In every case, it's been a ruse. Pope has hollowed out every agency he turns; he takes the best pieces back to the Committee and leaves behind the stationery and all the dim lifers. This mailman guy will turn out to be the same. You watch."

"Whatever with that," said Mark, trying to get the room back. "I may have damaged my chances with Straw. And if Pope's guys are outside my hotel, I bet it's because he intends to keep me from Straw and from getting back on *Sine Wave Two*."

The others considered this. "Well, your doppel's holed up in his hotel, drinking," said Constance. "Just like you were going to be. As long as the Bluebirds think you're that guy in there, we can move you around freely."

The *just like you were going to be* was unnecessary, thought Mark. "Yeah, but it's going to be awfully hard to slip back on board without Pope's say-so. They run a tight ship."

"Think of a way, Dixon," said Constance.

Mark thought.

"You guys got an outside line here?" he asked her.

Leila found Leo in the barn with his head pressed against the pony's brown neck, his eyes closed, a serene smile on his face.

"Leo? You okay?" she said.

He opened his eyes, looked at her. "You smell this pony?"

She had been olfactorily aware of the pony since it showed up at the landing strip; pony was indeed a pleasant smell, or this pony was, anyway. "Okay, but you know how you're in recovery? Or sober? Or whatever you're calling it?"

"Yeah. You think this isn't allowed?"

"What? Pony sniffing?"

"No. The eye test."

"No. No. I'm sure it's allowed. But if you're feeling kind of ecstatic right now, don't let it confuse you. This patch will be over in a few hours."

"That's no reason not to enjoy it," said Leo. Then he looked the pony in her spheroid eye and asked: "Wouldn't you agree, beast?"

Seeing him there, so blithe and pony-intrigued, Leila was angry. It felt misdirected from the get-go, the anger toward him. But it was a strong feeling, and she wanted to give it words. "And it's not the important part of this, anyway."

"What's not the important part of what?"

"Feeling transcendentally interesting or sublime or even connected is not the important part of Dear Diary. Or of life, really. We have work to do, Leo."

She had his attention. He stopped petting the pony and turned more squarely to her. "Those things you mentioned are pretty important to me, you know."

"I know," she said. "I mean, I let go and slip out into the big void too sometimes, you know. But I think most of the work we're supposed to do is self-tethering. You have to at least *try* to connect yourself to the plain old world you live in." A scrap of a poem came back to her. "'For us, there is only the trying.'"

"Yeah, I know," said Leo. "'The rest is none of our business.'"

He knew that one! "But do you really get that? If things don't go the way you want them to go, are you going to think you're a failure?"

"What are we talking about, Leila?"

He was so disarming. She'd meant to be scolding him, and here he had ducked it like an aikido master and moved in closer to her. She could smell the salt of him.

"The letter you wrote to me."

"Yeah, well, listen, if I was way off base, I'm sorry. It was worth a shot." He didn't look sorry.

"You weren't off base, Leo." They were standing close again, charged particles between them like fireflies. "But that teepee-wigwam thing of yours is a bad system. You're either a genius or a loser? What if you're neither? What if you're in between, a little of both? That's much more likely."

He didn't look loony anymore. He looked as clear-eyed as a raptor. "I know that. I know how I'm *supposed* to feel. I'm supposed to be okay with myself or change what I'm not okay with. But I'm halfway through my life, Leila, and it's always been this way. Most of the time, I'm a loser.

When I'm a genius, why shouldn't I grab hold of the feeling? At least that way I can pull up the average."

"Well, when you put it like that," she said. "But feelings aren't vines in a jungle; you don't grab hold of them. You get through them or you enjoy them or whatever." She was thinking of the plate smasher, and her one girlfriend, in college, and a maternal uncle—addicts all—who seemed always to be at the center of storms they could just as easily have steered around. "There's a basic problem in the way you're approaching this."

"Well, when you put it like that," he said.

"Sorry. No. That's kind of an asshole thing for me to say."

"I don't think it rises to asshole," he said. "But why do you care, Leila? I mean, about these habits of mine."

Why did she care? Was that love, or whatever was preliminary to love? It felt more like a tapeworm, or like that Alpine-hatted worm from the Richard Scarry books, with a little suitcase, come to live behind her sternum. Leila had always suffered from what she feared was a deficit in romantic drive, a condition stigmatized in women. Even the people she had most loved she could not exactly recall *falling* in love with. It had felt rather more like moving slowly up a steep grade.

"Because you were right," she said. "What you said in the letter. That there was more supposed to happen between us. It's happening now, isn't it?"

He nodded. The pony lifted her head. Her wild black nostrils flared and sniffed.

"Okay, but I'm not just some experience," she said. "I go forward and backward in time. And if we're going to do this, I want to know that you're reliable. Are you reliable?"

He was looking out at the sky through the door behind her. She let twice the reasonable amount of time go by and then said, "Leo?"

"Yeah. I'm thinking."

"You shouldn't have to think so long to answer that question," said Leila.

"I would like to one day live with you in Rome and bathe our child in an iron tub. Actually, any kind of tub, really. With you, I would always try my hardest—God loves a trier, they say. And I wouldn't lie or hide. I want to feed you and fuck you and ask you what's up and walk with you through whatever searing desert, down any choked street, into what joy and trouble might be ours."

The words brought her to the edge of a high cliff. *Rome? Our child?* Why, how, did he let himself race forward like this? She could have fallen into him then, but he kept speaking: "But all those are just promises and fantasies, so I don't see why they should mean that much to you. And reliable?" He made a little orchestra conductor's flourish before his temple.

"What does that mean?" she asked, imitating the gesture, gutted by his swerve and disclaimer.

"It means that I feel like my mind's a wild card. I don't want to say I'm reliable and then spend my life trying to live up to that."

She thought: *His mind's a wild card? Sounds worrisome.* She said: "I think that's exactly what you should do."

"What?"

"Spend your life trying to live up to ideals. The rest is none of our business." She could see him take that in.

"But what about when two or more of the ideals you're trying to live up to come into conflict?" he said. "Like when you get to some door and you can't be both reliable and adventurous and still get through the door?"

She left him there then, with the pony and his stupid angst, his Hamletian hemming. Why would he not just settle on one or the other? Their child in a bath in Rome, or not? It would be too much work, loving a man like that, torn as he was by twenty decisions a day. She walked back across the still meadow; the moon had set, and the sky was a blue speckled bowl.

She went back inside and found Mark and Constance and Roman clustered around a computer. Not one of the computers that Dear Diary appeared to fabricate here—the old laptops gutted and re-filled with the novophylum plants. The computer they were sitting around looked like an old PC, with a tower and a big monitor. Both were wrapped in tinfoil. Mark's Node was attached to the computer's tower with a short USB cord. A cable the gauge of a garden hose ran from the back of this setup along the floor and into the butt of a rifle that Trip was holding. He was making himself comfortable in a wooden chair by the window. Then he used another chair, overturned, to make a sort of aiming cradle, and he pointed the rifle out the window, at the sky.

Leila saw then that it wasn't a rifle but a sort of a telescope. Where there should have been a muzzle, there was a tiny ceramic parabolic antenna.

Constance made a finger-to-lips be-quiet sign at Leila. Leila stopped where she was.

"Wait for it," Trip said without looking at the people behind him. He trained the rifle telescope low over the far horizon. "Okay. Keyhole access in three seconds. Two. One. Established." Leila could see he was concentrating keenly on his aim.

"Go," said Constance to Mark.

Mark pressed a button on his Node. Leila heard the bubbly ring of the call he was making.

"Hello?" said a voice from the PC.

Mark spoke at his phone. "James. It's me. Mark."

"Mark? That's not what the screen says. Why are you calling cloaked? Parker says that's for emergencies only."

"I know, James. It's just that it's Parker I'd rather not talk to right now. I was afraid he might intercept the call. He seems rather upset with me."

"He *is* upset with you, Mark. We all are. I heard about your performance at Nike. You know I've really done a lot for you, Mark."

"I know, James. I know. And the thing at Nike, that was bad shellfish I had the night previous. I'm mortified, I assure you."

Silence from Straw.

"But the thing is, James, I'm not sure Parker understands us. I'm not sure he is able to appreciate the . . . nature of the connection between us.

Maybe even *I* have wanted to turn away from it at times, you know? Because I was afraid, because I have been afraid . . . of accepting the closeness that you've offered me."

"Closeness?" said Straw. The line a bit crackly.

Mark shut his eyes and continued. "Our minds, James. The way our minds have become close. If I could just talk to you again, about this job you want me to do."

"You're accepting the job?"

"Oh, yes, James, yes. But I want to accept it in person, with you. Maybe by the pool. I'm sorry I was seasick that last time. I want you to show me more. I want to learn from you now. I want *you* to teach *me*."

"This is wonderful news, Mark. I hoped you would come to see it this way."

"When can I come back to you, James? Can it be soon? Where are you? I'm still in Portland." Mark really did manage to sound ardent.

"Nils!" they could hear Straw shout at someone on his end. "Nils!" Then an inaudible reply. "Where are we?" Then a hard-to-understand response from Nils. "An auspicious stroke, Mark," said Straw. "We're gleaning the transpacific cable-five network." More crackly static. "We're nearby." He conferred again with Nils in the background.

In the corner by the window, Trip made a *wrap it up* gesture by spinning an index finger above his head. He was still aiming keenly.

"Can you get to the coast by tomorrow evening?" came the old man's voice through the computer. "Can you get to these coordinates?" He read out a GPS point.

Mark looked quickly at Constance, who looked at Roman, who thought for a sec and nodded once.

"Of course, James," he said. "But, listen. Can we keep Mr. Pope out of this for now? He and his people are such brutes. I do see why we need men like him, but he's taken against me, and I'm not even certain he wants the same things you want from New Alexandria. We should speak before anything else happens. Just you and me."

"Very well, Mark. I'll send a Zodiac to collect you. What shall we dine on tomorrow? *Bucatini al vongole?* Melon balls and a crisp Riesling? I'll speak to Chef."

"Sounds delicious, James. Until tomorrow, then." Mark hung up.

In the corner, Trip relaxed his rifle. "I didn't like that at all," he said. "That was one hundred and ten seconds. That's a long time to keyhole-connect."

"It was worth it. Mark will be on board in less than twenty-four hours," said Roman.

Leila could tell that Trip still didn't like it. "Let's hope the Committee won't notice two minutes of anomalous satellite cross-feeds over southwest Oregon," he said.

Leila looked at Mark. "You okay?" she asked him. "Nice work with Straw. I was getting a little steamed up there."

Mark smiled. "I read some Oscar Wilde at Harvard."

In the blue dark of the little loft, Leo could make out potted ferns and begonias running up the eaved walls toward the skylight. Mark was slack-jawed asleep on a sort of chaise or fainting couch. His socked feet stuck out like two spokes of a ship's wheel.

Leo and Leila made their beds on the floor, quickly and quietly, like soldiers.

"'Night, Leo," said Leila, and turned herself away from him.

He figured she was steamed at him for not calling her back when she walked out of the barn. "Good night, Leila," he said.

He still wasn't really tired. How could these two just sack out? Big day, he thought. Definitely should journal about this one. He slowed his breathing, counted the begonia leaves backlit by the night sky.

But his sleeping bag was made for a little girl. It was printed with the image of a cartoon heroine, and only about three quarters of him fit into it, so he appeared to be emerging from it, as if interrupted between pupa and imago. Leila was in a man-size green sleeping bag. But she was asleep already. Was she really asleep? He felt such a charge between them, her shoulders maybe eighteen inches from his sternum. She was a shell and he was the sea.

"Leila," he whispered at the back of her neck, which he saw now was downy. Maybe her shoulder stirred. There was a catch in her breath. Leo, his nervous system in a sort of flare, was aware of all of it. But after a minute, she had not responded. Outside, a night bug *skritch-skreek*ed at intervals. He didn't say her name again. If she was really asleep, he did not want to wake her. So he just lay there, half out of his sleeping bag, like a banana begun.

He fell into a sleep, and dreamed that he and Leila were trying to re-place a lightbulb together, climbing two sides of the same ladder. The higher they climbed, the closer they came to each other. But the light they had to reach kept receding, until, just to keep from falling, they had to hold each other. They fumbled tools between them. At one point, Leila was wearing only a tool belt. But then he was alone at the top of the ladder, standing on a step that bore the warning THIS IS NOT A STEP and he felt that he would fall at any moment. He tipped forward and woke from the hypnagogic jolt. His sleeping bag had ridden down and now was more just a sack around his lower half. He felt, beneath the sleeping pad and the gritty carpet, a crude transition in floorboards that his ribs were straddling. He was cold.

"Leila," he whispered. "Leila."

She made a sound with *n*'s and *h*'s.

"Leila, can we switch sleeping bags?"

Nothing.

"Leila," he whispered again. "You awake?"

She sat upright in her bag like a woken zombie. "Yeah. Sure." Then she slipped from her sleeping bag, all waist and hips and static cling. She was by far the most beautiful girl he had ever laid eyes on, and the whole thing was pretty much in slow motion. But Leila was just as quickly asleep in the smaller bag. No buzz came off her body as it was coming off his. He was pulled toward her; he was the sea and she the moon. He remembered that a high-school physics teacher once told him that the moon was always falling. That's what orbit is, after all.

Leo tried to tip himself back into sleep. But he was distracted by a tiny orange light playing on the cabin window below him. He looked closer and made out the shapes of Constance and Trip and Roman. They were out on the porch, in a sort of conclave. The orange light was the embered tip of Trip's cigarette. Their voices were indistinct and night-muffled, but the tempo and the interruption rate made Leo know that they were worried. He hoped they had this all in hand. Constance had said there would be scones for breakfast.

He fell asleep again, and this time his dreams were too abstract to decoct. The ladder scenario was not reprised, except possibly as a dream within a dream, but this time in Aramaic or something.

Everybody up!"

Leila sat upright. She was in a different sleeping bag. *Oh, yeah.*

A too-bright lantern came to life in the main room below them. Trip was down there, clapping his hands loudly.

"Diarists," he yelled. "There's been a breach and we're evacuating the farm. We're leaving now. I'm going to the greenhouse. I'll be back in eight minutes." He moved, then stopped. "Scratch that. Constance, check the go-bags, and see that the cabin is clean. Roman, go get the saddle and panniers on Little Nell. Whiskey, Tango, and Foxtrot up there, you guys grab your shit and get outside. Scratch that. I need one of you with me. Mark, you ever use a flamethrower?"

Mark was sitting up in bed, buckling his ruined shoes. "I have not," he called hoarsely. "But I'm game to try."

Leila was quick down the loft ladder. Leo behind her.

"What can I do, Constance?" Leila asked.

"You and Leo stand there. Await my instructions." Constance began to remove fancy backpacks from a wardrobe. She was opening and checking each one.

It was just Leila and Leo, waiting in a corner.

"About last night, in the barn," he said to her.

Really? she thought. *Now?*

"I definitely do want to live in Rome with you," he said. "I just don't know what comes between here and there, now and then. I think I'm strong enough for almost anything, but I've thought that before."

"Can't you just settle for a minute?" she said. "You sound so certain, and then you get all *Or it could be this other way too.*" He nodded to concede the point, which annoyed her even more. "How can you be sure about us, then, Leo, that we have this big story in front of us?"

"Because of our numbers," he said.

"What do you mean?"

He looked almost embarrassed to have to tell her. "I'm your square root, Leila."

A zap in the air between them, audible, like the snap of twig, the *thwang* of a snapped trap. In her mind, his number leaped up, its digits sparking, marrying, and multiplying. Indeed, multiplied by itself, it was her number. She felt the key find its tumblers and then a door open inside her. Nothing about eye tests or shadow governments. Just love. That expansion of the soul, that reaching out. Her story ran through his.

"The bags, Montes," said Constance. "Out to the barn. Chop-fucking-chop. I want us over the ridge in twenty minutes."

Leo moved to grab the bags, but Leila stood there, dazed.

"Lola?" said Constance, more loudly, waving a hand impatiently at Leila. "You with us?"

"Leo says he's my square root."

Constance looked at Leila and then at Leo. Roman turned and did the same. Then they each nodded.

"Well, that *is* remarkable," said Constance.

Leo wished Trip had given him a job. Mark was getting to use a flamethrower. But this way, he could stay near Leila. He had woken with such desire for her. Her face was still soft from sleep.

He and Leila each grabbed three of the fancy knapsacks, heavy and full. They left the cabin and walked into the creeping dawn outside. The eastern horizon was the color of a peach, but the sky above them was still an azure bowl. *A brand-new day,* he thought.

He looked back. A thick plume of gray smoke, darker against the dark sky, rose from inside the forest of novophylum. Leo could hear *whumps* and a rising *crackle,* presumably the sound that a greenhouse makes as it's being flamethrown.

"Which one of us is which, did he mean, do you think?" he asked Leila as they crossed the wide meadow.

"Which one of us is *which* which?" she said.

"Trip said Whiskey, Tango, Foxtrot. You think I'm Foxtrot? I bet you're Tango. I'm probably Foxtrot."

With a nod, she allowed that he was Foxtrot.

"What about my code name?" she said. "You think I should stick with Lola Montes? I didn't choose it."

"Stick with it. It suits you."

"You chosen a name yet?"

"Pace Backenforth?" He saw that she saw the joke in that. "No. I'm going with Leo Crane."

"I see what you did there," she said.

Did she? Did she see that he had forgiven himself for not being a genius? Did she see that he was ready to stand up and start pushing back against the world, no longer a fugitive or an apologizer; that he wanted a child and a task and to row in with all he had; that it was all due to her somehow, that she had turned a key? Of all the times and places, she lived in this one, and he did too, and they had come upon each other. That could be luck or something grander; either way worked for him.

"Did you have any dreams?" he asked her. His dream of her had been so vivid, she must have dreamed of him also. The world turned out to have hidden languages and plant computers. Probably, in such a world, you can co-dream with your square root.

She squinted up at him. So beautiful. So close.

"Oh. They were amazing. Something about my dad driving his hospital bed around an apple orchard. But then I was driving it instead, and it was a boat instead of a bed, and my mother was throwing baby rabbits at me from the top of the Golden Gate Bridge."

Nope. Still a mystery.

Mark caught up with them, huffing, sweating. He smelled like he'd just rolled in a bonfire. "You know where we're going?" he asked them both.

"No idea," said Leo. Through the open door of the barn ahead of them, he could see Roman slipping a bridle over Little Nell's head. Then he saw another man in the barn. But who? Trip and Constance were behind them. "Stay here a sec, you guys," he said. He slipped up to the barn door and peeked in. He came back.

"Who's the other guy?" Leila asked.

"I dunno. Some guy. Maybe our ride out. There's also a Thing in there."

"What kind of a thing, Leo?" asked Mark, with strained patience.

"A Thing. You know. Like a buggy."

"A *Volkswagen* Thing?" said Mark.

Constance rolled up behind them, pushing a wheelbarrow full of laptops.

"Where are we going, Constance?" asked Leila.

"Mark's going to the coast, quickly. The rest of us are going to Seven Ranch, in Enterprise."

"Is that my ride in there?" asked Mark. Constance nodded.

The man stepped out of the barn. Leila craned her neck and squinted at him.

"He's one of us?" asked Leo.

"He may be. But he's also a government agent, and he hasn't been tested," said Constance.

"That's no good," said Leila.

With a nod, Constance confirmed it was sub-ideal. "But we need him right now. He backs up what Mark told us, that our SineCo asset has been playing us. But he has real assets, inside Pope's shop. Double agents."

"Triple, if you think about it," said Leo.

"He's got someone on that boat. Someone you'll need, Mark, when you get there."

"So I'm supposed to ride down the mountain, alone, with an untested government agent?" said Mark. "I thought you people had rules."

Leila went intently toward the barn. *There was something about that man.* When she walked in, yellow light spilled from an overhead fixture. Her eyes took a moment to adjust. Roman was putting panniers on the pony. The new man was checking under the hood of a car. It was one of those faceted VW buggies from the seventies, faded orange. When he turned and nodded at her, she knew exactly who he was. It was Ned. The one who'd first turned her onto Ding-Dong.com. In Mandalay, he'd looked like a doughy, slightly-too-large-headed guy. That cologne he'd worn to their meeting. Here in the barn, he was handsome and strong-jawed.

The others came in behind her. Mark and Leo flanked her like lieutenants. "Lola Montes, this is Inspector Ned Swain," said Constance. "Of the U.S. Postal Inspection Service —"

Leila cut her off. "Yeah, I know Swain," she said. "He lied to me."

"You know this guy, Leila?" said Leo, stepping up beside her.

"Sorry about that, Leila," said Ned Swain.

"It's Lola," she said evenly.

"Swain represents the last of the uncorrupted U.S. intelligence apparatus," said Constance. "He's the one who says we need to evacuate."

"Don't those guys guard mailboxes?" asked Mark.

"That's the Postal Police," Ned answered. "I work for the Postal Inspection Service." He closed the hood of the silly car. "America's oldest intelligence agency. Born before the Republic. Ben Franklin's shop, originally."

"Swain's been trying to find us for a while," said Constance. "He followed you in, Lola. You're why we have to leave here. And this has been my home for five years."

Leila nodded to say sorry.

"He was probably running that Committee team that was trying to find you, but actually he must have been trying *to keep them* from finding you."

Ned nodded proudly. "I also had to *really* find and follow you, using only postal resources," he said, addressing Leila. "Tricky. We had you in Heathrow, but we lost you there, picked you up in LA, and then followed you to Portland. I had the bad guys lose you at that gas station but then I lost you on the bridge."

"Then how'd you find us here?" queried Leo.

"We spotted an anomalous satellite cross-feed at nine thirteen last night. Pot farmers can't do that."

"How'd you get here so fast? You drive?" asked Mark, pointing to the Thing.

"He parachuted out of a drone half an hour ago," said Constance. "He came to warn us. And he came alone."

"Yeah," said Ned. "You guys could have made me into plant food."

"Make him take the eye test," said Leila.

"Not at this time," said Ned.

"It's okay, Lola," said Constance. "There are extenuating circumstances. Roman and I waived the eye test. We invoked the common-cause clause."

"You wouldn't want to overuse that clause," said Mark. The three of them were still standing together, a united front.

"Look," said Ned. "We both want to save America from a clutch of greedy dukes, right? That's our common cause."

"I'm not really in this for America," said Leila.

"Do we still have to call it America after we save it?" asked Leo.

Swain was caught off guard by Leo's question. "We'll have to table that point, Crane. There's no time now. The Postal Inspection Service isn't the only shop that can locate people. I managed to slow their feed, but if I'm here, the Bluebirds won't be far behind. We have an hour, maybe."

"Your friends' black helicopters?" said Leila.

"They're not my friends and they're not helicopters. They're called Kestrels and you won't see them coming."

"He's right," said Constance. "We have to move. Right now." She started loading laptops from her wheelbarrow into the pony panniers. She was losing her cool, moving too fast.

Trip Hazards staggered into the barn, his eyes wide and white and bloodshot in his soot-blackened face. A corner of his heavy coat was still smoldering. He hacked and spit and hunkered down on his knees.

Constance ran to him. "Tom, are you okay?" She held him and batted at his smoldering coat.

"I'm high as fuck. But yeah."

"You destroyed everything?"

"All but the latest cultivars," said Trip, lifting proudly a bouquet of novophylum wrapped in a big cone of soggy paper.

His smoky entrance had dumped a bunch of haste and urgency into the barn. Leo moved to load laptops onto the pony. Mark went to the silly car.

Leila didn't move. She needed a few more seconds. She thought of her little family behind her, and the maybe-one-day baby inside of her. Was this the best way to help them? Like on a Magic 8 Ball, the answer soon floated up. *All signs point to yes.* Then she heard Constance say to Trip, quietly, "Baby. Outside just now, Ticonderoga mis-pronouned. He said *you people*, not *we*. You have to verify him."

Mark was scoping the VW that was supposed to get him down a mountain thick with forest and then two hundred fifty miles up the Oregon coast. The seats looked like lawn chairs. The floor was bare metal. The windshield was folded down, its glass badly cracked.

"This thing really gonna get us outta here?" he asked Ned.

"Well, we can't parachute *up,* you know?" said Ned. "But, yeah, don't worry. I'll get you to those coordinates. And this is no ordinary Thing, I gotta say. I think these came with those one-point-six, flat-four, air-cooled engines. This has a big-bore kit. Two-point-six, two-point-seven, maybe. Plus six inches more suspension. Bigger brakes."

It meant nothing to Mark. He was annoyed when men assumed shared mechanical knowledge; he didn't know how anything worked, or ran. But this was no Gulfstream V. Then Mark realized with disappointment that if all this went down the way it should, his private-aircraft days were over. That eye test had made him more open to the politics, but he knew that he still liked nice stuff, probably always would. The kind of stuff that there wasn't enough of to go around. That six-burner French cast-iron stove. The wine fridge.

He was getting into the passenger seat of the Thing when he saw Hazards coming at him quickly. Smudged as he was, and red-eyed, he looked like a demon. In a swift motion, he had the back of Mark's neck held tight in one of his huge hands.

"What the fuck!" Mark yelled, resisting as Hazards put his other hand on Mark's sternum, and brought their faces close together. Mark was about to deploy the head-butt for the second time in two days, but then he felt the other man's hand lying soft on his own heart; no threat, no danger. On the contrary, there was a sort of rise in Mark that he was not at all comfortable feeling so close to another man's face and looming body. Hazards held Mark's head and gaze for a long time—four syrupy seconds, maybe—and then released.

"He's good," Hazards called back to Constance. "He still wants stuff. But he's good."

"I'm glad we got that out of the way," said Mark huffily; he sat down quickly in the Thing. Roman rolled open a door at the other end of the barn. Ned Swain got in the driver's seat and started the engine, which did indeed sound more powerful than such a vehicle's engine is supposed to sound. He handed Mark a World War I Flying Ace sort of goggled leather helmet and put one on himself. Mark donned the headgear and looked around to show Leo and Leila. Leo was putting a heavy-looking backpack on Leila. Mark whistled sharply, and they both turned. Though burdened beneath her pack, Leila gave him a real thumbs-up.

"Be careful, Mark," she said.

"Go with God," said Leo Crane.

45°40'04.4"N 123°56'27.9"W

Evening had fallen. The surf growled Pacifically at the dusk-dappled sand. Mark was standing on a wide and log-strewn beach in the lee of a house-size boulder. A chill breeze was coming off the sea and he had only his corduroy jacket for outerwear.

He had been waiting for over an hour; had watched the sun drop below the sea, turning the sky orange, then vermilion, then bloodred. Was it Patel coming for him? Singh? Straw had said only *I'll send a Zodiac.*

Mark and Swain had been thirteen hours in that Thing. Swain really pushed it down the mountain and across the 5, and then back into a network of small roads through the Coast Range. A Cascadian Paris–Dakar.

There was no conversation on the journey. The leather helmets and the roaring engine made it impossible. They'd stopped for gas twice, though, at unattended pumps in gated maintenance stations deep in the national forest. At the first one of these, both men took off their helmets and drank from a canteen.

"It's Tessa Bright, isn't it?" asked Mark. "Your Bluebird asset."

"She's our most valuable one, yes," said Swain. He was running a handkerchief around his dirty neck.

Mark had known a lesbian attorney for an evil cabal would never smoke Lucky Strikes.

And at the second stop, leaning on the bumper of the car and wishing for a cigarette, Mark asked Swain, "So you postal guys are really the last uncorrupted law enforcement in the U.S. government?"

"Last uncorrupted intelligence agency," Swain clarified. "Pope hasn't turned the Forest Service yet." He clunked the nozzle back into the gas pump and replaced the little padlock that prevented its use.

Mark thought he could see something on the horizon, a black mote against the deep blue. Was it coming closer? He stepped out from behind his boulder and walked nearer the lapping shore. He still couldn't tell whether the speck was approaching. Why had this chance been offered him? To change course midlife, to earn back his friends, to strike a blow for someone other than himself. The speck resolved itself. It was an inflatable boat, a Zodiac, coming in at high speed. He could hear the whine of its engine now and see a little green light blinking on a tiny mast at its stern.

Look, Ma. While you still can. The greater good of the world is partly dependent on my unhistoric act. You will be proud.

The craft was a hundred feet out now, riding the swells. Mark tried to make out the driver or captain or whatever. It slowed and eased close to the shore, its engines bass and throaty. And then he saw that what he'd thought was the captain was actually just the little pilot station and steering-wheel platform. There was no one at the helm of the craft.

His Node vibrated in his pocket. He fished it out and read its glowing screen: **Board the Zodiac, Mark. Dinner awaits. James.**

If this goes wrong, he thought, *I will deffo rest in an unvisited tomb.*

With each step Mark took nearer the water, the wet sand pulled with more force on his bloated shoes. He stepped out of them, rolled the cuffs of his pants, and walked into the lapping waves. *Come in. The water's fine,* Lola had said. His legs went quickly numb as he waded out, the cold sending a plume of clarity up his body and into his head. His pants were soaked to midthigh by the time he was able to heave himself onto the black raft. For a moment he lay on its rigid floor, catching his breath and looking up at the first few stars in the east. The grandest mystery, strung over our heads every night. There was the North Star. And there, still faint, was the Big Dipper. The handle of the Big Dipper makes an arc, his dad had taught him long ago. Follow that arc to a star called Arcturus. *Arc to Arcturus*.

RIP, Pops, he thought, for the first time without bitterness. *You will be proud also.* Mark would get to write his great work, but maybe only on his heart, and for an audience of one.

He took stock. There was a tall ergonomic pilot's chair behind the little helm, a sort of neoprene blanket or cape folded on its seat. He stood up, wrapped himself in the blanket. He had to brace himself against the seat behind him as the craft executed a one-eighty, throttled up, and pointed into the horizon. The little boat barreled into the sea, thwacking occasionally into opposing swells. After a minute, Mark looked back. America was a gray humped shape below the new night. He was calm, full of self and secrets, but now with something else as well.

ACKNOWLEDGMENTS

Let's see. There were those very early readers, Christine Monk and Layla O'Mara, both of whom said *don't stop keep going*. Then there was Monica McInerney, who dashed up Arklow Street to say *don't stop keep going*, and who put me on to the canny and forthright literary agent Gráinne Fox, who has led me through some strange woods. There was the dynamic duo of Miranda Driscoll and Feargal Ward, friends and co-battlers and twin pillars of The Joinery—that mad, true place in Arbour Hill. There were my other mates there, all of us just tipping away, forging in our smithies. And the Lilliputians downstairs, who kept me bright-eyed and pacing. There was David Mitchell, who told me about helmets. Thank you to the Paul and Amy Foundation, off the South Circular. They made room for us, big time. Also many thanks to the CroMara Institute on Swinemünderstrasse, and Tucker Malarkey at the Dant Conclave. And to Tom and Constance Corlafsky, and the pleasures of their place. Much is owed to N. Lowry, his friendship, and his network of East London safe houses. Katharine Johnson never doubted I could do it. Heather Watkins let me use her truck-rumbled studio and gave me a squeaky chair, sharp pencils, and snacks in ramekins. Nicole Morantz said, "See. It wasn't for nothing." Dharma Nicotera and Andrew Land never let me down. Patrick Abbey came through in the end. Lola Oyibo cheered me on. My co-stroller MacGregor Campbell acted as conspiracy consultant. Big ups to my crim def advisors Celia and Ben. And mad props to Edward McBride, who showed me Burma, Beirut, and the Beqaa Valley.

At Fletcher & Company, Mink Choi boosted my spirits and prospects when she stood up early for this book and its author. Likewise, Rachel Crawford is a good woman to have in one's corner. My editor at Mulholland Books, Joshua Kendall, saw within the early, teeming drafts of the novel what *WTF* was to become. I had to trust him and I am so damn glad that I did. My sincere thanks also to Wes Miller and Garrett McGrath. And to Pamela Brown, Carrie Neill, Andy LeCount, Ben Allen, Nicole Dewey, Heather Fain, Judy Clain, and Reagan Arthur. They are the village that this book took. I owe a serious debt to all the designers at Little, Brown and the cover artist at Faceout Studio; I think they nailed it. And I thank my stars that *WTF* had to go through copyeditor Tracy Roe before it got to you, dear reader.

Thanks also to Isaac Hall, from whom I learned about the examined life, the joys and perils of examination. And to Chris Hollern (RIP), who gave me this city. And to my sisters, ever behind me, and my mom and dad, who made me read and let me write.

ABOUT THE AUTHOR

David Shafer is a graduate of Harvard and the Columbia Journalism School. He was born and raised in New York City. He has traveled widely, and has lived in Dublin and Buenos Aires. He has been a journalist, a carpenter, a taxi driver, and, briefly, a flack for an NGO. He now lives in Portland with his wife and daughter and son and dog.